1

Beyond All Doubt

Peter A. Moscovita

The sequel to the first book The Following Storm.
This book is mostly fictional based on many historic events commencing in 1940.
Characters in this book are also, fictitious. Any similarity to real, living or deceased, is
coincidental and not intended by the author

For information regarding permissions, contact the author at:
peteramoscovita@aol.com

ISBN: 978-1-7346839-1-2

Credits:
- E-book Formatting Fairies
- Ashley Lopez. Graphic Design
- Martine Moscovita
- Mary Storsteen

This second book has been written as a sequel to The Following Storm.
Once again, I have turned to the people that helped me with the first book.
Their encouragement to continue writing is greatly appreciated.

To my wife Martine, again my appreciation for the countless hours helping with the draft.
Your tireless encourage is the drive behind all that I do.

To our close friend, Mary Storsteen for again helping me with the draft.

Foreword

The thrilling sequel to *The Following Storm* throws the main caricature Karl Vita once again into the dangers of a World now at war. Starting with evacuation of the British Expeditionary Force off the beaches of Dunkirk France May 27th June 4[th.] 1940

Although this story is fictional it is based on many events that changed and scarred the countries in Europe.
This book starts in 1940 and continues through to the 1945. As a British Intelligence Officer Karl Vita is deeply involved in the planning and implementing of intelligence missions into occupied France. These hazardous operations leave him injured on several occasions. Recuperating he becomes romantically involved with several ladies but no wedding bells until he buys a car and a lasting new romance flourishes from that purchase, opening the door to lasting happiness. Assuming he can survive the dangers of being a spy.

Dedication

To all the Men and Women that served their countries in times of war.

Beyond All Doubt
Chapter One
In Harms way

Book Two.

England can be damp and wet in the early summer and this day was no
exception. Lieutenant Karl Vita stood in the crowded isle of the double decker bus
holding on to a leather strap hanging from the ceiling, heading to his job at the
military camp outside of *Slough Berkshire England*. Hearing the conductor
announce his stop he moved to the open platform at the rear of the bus, squealing
brakes brought the old double decker bus to a shuddering stop, like a flood, the
passengers inside pushed towards the platform in a hurry to get off heading to
their places of employment, another workday was about to commence.

   The war was not going well for the English *Expeditionary Forces in France*, the
combined *German blitzkrieg* forces were driving the English, French and smaller
divisions of Belgium's and Canadian forces towards the English Channel and the
long open beaches of *Dunkirk,* their survival now questionable? Over three
hundred thousand English troops and approximately another hundred thousand
plus French troops along with their equipment were now in jeopardy of total
annihilation.

   The drizzling rain made the short walk miserable for Karl his umbrella not really
shielding him from the blowing rain. "Excuse me sir may I share your umbrella,"
asked a pretty ATS, (Auxiliary Territorial Service) sergeant. "Of course, you can
young lady, I am heading to the camp I'm assuming you are going that way as
well?" Replied Karl noticing how striking she was in her khaki raincoat. "Excuse me
for asking sir, are you one of those International chaps stationed here at the camp,
there seems to be an awful lot of you? By the way, my name is *Gwen Phillips*." Said
the young ATS girl looking up at the handsome Lieutenant.   At the main gate they
presented their I.D.'s to the Military Police guard then proceeded towards building
B-3, located on the left side of the compound. "This is where we must part
sergeant, keep the umbrella I'm sure you will return it one day soon." Said Karl as

he started walking away from Gwen. "Sir how do I find you and who do I ask for in this building, to return the umbrella that is." Asked Gwen as she stood under the umbrella hoping that their brief encounter would not be the last. "Just ask for Lieutenant Karl Vita." Replied Karl continuing to walk briskly towards the entrance of the building marked B-3 in large red letters. Once inside he was greeted by the receptionist, "Good morning Sir, you look rather wet," Asked the jovial receptionist. "You are so right," replied Karl as he took off his raincoat. "Jean, would you get me the briefs for todays and an updated schedule," asked Karl as he headed towards his small cubical at the end of the row of workstations. Jean returned with a large steaming mug of coffee along with a stack of briefs for Karl to review. "Major Knight sends his complements and asked for you to join him at 0930 hrs in the main conference room and to remind you to bring the latest aerial photographs of the beaches at *Dunkirk*." Said Jean making sure her boss would not forget anything prior to the first meeting of the day. Karl arranged his briefs then placed them under his arm, he stopped momentarily to look at the framed photograph on his desk of his deceased fiancé *Kitty Johnson* killed on a mission in Germany almost two years ago, this he did every day without fail. The German military van she and another British Intelligence officer were being transported in was deliberately rammed by resistance fighter's lorry, in a brave attempt to rescue them before the dreaded Gestapo could interrogate and torture them for information. He picked up the picture kissing it tenderly, his love for Lieutenant Kitty Johnson was still that strong even after all this time it would be very difficult to let someone else into to his broken heart. On the opposite side of his desk Karl looked at the ship he had served on as its first officer back in 1936. With a war on the horizon, he had deserted his post to escape to England with his Mother, Sister and Nephew and a new life as an officer in British Intelligence Service.

"Morning, gentlemen please be seated," Said Major Knight as he entered the conference room. "The news from France is now critical, as of this morning all leave has been canceled and from here on you are confined to the base until your assignments have been issued, is that clear. Any, and all persons having prior experience with boating and seamanship are to report to this room at 1300 hrs as we are desperately short of skilled seamen.

Operation Dynamo will commence on *May 26th* from ports around the southern coast of England. Our boys in the British Expeditionary Force (BEF) are with their backs to the sea. *The Prime Minister, Winston Churchill* has directed all branches of the armed forces to aid in the evacuation of our forces back to England. Gentlemen this is a monumental undertaking, *Vice Admiral Bertram Ramsey* has been charged with directing the evacuation. Every seaworthy civilian vessel is to be requisitioned for this operation, as of this morning all private boats, yachts, ferries, merchant ships along with every available naval ship will gather to sail to Dunkirk. *Lieutenant Vita and Lieutenant Armstrong*, both of you have prior experience as senior merchant officers, you will both be given temporary command of an armed trawlers being reactivated from the reserve fleet. You will leave for *Lowestoft* after the meeting here *at 1300 hrs*. On your arrival you will be met by naval personnel who will brief you on the operation and direct you to your command. Your crews are all Royal Navy chaps, they are already working on the trawlers to make them seaworthy. When we adjourn after this meeting return to your quarters and pack a kit bag for at least one week. As for the rest of you, your orders will be assigned when you assemble here tomorrow morning at 0630 sharp. More than likely you will be assigned to a boat or dock support, so do the same pack lightly, is that clear."

Lewis Armstrong looked at Karl, fear and shock across his face," My God this is unbelievable there are somewhere near 400,000 troops on or near those beaches. How on earth can we rescue them all before the German forces capture or kill them out in the open like that. They are almost defenseless with no place to take cover or defend themselves while they wait to be evacuated." Lewis was reacting in a state of panic. Karl knew instinctively he must calm Lewis down, "Lewis get a hold of yourself man you are an officer in a room full of junior officers and none commissioned types, not a good way to set an example. Some of these chaps could well be with you on one of those trawlers, how confident will they be in your leadership seeing you like this, now straighten up." Karl's leadership was showing through. Major Clive Knight with a look of approval on his face was watching this interface thinking you can always rely on Karl to take charge. Back in his cubical Karl ran quickly through the briefs that needed his attention then called Jean to file them till he returned if ever! "Jean I'm in a rush please have a staff car brought over from the motor pool, I have to pick up a few thinks from my flat, looks like I'm out of town for a while." Karl started feeling exhilarated by the thought of returning to sea, he savored the idea of having his own command even though it was only a tired old armed trawler. Outside the building Karl walked quickly towards the staff car waiting by the curb. The roads were quite congested for this time of the morning, Karl asking the driver is there a quicker way to get to his flat and back again to the base. "Not really sir never easy this time of the morning I think it should be better returning though." The driver could see the lieutenant in the back seat was becoming very anxious. In his flat he packed a field uniform and essentials such as socks, underwear and a toilet kit then packed his trusty compass from the desk draw taking a last look around he returned to the waiting staff car.

Back at the base they showed their ID's at the gate followed by Karl instructing the corporal, "Drive me straight to Command," Almost jumping out of the car before it came to a stop, Karl thanked the driver grabbing his kit bag from the back seat and entered the Command Center, half running, half walking he covered the distance to the meeting room at the end of the long hallway in record time.
To his surprise he found the meeting room still full of military types milling around waiting for Major Knight to return. In a loud authoritative voice Karl yelled out over the group, "Has Lieutenant Armstrong arrived back yet?"
"Over here old man, are you all set to go." Replied Lewis. The door opened and in walked Major Knight along with two other officers." Vita and Armstrong, with me over here we need to go over your rolls in Operation Dynamo very quickly as the convoy of lorries will be leaving within the hour for *Lowestoft*. Once you arrive you will have only a day and a half to get your crew and trawlers ready to sail for *Ramsgate* to rendezvous with the flotilla of boat being assembled that are heading to Dunkirk. Your assigned vessels are both *Naval Admiralty Trawlers* from the reserve fleet they are about as ready as they ever will be so don't expect too much when you first see them. Here is a folder on each vessel try to read them on the way to Lowestoft. The operation details are on top so familiarize yourselves with the rendezvous points, traffic lanes in and out of the beaches and other details you need to familiarize yourselves with prior to the start of the rescue operation. Your crews are mostly Royal Navy reservist and Regulars about thirty-five in all, they are as we speak getting the boats ready. It is going to be up to you to whip them into shape prior to casting off, is that clear enough for you. This arm band and cap band will identify you as the ship's commanders, put them on now and keep them on till this evacuation is completed. Both Lieutenants stood saluting their commanding officer before turning towards the exit. "Good luck chaps may God keep you safe. Lieutenant Vita a word if you please." Said Major Knight. Karl turned and walked back to Clive standing by the desk. "Karl my dear friend please be very careful. The word from the Admiralty is they are expecting heavy casualties and heavy losses to the rescue vessels. Karl, make me this promise, you will not do anything reckless. I know you have a chip on your shoulder against Germany and especially the ones that coursed the death of Kitty." Clive showing genuine concern for the welfare of his close friend. "Don't worry about me Clive once this evacuation is over you can send me back into Europe where I can really get my revenge." Replied Karl being his usual sarcastic self. "Get out of here you crazy Austrian." Said Clive laughing.

Karl turned then adjusted his cap to one side like a seaman would do, he was returning to sea duty after all.

Chapter Two
Lowestoft and the HMT Reese

Outside there seemed to be much confusion about who was in what lorry. "This is ridiculous", said Lewis to Karl as they stood waiting for further instructions. "Sirs please follow me you will travel with these other officers in that bus at the head of the convoy." Said the Sergeant Major as he guided them towards the bus. On board Lewis and Karl introduced themselves to the other officers before sitting down together." Well old man I was getting worried we would be traveling in one of those drafty lorries, so this is so much better." Remarked Lewis. The journey of one hundred sixty miles would take about four to five hours with a quick stop halfway. Karl opened his folder and started to memorize the operation details; he was not in the mood for further talk.

The sun was still high when the convoy reached Lowestoft. Pulling into the shipyard they were totally surprised by the gathering of all types of boats and ships from civilian cabin cruisers to merchant ships. *HMT Reese and Twain were dockside with smaller boats rafted on the freeboard up to four deep. "Well Karl that's mine in front of yours, the Twain, so I guess the Reese is the one behind. There's a skippers meeting, at 0530 hrs tomorrow morning, so let's meet up dockside at say 0515 hrs shall we." Asked Lewis. Sounds good to me" Replied Karl. Walking down the dock towards the *Reese*, Karl was thinking out loud as he got closer, my God what a difference to the *Tristian*. A loud voice announced, "Captain arriving aboard." Came, the command from the ships First Officer standing at the top of the ramp with an ordinary seaman piping Karl aboard. "Thank you, *Lieutenant Adams*, please to make your acquaintance. Would you kindly assemble the crew on the fan tail so I can introduce myself and outline what I expect from them over the next few days? After that you can show me around the boat, considering her size that will not take long. My main concern at this point is the state of readiness of this boat and its crew." Said Karl finally realizing that this was his command, he was no longer a first officer? Mr. Adams, tomorrow morning you will join me at the flotilla operational meeting, I suspect this will take about two or three hours. Karl followed Adams to the stern of the Reese mentally taking note of the condition of this old trawler. The crew of thirty-five men formed up in rows on the fan tail, all in work overalls, some covered in grease and rust from working on the old triple expansion steam turbine engine, while others in standard dark blue overalls were working on servicing the armament and deck equipment. The last ones to join the assembly were the seamen working on the outdated bridge equipment. The crew stood apprehensively waiting to hear their new Captain give them his orders. Adam spoke quietly to Karl as they approached the rail on the fan tail, "Sir over the last four days these chaps have been frantically trying to get this old girl back into a state of readiness and believe me it shows, they are a terrific bunch of chaps as you will soon find out. Lieutenant Adams approached the rail ahead of Karl. In a controlled voice he ordered the crew to, "Attention!" "Thank your Number One." replied Karl as he placed both hands on the rail, he deliberately stood silently looking from left to right at his crew mustered below for what must have appeared to be an eternity to the crew. In a loud voice Karl started to speak, "Gentlemen, please stand at ease, we are all in this same boat it will make our work so much easier if we dispense with naval formalities. Up until two years ago I was an officer in a foreign merchant service but never served in any Navy. My accent as you can tell is not English, it's Austrian. And being a sailor was all I ever wanted to do till Adolf Hitler changed my career plans. For the last two years I have been active in the British Military Intelligence, I hope this will not deter you from following my orders as we make ready for a very dangerous but very necessary mission to save our troops. We have less than two days to get this old lady ready for that lifesaving mission. The British Expeditionary Forces and those of the French Army has been pushed back to the beaches of Dunkirk. With their backs now to the English Channel they have no place left to retreat to. This makeshift Armada being assembled has many types of vessels made up of merchant ships, tugs, all ferryboats that can float, privately owned power boats, sailing yachts and yes, we will be towing navy lifeboats. Gentlemen we have only one objective, to get to Dunkirk on May 26th to rescue as many troops as we can, hopefully it will be all of them, God willing we can make this happen. We depart for Ramsgate along with *HMT Twain* and the rest of the flotilla on the afternoon tide two days from now. Most of the vessels in the flotilla are unarmed, they will be under the protection of thirty-nine Royal Navy Destroyers with adding French and Norwegian Naval units, we will also provide screening to those unarmed vessels throughout the operation. Any questions before we map out the operation. "I have one Sir. How many vessels will take part in this rescue?" Asked one of the stockers. "Good question, what is your name," Asked Karl. *"Chief Petty Officer Charlie Brice* sir," Answered the seaman. "Glad to know you Charlie. From what I have been told it could be close to eight hundred or so that is the number we have been told." Karl scanning his crew as he gave them this information." "Crikey is there enough room for all these boats converging around the Dunkirk beaches," asked another seaman. "What makes you all believe the bloody German Navy and Luftwaffe are not going to do their best to sink the bloody lot of us." Asked another seaman. "The Royal Navy and Royal Airforce are mustering every available ship and fighter plane to protect us, hopefully they can keep the Germans at bay. Our biggest challenge right now is to get as many of those troops off the beaches before the Germans force them into surrendering." Karl was trying to make his crew understand that if this Army is forced into surrendering then England will more than likely be forced to negotiate a conditional armistice. "This plan was the brainchild of the Prime Minister Winston Churchill, all of us must give him our one hundred percent, let's give him something to be proud of, what do say boys." Karl now speaking more like a politician than a military officer. A loud cheering came back from all the crew. "We're with ya skipper." Yelled Charlie, this was the answer Karl was looking for. "Another crewman *Marvin Brown* with a real cockney accent yelled out loud, "They better not mess with Winnie he'll have their guts for garters." To this the entire crew started cheering out loud, sadly, this seaman would be the first fatality on the Reese off the beaches of Dunkirk on May 26th.

"Before dispersing the crew, number one, I would like to go down onto the deck to shake hands with each one of the crew. After that you can give me a tour of the old girl." Karl was now starting to feel good about his new crew. Meeting the crew took over thirty minutes, there was now genuine excitement and acceptance for their new foreign Skipper. "Okay number one show me around this old gal," Said Karl. Sailors on the forecastle were busy servicing the single
12-pound gun, other sailors were installing antiaircraft guns on either side mid ships, with two more being mounted on the stern for additional protection. Depth charge racks mounted on the stern gave them a limited four spread capability. "Better not waste those four charges if that's all we have, what's next" Remarked Karl to Adams. On the bridge two seamen explained the steering station and the limited outdated instrumentation. The radio shack only had room for one operator, it looked like an afterthought squeezed into the rear of the pilothouse. *Scotty* the chief engineer waiting patiently inside the pilothouse to take them

down into the bowls of engine room. As he spoke his Scottish accent was challenging for Karl, however he felt comfortable that the ship's engine and machinery were in capable hands. "Where is the navigation officer," asked Karl as he looked around the pilothouse. He will arrive later this evening got delayed in Portsmouth from what I was told." Replied Adams. "Well then Scotty, show me your engine room if you please." Asked Karl starting to feel more like the skipper of HMT Reese. "Follow me Sir it's going to be rather warm down there hope you'll be alright." Don't worry about me Scotty I've been in hot spots all too many times." Karl now in an almost jovial mood. The open steel stair well had two landing that turn back upon itself to reduce the rise in the stairs, this was nothing new to Karl, to the surprise of Adams and Scotty, he placed his hand on the steel handrails and slide down quickly to the first landing then again to the catwalk that made up the engine room floor, followed by Scotty and Adams. "I can see you are no stranger to navigating ships stair, you and I will get on just fine Sir." Said Scotty as he showed the way for his new Commanding Officer. "The engine is old but in reasonably good shape considering her age, way too many hours on that boiler though. She is oil fired compared to the older coal burners, that's one saving grace. The triple steam turbines are almost completely phased out, had to many years working on these old bugger's, Skipper." Karl was smiling to himself, thinking, he just calling me Skipper this is a good start. "Thank you, Scotty, see you topside for dinner." Adams and Karl climbed back up the steel stairs out onto the deck, into the twilight of May 24th. "I'm assuming we do not have a wardroom." Asked Karl as they walked towards the foredeck. "Not really skipper, we have a small galley that is for the officers only at this point it's almost supper time anyway so please follow me Sir." replied Adams a little embarrassed knowing his skipper had been a first officer on a large passenger freighter prior to coming to England. Karl sensed Adams uncomfortable tone as he apologized for the lack of a wardroom answered by saying. "You know Number One we must be kind to the old lady if we expect her to keep us safe, I'm sure the galley will serve us just fine." Karl following behind Adams feeling a whole lot better about how he had answered Adams. "Thank you skipper your making me feel so much better about being your Number One and your kind words about our old girl the Reese." Over dinner Karl listened intently to their stories of life and careers prior to being recalled to active duty in the Royal Navy. After they had their say, Karl described what he expected from each one of them as they prepared for this hazardous mission. All in all, it was a productive evening with Karl focusing on building the bridge of trust between his officers, excusing himself Karl asking to be shown to his quarters. Aft of the bridge a small corridor lead to the Captain quarters. Entering the cabin Karl's first thought was its only for a few days so no problem. The cabin had a narrow bed against the wall with a floor to ceiling wardrobe equally narrow. A small folding hand basin that had seen better days was in the corner next to a narrow desk that desperately needed refinishing. The old girl has been in hibernation far too long thought Karl as he stowed his sea bag in the wardrobe. Removing his jacket, tie and shoes Karl laid on the narrow bed his head spinning with thoughts of what will be waiting for them laying off the crowded beaches of Dunkirk.

0430 hrs came all to quickly for Karl as he reached for the light switch in the dim light of the small cabin. Dressing quickly, he headed to the galley downing a hot mug of tea before proceeding down the gang plank to meet Lieutenant Adams on the dock at 0515. "Morning Number One, did you sleep well." Asked Karl. "Finally dropped off about 2300 hrs feeling quite refreshed this morning thank you skipper." Replied Adams. On the opposite side of the dock a single overhead light fixture provided just enough light to aluminate the steel door to the converted warehouse. As they walked towards the entrance, they met up with Lieutenant Armstrong and his First Officer John Wright, many other Royal Navy officers, Merchant Marines Officers and a sizable number of Civilian Captains all heading to the same orientation for *Operation Dynamo*. Inside steel folding chairs had been hastily arranged in three columns across the center of the massive interior of the building. At the front of the building a makeshift platform had been built to accommodate the senior officers, three large blackboards were lined up behind the long table that faced the expanse of steel chairs. *Commander Alan Mathews* stood up holding his hands high in the air yelling "Gentleman, please find a chair and be seated, we have much to review this morning. This briefing covers how *Operation Dynamo* will be conducted by an armada of approximately 850 vessels all heading for the beaches of Dunkirk. This flotilla leaving from Lowestoft will rendezvous later today with other vessels off the harbor entrance to Ramsgate all enroute to Dunkirk. Please open your packets of instruction and charts given to you as you entered the building do not forget to take them with you at the conclusion of this briefing. Now please open your packets. We will be leaving for Ramsey tomorrow morning at 1030 hrs, the distance is 78 plus miles on a straight rum line. Stay together in the column you are assigned to and remember to allow for the slowest vessel in the flotilla. We expect to join the main body of vessels in about ten to eleven hours. Remember if you are towing smaller boats steer clear of the wake coming from larger vessels, we don't need to swamp these smaller vessels before reaching Dunkirk. Upon our arrival they will play a vital part in evacuating our blokes off those shallow beaches. Our approach to the beaches will be from the southwest in a counterclockwise pattern. Approach the beaches in a line astern formation in two columns the smaller boats that have a very shallow draft will ferry the chaps out to the bigger vessels waiting in the deeper waters. Do not attempt to get too shallow if you go aground you will be on your own so remember that we do not have the time or resources to come to your aid. If you are attacked and in danger of sinking, try to get your vessel out of the traffic pattern. Now once your vessel is loaded head straight back to Dover or if instructed one of the other arrival ports such as Folkestone to unload, on your return trip to Dunkirk follow the same approach pattern. Now I will turn this briefing over to *Captain John Tillerson* who will update you on defenses from the combined forces of the Royal Navy and the Royal Airforce." Concluded *Commander Alan Mathews* returning to his seat. "Thank you, commander, for those of you that don't know who I am well you could say you're lucky, ask the blokes around you they will tell you the truth." A loud applause came from many of the Royal Navy attendees. "Now that's out of the way, let's get serious about this briefing and the operation to save our boys. The Royal Navy has diverted 39 destroyers along with 3 French destroyers, we have also brought out of reserve fleet some Armed Admiralty Trawlers and Armed Merchantman that can provide additional protective air cover for the flotilla. These vessels will be dispersed on either side of the main body, we are expecting heavy aerial attack from the *Luftwaffe*, it goes without saying our loses are expected to be very high. If your vessel is unarmed, I'm assuming you have collected hand weapons and ammunition yesterday from the supply stores if you have not done so please see the supply officers before you depart this briefing they are on either side of the entrance at the back of this warehouse. Those machine guns could well save your life and those around you. Now let's review the operational details shall we. On the way out all vessels will monitor *Channel 168 on your VHF radio's*. On the return trip to England switch to Channel 180, using two dedicated channels will reduce the chatter and hopefully eliminate confusion. Now in the event you are hit and in danger of sinking, if your vessel is still capable of making headway try to get out of the shipping lanes if this is not possible call the vessel or vessels close to you to aid in your evacuation. Another very important point, if your vessel is still afloat, drop your anchor so it will not drift into other vessels. Keeping the traffic lanes clear will add in evacuating more blokes off those beaches. Many of the larger merchant ships will be using the Eastern breakwater which has a 1,400-yard-long dock with a wooden boardwalk, wide enough to traverse troops four abreast. Captain *William Tennant* has been assigned as the Beachmaster he has Tactical Oversight for entire evacuation. Our flotilla will take directions from him. This briefing will now adjourn to allow preparations to continue. When we depart have your radio set for channel 69 and wait for instruction on when to get underway. Gentlemen England is relying on all of you to save the *BEF*, God be with all of us. Lieutenant Adams approached Karl as they all left the warehouse, "Karl it looks like your shoving off ahead of me, it's a big job hopefully we will come through it in one piece take care be safe see you out there," with that he gave Karl a casual salute and headed towards the Twain with his First Officer. "Well Number One shall we get back to the Reese there is still work to be done and we don't have too much time left do we." Karl was talking to Adams in a rather subdued tone. "Are you alright Skipper you seem rather melancholy," Adams was seeing a side of Karl he had not seen before even though their time together had been very brief, he felt he knew his Skipper reasonably well." No Number One I'm fine it's that I've had a storm following me for so long I just feel it's about to catch up with me shortly.

Chapter Three
DUNKIRK

Back on the Reese Karl looked up to see smoke curling away from the smokestack. "Looks like Scotty is getting her fired ready for tomorrow that's a good sign?" That night the work continued till way past 2200 hrs, Karl and Adams were hard at work planning and marking the charts they received at the meeting. Karl rose at 0530 hrs dressing he headed to the galley for some hot tea and a buttered roll then undertook an inspection of the ship, satisfied with the results he returned to the bridge saying, "Morning all, I trust you had a good night's sleep and now are ready for this long day." At 0930 the deck crew were busy getting the tow lines ready for the eight smaller boat they would be towing. These smaller vessels had already left and were now waiting outside the harbor entrance to pick up the tow lines that would be laid off the Reeses stern by members of the deck crew. The VHF radio crackled into life, "Command to Reese, are you ready to drop your lines and pick up your ducklings outside the harbor over." Came the request from Captain Tillerson. "Reese to command ready to depart over." Adams replying to the command ship. "Take her out number one." Came Karl's first command." Aye, Aye Skipper came the response as Adams picked up the bullhorn and headed out onto the starboard pilothouse wing. "Single up all lines followed by, let go forward spring lines, let go rear spring lines," the deck crew pulled the heavy lines aboard and waited for the next set of commands. "Let go stern lines followed by a brief pause as Adams leaned over the bridge watching the lines come aboard." Let go of the bow lines, looking back into the pilothouse he gave the order to the helmsman, "helm over five degrees make revolutions ten." The Reese gave a slight tremor as her big single propeller screwed itself through the dirty waters of the harbor. "Helmsman come left to make the harbor entrance, set revolutions for three knots." The Reese was now moving very slowly towards the entrance passing larger vessels waiting their turn to cast off. Once through the harbor entrance Adams barked another command, "Helmsman put your helm amidships, stop engine." Adams then picked up the bullhorn once again giving his next command," Lay off towlines to the ducklings as they approach our stern." Adams turned to Karl with a big grin on his face," Sir will you take it from here or do you wish me to continue the maneuvering." Karl responded by saying, "Nice job number one, get the ducklings rafted and secured to our lines then take her out to the marshaling area the command ship will give us instructions and positioning in the flotilla once we are there." Karl was enjoying being the Captain and more than confident in Adams ability as a seaman. The Reese slowly answered the helm as she turned southerly towards the merchantman in front. With a bullhorn in hand Adams went out onto the deck giving instructions for seaman Wilson to remain at the stern, keeping an eye on the tow lines and the little ducklings. "Thanks' number one I'll take her from here, why you don't get some rest you will need to be alert once we close on *Ramsgate*." Karl now picked up the PA microphone telling all deck hands to be vigilant in watching the skies for enemy aircraft. "Stand ready at your gun positions, you are clear to check your weapons now, try not to sink any of the flotilla while you do so." Karl smiled as he said that, it brought back memories several years back when training in Scotland with an instructor that loved to torment his pupils with sarcastic remarks. Four Royal Navy destroyers and two smaller Corvettes took up their screening position on either side of the growing flotilla as they headed south west towards Ramsgate. Helmsman, keep your distance at three hundred feet, no need to bump that merchantman in front of us, right! "Command to Flotilla please report." A crackling message from the Command ship came back. "Sparky make to Command Reese underway." Karl listened as Sparky reported back to command, so far so good. Karl walked out onto the pilothouse wing deck, looking up first then around the ship to see that everyone was paying attention. Satisfied that the Reese was ready for any incident he placed his hands on the railings of the steel steps leading down from the bridge, like an old salt he half walked half slide down to the deck below. Approaching the gang of seamen that would be boarding the troops from the beach he elevated his voice to make sure all could hear him speak." Alright listen up chaps, when we give way, we will stay on station long enough to board as many troops as we can. Jones you and your gang will let go the ducklings make sure no lines get fouled in their props. Once that is done lay off on the starboard side the boarding nets and both boarding ladders. When the ducklings arrive back with troops help the men up onto the deck. Now I need you all to pay attention to what I say next, we need to distribute the troops evenly once on board. Lieutenant Adams and you Jones will direct them first to the stern say a boat load at a time then to the bow with the next load, make sure they understand not to congregate on one side only, balancing the ship as we load will help us get underway back to England that much faster, are you all clear on that? Right now, organize your gang Jones so they all know the drill, no need for us to act like blue-arsed flies do we," Karl was trying to get them all relaxed and focused on the task ahead a little humor was going a long way. One of the seamen asked, "Sir when we depart what will happen to our ducklings." "Good question, they will continue ferrying troops out to the other boats and ships waiting behind us with any luck they can get a tow when their job is done, assuming they don't get sunk." replied Karl. The semaphore signalman received a message from command, silence radio activities use signal lamp from here on. Use designated outbound VHF channel for emergency use only. The Ramsgate contingency is already ahead of us, helmsman make your course 220 degrees. All vessels acknowledge signal by position came the final instruction. Reese to command acknowledge and understood. Karl could feel the tension building as the armada of miss matched boats and ships headed south west to their destiny off the beaches of Dunkirk.

The seas were choppy with clear skies the smaller vessels rolling on and off the wave tops. All eyes were searching the sky looking for enemy aircraft and the first signs of the French coast. The waiting was playing on everybody's nerves, this was quite disturbing until a loud horn sounded from one of the merchantmen followed by anti-aircraft fire from one of the flanking destroyers ahead of them. "Aircraft approaching from the East," a sailor screams out. Out of the sun three black dots diving at high speed made everyone run to their gun stations. "Hold your fire repeat hold your fire until we can confirm if they are friend or foe, those nitwits have opened fire before verifying that they are enemy aircraft." Yelled Karl. As they watched a signal lamp from the lead destroyer, hold your fire repeat do not open fire incoming aircraft are RAF planes, please acknowledge this signal. Signalman "Make to command, understood." Karl removed his cap to scratch the top of his head in frustration then throwing his hands in the air yelling loudly, "We are still an hour away and those trigger-happy morons are trying to shoot down our own fighter aircraft." The three aircraft could now be seen quite clearly, "Look like bloody Hurricanes to me Sir," yelled Charlie from his gun position, "those blokes on that destroyer should be thrown overboard, not like we have hundreds of spare planes right now do we?" Karl and Adams could not contain themselves as they watched Charlie gyrating around his gun position. The three Hurricanes approached the flotilla almost a mast height saluting their countryman by rolling their aircraft from side to side then peeling off towards Dunkirk. Everyone's attention was now concentrated on the coast of France as it came into view through the columns of black smoke and the sounds of bombs detonating as the screaming Stuka dive bombers released their deadly ordinances on the columns of soldiers and abandoned military vehicles scattered along the beach. Heavy caliber gun fire added to the continuous music of war. "Number one let's get the boys ready shall we. Signal from command skipper close ranks and get your boarding nets ready, watch out for submerged wrecks as we get closer."

The images that were now confronting them as the flotilla arrived within a few miles of the beaches was one of horrendous chaos, men and equipment stained their vision shocking them to the core. Thousands of soldiers, their uniforms resembling brown lines of ants rather than soldiers of the BEF. From their location the columns stretching out over the sand dunes for as far as the eye could see, the ones in the front were shoulder deep in the braking surf waiting their turn to board one of the small boats. Half sunk vessels were all around the approach lanes, others were clinging to sinking boats some on fire sending soldiers and sailors into the oily waters around the wreck. "My God this is worse than I expected, how can we evacuate all those poor blokes when so many boats and ships are being sunk or damaged. Cried out Adams tears filling his eyes. "Thank God we have all these boats coming in behind us" said Charlie as he placed his metal helmet back on his head. "Boats approaching on the starboard side man the boarding nets, stand by to assist on the railing." Yield out Jones. Six of the ducklings approached line astern. Two boats at a time banged against Reeses steel hull. "Climb up as many as you can chap's we need to load and depart as quickly as we can." Jones was making sure they used as much of the clumsy rope ladder, six to eight men at a time. In less than forty-five minutes all six ducklings had unloaded and cleared the side of the Reese ready for more small boats to unload. "This will have to be the last load for this trip," Called out Adams. "Pull the boarding nets and boarding ladders up after taking on those last two boats, so we can get underway." He had just finished saying that when the waters close to the starboard side irrupted in massive columns of sea water. The ship shook violently as the compression of water slammed the old ship's hull. Two Stuka dive bombers screamed back into the safety of the sky after releasing their deadly bombs on the ship below thankfully both missed the Reese but annihilated two of the ducklings that now were now no more than splintered pieces of wood with dead bodies floating in the debris field. Every available gun was sending the Stuka's a message of lead, you're not safe yet. One of the planes started streaming black smoke from its engine banking sharply to the North. "Keep your firepower on that engine," yelled out Adams as all the guns made an ear splitting 'ratatat' sound. The other Stuka dived down to sea level making its escape back to its base. Less than two miles away a loud explosion and massive plume of water could be seen and heard as the critically wounded Stuka hit the water, its tail and part of the cockpit was all that remained above the water. Everyone watched in silence as its crew tried to climb out to no avail the canopy was jammed. Through his binoculars Karl could see both men banging against the plexiglass their fate was sealed as the Stuka slide slowly below the waves. "Poor buggers," said Adams as they all watched the drama unfold in front of them. "They would have cheered if they could have blasted this ship and all these blokes to kingdom come," replied Karl with a stone face and ice in his veins. Karl turned shouldering his way towards the pilothouse without looking back. "Gov your skipper is a hard-nosed bugger ain't he." Said one of the soldiers. "If you had lived through what he has lived through you might think very differently." Replied Adams as his eyes followed the skipper pushing his way slowly back towards the pilothouse. Every foot of the pilothouse wing deck was occupied by military evacuees. "You chaps make a hole for the skipper." Yelled Adams to the soldier standing in the path of the skipper. Karl entered the pilothouse Adams close behind. "Thank your number one it is getting a little crowded out there." Said Karl trying to remain calm. "Once we are clear of the area have the six sailors on watch duty report to pilothouse." Karl restraining himself as he thought through what had just happened. Around them fully laden vessels were making their way back to English ports to discharge their live and wounded cargo. Ahead of the Reese about a mile a merchantman was struggling to maintain headway, its forward cargo hatch was belching smoke from an aerial attach while it lay waiting for its human cargo. Its decks from the superstructure back were overloaded as the troops were pushed back away from the damaged bow area of the ship. "Signalman, make to the *Hampton* are you in danger of sinking, do you need us to stand by? Can you maintain headway?" Karl looking at the laboring merchantman through his binoculars. The Hampton responded with a signal pumps are handling the seawater entering from our bow. The fire has been put out only the smoke left now. We are steady at six knots. Can't take another hit though, Hampton clear. Karl leaning back against the pilothouse windows his legs crossed and arms folded across his chest. "Sparky, break silence and make to command we are escorting a stricken merchantman, please send a naval escort vessel or at least an ocean-going tug to relieve us, not able to transfer troops should the transport founder, Reese out. "Navigator, give me a plot and estimated time of arrival at our present speed." Karl was formulating a plan in his head should the Hampton succumb to her damaged hull how would they assist in recovery? "Message back from Command sir," called the radio operator. Command to Reese continue to stand by, have an empty returning freighter being diverted to the Hampton's position, will be with you within the next ninety minutes. Signalman, make to Hampton we will continue to standby until the relief merchantman arrives in approximately ninety minutes. Adams entered the pilothouse again asking Karl should he now bring in the watch crew, "Yes number one let's get this out of the way." The pilothouse door opened in walked six sailors the leader asking, "You wanted to see us?" Karl with anger in his eyes looked up and in a loud authoritative voice yelled. "It is customary to address the captain of a vessel by referring to him as Sir or Captain and stand at attention when doing so." The sailors looking at each quickly came to attention apologizing for the lack of discipline. "Earlier today I specifically gave you an order to remain alert by scanning the skies for enemy aircraft with your binoculars. What did you do as we started loading troops from the beaches, you took your eyes off the skies and that action allowed two enemy aircraft to take advantage of the lack of antiaircraft fire making a direct hit on two of our support boats killing everyone in those boats? Given adequate warning we may have had a chance to defend those chaps. Number one, make an entry in the log that these sailors have been charged with dereliction of their duties. It is the decision of this command that their lack of defensive action or warning brought about the loss of two boats their crews and the soldier they were transporting. This reckless action will be reported to command on our arrival back in Dover." Karl was venting his anger on these sailors, fear written all over their faces. "Now get off my bridge, number one you will take charge of turning them over to the MP's, on arrival back in Dover is that understood." Instructed Karl. "Yes, sir replied Adams now seeing another side to this kind and carrying Captain. Once the sailors had left the bridge, Adams turn to Karl saying, "Don't you think that's a little harsh skipper?" Adams was thinking about the available manpower for the next evacuation operation, loosing six sailors would put them at a big disadvantage. "Yes, it is number one let them stew for a while then tell them you talked me out of reporting them. Their opinion of you will be elevated defending them in that manner and their respect for how I address slackers will have a very positive effect on how they perform their duties from now on, one other thing, forget that entry in the log." Karl once again showing his leadership strength. "Thank you skipper, I should have had the common sense to follow your handling of this situation." Adams walked out of the pilothouse with a much higher opinion for the Captain of HMT Reese.

The navigator turned to Karl saying, "Should be in line to discharge our troops in less than hour sir, we should notify command that we will lay offshore till called into the harbor." The navigator did not have much to do so far on this mission so handling this phase of the operation gave him a purpose. "Thank you, *Manning*, send a coded message, laying off Dover." Karl walking out onto the bridge wing as he gave the order. Looking down now at the mass of returning troops below, he allowed his mind to drift back to another time when he was the first officer on his last voyage aboard the *Tristian*, how things had changed in his life as he looked around, a voice behind him snapped him back. "Excuse me sir may I speak to you," asked one of the seamen that he had reprimanded earlier. "Of course, speak your mind," replied Karl in a very short tone. "Speaking for the watch crew sir, we just wanted to thank you for resending the order to report us. From here on you can rely on us, we will not let you down again should any Hun come anywhere near the Reese they will regret it." With that the sailor came to attention saluting his Captain. Karl responded by saying "All of us on this ship must act as a single unit relying on the action of the man next to you, so thank you apologies excepted, dismiss." Karl was feeling good about how he handled this incident the results of which would prove to be a tremendous contribution so very soon!

"Incoming communication from command, sir, we are instructed to rendezvous with the navy tug B-1240, two miles off the arrival port." Said Sparky as he read the communication to Karl. "Excellent what else did it say." "It goes on to instruct us to enter the harbor and raft up alongside the merchantman *Cornish Lady*, the tugs will turn us around once inside the harbor." Slowly the Reese was turned around being pushed by the tugs abeam of the much bigger Cornish Lady its boarding gangplanks already swung out to come aboard once they were secure, the tugs held the Reese in position as lines fore and aft were secured. Now the boarding gangplanks were quickly lowered down to the smaller ship. "Alright lads up those gangplanks at the double, we need to return quickly to Dunkirk." Yelled Adams through the bullhorn. Karl stood on the wing deck watching how fast the troops transferred to the bigger ship and onto the dock. "Mr. Adams, Stand by to cast off." Came the command from Karl speaking through his bullhorn, it's your boat Mr. Adams, take her out," "Aye, Aye Skipper." Came the replied from Adams. "Helmsman come left to clear the harbor breakwater then make your heading 180 degrees, Mr. Arnold ring up the telegraph for full ahead as we clear the seawall, we need to push her as hard as we can." "Aye, aye Sir," Answered both bridge seamen. Karl entered the bridge saying, "Number one I am going to get forty winks before it gets crazy back at Dunkirk." "Sounds like a good move skipper will let you know when we're about one hour out." Replied Adams as he watched Karl leave the bridge. "Poor chap he looks like he has the world on his shoulders." Adams in the short time he had served with Karl had come to trust and respect him very highly. The now familiar sounds of gunfire and explosions were getting louder as the Reese and many other vessels approached the devastation ahead of them on the beaches of Dunkirk. "Mr. Arnold be so kind as to wake the skipper and request his presents on the bridge." Lieutenant Adams was liking his responsibilities as the officer in charge even if it was an armed trawler and only its first officer. "Yes Sir, shall I bring you a cuppa as well before it gets too hectic?" *Arnold* was a real Londoner, older than the rest of the crew, tall and well-built for his age. He had jumped at the chance to volunteer for this temporary assignment getting back on a ship and on the sea again it was another chance to serve since his retirement as a Chief Petty Officer in the Royal Navy back in 1928. As a civilian he had joined the Greater London Ambulance Corp, a job he felt would allow him to continue with the skills he enjoyed as a sailor, providing aid to those less fortune, in the day ahead this expertise would prove to be invaluable. Knocking on Captain's cabin door he entered to find Karl seating at the small desk pouring over charts of Dunkirk. "Sorry to disturb you Skipper, Mr. Adams sends his complements to join him on the bridge we are getting close to Dunkirk." "Thank you, Mr. Arnold, tell Lieutenant Adams I'll be along shortly." Karl stood up carefully folding his charts then put his jacket on. "Shall I get you a cuppa Skipper and deliver it to the bridge?" Arnold was another seaman that had very high regards for his Austrian Captain. "Thank you, Mr. Arnold please tell cookie to make it real strong must stay alert from here on, right." Karl smiled at the older gentlemen. "Will do Skip," came the response. On the bridge the view ahead was one of continued chaos and destruction, billowing smoke, ships half sunk belching fire and burring oil around the wrecks could be seen off the beach. "Steady as you go helmsman there are men in those waters, slow ahead one third." Said Karl unable to finish calling his command, when screams from all over the deck froze him to his core. Rushing out to wing deck Karl just had time to see two enemy planes dive down towards them. Antiaircraft fire and every available seaman that could fire a submachine gun were focusing their combined firepower towards the menacing incoming aircraft. As Karl spun around to look up a rain of 20mm cannon fire from the lead Messersmith-109 starting to shred a path along the deck and superstructure. Pieces of scolding hot shrapnel were flying in all directions. Sailors were being thrown everywhere blood and body parts painting a picture of horrifying destruction. Karl dove to save the sailor next to him as he gyrated towards the deck his left leg at a sickening angle, his death screams of agonizing pain was also coursed by the red stains spreading across his turtleneck jumper. Karl seeing this reacted immediately diving towards the deck, to save the sailors head from crashing into the steel deck. As his hand scooped up the already dead sailors head the ship shuddered violently throwing Karl against the superstructure excruciating pain in his neck and upper right thigh consumed all his power to remain conscious. Another massive explosion sends him back across the deck again and very close to being thrown overboard. The forward twelve pounders would fire no more, it lay on its side smoke coming from the remains of the muzzle, split down the length of the barrel. The four-man gun crew lay dead and disfigured, smoldering from the bomb blast. The *Stuka Ju-87* dive bomber had found its mark with precision it released its deadly bomb on the gun and its crew below. "The skipper is down yield Arnold as he rushed out of the bridge to aid the lifeless body of Captain Vita." Oh my God he has shrapnel sticking out of his neck and right leg. The nasty bang to his head has knocked him out, that gash is deep across the top of his head, he is bleeding badly. Someone help me I've got to stop the bleeding." Arnold's ambulatory experience was taking over, Adams rushed out yelling," My God Arnold how bad is he, will he make it." "Not if you just stand there, get me that first aid kit from inside, I'm staying with the skipper, your job right now is to keep us afloat, you're the acting Skipper as of right now, now go." Arnolds leadership and cool head was taking over. Back in the pilothouse Adams sent seaman Bennett with the first aid kit to assist Arnold with the skipper. Adams picked up the P.A. calling all department to report their damage. Looking through the broken bridge window gave him his answer, "My God we are sinking by the head." He turned towards the voice tube yelling into it, "Scotty how bad are we down there." His answer came back quickly. "At this point the pumps are barely keeping up, we need to get her out of the shipping lane while we can still make headway. Once we are out of the shipping lanes, we can lay the anchor to stop her drifting back into the shipping lanes. Once we are done with the engine, I'll blow the high-pressure steam valves to stop her from blowing up around us." Scotty talking in a very calm tone had been in a similar situation some years back and knew exactly what to do. "Sparkie send a distress signal to command that we are sinking by the head and need immediate assistance, add we have wounded including our captain." Adams answer, came back almost immediately. Command to Reese, standby we have a Frigate returning to England they can be with you in less than thirty minutes. They are overloaded but they are also the closest to your location. We need to give them a personnel count, are you capable of giving us that number? Command standing by. Adams put the mic down saying to Sparkie, "Once we confirm a rescue plan you may as well join the others gathering on the port side alright." Command to Reese, they can assist you how many souls are you? "Including the wounded approximately eighteen," answered Adams. Command to Reese do you still have a usable lifeboat? "Affirmative we have two. Will start boarding the lifeboats once we clear the shipping lane and laid out the hook. Reese over and out. Helmsman I will handle the telegraph for you, I'm taking her astern can't take a chance with that damaged bow, stand by. Scotty make your revs for slow astern, once you see the telegraph signal all stop, proceed with releasing the steam valves." Adams now yelled out the broken center window of the bridge to Charlie down below on the main deck, "Can you take two blokes and stand by to release the bow anchor." Adams was moving very quickly to make everything happen while the Reese was still afloat. "Will do skipper, Brown and Hepworth follow me, we need to lay the anchor when the Skipper gives the command." Charlies years of seamanship was very evident as he barked out orders," Chief will we have enough time, she is settling much faster now?" Asked Brown as the three sailors made their way forward to the anchor equipment seawater now close to the bow's freeboard. The Reese rumbled as she started to move backwards, her propeller blades throwing seawater high in the air protesting as the screw neared the surface. Adams standing on the bridge wing studied their progress, when he felt they were clear he rushed back into the pilothouse slamming the telegraph into all stop. With the bullhorn in hand he yelled to Charlie, "Let go the anchor for two hundred feet then get the hell off that bow. Returning to bridge he dismissed the sailors that were still at their stations, just as he was about to yell down the voice tube for Scotty and his three other boiler room gang to release the steam valves and get topsides, an ear splinting scream came from the funnel as a column of steam shot high in the air. Reese was no longer able to function as a trawler she had done her country proud and soon would lay silently on the seabed off the coast of France. Arnold along with Charlie and Brown carefully lifted their Captain's limp blood soaked form, onto a stretcher. "Keep his head in the center can't take a chance with that shrapnel so close to his jugular vein, stuff those towels on either side of his head, but be careful. When we abandon ship, we can walk the stretcher forward to where the deck railing is almost at sea level, that way we can move him into the lifeboat without tilting him down alright." Said Arnold. Adam's with bullhorn in hand was the last to leave the bridge his last act was to place the ships logbook into an oilskin bag. Taking a last look around, a lump in his throat lifted the bullhorn to his mouth announcing his last command. "Abandon ship repeat abandon ship, clear the wounded first, Scotty take a head count before we cast off." Adams helped to transfer Karl and the other wounded to the first lifeboat then helped the other survivors climb into the second boat. Looking around at the wrecked and now silent deck, he came to parade attention saluting the ship that had served them faithfully. "Goodbye old girl not the way I thought we would part. Push off and clear the ship before she goes under." Adams now turn his attention to coordinating the two lifeboats. Each boat had four rowing stations two on either side," All together now lads, row us out into the shipping lane and away from the Reese. About fifteen minutes passed Adams felt they should remain on station till the rescue Frigate arrives, "Alright lads ship your oars, we will wait here till the frigate arrives. A loud bubbling hissing sound made them all turn around to see Reese's stern rise out of the water then in slow motion she slipped without protest to her resting place on the ocean floor. She would however leave her funnel and two mast protruding above the waves in the shallow water.

"Mr. Adams that looks like a Frigate steaming towards us, is it?" Asked Brice as he stood up in the bow of the lifeboat. "Think your right, who has the portable signal lamp," asked Adams. "I do sir," said Hepworth the signalman. "Send a signal that we will come along side with the wounded first. Request they lower their boarding ladder, add our Captain is badly injured and cannot be boarded vertically, please confirm this request." The frigates signal lamp flashed back a reply, we are lowering it now stand by, F64 out. "Alright lads let's get those oars back in the water and start rowing towards the frigate, you blokes over there in the second boat get closer once we come along side and upload you can follow us in, is that clear. We need to board quickly then cast of. Charlie it will be your job to blow a clip of ammo into the bottom of our boat to sink it. Is that clear? Thompson use your bren gun to do the same to your boat, now stand by." Adams had saved many of the crew, his training as a naval officer and now leader had saved all of those around him with his quick thinking and a well-executed abandon ship plan." She is slowing down sir I can see some blokes lowering their starboard boarding ladder, shall we continue rowing towards them Skipper." One of the sailors yelled out. "Of course, now pull for all your worth." Adams replied. From their location they could see and hear the powerful props churn up the water as the frigate slowed in reverse to an almost stop. All along the railings on every deck, soldiers packed in looking down to watch the rescue. The first lifeboat banged against the boarding ladder, helping hands quickly and very carefully lifted Karl out of the lifeboat carrying him up the boarding ladder in such a way the stretcher remain level. Arnold staying right behind reminding them to be careful with their Captain. A few minutes later Brice opened fire with his bren-gun sinking the lifeboat in a hail of bullets. Next came the second boat with its complement of able-bodied seamen, in a very orderly fashion they all scrambled up the ladder to the deck above. Thompson shouldered his bren-gun then standing on the first run of the boarding ladder opened fire with ear-splitting rapid fire into the bottom of the lifeboat with that many holes it sank to the gunwales, wallowed for a moment then disappeared below the waves. "Come on you blokes get up here and off this bloody ladder," yelled out a sailor waiting with four others to hoist the ladder back on deck. The frigate trembled as all its power was sent to its twin screws churning the seawater at the stern. Up on the deck it was standing room only, a warrant officer yelled out, "All you lot from the trawler follow me, make way for the bloke on that stretcher." "Hey you that's our Captain your calling a bloke show some respect, or my right fist will do it for you." called out an irritated Charlie Brice, every soldier and sailor on the deck broke out in a cheer for Charlie and the tongue lashing he gave the warrant officer. "Look I'm sorry I meant no offense or disrespect for your Captain I am only trying to get you all into our sick bay as quickly as possible and right now we are so overloaded it can get very frustrating trying to make any headway, again I'm sorry." The warrant office was showing a little more humility now that someone had put him in his place. Adams was following smiling and shaking his head suddenly he yelled out, "Three cheers for Chief Petty Officer Charlie Brice." The response that came back from the remanence of HMT Reese crew was one that lightened up the tension for everyone on board.

Inside the frigate sick bay, the surgeon made his way over to were Arnold and Charlie sat next to the unconscious form of their Captain Vita. "Let's look at your captain shall we, how long has he been out?" Asked the surgeon. "More or less about four hours I'd say," Said Arnold as he looked at the concerned face of the surgeon. "Those cuts on top of his head I can clean up and stich up right away that will stop some of the bleeding, the bigger concern right now is that shrapnel in his neck it's in a very difficult position to remove here on the ship, way too dangerous if not done correctly it could sever a main artery, this needs to be done in a surgical suite with the correct instruments. At our current speed we will be back in Dover, no I stand corrected that was our previous load, this time we are heading for Folkstone in about fifty minutes or so. Anyway, once ashore we can move him quickly to one of the temporary triage centers that have been set up to handle the returning wounded. Now let's get him sewn up and see if I can bring him around being out this long has me concerned that his head injury could be worse than they appear." Concluded the surgeon. Adams by now had joined the ship's Captain on the bridge, like himself a first lieutenant only a regular career navy officer. "Captain I'd like to thank you for the quick response to our distress call, with the wounded and the critical condition of our Captain, the thought of being in open lifeboats for any extended period of time surely would of lead to more deaths, so thank you." Concluded Adams. "Sometimes things have a way of working out, glad we were so close to your location and may I say how efficient your crew squared away the boarding and sinking of your lifeboats they knew exactly what to do, we hardly lost any time rescuing you." The Captain's comments made Adams even more proud of how he had handled the whole operation, pity the Skipper never got to see it thought Adams as he sipped his mug of hot tea. Back in the sick bay Arnold and Charlie sat watching the corpsman as he gave Karl medicated oxygen supply through a facemask. "We are getting close to Folkstone should be pulling in in about twenty minutes" Said a sailor to the corpsman as he entered the sick bay. "Gentlemen you have to leave the sick bay we must get all these wounded ready to move ashore." Directed the friendly corpsman. "Arnold pleaded to remain with his Captain to no avail he would have to wait on the dock. The dime lights on the dock were focused on the boarding ladders as the troops lined up to disembark." Keep the gangplank clear till we have moved all the wounded ashore." Yelled the first lieutenant in charge of clearing the ship. One by one the wounded were taken up the gangplank some helped by corpsman many carried off on stretchers. Back in the sick bay the surgeon worked on Karl trying to revive him. "Sir we must move the Captain ashore can your men stay with him?" looking at Arnold and Brice. Once he is loaded into an ambulance give the attendant this note not to touch or move his head is that clear." The surgeon was concerned that his lack of response and the dangerous piece of shrapnel in his neck could become a problem moving him ashore. Arnold pleading with the ships surgeon to instruct the attending corpsmen to let them stay with the skipper till he is moved in the ambulance. "Once we are dockside only one of you can go with the Captain to the triage center, so which one of you will that be?" Asked the attending corpsman. "Guess that will be you Arnold you have been with him since it happened." Replied Brice. Two strong sailors carefully lifted the stretcher and walked towards the door leading to the deck, Arnold and Brice following behind at the door Brice turned around to thank the surgeon. "Thank you, sir, all of us appreciate the attention you gave our Captain." "Only wish I could have done more." Came the response.

On the dock ambulances lined up for the wounded and another long line of military lorries taking the troops to the waiting trains returning them to the numerous dispersal stations. "So long Charlie take care of yourself hope our paths cross again under better circumstances." Said Arnold as they parted. "Wait a minute mate let me give you my address at home and you can give me yours that way we can make a date to visit the skipper, hey there you in the white do you have a pencil and some paper, we can use?" barked Charlie in that London slang of his. "Got a medical form you can use the back of its blank and here is a pencil you can use." Replied the corpsman Charlie ripped the form in half giving one piece to Arnold." Once I know my new posting, I'll drop you a line we can make arrangements to visit the skipper after that." Both men faced each other, first a hand shack then a big hug. Charlie marched off towards a lorry that was loading, and Arnold climbed into the ambulance seating across from Karl on the stretcher. "Looks like he's is in a bad way," said the nurse seating at the side of Karl attending to the I.V. drip and oxygen mask. "He will need a blood transfusion once we reach the hospital." Fifteen minutes later the ambulance entered the makeshift triage area. Two burly soldiers with a red cross armband opened the ambulance door saying. "We'll take him from here please follow us." You will have to be very careful he must be kept level there is shrapnel in his neck very close to a major artery." Said Arnold staying very close to Karl's head as they offloaded the stretcher just to make sure. Inside the center, injured soldiers and sailors lay on beds lining both sides of the corridor. Nurses, corpsmen and military types, were half running up and down doing God know what. "Follow us Chief we are taking him right into the prep waiting area, once inside you can find someplace to wait." "I think once you go inside, I'll head back to the processing area at the docks there nothing I can do now but pray." Arnold would of prefer to stay but he needed to find out where he should be going. A tall surgeon wearing a blood-stained white lab coat came over to where Arnold was standing saying. "I say have you been with this officer since he was injured, if so I would prefer you remain here in case we have questions, by the look of him I would venture to say he's in bad shape so can't waist time getting him into surgery. By the way I'm Captain *Terry Mills* and your name?" asked the surgeon. "Chief Petty John Arnolds Sir. Thank you so much for asking me to stay I would much prefer to stay here with the skipper." Arnold was feeling much better now he knew he could remain with his Captain. "I have a question sir? I never registered when we go off the ship, I don't think anyone knows I'm here should I go back just to let them know?" asked Arnold. "Come with me chief, see that lieutenant over there, I'll tell him that I need you to remain here." The surgeon walked over to where the young naval Lieutenant was seating at his desk. "I say old chap I need this Chief Petty officer to remain here till we get his commanding officer out of trouble, be a good chap and notify whoever is responsible for registering returning chaps from Dunkirk will you." The surgeon looked at Arnold saying, "Give the lieutenant your information and tag numbers then follow me. Now that's done get yourself some food and drink from the cafeteria down the hall on the left. Return here after you have eaten, I would say you could do with forty winks. Use the couch in my office right over there. I'll wake you up after his surgery." Captain Mills could see the older gentleman needed some sleep. "Thank you so very much Sir you are so kind." replied Arnold. "It's me and everyone around us that should be thanking you Chief, I can only imagine the hell conditions you have survived through, now excuse me I must scrub up for surgery," with that the Surgeon walked off swiftly calling out to the operating nurses to get Karl ready. Arnold walked out of the prep-surgery area, turning left he walked down the hallway till he saw an overhead sign that said cafeteria. Inside he cast his sight on rows of long tables some occupied by soldiers and a few naval chaps, others sat with field dressing on their heads, arms, and legs. As Arnold stood there, he could not help thinking poor bugger's, most of them look like death warmed over, I must look about the same in this dirty blood stained and ripped uniforms, how will England survive? Waiting in line he picked up a metal tray and slide it down the chow line. "Got some scrambled eggs and chips for ya mate alright, there plenty of hot tea in those big urns at the end, glad you made it home." Said the older gentleman a civilian volunteer behind the counter "Thanks, it hasn't sunk in yet that I'm in one piece with no injuries." Arnold was starting to show signs of fatigue and maybe remorse. The old man just smiled as Arnold took his plate sliding it towards the tea urn. Arnold devoured the food on his plate wiping it clean with a slice of bread and butter. "Cor you look like you haven't eaten in a week said a cheerful Grenadier Guard sitting next to him. "Well not since yesterday anyway." Replied Arnold. "You're a sailor so you must be off one of the rescue ships is that right." The kindly soldier was trying to encourage conversation with the older sailor. "Well yes, I was on a rescue ship unfortunately my ship was sunk off Dunkirk, I'm here with our commanding officer he's in real bad shape and only now going into surgery. I've been asked to stay here till he's out of surgery, by the way my name is Chief Petty Officer John Adams what's yours." "Sergeant Mark Williams and from your accent would say you're a Londoner as well, glad we made it mate I am dreading to hear the casualty list, it was a miracle me and my boys got off the bloody beach at all we had to stand almost to our shoulders in sea water, waves washing over our heads at times waiting for one of those small boats to take us out to a merchantman. Bloody mad house scrabbling up the side of that ship and once on the deck we literally had to stand shoulder to shoulder, not going to complain though we are seating here safe and warm now ain't we." Mark held out a big hand to shake John's. "Really nice to meet you to Mark now I must be getting back to the waiting area, stay safe." John stood up collected his tray and headed for used tray bin. Back in the surgical area he asked a nurse if there was any news on Captain Karl Vita yet." Not yet still too early! Do you need anything before you take a nap in Captain Milles's office?" replied the nurse. "Nice of you to offer I think catching up on some sleep is what I need right now," replied Arnold heading for that couch.

The time was 0330 hrs, a gentle push on Arnold's shoulder woke him up from the deep sound sleep." Sorry to wake you Chief, there is someone very anxious to see you, I've also brought you a nice hot mug of tea which I'm sure will go down nicely right now." The friendly nurse had a smile on her face that told Arnold the Skipper was out of surgery. Following the nurse and sipping his tea as he followed her through a door marked authorized personnel only. White cloth partitions hung between the row of beds lined up on either side of the ward. Arnold walking behind the nurse could not help noticing the condition of the patience's in each bed they passed. The nurse stopped in front of a partition that had a curtain pulled across its front. Arnold could feel himself tense up waiting for the sight he would see as the nurse slide the curtain to one side. "Come in Chief, someone here would like to speak to you, not to long though, Lieutenant Vita is still quite weak." Said a cheerful Captain Mills now addressing Karl by his rightful rank as an officer in the BIS and not the temporary rank of Captain. Karl's head was bandaged across the top and one side, a neck support over the dressing held his head straight making it hard for him to talk. His injured right leg was not visible it was covered by a device that kept the bed covers off his leg. "Arnold so pleased you are here how can I ever thank you for saving my life." Said Karl in a very low strained voice. "It's a life worth saving sir, you would do it for me I'm sure." Replied Arnold. "Please tell me what happened I can only remember trying to save a sailor as he was falling to the deck then nothing, till a little while ago. What happened to the Reese did they save her and what about the crew." Karl was getting anxious to find out all the details. Captain Mills stopped Karl by saying. "There will be time for all those details at another time but right now I need you to rest. Chief there is a military ambulance going back to the docks in Folkestone, I asked them to wait for you so you can say your goodbyes, I'm sure when you can get back here the Lieutenant will demand to hear the rest of your story" Said Captain Mills. "Goodbye sir, get well, and be assured we will visit you when we are given leave. Before leaving with you in the ambulance, Lieutenant Adams did yell to me that he would try to get, Charlie and I assigned to a ferry going back to Dunkirk, so I'll have to find them somehow! Arnold had accidently let the cat out of the bag. "Arnold she's gone is that right at least tell me that before you leave." Karl was not about to let them leave till he at least knew that. "Yes, sir she is gone, goodbye again." Arnold regretted making a slip like that he would have preferred to address that at another time when his skipper was stronger. He took one more look at the injured person laying in the bed as he walked out with Captain Mills. The evacuation of Dunkirk was over, what would have been a crushing defeat was now viewed as the miracle of Dunkirk. An overwhelming victory against a superior enemy force saved over 300,000 English troops of the BEF and an additional 125,000 French, Belgium, and Canadian forces. Although the feeling of jubilations for the evacuation were being heralded across all of England the tragic loss of equipment would now put a tremendous strain on England's industrial capability to rebuild and reequip its army ready for the next confrontation with its enemy, the Germans.

CHAPTER FOUR
The Long Road Back

 Ten painfully slow days passed by one by one, for Karl every hour felt like a lifetime since he arrived at the field hospital. Once out of immediate danger and stable enough after the surgery, they had transported him by ambulance to this facility where he would be nursed back to health. He was still confined to his bed and getting very restless with little to occupy his mind and time other than some old books. The Matron for the ward was a charming lady in her twenties, started visiting Karl in the late afternoons after her shift had ended. She would sit by his bedside trying to make him think of something other than what was happening with the war. "Come on Lieutenant Vita loosen that load and talk to me of something else will you, this obsession with the war is not helping your recovery in any way, why don't you start by telling me how you arrived in England." Said *Sara* trying very hard to distract him. In a voice laboring with every breath Karl reached out taking Sara's hand shocking her by saying, "Sister when I get a little stronger you can show me more of those beautiful legs and thighs is that a deal." Karl was trying to smile holding her hand as tightly as he could. "Lieutenant Vita, I must say you are rather bold and very forward." She stood up still holding his hand leaning over him she whispered softly in his ear. "Promise me you will cooperate with the nursing staff and strive to get better with the therapy program, and I will gladly show you more than that, is that a deal." Sara was sending Karl a message that she liked him a lot more than she had let on to, it would not be too long before the nursing staff also knew her secret!

   The days remained quite warm and sunny, the patience's were encouraged to take advantage of the weather conditions outside, some could walk out, some needed crutches and many needed wheelchairs as did Karl. Nurse *Julia* would help him out of bed and into his wheelchair, taking him outside. At the lower part of the garden, she would wheel him under the shade of a large old oak tree, then check in on him ever thirty minutes to make sure all was alright. On one of this days Karl was reading a newspaper when a familiar voice behind him announced," Lieutenant you have visitors, let me turn you around." Said Sara turning the wheelchair around in front of three uniformed officers." You bugger's it's taken you long enough to come and see me." Said the now very upbeat Karl. "Thank you nurse Wilkinson guess I will have to behave myself now we have witnesses, won't I?" Karl happier now than he had been in for over a month seeing his friends was the medicine he needed. "Lieutenant Vita I swear to God you are the most incorrigible patient in the entire hospital," said Sara. "And my dear that's why you love me." replied Karl. "Please excuse me, I will be back in about an hour, can I have some tea and biscuits brought out for you? One of the stewards is on his way with folding chairs." Sara turned towards Karl fussing over him by adjusting the blanket and fixing his pajama collar. "What a sight you three are, Hazel have not seen you in over a year, think it was a few months after you returned to England with Bill. Clive, I expected to see you weeks ago guess I rate low on your priority list." Karl could not be happier. His closest friends had come to see him. "I say old man you really embarrassed that nurse, some things never change." Said Clive as he unfolded one of the chairs. "Sara is a wonderful nurse and by the way she is the matron of my ward, she has spent many, many hours pulling and pushing me through some difficult times including some rough therapy sessions. Did you bring me the statistics on Dunkirk I wrote you about and the files on my crew that did not make it back, I need to write to their families, not sure how to write those letters though." Without realizing it, Karl was now conversing in a much stronger sounding voice, a sign he was on the mend. "Why don't you let me help you with those letters Karl, my family only lives about thirty minutes from here. These chaps are dropping me off once we leave you today. Our boss here authorized a four-day leave so I'd be glad to help you with those letters." Said Hazel as she poured four cups of tea from the large tea pot. Hazel still had feelings for Karl that dated back some years when they were training in Scotland. Bill was the last person to see Kitty alive, Hazel was the radio operator on that fateful mission, and it was she that send the morse coded message about Kitty's demise. "Why don't we start tomorrow what time should I be here, in the afternoon would that work." Hazel was moving in on Karl before that matron beat her to the punch. "That sounds like a plan Hazel, I'll have to check with Sara first to see when my next therapy session is scheduled, alright." Karl answering Hazel then turned his attention to what plans the BIS had for him when he returned to duty." Karl, here are the reports but can you put them aside while we visit with you alright." Clive was not prepared to spoil this time together by allowing Karl to see casualties and equipment losses quite yet. "Of course, that would be rude of me to start looking at those reports while you are visiting." In the back of Karl's mind, he had already determined the extent of the destruction and deaths those reports would detail. Over the next couple of hours, the four enjoyed talking about the good times shared while in Scotland training and partying in the cold of winter. "Hazel I can remember one night at the officers club, you got me to dance with you, my God how drunk you were." Karl saying that also remembered Kitty cutting in ending any further advances Hazel could be contemplating. "Well, if my memory serves me correctly Kitty put a stop to that night of fun for me, guess I got the short end of the stick or should I say no stick at all." Hazel realizing what she had just said, with a smirk on her face she looked at the straight faces of Karl, Clive, and Bill for what seemed like an eternity before Bill broke out laughing melting the ice to what now could only be viewed as funny. All four of them continued laughing and adding other instances that made the time go by all too fast for Karl. Sara returned to find the mood light and very cheerful. "Time to get you back inside and thank you for making this afternoon so enjoyable for Lieutenant Vita." She could not believe the transformation Karl had made in just a few hours with his fellow officers, his energy was recovering he was gaining his old self back, the side of him she had never seen before. "Sara, Hazel and I are going to be working on some very important letters tomorrow afternoon, I know I have a visit with Doctor Mills first thing then therapy that pretty well takes up most of the morning so if she arrives say at 1350 hrs will that be alright." Asked Karl. "I'm sure that will be perfectly expectable, would you like me to see if I can find you an empty room or maybe an office that is not in use." Asked Sara as she folded the blanket from Karl's lap. "That would be super that way we can spread out." Replied Karl. Clive stood offering to push Karl back up the inclined pathway that led up to the French doors in front of Karl's ward. "So, matron what's the story behind this mansion," asked Bill walking beside Sara and following behind Clive pushing Karl with Hazel close by.

"Up until six weeks ago this magnificent mansion had been the home of a leading industrialist. The army requisitioned it for a field hospital based on its proximity to Dover and Folkstone Harbors. Colonel Benjamin Warren, the owner retired from the army a year after the first world war that ended in 1918. He made his fortune building a manufacturing company that made farm equipment. When he was approached by the Army, he jumped at the chance too once again serve his country giving up this magnificent home, he just couldn't do enough to assist. Colonel Warren instructed his management team to clear all the furniture out of the first level and part of the second floor. His purchasing department was instructed to buy as many hospital bed's that could be used to set up the wards, that also included other furniture the hospital would need. His factory workers were also eager to contribute by feverishly working to make the transformation happen. That whole month everyone involved worked day and night including the nursing staff and many of the doctors to set up the surgical theatres, treatment rooms and of course the six wards. It truly is quite an accomplishment getting this mansion transformed and may I say just in time for the large numbers of casualties we have here right now." Sara was enjoying telling Bill this story and it showed. "Well, this is where we must take our leave of you for today anyway, I'll put your file in the top draw of your bed stand, remember to lock it up in Matron's file cabinet," Said Clive as he parked the wheelchair next to Karl's bed. "Will do Major Knight I'll start reviewing it after supper tonight." Karl was enjoying kidding Clive like this. Their friendship had been through some wonderful highs, the lows however had been extremely painful, it was this bond that bound, Karl, Clive, and Bill together as lasting friends. "Up yours," said Clive grasping Karl's hand tightly laughing to how Karl had addressed him. "Bill don't wait for this bugger to bring you here come anytime I really would like the company and updates alright your gimpy old bugger." Karl now turned his attention to the striking Hazel standing next to Clive. "Hazel I guess I'll see tomorrow afternoon then hope you will be out of uniform or should I ask pretty please." Karl was rebounding back into his old sarcastic and flirtatious self. Clive looked at the other two with a smile that said it all, he is going to be all right. As they turned to depart Clive stopped and in a jovial tone said to Sara now standing next to the Karl's wheelchair. "Matron one word of caution, now this Vita chap is on the mend you will have to watch him he has a reputation with the ladies especially if they're in nursing uniforms." Clive had got the last word in for the day, so he thought. "Well Major I'm glad you told me that because I'm about to give him a sponge bath once you're gone." Sara had a big smile across her face that had a hidden meaning. If they only knew he can have anything he wants, whenever he wants thought Sara still smiling. "See you tomorrow," said Hazel as they walked down the ward and out the door. Sara helped Karl back into bed thinking he is getting stronger, what a difference from this morning don't think I've seen anyone bounce back quite this fast. She left then, returning pushing a cart that had a big white enamel bowl full of warmish water in it. Two sponges and two towels lay across the side. "Well let's get you ready for supper shall we." Said Sara as she pulled the curtain shut for privacy. "Sara we can do this, but you made a commitment to me earlier today and I demand you live up to it." Karl was only fooling with her but Sara on the other hand was going to take advantage of this challenge. Placing her finger across her mouth for Karl be quiet she started to undress him then carefully sponged him all over with sweet smelling soap. Karl lay back enjoying the feel of her touch, he closed his eyes and lay perfectly still when suddenly he felt soft moist lips on his. Sara pushing against his lips with her tongue made him thoroughly aroused for the first time in years. He moved to rap his arms around her neck when Sara stopped, stood straight up saying in a very low voice, "There's more of that, you big tease when you are much stronger. Now let's get you into fresh pajamas shall we." Karl motioned to Sara to come closer almost whispering into her ear he said quietly. "Matron I will do as you ask, but for now I want that private viewing you promised." Karl holding her hand and stopping her from pulling away kissed the back of her hand waiting for a reply. Sara walked to the curtain opening it just wide enough to look up and down the ward. Once she was comfortable that all was quiet and safe for her, she turned in front of Karl her eyes burning into his and quietly said, "This is a deposit on my promise." Slowly and very deliberately she bent over taking the hem of her uniform with both hands and proceeded to raise it slowly up to almost her waist for just a very few seconds then dropped it back down again. Sara returned to his bed side smiling that she had wiped that look off his face. "You realize I could be dismissed for what just happened don't you, so I guess you're in the driver's seat right now. I will have to do whatever you ask for to keep you quiet won't I?" Sara bent over to kiss him once again stroking his face with her left hand. "I'll come by after supper to say good night hope you enjoyed yourself." With that Sara opened the curtain wide and rolled the cart out into the center of the ward thinking that would carry some weight till tomorrow when that Hazel is here. Karl sat starring at the ceiling processing what had just happened. The picture in his mind was the very attractive Sara in dark hose and black suspenders, her piercing eyes never leaving his. This vision was quickly crowded, falling back into another time when a very attractive lady in similar hose and black suspenders had done the very same thing, this new vision was *Kitty his deceased fiancé*.

Julia and another nurse entered his partition with a wheeled bed stand designed to fit over the bed on it was his supper with a pot of hot tea. "Eat it while its hot Lieutenant got to get your strength back." Said the pretty young Julia, "We will be around later to remove the tray and get you ready for the evening. After the supper things were removed, he laid back and without realizing it was reverting into his military mode of thinking. He had been out of contact for too long and this was making him angry at being so laxed in a time of survival for his adopted homeland of England and even more so now after the evacuation at Dunkirk. I need to put all this foolishness aside and stop this flirtation with Sara it's not fair to her what I've started something I know will eventually hurt her when it's time for me to leave. Karl when will you ever learn? When she comes by tonight I must be firm and sincere about putting this flirting aside till England is safe once more. Pouring his last cup of tea, he stretched over to retrieve the locked fabric document pouch Clive had given him earlier. From the draw he also retrieved a small leather key holder. Karl unlocked the document pouch and removed a folder that had Private and Confidential stamped in big red letters across the outside.

Operation Dynamo date: May 26th. June 4th. 1940 (Condensed Statistics)

1. The total Flotilla 900 vessels. This included naval and civilian craft, French and Norwegian units. Reported as of the May 26th and 27th.
2. Reported losses 235 vessels sunk. Royal Navy, French Navy and units from Norway, Merchantmen, English and French. Channel Ferries, and a fleet of small private craft. The final report is still being compiled by type and registry.
3. Approximately 106 RAF aircraft destroyed
4. Estimated deaths during the evacuation 5,000 BEF soldiers
6. Other allied troops were rescued by mostly British ships
    from French ports: Cherbourg, Saint-Malo, Brest, and Saint Nazaire.
7. Allied troops rescued 558,000 from all locations.
8. Reports as of June 5th estimate that over a 1,000,000 allied soldier from England- France and Belgium had surrendered.
9. The main rallying point the town of Dunkirk was reduced to rubble by heavy German artillery and aerial bombardment.

Projected Equipment loss

1. 2,472, Artillery pieces, (Large Caliber only) and 76,097 tons of ammunition
2. 63,879 vehicles, includes battle tanks, armor cars, lorry's, staff cars and 20,548 motorcycles
3. 416,940 tons of assorted stores.

The reports went on to say that units of the BEF, French and Belgium Armies held back the German forces in a rear-guard action during the evacuation. *Lord Gort,* Commander-in- chief, arrived back in England June 1st, feted as a hero.
Prior to departing, Major-General Harold Alexander inspected the shores of Dunkirk from a motorboat before boarding a Royal Navy destroyer vowing, we may be forced to leave today, be assure we will return and on that day, Germany will regret her actions. Karl laid there reading five more pages of data before he came to a transcript of Winston Churchill address to the House of Lords the day after the

last of the returning troops arrived back in England. *Prime Minister Churchill* describing the evacuation as:

The Miracle of Dunkirk.

We shall not fail or falter. We shall go on to the end. We shall fight in France. We shall fight on the seas and on the oceans. We shall fight with growing confidence and growing strength in the air. We shall defend our island, whatever the cost may be. We shall fight on the beaches, we shall fight on the landing grounds, we shall fight in the fields and in the streets, we shall fight in the hills, we shall never surrender.

Karl reviewed the file several more times, slowly shaking his head in disbelief. He gathered the documents returning them all to the pouch then made sure it was firmly locked. He could feel the sorrow welling up in his eyes and the realization that from this moment on he would be all business, he would try anyway? Tomorrow I must call Mama at the bungalow to see if they received any news about Papa and my brothers, I pray their escape from Wien (Vienna) was successful, but where are they, and are they in a safe place? In this time of melancholy, he allowed himself to catalog what he needed to accomplish before returning to the BIS. He would insist on assignment back into occupied Europe, field agents would be key in assessing how the conquering Germany forces would be enforcing their will and demands on the people of occupied Europe. Staring at the ceiling he was brought back to the present by the sound of the privacy curtain being moved back just wide enough for Sara to walk through. Smiling she closed it once again. At his bedside she sat on the side of the bed quietly reaching for his hand. "Sara, stop I must talk to you and you must listen very carefully to what I have to say. Earlier today we both got carried away in a heated flirtation. As much as we both may have enjoyed that foreplay, it must now stop, it will not and cannot go any further. From this moment on I need your help to regain my health enough to pass the medical discharge exam. What has happened recently to this country means the BIS will need every available Intelligence officer. I need to return to my post as soon as possible. Sara will you do that for me and please and again except my apologies for any notion you may have had that I was suggesting a more meaningful relationship. My actions were simply an escape from the frustration and boredom having to stay here, immobilized and not doing my part back in the BIS." Karl stopped talking waiting for her response. Sara did not move or say a word, she remained still her emotions controlled by her training. She continued holding his hand sitting on the side of his bed. Collecting her thoughts, she returned his hand to his side. "Karl or should I call you by your rank of

Lieutenant, like you I have a responsibility to this hospital. Hearing you talk like this makes me also realize that we are in a war for survival those girlish actions may not be appropriate at times like these, as much as I would love to make it more, it's just selfish on my part. I have worked hard to become a Matron and it's that responsibility that must now keep me from straying till times are more appropriate. So, my dearest Karl I understand completely. As a nurse I will do everything in my power to help you get back on your feet. When the time comes for you to leave, I expect a big kiss on the cheek, of course. When this war is over hopefully, we will come through as the victors, I can assure you I will find you so get that through your thick Austrian head, do you understand me." Sara with a smile on her face showing her strong professional side as well making it clear he was not off the hook by any means. Sara stood up looking Karl in the eyes that tender smile still on her face. "Sara would you kindly put this pouch in your locking file for me, can't take the risk of it being opened." Asked Karl feeling relieved by this brief talk. "Sure, now give me a lasting big kiss, no strings attached of course," Sara needed a lasting memory of what could have been or might be in the future? "Help me stand up then can't appear to be half a man when asked to kiss such a beautiful lady or should I call you Matron." Karl was almost his old self, well almost. "Do you realize this is really the first time I have stood up without the use of a walker, now let's have that last big kiss shall we." Sara gave a hearty laugh her eyes told a different story though. Karl placed his hands slowly and softly on Sara's checks his facial expression becoming very serious. Sara made the first move by reaching up to his lips her mouth partially open hunger in her eyes, embracing they kissed allowing their mouths to open as Sara thrust her tongue into Karl's mouth this was more than either one of them expected. Karl stiffened at first then relaxed knowing that when they parted it would be over for now anyway. "God Karl you are a wonderful kisser got my juices going and by the look on your face, I would say it's going to stay with you for a long time." As Sara said that she knew she would think of this moment often in the months ahead and prayed Karl would return to her when this war comes to an end. The following morning, he was wakened at 0530 hrs by Nurse Julia, she helped him dress then brought his breakfast tray in noticing how well he was moving and now standing without any help. "I say lieutenant you are making a miraculous recovery, at this rate you could be out of here by next week, we will be sorry to see you go though, after I have cleared your breakfast tray I'll walk you down the hall to Doctor Mills office ." Said Julia as she cleared the tray. Karl tried to walk without the walker but reverted to using it after only a few yards. "You're not ready to walk without that walker yet sir give it time."

Julia could see that Karl was pushing too hard concerned the stitches on his right thigh might open if he continued like this. "Good morning Lieutenant your looking so much better than a few days ago, how's the neck and thigh doing let's get a look shall we. "Doctor Mills help Karl onto the end of the examination table followed by nurse Julia removing the dressings on his upper thigh. "Well, that looks so much better a little inflamed at the stitches has me a little concerned though.

"I reminded the lieutenant earlier he's not ready yet to put too much pressure on those stitches yet." Julia was trying to make Karl take heed of the Doctors comment. "Let that stay open nurse till I have looked at Karl's neck please." Doctor Mills stood next to Julia as she carefully removed the neck support and then the dressing. "This is the one that worries me the most Karl, when we operated, we removed nearly all the shrapnel, what we did not remove is a longish slither laying under a main artery. Your neck was too much of a mess so at the suggestion of Doctor *Burgess* we did not remove it we secured it instead. There may come a time sometime in the future when we can look at that wound again but not in a field hospital like this, that will have to be done in London probably at *Saint Mary's* by Doctor Burgess himself. For the meantime we are satisfied it should not give you any problems other than an occasional pain for a minute or two." Doctor Mills moved to the sink washing his hands firmly saying, "He is all yours now nurse." then left the room wishing Karl a good day and continued progress with the therapy. "Are you ready to see Matron and continue with your therapy, you heard the Doctor don't overdo it alright?" Nurse Julia was hoping he would take note of the Doctors advise.

In the converted ballroom Karl met up with Sara and a male therapist named Harry, Julia handed the clipboard with the Doctors notes over to Harry to review then helped Karl up onto the therapy table. "We are going to start with slow leg bends then work the upper thigh, Matron would you help the lieutenant to raise and lowering his right leg very slowly for a count of twenty." Instructed Harry as he moved off to attend to another patient. Sara true to her word carefully helped Karl for the best part of an hour then worked on his neck wound without that annoying neck brace. "Alright Karl time to get you back and washed up for your visit with lieutenant Collins after lunch is that still on?" Asked Sara, now holding Karl's arm as they walked through the ward, Karl trying hard not to show the pain he was enduring as he labored with ever step down the ward. "Karl why don't you take a break and allow me to get a wheelchair, you're in no condition to walk all the way yet." Sara could see the stress on his face knowing full well he was determined to walk to the bathroom. "Karl please listen to me if that wound opens up again it will set you back weeks, now stop being a thick-headed Austrian and sit-down in this wheelchair and that is an order." Sara knew if she didn't demand he would continue to limp down the ward. "Alright Karl let's get you into the bathroom for a shower and shave, will you be alright, or would you like me to help you." Sara saying that looked at Karl now with a big grin on his face. "Karl what happened to our promise made earlier this morning or have you already changed the rules." Smirked Sara as she wheeled him into the bathroom. "As usual Sara you are right, I was merely kidding around." Responded Karl. "As I told you I take my work very seriously as much as I would like to sponge you down in the shower stall it's not going to happen." Sara had a way of coming back at him with a sarcastic remark and Karl enjoy her spirit so much. Sara left him in the bathroom saying she would be back in about thirty minutes to help him get dressed ready to receive his visitor.

Hazel Collins sat at the small make up mirror in her bedroom modestly applying her makeup her beautiful features did not need to much makeup to enhance her striking beauty. She had decided to wear a pair of grey pleated wool trousers with large turnup at the bottom that would go nicely with the cream-colored silk blouse she already had on. Her long brown hair was perfectly brushed, normally when in uniform she would wear it up in a French twist, but not today and especially considering who she was driving to meet! Downstairs she entered the kitchen to have an early lunch with her mother and father already seating at the table. "My don't you look spiffy out of your uniform said her father as she sat down next to him. Hazel took his hand and kissed the back of it she adored her parents so very much any chance to spend time with them was a real treat. "Thank you, dad, it feels so nice to be in civvy cloths even though its only for a few days. What's for lunch mum, whatever it is smells delicious." Sara was always careful about letting her parents know what she really did in the BIS. When asked years back why she had joined the bloody spy blokes as her father called them. She had fabricated a cover story that her job was to train new recruits how to speak German and French that included reading and writing. She had majored in English Literature at University, she was however intrigued with other languages, so it was easy decision to add German and French to her studies. Growing up in this thatched cottage on the outskirts of *Sandwich in Kent* with her parents and older brother currently station with the Royal Airforce in Singapore. Life in those early days was as perfect as it could be for young Hazel and brother *James* to grow up in. Her Mother, *Mary* had been a schoolteacher and married her husband *Bill* when he was still in The Royal Corps of Engineers before retiring into a civilian position with the *Dutton Company Ltd* as a mechanical engineer that manufactured bicycles. This environment was perfect to mold life values into both Bill and Mary's children. "Dad, are you sure about letting me borrow your car, I know how you love that *Morris 10*, Major Knight gave me some petrol voucher yesterday so I will not be depleting your precious fuel." Sara knew her father would not object he would gladly give his children the world and sometime forgot they both were adults in military service. "Must be off will probably be home about six alright. Her mother could always read her daughter's face, as she said. "Behave yourself young lady your Father and I are not ready to start babysitting just yet." Mary was smiling almost laughing as her daughter picked up the car keys heading to the kitchen back door. "Mother please how can you think like that." Hazel was also thinking how she would do anything to win Karl over and that was probably showing in her facial expressions. "My sweet girl we may be getting older, but I can assure you when we were much, much younger we probably would have made you blush, as the old saying goes if you can't be good then try to be careful. Now off with you that young man won't wait forever." Hazel threw a kiss to her parents as she walked out the back door into the driveway. Outside the air was sweet from the colorful flower beds on either side of the doorway and others growing up the side of the house. As she walked over to the car she was thinking, I am so fortunate to have parents that are very much with it and still young at heart. My mother must have been quite the lady when she landed good old dad. Hazel was quietly laughing as she unlocked the driver's door to the Morris. Once inside she looked around noticing that everything was spotless, her father took so much pride in his car, purchasing it three years earlier from the Morris dealer in Sandwich. She started the engine turning around in front of the house then proceeded to the driveway turned left into the very narrow lane that led to the main road two miles ahead.

She covered the distance to the hospital in less than twenty minutes, parking the car she checked her makeup and hair in the small rearview mirror before stepping out into the bright sunshine. Once inside she asked the nurse sitting at the information desk how to find a Lieutenant Vita a patient in the hospital. "One moment and your name please," answered the nurse. "Lieutenant Collins," replied Hazel. The nurse picked up the desk phone dialed the extension number from the book in front of her and waited for someone to answer. "Hello Nurse *Ambone*, here, a Lieutenant Collins has arrived to see Lieutenant Vita," The nurse waiting for an answer then said, "Right I'll send her down. Nurse Ambone wrote a visitor pass handing it to Hazel, "Your party is expecting you in meeting room B-2, it's easy to find just turn right at that big column then it will be on the right side just a little way down." Hazel thanked the nurse then proceeded to the meeting room. She could feel the excitement build in her chest as she opened the door. "Hazel come on in so pleased you made it," said Karl as he slowly stood up. Hazel closing the door crossed over to Karl standing at the small table saying. "Well look at you standing there it's like you're ready to come back to work. Really wonderful to see the old Karl on the mend you heal really quickly." Said Hazel as she put her arms around him giving him a big hug. "Well Hazel I'm glad you noticed. I seem to be getting stronger with each passing day and yes I'm ready to return to work the sooner the better." Replied Karl. "Well let's get these letters written shall we, then perhaps we can take in the afternoon air it is so nice outside, does that seem like a good idea." Hazel was happy to help Karl with these sensitive letters but equally intent of spending some quiet time along with him outside of this hospital. "How did you get here." asked Karl as they sat down at the table. "Borrowed my Dad's car only took me twenty minutes it was very pleasant driving here such a pretty part of England in summertime." Replied Hazel pouring herself a tall glass of water from the pitcher on the table. "Must say Hazel you look fantastic out of uniform, never realized your hair was so long really transforms you." Remarked Karl taking in this new look on Hazel. "Glad you noticed. You know it's all for you, don't you?" Hazels eyes found Karl's as she said that waiting for his reaction. "Well in that case all I can say is thank you for doing this for me." That voice in the back of his head kept repeating, don't start anything Karl remember yesterday. "Shall we get started," said Hazel as she opened the list in front of them. "Why don't you tell me what it is you would like to say, will each letter be the same except for their names and addresses? You take half the names and I take the rest alright." Hazel quickly drafted a form letter then passed it to Karl for his input. "Very well written Hazel I think that says exactly how I feel. Make sure you sign it Lieutenant Karl Vita, acting Captain HMT Reese." "Alright then let's get to work." Answered Hazel. With two of them writing the letters they were finished in less than two hours. "Ready to venture outside Karl," Asked Hazel as she collected all the envelopes from the table then stood ready to help Karl stand up. "Do you want that wheelchair Karl, or would you prefer to walk I'll hold your arm if that's what you prefer." Hazel could not do enough for Karl and he knew it. "Would much prefer to walk if you're alright with going really slowly." Said Karl as she helped him to his feet. Leaving the meeting room, she held his arm firmly keeping him close to her side, this added support enabled Karl to walk with less of a limp than earlier in the day. At the reception desk Karl explained that the box of letters had to go out that afternoon and somebody needs to stamp them. "I'll make sure that is taken care of sir. "Replied nurse Ambone. Outside the bright sunshine made them squint momentarily, Hazel reached for her handbag and removed a pair of sunglasses. "Karl you don't have any sunglasses with you, would you like me to go back inside and get yours for you?" Asked Hazel. "Could you please I never thought it would be this bright this late in the afternoon, let me sit right here on this bench and wait for you." Karl sat down with the assistance of Hazel, as she bent over to help him Karl caught himself looking down the front of her blouse at perfectly formed breasts in a very lacy white bra. This vision aroused him and stayed in front of him as she stood up again. "I'll ask one of the nurses in your ward to find them for me, where would they find them." Asked Hazel. "Should be in the dresser top draw." Karl watched her walk back towards the main entrance thinking she is a very striking woman. Don't think I ever looked at her like I'm looking now, there again I only had eyes for Kitty back then. About five minutes pasted before Hazel walked back waving his glasses. "Found them here put them on before we go walking. Spoke to the Matron and nurse Julia, they told me to tell you not to overdo it and be back no later than 1750 hrs. Ready for that stroll, you good looking hunk." Hazel looped her arm under his and helped him to his feet then started walking around the end of the building towards the beautiful landscaped garden at the end of the hedgerow they turned towards the lake surrounded by large oak trees and beds of colorful flowers. "Looks like we are all alone back here, let's not overdo it, why don't we seat awhile on that bench in the shade if that sounds good to you." Came the suggestion from Hazel as she guided them towards the bench. Carefully she lowered Karl down then sat next to him saying. "Karl there is something I need to tell you and wanted to for a very long time. Seating here alone and together is the perfect time for me to get it off my chest and I want you to listen without responding till I have finished will you do this for me?" Asked Hazel turning in towards Karl taking his hand and cradling in between hers. "You have my undivided attention, what's on your mind you have a different look on your face that tells me this is way overdue, is it?" Karl had a feeling he knew what was coming, is this the right time to continue or was he letting another opportunity for happiness pass him by? Best to wait till she has finished he thought. "Karl, we have known each other for a few years now, although most of that time has been work related. When I was on assignment with Kitty and Bill into Germany, she confided in me one night that she had a bad feeling that she would not be returning to England at the completion of the mission. Her biggest fear was how you would react hearing this devasting news, she continued saying that your temper may get the better of you against any German you come across. Karl, I know how in love you two were and that torch you still carry for her, but as I said she did not want you to go on without another love or lady in your life. You must know?" Hazel hesitating before continuing, "Karl, I know you know I have always had a special place for you in my heart. Kitty knew that also, so it came as no surprise when she asked me to make her a promise that if she fell in the course of her duty, I would try to replace her, of course that's assuming you would come around to excepting me. Karl I would never try to replace the love you had for Kitty she was a wonderful remarkable lady, but when she asked me to do that for her, I also knew she trusted me to make that happen. You may be thinking, why have I never approached you before? It's been several years after all, well needless to say I was too scared to make that move, I did not want to face rejection from you either?" Hazel stopped talking turning away from Karl ready for his response whatever that may be.

"Hazel I can only imagine how difficult that was for you to tell me this. Kitty and I found something very special in these times, we live in has shattered any chance of a life together happening. My heart is almost permanently damaged the thought of enduring that again is too much to consider. The only thing I'm capable of is a casual relationship, I'm not sure that's enough for you. Hazel would you consider such a friendship and let's see how that plays out, simply enjoying each other's company and if something happens during those times well let's just say war is war and hormones because of war have a tendency, to erupt without notice. I think you have an idea where this is going. I have built a wall around myself and by doing so have lived other than work in this lonely existence without the tenderness of a lady to turn to. Our jobs are such that looking too far ahead is dangerous, here today and sometimes gone tomorrow." Karl stopped rambling on and now put his arm around Hazel hoping what he is suggesting will be enough for her. "Karl, I feel like a big load has been lifted from my shoulder and of course I understand where you are right now. If we can be special friends with needs such as making love, enjoying being out together, basically having each other in our lives is all we can really expect with jobs in the bloody BIS, doesn't leave much time for little else. One thing I must add and caution you on if I find myself unable to continue because I need more from you, you will seriously consider making this relationship more than casual, or just walk away with no hard feelings, alright." Hazel had to add this because she could not tell Karl that she had been in love with him for a very long time. Making love and spending time together would have to do but she knew deep down she would be going down the same road as Kitty did. Karl pulled her towards him tenderly lifted her head towards his and kissed her softly. Hazel's head was spinning she was being kissed by someone she had dreamed about for such a long time. Her left arm went behind his head pulling him into her mindful of his neck wound, this was going to be an end to a perfect day. Back in the ward Sara looked at her watch realizing it was now passed 1800 hrs. "Julia lets go find Karl and his friend Hazel shall we they probably have not been keeping an eye on the time and we need him back in the ward." Sara was also concerned Hazel had got what she really came for and that was Karl. As they rounded the corner of the building they could see down to the lake and there on the bench, they saw Karl and Hazel locked in an embrace. "Well, there is your answer to why they are late returning," Said Julia with a big grin on her face. "Julia that's what I was thinking also, now let's remind them it's time for Hazel to go home shall we." Sara was obviously put out even though she suspected that Hazel was in a far better position than she was. Hate to break up the party you two, but our patient needs to return to his ward." Sara turned quickly to avoid Karl seeing the expression on her face and with Julia by her side walked back towards the building. "Karl, I think the Matron is a little put out by me being here with you so long, better we walk back to the entrance and get you into the ward then I must be off.

Karl when can I see you again, let me ask Clive if I can return next weekend that's of course if you would like me to." Hazel stood facing Karl as she said this waiting for a positive response. "That Hazel would be very nice what would be even better is for me to request a weekend pass, I think I'm well enough for that to happen. I'll look into available Inns close by does that make sense to you darling." For the first time in a long time Karl had just called Hazel darling without even giving it another thought. "Oh, by the way if Clive gives you any trouble have him call me." At that very moment Karl could feel sunshine breaking through the black cloud that had been over his head since Kitty was killed. Back at the entrance Hazel walked him inside gave him an affectionate kiss then said she would call him tomorrow at about 1130 hrs to confirm her leave and he should investigate the Inns close by. "Guess I'll be off then wish we could be staying together tonight but this will give me something to look forward to during the week." Hazel turned towards the steps stopped momentarily looked back at Karl saying with a glow to her face. "There are nice looking nurses in there, lover boy remember I've got first dibs on you." With that Hazel walked quickly to her car, she had got what she came for, well almost!

Chapter Five
Time to leave.

At 1130 hrs the following day Karl waited patiently for Hazel to call but that did not happen nor did she call the following week, something big has had to happen back in Slough there must be a lockdown at the camp with no outgoing calls. Karl seating outside felt the warmth of the midday sun in the cloudless sky but deep inside that black cloud was forming once again. God please don't put me through that stress again haven't I paid my dues and just when I was starting to believe there was a new lady in my life. Once again Karl was sinking back into that dark state of despair. Trying to drive those bleak thoughts from his mind he turned his attention to getting fit again, with each passing day he worked diligently with Harry and occasionally with the help of Sara in his therapy sessions, their encouragement to go further was the drive he needed but always mindful of his wounded leg and neck. The visible signs that he was firmly on the mend was encouraging to the staff and the watchful eye of Doctor Mills. Karl tried to put on a cheerful face, but Sara knew differently, he was not his normal cocky sarcastic self, remaining mostly on his own that cloud that had been following him since leaving his ship in Marseilles was forming again and this was not doing anything for his self-esteem. Karl had by now discarded the walker reverting to only using his cane to help himself. As for the dressing and support around his neck that still gave him some discomfort when trying to wear a shirt with a collar, however this seemed a small price to pay considering the alternatives. On Thursday afternoon almost three weeks since he said goodbye to Hazel, nurse Julia found him seating on the veranda reading the Daily Mirror newspaper. "Sir you have a telephone call, you can take it in Matron's office. Do you need help, or would you prefer to use you cane to walk there?" Asked Julia. Karl thought for moment then said. "That can only be Hazel," as he hobbled towards the office. Once inside he picked up the receiver hesitantly putting it to his ear, about to ask Hazel what had happened, before he could utter a word, she cut him off saying." Karl thank God they let me telephone you I have some bad news darling any plans we made will have to wait I have been confined to base here in Slough. Can't say too much on an unsecure phone line but I'm sure you can figure out the reason, Gunther and Herbert send you their regards they are meeting up with me in about fifteen or so minutes. Not too sure when I can contact you again, please think of me often and those wonderful plans we made only a few weeks ago, must go now I think Gunther is at the door. Keep getting stronger, bye darling." Karl returned the receiver to its cradle his mind now in overload. If Gunther and Herbert are joining up with Hazel, can only mean one thing they are getting ready to leave on a mission back to the Continent, Hazel had got her message through to him. As he sat there processing her call, he felt a cold chill cross his check once again thinking, I have been down this road before, God take care of them if it's into harm's way that they are heading? I've got to find out immediately when I can return to Slough, they must be scrabbling for help after the beating we took at Dunkirk.

Karl in a very loud voice called Julia back into the office. "Julia on the double, please find Doctor Mills for me don't come back without him do you hear me now go." How can I convince the Doctor that I'm well enough to return to my post? We are almost at the end of July. If I'm not strong enough to return to field work, I'm strong enough to work at a desk in an intelligence position. Karl had started to walk back to his cubicle when he stopped turn around and heading back to Sara office fully expecting to see Doctor Mills heading towards him. Reaching the office, he entered to find Doctor Mills, Sara and Julia talking by the scheduling board. "Karl come join us and tell me what's all this flap is about." Asked Doctor Mills. Karl sat opposite Doctor Mills and in a very controlled voice explained why he needed to return to Slough as quickly as possible and to do that he would need the Doctors help to give him a conditional release. He looked at the three as they hung on every word he spoke. "Well Lieutenant under normal circumstances I would refuse such a request to return to active duty even on a limited basis, however these are not normal times, are they? If I approved this it must be with your assurance, no with your promise you will follow the plan we put together for you is that understood." Doctor Mills knew without having to say another word that officers like Karl would be much in demand in the weeks and months ahead. "Matron why don't we get a supply of Karl's medication for about a week, that will give me time to contact Major Burns at the base medical center tomorrow morning and explain that one of my patience will be returning to Slough in a couple of days, I'll also give him a list of medication Karl will require during his recuperation. Could you and Harry get together and draw up a therapy exercise routine for Karl to follow. As for you Lieutenant you must make me that promise to follow them religiously. Matron you will also need to contact whomever, will be taking care of him on that regiment get their name rank and telephone extension so we can check up on him regularly. Now Karl our transportation is spread thin, I will not allow you return on public transportation you are simply not strong enough for that amount of traveling. Can you call your commanding office to see if they can lay on a car, I'll be glad to make that call for you if you're not comfortable with making it yourself?" Doctor Mills looked at Karl now displaying a smile of confidence. "I'll be glad to make that call to Major Knight once we have finished here, he and I have a long-standing relationship, I'm sure there will not be a problem. So, to clarify I should be ready to leave the day after tomorrow is that correct." Reinforced Karl now looking at Sara for her approval. "That is correct I will see you tomorrow afternoon for a checkup alright, now I must return to my other patience, you know the ones that don't give me problems like you." Doctor Mills patted Karl on the shoulder chuckling and shaking his head as he departed. Sara dismissed Julia then sat down next to Karl saying. "Glad to see the Doctor is allowing you to return to your base. We shall all miss you and I will always think of you as a wonderful excursion away from my hectic daily duties. When I saw you and Hazel sitting embracing on that bench, I knew there was history between you both, any notion I may have had that we could share more went out the window seeing you both like that. Karl I will always think of you fondly, men like you are very hard to come across. Will you at least stay in touch, I would like that very much?" Karl took her hand firmly saying. "You will forever be my lady with the lamp that carried me through a very difficult time. Yes, Sara I will write to you whenever time permits. My sweet Sara until Hazel came back into my life, I truly believe we would have become so much more." Karl gently kissed her damp check then stood up saying. "See you before lights out." As Karl limped away be could feel Sara watching him feeling very let down by a romance that never really got started. Karl could not sleep there was just too much going through his brain like Kitty's first and only visit to Baldock, the wonderful emotionally charged memory of his mother giving Kitty her engagement ring. Those few days spent with his sister, her husband Ronny, and their son Franchot made them both look forward to similar life in a town much like Baldock, that vision of living in peace was shattered by Kitty's tragic death, held captive in Germany by the despised Gestapo. To escape these upsetting thoughts Karl drifted off to sleep only to be woke up by nurse Julia at 0530 hrs. "Time to get up lieutenant," said Julia as she handed Karl his bath robe. "Must have dropped off again I have been awake most of the night, too much going through my mind about now." Said Karl as he struggled to stand up. "You're leaving us tomorrow I will miss having you in this ward, kind of got used to having you around I guess." Julia was just making small talk as she helped him into his bathrobe and slippers. After getting ready he ate a quick breakfast then headed to Sara's office. "Morning

Sara can I use your telephone to call Major Knight." Asked Karl. "Certainly, I've got rounds to do with Doctor Mills so you will have privacy." Sara was all business this morning no need to labor an uncomfortable situation. Sitting at the desk Karl dialed nine for the operator then gave the switchboard operator the phone number. A voice on the other end answered. "Morning Major Knights extension." Answered a familiar voice. "*Pat*, it's me Karl Vita so good to hear your voice, is Major Knight in his office really need to speak to him right away." Asked Karl. "So nice to hear you too Lieutenant it's been a rough couple of months for you I hear, miss seeing that face of yours when are you returning back to us?" Asked Pat. "All going well probably tomorrow." Answered Karl. "Now that's the best news I've heard all morning, let me transfer you, see you tomorrow, please hold." Said Pat as she dialed the interoffice number. "Vita is that you so pleased to hear from you." Said Clive to his friend. "Clive I am returning to base tomorrow however I need your help to get me back." Karl explained the situation and that Doctor Mills will only conditionally release me if the base would provide a car. "Well, you know it's not usual to have a sailor picked up from an extended holiday, however for you my friend, call it a done deal what time should the car arrive?" Concluded Clive knowing full well that Karl would be laughing at the other end hearing his sarcastic remarks like sailor and extended holiday, their friendship had withstood the test of time and tragedy. "How about 1300 hrs will that work." Replied Karl. "Pat, get me the motor pool and then let everyone in the department know the crazy Austrian will be back tomorrow so plan on a get together after hours everyone will attend and that's an order." Clive could not be happier. Karl hung up the receiver chuckling at Clive's wisecrack remarks. The weather was still sunny and warm, so Karl grabbed his walking cane and headed outside for a walk around the beautiful grounds, he so wanted to inhale clean fresh air it was good to still be alive. Down by the lake he decided to sit on the bench for a while watching the ducks as they paddled around not a care in the world. From his inside pocket he took out a small notebook and pencil, turning the pages till he found his to do list. One: was done next Two: Call Mama at the bungalow need to schedule some time with the family. Three: See Doctor Mills for the last examination and discharge papers. His thoughts now turned to calling Gunther to ask him to pick up his spare uniform from his flat with his spare key, then give it to the driver picking me up, can't return to the base in borrowed shirt and trousers, oh need to add a shirt, tie and shoes to that list. Karl could feel the excitement building as he wrote in his notebook. Nearly forgot I need to get Sara's address I made her a promise and I intend to keep it. Without realizing the time Karl had been sitting there for the best part of an hour, a tap on the shoulder made him spin around to see the smiling face of Sara. "My you made me jump did not see you coming." Said Karl not expecting to see her down here by the lake. "I have just made myself a note to get your address when I got back to ward and just like that you turn up, great minds think alike I suppose." Karl saying that could see through the smile that she wanted to talk. "Karl I am wrestling with the fact that tomorrow you will be gone, will I ever see you again, probable not? There always remains that possibility you'll turn up on a stretcher because you got yourself shot up again, so I decided to find you while you're in one piece, well kind of. Since you were nowhere to be found in the building, I figured that I would find you down here enjoying the solitude." Said Sara. "You know me so well Sara, yes I love my quiet time to reflect on the times around us and where will I be by years end." Karl was also wrestling with the right words he did not want to get her hopes up that there could still be a relationship. "Shall we walk back to the hospital together or would you still prefer to be alone." Asked Sara hoping he would kiss her goodbye while they were still alone down by the lake. "Sara, I think I know what's on your mind and quite honestly it makes me somewhat uncomfortable. As much as I would love to kiss you, goodbye, it might send the wrong message, and Sara I have far too much respect for you to allow that to happen." Karl was now standing facing Sara trying to find the appropriate thing to say without upsetting her more than she already was. "Why don't you let me be the judge of that?" replied Sara as she placed her right arm around his neck followed by a very moist kiss squarely on his lips. "Did you honestly think I was going to let you run off without this if you did you are very naïve Mr. Vita. I am a big girl in times like these we all should grab at any chance for happiness, Karl, stay the night with me, so I'll know what has slipped away from me." Sara moved again to kiss Karl. "Sara that's enough I cannot allow this to go on any further, let's go back right now." Karl was getting angry, and Sara realized she had crossed the line. "I'm sorry Karl I should not have taken that liberty with you, as I said I'm a big girl, so no harm done hope you're not too offended by my actions now let's walk back, how's that leg feeling walking around this much as you are could course those stitches to bleed, I'll take a look at them once we are back inside." Just like that Sara had reverted to being the Matron she was. Back in the ward Sara along with Julia cleaned Karl's wounded thigh then put him to bed wishing him a good night's sleep. Tomorrow would come quickly but not fast enough for Karl.

The staff car turned into the circular driveway of the hospital, the army corporal entered the hospital walked to up to the attendant and said, "Morning Corporal *John Webley,* I'm here to drive Lieutenant Vita back to Slough, could you please let him know I'm here." "One moment I'll let the Matron know, would you like some tea while you wait." Said the nurse. Sara answered the phone then asked Julia to get Karl from the breakfast room and bring him out to the lobby as his driver was waiting for him there. She then called Doctor Mills to inform him that Lieutenant Vita was ready to depart. "Matron let me take a look at his wounds again before he leaves us." Doctor Mills would only sign the discharge papers once he had examined Karl for the last time. Sara walked briskly to the breakfast room just as Julia was leaving with Karl. "Hold on you two, Doctor Mills would like to examine Lieutenant Vita before he leaves us." Sara reached out and took Karl's arm leading him down the hall, followed by Julia. As they entered the examination room a cheerful Doctor Mills rose from his desk extending his hand towards Karl. "Well let's give you a last look shall we, I've arranged your medical care with Slough, so everything is arranged. Now up on the table, nurse please remove the dressing on his neck then we can look at that nasty wound in your leg, need to lower your trousers old man for that." Carefully new dressings were applied, the Doctor very pleased at how Karl was healing. Karl thanked Doctor Mills for the exceptional care he administered during the weeks he had been there. "I hope our paths cross again Doctor when things are less hectic maybe we can have dinner when you find yourself in town." Karl stood up excepting Sara's hand to steady himself from the table. "Shall we go, I have a bag here with your medication enough for the first week make sure this medication list is given to the attending physician once you arrive at your base. The therapy instructions are in an envelope marked therapy instructions, don't lose them. The nurse from reception asked me to give you this bag with your uniform in it." said Julia. Karl just laughed. "That bugger Clive forgets nothing, where can I change?" Asked Karl. Julia opened a door to an examination room hanging up the uniform on a hanger then put the accessories on the table. "There you are handsome, we'll wait outside." Julia had always taken exceptional care of the handsome Austrian officer he was not your ordinary officer for sure. The door opened and out walked a striking Lieutenant Vita minus his forage cap which had been forgotten in the rush to pick up his spare uniform. "Wow will you look at the new Lieutenant Vita." Said a cheerful Julia. Sara stood with her arms crossed shaking her head slowly and smiling at Karl in his uniform, thinking, almost mine well guess it wasn't meant to be? Sara moved over to take his arm, Julia on the opposite side and Doctor Mills bringing up the rear as they walked towards the lobby. "How can I thank you for the care and attention you all have shown me, from the bottom of my heart I will always remember my time here." While Karl was talking, he turned addressing the sizable group that had turned out to see him off. Karl went around shaking hands then stopped in front of Sara. "Thank you Matron my lady with the lamp. I will write you once I'm settled back in Slough thank you." Karl could see the look in her eyes he reached over and kissed her on the check saying out loud, "That's the one I promised you when I first arrived, remember." Turning around he raised his hand in a parting gesture then with his walking cane as support he limped out the front door down the step to the waiting Humber staff car. The kindly corporal driving the car helped him into the rear passenger seat, inside he rolled down the window and waved once more to those that had walked out to see him off. Karl sat back in the rear seat feeling tears welling up in the corner of his eyes. At the end of the driveway the car stopped momentarily while traffic passed in front of them something made Karl turn in his seat looking back towards the entrance, there she was standing alone waiting to see the car disappear around the corner. It would be a long time till he saw Sara again, even though they occasionally write letters to each other. They had met under trying conditions, during his recovery that attention turning into a brief flirtation, they had started something that would never come to fruition even though Sara tried to make it so much more, it was simply not to be and now it was time to start a new chapter back in the BIS.

Chapter Six
Returning to the Intelligence Service

The ride back to the camp in Slough was slow going, too many military convoys heading God knows where, added close to an hour to the trip. Karl drifted in and out of a shallow sleep which perhaps was a good thing. Finally, the driver said, "Almost there, Sir. Sorry it took longer than normal the Army is on the move for sure." Karl could see the familiar signs that led up to the entrance barrier. The Military Police guard approach the staff car, Karl had already wind down the window and had his military Identification ready. The guard looked at the ID then saluted saying. "Welcome back sir proceeding to raise the barrier." The guard stepped back as the big Humber drove through the entrance, Karl feeling as though he had returned home. "Excuse me sir, Major Knight instructed me to take you to the main building then leave your things in his office. You are to meet him in the cafeteria do you need me to help you sir or can you manage on your own." Asked Corporal Webley. "I'll be fine Corporal, thank you for offering though." Replied Karl feeling the excitement of being back in familiar surrounds. The car came to a complete stop in front of the entrance, Corporal Webley smartly walked around the car to open the rear door helping Karl onto the pavement. The front door opened and out came an ATS private covering the steps two at a time. "Welcome back so pleased to see you back safely in one piece, we have all been very worried about you." Crossing over to where Karl was standing, she told the Corporal I will help Lieutenant Vita climb the steps, thank you I've got him now." Said Jean as she handed him his walking cane then looped his arm with hers. "You look smashing sir after what you have been through, never expected to see you look this good." Jean always liked seeing him when he came through the door first thing in the morning, he would greet everyone with a big smile, today was no exception seeing that smile once again. Climbing the steps one at a time was a painful exercise for Karl hiding that pain from Jean and relying heavily on his cane. "I have been asked to help you to the cafeteria to meet up with your pals, would you like to rest awhile or go straight there." Asked Jean not sure if those steps were a little too much for him. "No Jean, I'm fine let me lean on you a little if you don't mind this leg can give me problems if I put too much weight on it." Karl would of much preferred to sit for a few minutes but that to him would be a sign of weakness. The lights that normally shone through the cafeteria door windows looked dark. "Are you sure I'm supposed to meet them here it looks kind of dark don't you think." Asked Karl. "No sir, Major Knight was pretty emphatic about were to deliver you, could be because you arrived a little late?" Jean was trying to hold back the urge to laugh, she knew precisely what was waiting for them on the opposite side of those doors. "Let me open the door sir and put the lights back on, I'm sure they will be along shortly." Jean quickly opened the door and at that moment all the lights came on followed by a very loud cheer from everyone in the department. Karl was back. "You bugger Clive should have known you would pull a stunt like this, thank you, thank you for making this such a wonderful way to welcome me back." For once the cocky sarcastic Karl was lost for words. Everybody pushed forward to welcome him back. Jean helped Karl sit down with old friends Bill putting a chair under his wounded leg. Karl was now the center of attention. "Jean thank you for helping me, your sneaky bugger, give me a big kiss on the cheek." Karl was sliding back into his old self. "On the cheek, like buggery I will, I'm not a schoolgirl you know, now give me a real kiss." Jean and everyone cheered as she bent over giving Karl a real lip-smacking kiss, she was laughing out loud obviously enjoying the liberty she had just taken. "Gunther and Herbert so pleased to see you chaps, I was under the impression you both were on assignment. Isn't Hazel on your team? If so, is she here?" Karl was trying to downplay his excitement at seeing Hazel before she left on their mission to someplace in Europe. "Right behind you lover boy." Said Hazel as she worked her way up to Karl. "Well, if young Jean got a lip smacker, I want one even bigger." Hazel had a way about her that reminded Karl of his dead fiancé Kitty, as much as he enjoyed the attention Hazel showered upon him it still brought back memories of his only true love. "Well, I'm waiting said the laughing Hazel as she bent down to kiss Karl squarely on the lips. Hazel satisfied with her kiss pulled up a chair next to Karl. After about an hour the party started winding down, everyone filed by to bid farewell to their returning hero. Clive stood saying, "We have made arrangements for you take one of the duty doctor's quarters in the medical center, he will not be back for quite a while so that works out well. In your present condition you aren't going to be able to climb those stairs to your flat. As much as I would love to spend more time with you there is still a war to attend to, ready Bill?" Clive and Bill had to return to planning the upcoming mission only days away. Hazel looked around the cafeteria then sat back down next to Karl. "Well lover boy, guess everyone has left us, Clive has already moved your things to your temporary quarters, Gunther yesterday went to your flat and picked up everything you will need, so your well taken care of. I know where it is in the medical center so why don't we take a slow walk over there and get you settled in shall we." Hazel was still tickled pink she would have this time along with Karl, she was trying hard to win him over and that would not be easy there was still a tender memory stopping that from happening. "How much further Hazel my leg is starting to hurt me." Asked Karl as they crossed over the small courtyard that led to the medical center. Hazel opened the side door then guided Karl into the small hallway. "The first door on the left Karl, it should still be locked I have the key in my purse. Gunther gave it to me earlier before you arrived. I have about an hour before I need to meet up with my team, let's get you comfortable on the bed this way you can rest up while I'm in my meeting how does that sound, should be back in about an hour could be longer if we run into overtime though. Before leaving I will stop down at the nursing station to let them know you are in the room and ask the Matron to stop in to see you, she can give you the once over and make the arrangements for the camp doctor to see you in the morning, alright." Hazel helped him remove his shoes and uniform tunic hanging them neatly in the wardrobe. "There does that feel better, earlier I put a pitcher of water on the shelf in the bathroom for you, if you need anything else like coffee or a sandwich the NAAFI (*Navy, Army and Airforce Institutes*) stays open till 2000 hrs, just call ext. 108, you Lieutenant Vita are very lucky these rooms have their own bathrooms, surgeons around here live good. When I get back, we can get dinner, would you like me to ask Clive, Bill, Gunther, and Herbert to join us, that's if you would enjoy that, it's up to you?" Hazel was fussing over him and Karl was enjoying it. "Hazel if everyone is restricted to camp, where are you staying?" asked Karl as he propped up his pillows. "I'm billeted in the female officer's quarters two buildings down from here." Answered Hazel as she took off her khaki tunic draping it over the chair in front of the desk. "There that's better even if it's for forty minutes or so, can I join you on your bed." Hazel thought again about what she had just asked. "Or would you prefer I sit on the chair next to it?" Hazel was looking straight at Karl waiting for a reaction to what she had just asked. "Hazel, you're trying to be coy with me come over here and share this pillow with me not much can happen in forty minute or can it?" Hazel with a big smile on her face lay down besides Karl wrapping her right arm over his chest. "When I heard you were returning before we left on out mission my heart would not stop pounding, I felt like a skittish lovesick schoolgirl, well maybe not lovesick schoolgirl." Hazel did not mean to use those words especially knowing how sensitive Karl was about love and commitment. "Well, you know what I mean don't you." Hazel said brushing off what she had just said. "That's alright Hazel I was looking forward to seeing you as well, glad we have established that." Concluded

Karl trying not to laugh. Hazel's face went from smiling to one of concern. "Karl, my darling there is so much I want to say to you, but quite honestly I'm still walking on pins and needles when it comes to you and me." Hazel knew she had to bring that up, weighing ever word was not the way to start a relationship and Karl had to decide if there would be one. "Hazel as I told you only a few weeks ago since Kitty's tragic death I closed my feelings so I would not be hurt again. Look I have dated other ladies some in the military not many civilians though and that suited me just fine. No commitment just fun and making love and that was it, short term mostly one or two dates. Then you came back into my life, Kitty was smart encouraging you to become part of my life, that is just like her to do that you two are very much alike, I told you as much back at the field hospital when you told me if a casual, relationship was not for you, you would tell me, are we already at that point? If so, you need to tell me right now." Said Karl trying to read between the lines. Unbeknown to Hazel, Karl had already made up his mind he did not want to go on in his lonely existence without someone special to share his time with, this could well be that right time. "Karl let me be very open with you, you must realize I'm very much in love with you and have been since Scotland. Kitty guessed as much and that's probably why she confided in me the way she did. There now you know, are we finished before we've begun?" Hazel had tears in her eyes, she was going on a mission and this distraction was not helping. "Hazel, you sweet sensitive lady you don't have to worry I have already made up my mind an empty life without you is not going to work for me either." Karl stopped short of telling her he was slowly falling for her in a big way and yes that meant love. "Now come here and give me a big kiss I could use one about now." They both looked at each other in a whole new way but no wedding bells would chime not while there was a war going on, Karl would not open that door for a very long time and telling Hazel at this point would not be the right thing to do, not right now anyway. Hazel kissed him passionately her tongue thrusting into his mouth to find his waiting for her. With only thirty minutes left she trembled with excitement she wanted him so much but that would have to wait till tonight or even tomorrow. There is no way I'm going on this mission till I have had my time with Karl, I want him so very much I can understand now how Kitty felt before she left at least she had the time for those romantic interludes with him those private times in a bed skin to skin, I want that also before I leave. "Karl, you know my time is getting really short but darling I need this time for us alone in bed making love is that so much to ask before I leave you, if it's to be just one time that's better than no time don't you agree. Tomorrow afternoon I will make sure I have no commitments nor should you.

Thanks to good old Major Knight we have this private room it's the closest place to heaven for me right now. Now let me put my tunic and shoes back on and find that Matron, hopefully this one is old, fat and ugly." They both laughed at Hazels wise crack remark, see you later don't lock the door as the Matron will be around shortly. Karl lay there his head swimming with excitement and the ever-present fear that he was going down that same road that took Kitty from him back in 1938. With his eyes closed, his cluttered mind running a hundred miles an hour Karl was about to make a big decision better to have love in his life than the emptiness of none, even though the risk would be painfully high. Somewhere down the road the likelihood of being hurt again was a real possibility with that decision made he sat up feeling so much better than an hour before. A knock on the door snapped him out of the twilight he had been in. "Come in please." Said Karl as he looked towards the door and the new Matron. The door opened and in walked the Matron along with the duty nurse. "Well, we finally meet the popular Lieutenant Vita. My name is *Elizabeth* and the nurse here is *Ann,*" Said, the friendly Matron. "Nurse please hand me the clipboard let's see what we need to take care of shall we? Can you turn towards me Lieutenant need to remove that dressing around your neck, the instruction are to clean and replace this dressing every evening making sure the neck brace is securely put back on. As for your thigh we are instructed to change that one twice a day, I can see why, it's a very nasty gash and it's still weeping. Are you comfortable with us calling you Karl? It makes it less formal." Said the Matron. "I would prefer that may I also call you Liz and Ann. I'm assuming Ann it will be you that will be taking care of my dressings, is that right?" Karl already liked the middle-aged Matron her accent would indicate she came from the Midlands. As for Ann, she was in her early twenties with a noticeable Scottish accent. "If I need your assistance, how do I get hold of you?" Asked Karl. "There is a two-way control next to your bed and another in the bathroom, they are really for the doctor on duty if we need to contact him, by the way it goes straight to the nursing station. Nurse would you please refresh Karl's water pitcher once we are done with changing his dressing." Instructed the Matron. "Liz I would like to have a shower could one of you help me in and out of the shower, still a little wobbly on my own." Asked Karl as he sat up on the edge of the bed. "Wish you would have asked that question before we changed your dressings." Said Liz. "I'm so sorry ladies guess you got me excited." Karl was enjoying this new hospital staff members. "Well that shower may be out for today, so let's settle on a sponge bath shall we." Liz giving a little chuckle as she said that. "Oh yes please." Replied Karl. "I heard that about you, best to be careful with what you say to Lieutenant

Vita, he usually has a comeback that has a double meaning." Said Liz laughing along with Ann. "Oh, ladies you really don't believe any of that silly stuff surely." Karl was enjoying himself. After a somewhat limited sponge bath, Ann helped him change into a fresh shirt, his uniform trousers, socks and finally she helped him tie his shoes. "There you are Karl now you are ready for Lieutenant Collins when she returns." Ann's strong Scottish accent intrigued Karl, it reminded him so much of the friendly staff at the training camp in Scotland years back. "It's such a nice day I think I would like to sit outside and freshen my tan till Lieutenant Collins arrives back, could you please be so kind as to find me a deckchair." Asked Karl. Outside in the fresh air the warm sun was very therapeutic to Karl's condition, within thirty minutes he fell into a deep relaxing sleep which he needed so much.

A warm kiss on the lips awoke him, squinting from the sun brought him back to a vision of beautiful Hazel leaning over him. "Welcome back lover boy guess you needed this time sleeping in the sun." Hazel looking at him was the perfect picture of a young English woman. "Let's get you ready, where should I put this deck chair before we go back to your room?" Asked Hazel. "Why don't we stash it in my room so I can use it again, I believe this nice weather will continue tomorrow. In the room Hazel kissed him passionately then retrieved his tunic from the wardrobe, saying. "Ready to do some walking, lover boy." Yes, so long as you don't think I'm going to power walk to the club." replied Karl.

Inside the officer club Clive, Gunther and Herbert sat in a corner table talking and drinking pint size glasses of beer. "Well look what the cat dragged in." Gunther taking a jovial shot at Karl, he responded by saying, "Hazel do you really want to have drinks with these blokes they're not the best company to spend time with." returning the sarcastic banter at his friends. "Seat down, you crazy bugger, what can I get you two from the bar?" said Clive getting up to buy another round. "We will have a gin and tonic please." Hazel answering for Karl. When Clive returned, he asked if he could change the subject while they were all together and in a quiet corner of the room. "The day after tomorrow you three will depart, if all goes according to plan you will rendezvous with the team embedded with the resistance group early next week. We are not expecting any major problems with this mission as its more of a fact finding than anything else, still need to be very careful though. As for you Karl now that you are back you will be their inside liaison back here in Slough. Your responsibility will be to keep the lines of communications open for incoming encrypted messages. Karl your knowledge of the local area they will be operating in will be invaluable when we start to review that data on troop buildup and movements in strategic locations to our planning people. I cannot stress enough Karl your team will man the radio twenty-four seven. Starting the day after these three leave our strategy will be to outthink those bloody German excluding present company of course. The evacuation of Dunkirk is over, now we must brace ourselves for the next major offensive by Herr Hitler. Our intelligence chaps are predicting a direct assault, probably airborne in conjunction with a seaborn assault somewhere along the south coast. Our readiness will be reliant on where to concentrate troops and artillery will be key to saving this country. Our massive losses from the enormous amount of equipment left behind in Dunkirk has left us desperately short of equipment for a sustained campaign. As for the RAF, well they have been working around the clock training new pilots. Aircraft production is in better shape they are building parts in every spare garage around the country then shipping them to the aircraft manufacturers for final assembly, quite amazing really. The Air Ministry believes our reserve of new aircraft should put us in a survivable position, who knows? Karl, I have already cleared your return to duty with the medical chaps. They understand the importance of having you directly involved during this next phase of the expected attack, just promise me and your friends here, you will not overdo it alright." Clive stopped talking taking a long swig of beer and silently waiting for the response he knew would come from Karl and it did. "Clive thank you for allowing me to be part of the operation, you can rely on me to back them up. The Germans are acutely aware the RAF pilots and their fighters are equal match to those of their Luftwaffe. They obviously are concerned without dominating the skies over the channel could be devastating for any sea assault. If I were Hitler, I would throw every available fighter at the RAF, to gain aerial supremacy before launching an amphibious assault. Now let me ask Gunther and Herbert to do something for me, Hazel will be your radio operator on this mission, she is special to me, as you know I have been down this path before, please keep her safe. Look I know a promise like this can't really be kept, but please shield her as much as you can that's all I can hope for." Karl saying that reached over for Hazel's hand he felt they should know that he and Hazel were becoming an item, no wedding bells though. Clive lightened the conversation by say, "No throwing kisses on those communications Hazel it could confuse the Germans." That line made them all start laughing breaking the tension that was building around the table. Clive was eyeballing Karl and Hazel looking for a telltale expression, that did not happen they were painfully aware of the danger confronting them only a few days away. At 1700 hrs Hazel stood saying it's time to get you back to the room, they will be coming to change the dressings soon. she knew the longer they stayed in the club the less time she would have along with

Karl. "Of course, you must be getting fatigued by now Karl, why don't you make your way over to my office tomorrow morning after you have had therapy and seen the Doctor alright. As for your young lady I'll see you and these two geezers at 0600 sharp, now be off with you." Clive recognized they needed some private time to say their goodbyes. As Karl with Hazel holding his arm hobbled away Clive turned to the other two saying. "I can't help thinking its Kitty all over again you know how Karl has a habit of diving in headfirst into most situations, he could well be heading down that same road again? If I had more time to replace Hazel in this operation, someone with equal field experience I would pull her out of this mission but there is no one to replace her at this late date." Clive remembering the hell Karl went through when Kitty was killed. "Clive, Hazel has already pleaded with me not to cut her from this mission when I confronted her about this blooming romance with Karl. She is very much like Kitty we are at war and she has a duty to perform, nothing will stop her from performing that mission. I have known about her feelings for Karl since we were in Scotland, she has been carrying that heartache over the past several years. Giving them their time together will fortify her commitment to the BIS and this mission. If she holds on tight to the notion, she is returning to someone special waiting for her return, will give her strength." Said Gunther, thinking of his own family back in Hamburg and the daily heartache he also lives with.

Back in Karl's small room Hazel helped him remove his tunic and shoes then helped him onto the bed. "Well lady now you have me where you want me, what do you propose we do now? "Well playing chess is really out of the question don't you think?" Answered Hazel her hormones in high gear. "Did you say play chess or was that playing with your chest." The old Karl was back in action even though it would be for two nights only in his mind he had blocked out anything beyond that. "Well since you asked might as well get comfortable, should I?" Hazel was going to tease him into submission, well maybe not submission because she could see he was already ready for her on the bed. "Where is that small radio I brought you, could do with some romantic music about now, there it is, I'll plug it in on that desk. "Now that's more like it the Glenn Miller orchestra, what was I going to do next?" Hazel was enjoying this immensely she crossed over to the bed leaning over Karl and gave him a moist kiss remaining there her blouse without a tie gave Karl a commanding view much like that day by the lake. "Hazel this is the second time you have got me going with that marvelous view down your blouse." Karl was being teased by the beautiful Hazel and he loved it. "Darling are you so naive you think I did not know that?" replied Hazel as she slowly unbuttoned her blouse then removed her skirt. She stood there, love beaming across her face. "Well, what do you think lover boy?" Hazel now had his full attention. When she had dressed that morning, she did not put on the regulation military underwear, instead she elected to wear seductive silk and lace, thinking no one will know only Karl when I remove my uniform. Her seduction was going as planned now it was time to make love to this Austrian, she had waited so long for. "Darling as much as I want to screw your brains out, we must be careful don't want to put you back in surgery now do we? Please let me take care of you first, I really want too anyway." Said Hazel seating down on the edge of the bed. "Hazel you better lock the door first." Said Karl in a controlled voice. "Already done that when we arrived, I confided in that lovely nurse Ann that we would like to be alone for a couple of hours, so now you can relax and enjoy our time together." Hazel was slowly pulling the bed sheet down, unfortunately that revealed the bloody bandage around Karl's upper thigh. "Oh my God Karl I did not realize the wound to your leg was still weeping like that, I was more worried about your neck and movement of your head, darling this might not be a good idea right now." As much as Hazel wanted to make love, she certainly did not want to jeopardize his recovery by any movement that could be dangerous. "I know what Ann meant when she said to me be aware of his condition, one false move could set him back weeks." Hazel now sat upright holding Karl's hand. "Darling I'm sorry you have to see my leg like this it really looks so much worse than it is, my neck well that will be a problem till such times as they remove that blasted piece of steel." Karl trying to comfort her took his other hand placing it over the tears on Hazel's check. "There is always another way to skin a cat and I have an idea that will give us what we both need." Karl feeling, he needed to be creative and find a way to make love to this beautiful women seating in front of him that would not course a problem to his wounds, this might be the only time before she left on a very dangerous mission. "Hazel please help me up from this bed, then get me into the bathroom." Said Karl a plan firmly in his mind. "Alright do you need to use the bathroom?" she asked. "Not for that, take those towels and put one on either side of my neck, now lady back up to the wall reach as high as you can so I will not have to bend too much to enter you." Karl had found the way to make love to Hazel. "Oh, Karl I could not follow what you were up to, now I know why they always say Karl never does things in the excepted manner." As she spoke his hand found her wet mound the last words she spoke changed to a moan as Karl continued to massage her with his thumb and index finger. "Hazel stood shaking as a wave of ecstasy drove her to her first orgasm. "Karl, what you just did put a powerful torque on this body of mine." Hazel with a noticeable quiver in her

voice was about to say something when she felt a thrust inside of her that stopped her cold, Karl had entered her without her noticing what he was doing in front of her. No wonder he wanted me to stand as high as I could? oh God this is beyond heaven. "Karl please don't stop I want all you can give me, darling I love you so much you can have anything you want. As she tried to finish that line, she felt that intense feeling come over her again and with a loud sigh she surrenders to another powerful orgasm which triggered Karl into doing the same. The two stood there locked together in an embrace for just a few minutes that felt like an hour. "How do you feel darling, now that you have got rid of all that dirty water." Karl had a grin on his face like a Cheshire cat. "Karl honestly you come up with the most bizarre things to say especially after giving me a work over like this. Thank God you can only function at half speed, I dread to think what's in store for me when your all together again. Hazel helped Karl stand back from her as she said that. In the back of Karl's mind, a voice was telling him he had heard someone say almost the identical thing. That black cloud was trying to move in again only this time he said, "Stop!" "Stop what?" asked Hazel as she was putting her blouse on in front of the mirror. "It's nothing darling just some thought that cropped into my head." Replied Karl starring at Hazel in a different manner. He hobbled over to her turning her around he pulled her to him rapped his strong arms around her kissing her softly on the lips not in an animal way but more in an affectionate loving manner. Pulling back, he held her face between his big hands starring into her eyes saying nothing. "Karl is everything alright you look so sad what's bothering you like this?"
"For too long I have felt nothing when making love it was only a means to escape and relieve my tension. Today we were not having sex, we were making love and for the first time in over two and half years I feel alive again, you my darling Hazel gave me that. So, no I'm far from sad, feel like another round?" Karl breaking out laughing. "Are you crazy they will be doing rounds shortly can you image the look on their facing seeing the two of us up against that wall banging away with hardily anything on. Come on let's get you dressed then I'll make the bed before they come in to change your dressing. Over here lover boy, let me wash you down need to get rid of that love scent before Ann gets the wrong idea." After they had made themselves presentable again, Hazel said, "While you wait for the nurse to arrive, I'm going over to command to get an update on the mission status." Hazel kissed him on the forehead and headed for the door. Hearing her last statement about checking in on the mission cast a dark shadow again in Karl's mind, he had been here before! A knock on the door brought Karl back, "Come in its open," Karl calling to Ann. "Alright Karl let me get those stained dressing off shall we, did you

have a nice afternoon just saw Lieutenant Collins going down the hall, such a lovely lady you should be very thankful she is your girlfriend." Ann was just making small talk as she cleaned and replace his dressings.

Over dinner Gunther asked Karl once again was he still up to being, their mission contact. "You know I am, must interject though I will be going up to London shortly for a second operation to remove this chunk of steel in my neck, not sure what it entails. I venture to say if it goes wrong, you will need another inside contact for the mission." Karl trying to make light of what could happen in that operating theatre. "Don't talk like that Karl, you will have two of the best surgeons working on you, Doctors Burgers and Mills so stop scaring me." Said Hazel reaching for his hand. "Now that everyone around here knows you two are an item will it create a problem for us out there in the middle of God knows where?" Asked Helmut looking at them both. "Helmut my dear friend you should know that neither one of us will let our personal lives interfere with this or any future mission either one of us may be involved with, is that correct Hazel?" Said Karl as he squeezed Hazel's hand. "That is very true, both of you have worked with me before in Germany so you know how I conduct myself. There is a time for everything as of tomorrow morning I will be covering your backs as you cover mine, are we clear on that?" Replied Hazel with a stern look on her face, when called upon to be all business she could focus extremely well. Clive came in pulled up a chair then flagged the steward to bring him his usual pint of mild and bitter beer. "Anyone else like a drink while I'm buying." Clive had joined them with some long-awaited news for Karl. "Just got off the phone with Doctor Burgess looks like he would like to schedule your neck operation for next Wednesday. Doctor Mills will be returning to London and has agreed to swing by and drive you to St. Mary's Hospital so that works out nicely. Once I knew the date, I took the liberty of calling your brother-in-law Ronny at his base in Duxford to give him the update on when the operation is scheduled. Here's the good news old boy, Ronny will be driving your Mother down from Baldock next Wednesday, this must be fabulous news for you Karl considering you have not been the best at staying in touch with her." Said Clive as he lifted his pint to celebrate this long overdue announcement. "Now as for you three I'm assuming all your gear is ready for tomorrow morning if not get it done today and that is an order, I'll be there to see you off at 1850 hours, care to join me Karl?" asked Clive. "Would not miss it, are there any additional instructions I should be aware of before your departure tomorrow?" Asked Karl. "How about joining us after breakfast for a quick refresher." Answered Gunther. "Sounds great to me, Clive will you be there as well, don't forget as of next Wednesday I'm going to be out of circulation for a while. Replied Karl. "Oh, on that subject Ronny will be picking you up on the Friday after the operation. Your medical leave has been approved by Doctor Burgess. He notified me that two or maybe three weeks of rest is mandatory in this case, so please convey to your mother I am keeping my promise to send you home for a while." Said Clive beaming with a smile on his face. "She asked you that Clive? When did you talk to her last?" asked Karl. "Well, I took it upon myself to call her at least once every other week seeing as you very rarely do that and by the way Hazel and Gunther from time to time have also been keeping her abreast on your recovery." Clive sending Karl a message to stay in touch more often with his mother. "Sounds to me you have everything under control, so thank you very much." Karl feeling humbled by the way his friends kept his mother updated. "Karl, I think we need to get you off your feet you are starting to look really tired, let's say goodnight shall we." Hazel could see the pain was returning and as much as he was trying to make light of it, he knew he needed to lay down. "See you tomorrow morning then, good night chaps." Said Karl as he stood up with the help of Hazel. After they had left Gunther making small talk remarked that he thought they made a good-looking couple and that he and Herbert would do all within their power to shield her from danger. "Very commendable of you Gunther just remember she is your radio operator, and we all know the survival rate for an operator these days, don't we?" Clive knew all too well that this mission was safer than most but felt he still had to interject that question. Back in the small room Hazel helped Karl out of his uniform hanging it up in the wardrobe. "I can't stay long darling, have a lot of preparations to take care of before tomorrow." Said Hazel as she moved back to sit next to him on the bed. "I can see from your face you are already in mission mode am I correct." Karl was giving her the out to leave. "You're getting to know me very well my darling. Guess you know the feeling you get when it gets close to leaving on a mission, so yes I think I'm going to tuck you in and return to getting my equipment sorted out, hope you're not too disappointed?" Hazel answering him could feel the tears welling up in her eyes and this she did not want him to see. Hazel sat down again next to him on the narrow bed, thinking I hope I can come back to you Karl I have never felt so alone as I do right now and there is nothing, I can do to prevent it. "Come here Hazel let me hold you for a few minutes." Said Karl as he looked at her, knowing full well what was going through her head, he had been in this position once before only a few years back. Lying together Karl's strong arms around her he could feel her tension. "Hazel, it's time to put your feelings in a safe place at the back of your mind till you return. No need to worry about me I am getting better and stronger with each day and once that hunk of steel is out, I will be able to return to my normal duties after a lengthy recuperation. "When you send a message add this word occasionally in a sentence, *better*. Never use it in a way it could be construed as a pattern, I'll see it and know you're alright." Karl kept stroking her face and hair as he said this. "One last kiss then I'll be off." Hazel was over that brief period of melancholy. Sitting upright once again she leant over and kiss him good night. Any devilish thoughts Karl may have had, such as sliding his hand up her skirt were now gone. He knew she had to focus her mind and concentration back into military mode and he had no intentions of complicating matters. Hazel opened the door turned and blew him a kiss, "See you tomorrow morning for breakfast better still I'll come over early and help you then we can go together how's that sound?" Hazel saying that had a thought go through her head. If I come to early Karl will surely try something so I'll go get him just before its time to leave. As she brisky walked to the female quarters she realized what she was thinking. Change that idea tomorrow morning will be the last time I get to be alone with Karl for at least four months or maybe longer, so if he's up to fooling around I'm his girl, with this change in her head she smiled then laughed to herself as she entered her building.

Hazel's roommates woke her at 0530 hrs, "Come on lass, up and at 'em long day ahead for you." Said Claire, her Scottish roommate heading for the bathroom. Hazel lay there for a few minutes still half asleep her mind was drifting in and out of consciousness, Claire was correct this would be a long day with the strong possibility of real danger before it ends. Why am I getting up so early then? Now almost awake she sat up stretched then put on her dressing gown and slipper, picking up her toilet bag she headed for the door almost like a programmed zombie. Walking down the hallway her faculties slowly returning. You're getting up early you idiot to see Karl remember, with her vision and focus finally clear she picked up her stride covering the remainder of the distance to bathroom in just a few long steps. Back in their room Hazel finished dressing and applying her makeup giving the finishing touches to her hair in its French twist. Finally, she inspected the contents of her suitcase satisfied she locked it then placed it at the foot of her bed ready for later in the day. Her footlocker was alongside her bed packed and locked with everything that would go to the storage room. She was ready, turning to the three other roommates she said nervously, "Well girls I'm off to see Karl then on to a mission briefing, I'm not sure I'll get to see you before I leave later today, wish me luck and a speedy return." The three roommates closed in too hug Hazel each with tears in their eyes, as field agents they had all lived that fear which lay ahead for her, in their minds they saw that hell that lay ahead. "Bye then, see you soon, God willing I hope." Said Hazel heading for the door. Outside the air felt clean and fresh as she filled her lungs allowing the sun to warm her face. The brisk walk felt invigorating stretching her long legs helped her condition herself for what lay ahead. Entering the medical center, she walked up to the nursing station looking for familiar faces. "Morning Ann, how is he, are you finished with changing his dressing?" Hazel asked. "He's all yours Lieutenant, too much energy though, first thing in the morning maybe you could work on discharging that battery of his?" Said Ann laughing at what she had just said. Hazel knew exactly what the friendly nurse was implying. She must think I'm a nymphomaniac or something like that, chuckling Hazel. Entering the hallway, she walked down to Karl's room, still thinking about Ann's last remark well this morning she could be right. In front of the door, she took a moment to ensure her uniform and hair were perfect then tapped twice on the door. From the other side came a response, "Come on in Lieutenant your early." Hazel hearing his voice could feel her excitement building as she opened the door to see Karl standing fully dressed in his uniform minus the tie due to the neck collar. "Well look at you what a hansom devil you make in that uniform." Hazel stood there in the doorway just absorbing the feelings she could not contain. "Come over here you sweet thing and lock the door behind you." Instructed Karl. Hazel quickly looked at her wristwatch as she moved towards him. "Good morning darling did you manage to sleep well last night, I did not fall asleep till way after midnight, you know the things that race through your head prior to mission." Hazel saying that regretted it almost immediately thinking, You idiot you should know that would hit a nerve with him. "Oh, darling forgive me for rattling away like that I was so excited to be here with you this morning my nervous energy kicked in and has turned me into a babbling idiot." Hazel stood in front of Karl her hands holding his forearms tightly. "Darling, that's perfectly alright no apologizes necessary, I remember that feeling before being deployed, I think what may calm you down is a good romp in the hay, how does that sound?" Hazel hearing this let out a big sigh, "Let me remove my tunic and shoes these heels make me too tall for you." Said Hazel as she unbuttoned her tunic, this will have to be a quick one darling we only have a little over an hour. "That's alright darling an hour is better than nothing at all right." Karl could feel she was trying to rush this time together, making love to her this morning would be like running on autopilot. "Hazel you have way too much going on in that head of yours, cramming every thought into this moment, rushing like this will only frustrate things by trying too hard to please me, so let's just enjoy some quiet time instead shall we?" Karl saying this knew it would throw cold water on her advances. "Karl, forgive me I'm a mess right now I don't know what's the matter with me this morning I was all excited knowing I would have some time with you, now look at this train wreck I've created." Hazel was becoming unhinged not uncommon before the start of a covert operation. "Come lay down next to me Hazel you need to relax mentally as well as physically." Encouraged Karl, feeling this was not going very well. Hazel curled up next to him locking her arms around his chest, Karl cradled her head very carefully into the nap of his neck, making sure he kept his head upright. They lay there quietly for a few minutes. Karl could feel her tension subsiding. Slowly Hazel's right hand caressed his face then went down to the front of his trousers. Neither one spoke a word, Hazels long fingers with deliberate intent started unbuttoning them, then without looking at him she moved her head to his chest remaining there while she finished opening his trousers. Hazel placing her hand around his erection and with slow movements started stroking in long slow movements. Karl realized Hazel was trying to resurrect the mood she had started earlier, he decided there and then that he would not say a word, to do so would destroy the mood Hazel was desperately trying to rekindle. Hazel was aroused once again and she also knew that wound on his leg could course a problem, on the day she would leave she did not want to have that on her mind, with that thought in her head she moved over his very erect penis her mouth sliding down its length. Hazel moved in slow precise movements enjoying her conquest by doing this for the first time. Karl was in heaven well almost, two can play that game he thought as he pulled at her to move her legs towards him so he could slide his hand up under her skirt. With a little adjusting Hazel put herself in a position for Karl to make that happen and into her waiting mound. Hazel continued with slow movements until an electrifying feeling sent her into a frenzy with mounting excitement. Karl was giving her the same treatment as yesterday with almost the same results. Hazel lifted her head as she shook with in a powerful orgasm, Karl had done it again. "Darling don't move I need to feel you in my mouth, please I really want this." She cried out as she once again started to squeeze him in her mouth within seconds Karl exploded making her moan even more. "Well, my darling that did not take long at all did it." Said Hazel as she swung her legs over the side of the bed. "How did you like that lover boy, a little extra treatment to keep those vulturous nurses away from my man. I'm going to fix my hair and straighten myself out, you should think about doing the same." Karl lay there for a few minutes thinking about what had just happened. A feeling of extreme guilt started crowding his thoughts with a clear image, he was still in love with Kitty and that thought would stop any further romance with the beautiful Hazel. Damn you Karl, you are doing it again breaking poor Hazel's heart. Can't let on at this late stage of her deployment. When she returns you will face the music and tell her you really tried but there will always be Kitty between us. Karl started to dress once again. Hazel now neatly dressed came out of the bathroom, she was about to say something but froze in her tracks as she looked at the facial expression on Karl, it was giving him away and she immediately knew what that was. "My darling Karl there is more than two of us in this romance am I right? Your face is giving you away am I right? please talk to me Karl please." Hazel trying very hard not to lose her composure as she reached for his hands. Karl's disciplined mind jumped into defensive mode stood silently for a mere few seconds before answering her. "Hazel my mind is in turmoil. You know very well I've been in this same situation before. Later today you will leave on a very dangerous mission and it's that same feeling of emptiness that is turning me inside out feeling the way I do right now. Please forgive me I have no right to upset you like this." Answered Karl knowing full well he was deceiving her, I cannot let her go into harm's way with the thought of a broken romance on her mind, so I will play alone till she is back, maybe I will change in the following months who knows! For a few silent minutes they embraced speaking at this point would serve no purpose. Hazel spoke first, "We should think about joining the others for breakfast and the pre-mission briefing, are you ready to go." Karl could sense the difference in Hazels tone of voice was she sensing there was no future in this relationship and like him was just going through the motions? "Where did I leave my cap, is it in the wardrobe dear?" Asked Karl trying to salvage something from earlier this morning that she could hang on to.

The walk over to the main building was charged with silence, reaching the main entrance Hazel helped Karl navigate the few steps to the front door, Karl making small talk about how walking was becoming so much easier than yesterday even the steps were easier to climb. "Must admit my damn leg does feel stronger." Remarked Karl holding on to Hazel's arm. Once inside Hazel stopped and turned towards Karl saying. "Karl I was thinking as we walked over here after the mission briefing it may be easier if you did not come to see us off. I now understand what Kitty meant when she told me she did not want you to see her off either, are you alright with that?" Hazel was uncomfortable standing there what she really wanted was to hold him and cry her heart out, her world was coming apart. "Are you sure about this Hazel, I will do whatever you feel is best." Karl was going through the motions making him feel even more guilty. "I really think it's for the best, we are both to emotionally tense right now. When I return, God willing I will return, I'm hoping you will be there to throw your arms around me and smother me with kisses, Karl do you think that will happen?" Said Hazel holding back the tears she was feeling from a heart that was being broken. Karl just stood there momentarily before he wrapped his arms around her pulling her in tightly before he answered. "I will be there my darling Hazel. I have hurt you on this the day you should be leaving with love in your heart, can you forgive me. I was feeling too sorry for myself and that was not fair to burden you with that black cloud hanging overhead, **beyond all doubt,** you can count on me. As for seeing you off there is no way or no one that will stop me, are you listening to me." Karl in a matter of seconds had pushed that cloud out of his mind he would be there with open arms when Hazel returned or would he? Over breakfast their spirits were high, Karl and Hazel were holding hands under the table, Hazel had that wonderful smile back on her face knowing they had just gone through a war zone that nearly killed their relationship. The briefing went according to plan with Karl interfacing with Hazel on when to expect radio transmissions and when Hazel should schedule instructions from Slough. With the briefing over Hazel, Gunther and Herbert returned to their quarters to retrieve their luggage while Clive, Bill and Karl remained in the meeting room. "Karl how do you feel about next Wednesday, you must be anxious to get that dog collar off your neck." Asked Bill. "You have no idea how I'm looking forward to getting this behind me, I need to be over there where I can be most effective doing my job." Replied Karl. "We need everyone we can get to man the BIS in the months ahead, so hurry that recovery along Karl your needed back here right after your operation and home leave." Clive knew a lot more about what was expected for the English people and the painful steps needed to save their Island. The three returned, luggage in hand joining the others as they waited in front of the building for the van to arrive Karl excuse himself then said. "Major Knight, do you mind awfully if I borrow Lieutenant Collins for a few minutes there is something I must say that is of a private nature." Clive looked at Karl then Hazel then in a soft tone of voice said. "Of course, go right ahead you two but make sure your back here in fifteen minutes." Clive thinking, whatever happened this morning between those two looks like it has passed, I am willing to bet it has something to do with Kitty?

Inside the building they found an empty office, Hazel now dressed in wool trousers, turtleneck pullover, heavy boots and a field jacket fitted at the waist, her hair pulled back in a ponytail making her look so much different from the officer of this morning. "Hazel this morning I was not in control of my thoughts in fact I will admit to you that I was feeling pretty sorry for myself and by doing so allowed old memories to flood my mind, am I making any sense to you?" asked Karl as he held Hazel very tightly. "Karl, I asked you were there three of us in this relationship is that still the case?" Hazel felt she would rather know now than have her hopes shattered when she returned. "Honestly, I was questioning that myself but my darling Hazel as we stand here, I can tell you emphatically I will be here for you. There may come a time when that cloud brings me down again but know this if it does, I will be ready for it." Karl was stumbling trying to find the right words to tell her he was desperately struggling to bury the past. "Darling Karl, before I leave tell me honestly and please don't lie to save my feelings, do you love me if not can you see a time when that could possibly happen? I need something to hang onto while I'm away?" Karl, holding her face, looked deep into her wet eyes waiting a moment while he asked himself that same question, then reaching down for her hand and quietly whispered in her ear. "Yes, Hazel I do, I have not said that in so long it scares me so, again yes Hazel, I have fallen in love with you. Now you must promise me you will be careful and come home to me." Karl had finally made the commitment, Hazel so needed to hear. They walked back to the van parked in front of the group, "Well it looks like this is it, let's get loaded shall we." Said Gunther. Clive shook hands with each of them then saluted them as they boarded. As Hazel started to board, she stopped turned towards Karl standing next to Clive, with tears in her eyes but under control said very loudly, "Think of me lover boy while I'm away!"

Chapter. Seven
Time to Recoup
and face the German Invasion

The following Wednesday came quickly however the communications from the *Delta-1* Team did not, there again no one expected to hear from them till they reached the safe house in *Brittany France* the first stop on their mission. Karl sat in Clive's office drinking coffee whiling away the time till Doctor Mills arrived to take him to St, Mary's Hospital in London. Clive however was engrossed in a pile of documents awaiting his approval. "Sorry if I appear to be ignoring you old boy, I'm terrible at getting these documents signed, most are duplicates and some are triplicates that simply drives me absolutely crazy. If things could be changed, I would gladly swap this desk job for a field assignment." Remarked a frustrated Clive. "That's alright Clive you carry on I should be leaving shortly anyway." Replied Karl as he continued sipping his awful coffee. A rap on the door followed by a corporal saluting as he entered. "Sir, Doctor Mills has arrived to pick you up, I'll take your suitcase to the car for you, do you require any assistance getting down the steps or can you manage with your cane." Asked the young corporal. "I'll be fine yes take my suitcase and tell Doctor Mills, I'm on my way, thank you. Well Clive wish me luck and please let me know when Delta-1 makes contact, I will plan on hearing from you daily using Ronny's secure base phone at the bungalow, say 0900 hrs each morning with an update. Wish you would consider my Mothers offer to visit us in Baldock, that would work out perfectly for me to return to camp with you, try to make that happen." Asked Karl as he opened the office door. The weather outside was perfect sunny and dry with a few wispy cumulus clouds drifting by. "Morning Doctor so nice of you to drive me to St, Mary's." Said Karl as he approached the passenger door. "Karl please drop the formalities just call me Terry that will be fine, are you ready to go." Asked Terry as he slid in behind the steering wheel of the Humber staff car. "I spent many an hour in one of these big buggers." Said Karl realizing he was letting those haunting old memories slide back into his mind, reacting quickly he blocked them completely. "I think they are the most popular car on the road right now, they look more like an oversized pregnant saloon with those enormous tires, don't you think," Terry chuckling as he said that.

"Well let's get going shall we, it's about thirty-two miles so with moderate traffic we should be there in about ninety minutes. Once I get you checked in, I would like to look at that neck before tomorrow's surgery alright." Asked Terry. "You're in charge whatever you think is best. How long will the surgery take, and will I be able to get rid of this blasted neck collar after its over?" enquired Karl hoping the answer would be yes. "Once we have opened the incision and cleaned around the artery, we will know what we are dealing with. It's not a big surgical procedure but could be very dangerous for you if we run into problems removing that chunk of steel. However, once that shrapnel is removed the rest is straight forward, stitching you up and replacing the bandages around your neck. All going well you should be able to take them off permanently in about a week that does not mean you can return to duty does that answer your question. When you eventually return to Slough you can return to your regular quarters if the leg wound has healed sufficiently enough to climb the stairs to your flat, if not you'll have to stay in the officer's quarters at the camp for a while." Concluded Terry. The drive was very pleasant, except for the continuous convoys of military vehicles going in the opposite direction. "I would venture to say the army is fortifying the coastal approaches, what do you think? Sorry I suspect you are under some gage order what is going on, is that right?" Terry realized that was not the most appropriate thing to ask an intelligence officer at times like this.

Terry turned the car into the main entrance of St, Mary's Hospital parking in front of the door, then walked around to the passenger side to help Karl out of the car handing him over to an orderly that would help him into the lobby, once inside the lobby Karl's heart skipped a beat, there seating on a bench in the hallway was his mother and brother-in-law Ronny. "Mama, God it's so wonderful to see you and Ronny thank you for driving Mama here, come here Mama give me a hug, need to watch my neck though have not had surgery yet, alright." With his arm around his Mother, Karl reached out with his other arm to shack hands with Ronny. "I suppose Freida could not make it because she has to take care of Franchot, not to worry after this I will be home and we will have plenty of time to catch up." Karl spirits could not have been higher. Doctor Mills parked the car in the reserved physicians parking area then preceded to the rear entrance to meet up with Doctor Burgess. While the Doctors prepped, Nurse *Rachel* was instructed to fetch Karl from the main waiting area. "You must be Lieutenant Vita is that correct." Asked Rachel. "Yes nurse, that's me. I suppose you are here to collect me is that right." Asked Karl as he released himself from his mother's hold. "My Mother, and Brother-in-Law, are going to wait here while I'm in surgery, how long before they can come to see me?" asked Karl. "Not really sure the procedure itself will not take long, recovery well that's not for me to say, be assured I will keep them informed on your progress." Said Rachel leading Karl by the arm down the hall to the surgical prep room. Once inside two nurses in surgical gowns helped Karl remove his clothes and put on a hospital gown open at the back, this got a chuckle from Karl. One of the nurses now lowered the bed so Karl could climb onto it. "Sir, I will be rolling you onto your side after I have given you a shave, the next part I don't think you will like. Because of the surgical area I will need to cut your hair on that side of your head followed by a close shave up to the parting line. With thick hair like yours's sir I'm sure it will grow back in quickly. Two nurses entered the preop' area introducing themselves. "I'm sister *Julie* and this is sister *Ann* we will be with you through the procedure and recovery." "Another Ann," said Karl in a jovial mood he was so relieved at finally getting that piece of steel out from his neck. "I'm leaving now to go change for surgery, sister Julie will stay with you while the anesthesiologist administers the pre surgical medication." Said Ann, "See you shortly sir." Karl lay there on the bed for less than ten minutes before the anesthesiologist, Doctor *Michell* pulled back the curtain saying.

"Lieutenant Vita very nice to meet you, I see the sisters have got you ready. I am going to give you a couple of injections that will make you very sleepy, once inside the operating theatre I'll be administering medication to put you to sleep, do you have any questions for me before I start." Asked Doctor Mitchell. "No sir I am about as ready as I will ever be," replied Karl. Inside the operating theatre both surgeons welcomed Karl, already in the twilight zone. "Karl we are going to roll you over on your side then strap you in place, followed by another strap over the top of your head to ensure you don't make any sudden movement while we operate to remove that shrapnel in your neck." Explained Doctor Burgess as he stood back to let the sisters position Karl on the operating table. "Are we all ready?" said Doctor Burgess as he looked to Doctor Mitchell for that nod that Karl was under. Back in the waiting room, Mama sat quietly on one of the couches having been there a little over two hours, time was dragging. "Ronny, do you mind getting me a hot cup of coffee if they have it, tea will do if not." Asked Mama a bundle of nerves worrying over her youngest son. "Mama you have not eaten since early this morning let me get you a sandwich, you really must try to eat something, I know it's the furthest thing from your mind right now but try anyway." Ronny standing over his Mother-in-Law his heart heavy seeing her like this, stressing till some news came that her son was out of danger. Ronny came back with two mugs of coffee and two ham and cheese sandwiches then sat down next to Mama. Turning her attention towards Ronny saying, "Ronny you are such a good man we are really lucky to have you in our family." Mama reaching for his hand as she said this. The coffee and sandwiches were woofed down very quickly, "Did not realize I was that hungry, not sure I can eat both half's though Ronny would you like to finish the remainder? we must always be thankful for having food available, there are thousands going without in this evil world." Said Mama as she handed Ronny the remainder of her sandwich.

Mama resting her head on the armrest of the couch slipped into a shallow slumber to while away the waiting. About an hour later the surgeon came walking down the hall towards them, Ronny woke Mama just in time to get an update from the surgeon. "Mrs. Vita I'm Doctor Burgess, first let me apologize for the surgery taking longer than we originally anticipated, the good news however is we managed to remove all the shrapnel from Karl's neck. It was a very nerve-racking procedure that sharp piece of metal was lodge in an area that made removing it very difficult. Karl is in the recovery room he will be out for about another forty or so minutes. I will have sister Julie come and get you once he comes to. We will be keeping him overnight for observation all going well we shall be able to release him tomorrow afternoon. Doctor Mills will be driving himself to Cambridge tomorrow afternoon seeing as he will be driving right through Baldock he has offered to drive Karl right to your doorstep. Now I must caution you to be very careful with his neck any sudden movement could open those sutures so just remember that. When his leave is up, he should be fit enough to travel back to Slough." Concluded Doctor Burgess turning to walk back down the hall. "There you are Mama Karl is out of danger now try and relax till sister Julie comes to take us to his room." Said Ronny thinking forty minutes seemed like an eternity. Watching the clock Mama was very fidgety she was anxious to be with Karl and Ronny was doing his very best to keep her calm. The doors at the end of the hall swung open and through them came Julie now back in her regular uniform. "Mrs. Vita, ready to see your son? Please follow me." Julie had a big smile on her face thinking, when a procedure goes well it makes the day for the staff so much brighter and today was no exception. Julie held the door open to the recovery area allowing Mama and Ronny to pass through. Karl lying flat on his bed eyes open the bandages stopping his head from moving to the side to look at his Mother. Speaking in a semiconscious voice. "Mama, Ronny your still here how long has it been." Mama sat down carefully on the corner of the bed looking at her son, tears in her eyes saying. "Son it was a wait well worth waiting for. That nice Dr. Burgess told us you will be kept here overnight, and that Dr. Mills will be dropping you off tomorrow afternoon in

Baldock. Karl it's going to be wonderful having you home even though its only eight days." Mama holding her son's arm was secretly praying he would not be going on those mysterious operations to places they never could talk about. Wishful thinking will not stop that from happening I suppose! Karl's eyes were becoming heavy he was falling asleep trying to speak. "Sorry I'm having a hard time staying awake, see you tomorrow afternoon." With those last slurped words Karl went into a deep relaxing sleep. "Mama I think we can go now he will be out for the rest of the night and that's something he needs right now. Tomorrow will come quickly for all of us." Ronny helping his mother-in-law to her feet and guiding her towards the door. Back in Ronny's little Austin car driving the ninety minutes back to Baldock they had time to talk about Karl and Kitty's tragic demise. "Ronny, I wonder what this crazy life has in store for all of us? It's been almost ten months since I received a letter from Papa. I'm trying to keep that from Karl, he was his father's favorite son, probably because they were so much alike." Mama was making small talk to pass away the time on the drive home.

At 0530 hrs the low blue lights were replaced by the soft white overhead lights as the nursing staff started their morning ritual of getting their charges ready for the new day. "Well Lieutenant how are you feeling this morning after that real long sleep, we decided not to wake you last night for dinner, Dr. Burgess told us it would be better to let you sleep." Sister Ann helping him seat up propping his pillows behind him. "After you have had your breakfast Dr. Burgess or Dr. Mills will be along to examine your incision, after that you're free to use the bathroom and get dressed. I'll help you dress. I understand you will be going home today so we will get you a package of medication and bandages to cover you for the rest of the week." Ann was talking to Karl watching his movements as she applied the new smaller bandage around his neck replacing the large uncomfortable type he had been wearing since being injured. "Feeling bloody marvelous sister that constant pain in the side of my neck is almost gone still a little sore though, feel like a new man." Although Karl still had restricted movement from side to side this added range of motion was making him feel more like his old self, when the time came to returned to Slough, he would be able to move around much easier and that thought was driving him forwards. After breakfast Dr. Mills stopped by to examine Karl's neck and make the final decision to discharge him. "Morning old boy, your looking one hundred percent better now let's get those bandages off shall we nurse." Ann carefully removed the dressing to reveal a long line of heavy sutures running from Karl's shoulder to just below his ear. "You will have a great war story with that scare, old boy, sorry we could not hide it better however your collar will conceal quite a bit of it. Now Karl, I want you to turn slowly from right to left, then repeat it. It's going to feel very stiff at first, so don't expect too much at this point." Slowly Karl followed the instructions, he could feel the pulling from the sutures however that constant pain was almost gone. "Well done," said Doctor Mills. "You can buy me a pint one of these days is that a deal? Guess I'll sign the discharge papers now nurse Ann, as for you Lieutenant, plan on being ready after lunch, I'll pick you up at the front of the main entrance where I dropped you off yesterday alright, say 1230 hrs." With a cheerful wave Doctor Mills proceeded down the ward to his next patient. Karl without any assistance headed for the bathroom and a nice hot bath, Doctor Mills had cautioned him to keep the neck dressing dry. Karl relaxed feeling the hot water penetrate his entire body, after a careful close shave noticing the side of his head had been shaved clean made him feel like a circus clown, oh well he thought it's a small price to pay for being alive. Walking back to his cubical he realized the limp from the thigh wound was also feeling that much better, the hot water did not affect it whatsoever, amazing how fast a gash like that can heal, he thought as he entered the cubicle. sister Ann arrived at his bedside to find Karl dressed and packed ready to leave. "Well Karl you look very smart in your uniform. "Thank, you Ann we are blessed with another beautiful morning I think I will go sit outside till it's time to leave, could you be a sweetheart and get me todays Daily Mail might as well get caught up on what's happening with this bloody war!"

Sitting outside Karl tried hard to read the newspaper dated July 7th, his eyes kept crossing in the combination of warm sun, soft scented breezes and the feeling of relief lulled him into a deep relaxing sleep. "Wake up Karl it's time to go." Said Ann as she gently shook him. "My goodness, I guess I needed that, how long have I been out." Asked Karl. "About sixty or so minutes, I decided to leave you out here, you really needed the rest. The hospital requires me to walk you to the entrance, so if you're ready we can go." Said Ann, standing back while Karl stood up, she was watching to see how he would stand, followed by a walk down the length of long hallway. "Wait up a minute Ann will you hold this for me?" Karl had made up his mine that he would not rely on that walking cane anymore. "Karl should you be doing this so soon? Why don't you wait a few days before walking without that cane?" Ann was concerned that he was taking unnecessary chances by putting too much strain on that leg. Karl walked all the way down the hall carrying on a conversation with the very young nervous sister. "I feel wonderful, think that leg of mine is well and truly on the mend. As for this neck, well let's say it's so nice to be able to look around and specially when there is a beautiful young nurse walking by my side." Karl's flirtatious old self was almost back. Ann blushing at the attention Karl was bestowing on her. "Karl really you are such a big flirt, I really don't know how to react to your comments but thank you anyway." Ann could not be more pleased to see Karl walking without his cane, in her mind she imaged being out on a date with someone like Karl, oh well one can always dream I guess she concluded as she sat down next to him on the bench, looking at her watch she said. "Doctor Mills should be along momentarily, Karl you must be getting excited, spending time with your family." Asked Ann trying to fill the silence. "Tell me Ann do you have a young man, is he in the military?" Asked Karl. "Yes, I do. He is two years older than me, before the war he was studying to be a civil engineer but that had to be put on hold when war broke out. David is in the Royal Navy as a gunnery officer, his new orders just came through two weeks ago he is so thrilled, he is to report to *HMS Hood* in ten days. I'm sad to see him go but excited for him he wanted this posting so very much. Here he is Karl, so very nice to of met you, stay safe and who knows our paths may cross again when we are both out of uniform." Karl stood up turning towards Ann. "Would you mind if I give you a big hug and a kiss on the cheek for all your help." Asked Karl as he looked down at Ann. " It's against the hospital policy but heck there is a war going on so why not, don't squeeze to hard though I bruise easily." Karl put one arm around her neck and the other around her waist, as promised he kissed her softly on the cheek her soft skin and perfume against his cheek was awaking the images of loves that would forever hold a special place in his heart. "Karl are you getting sentimental on me?" asked Ann as she returned the kiss. "Yes, Ann its times like this that remind me why we put ourselves in harm's way we do it to give our future generations a chance to live in happiness in a world were war has no place, not really wanting to tell her what was really going through his mind. "Now young lady let me be off can't wait to return to my post and join all the men and women that are fighting to make peace a reality." Karl released Ann, picked up his small suitcase and walked towards the Humber staff car waiting at the curb. Karl opened the passenger door and as he slid into the cabin, one last gesture was to throw a kiss to Ann standing waiting to see him off. "Are you ready to be home Karl?" Asked Doctor Mills putting the Humber into gear pulling away from the hospital entrance. "Yes, I am it will be a wonderful to recharge my battery, but I must admit I can't wait to return to my post in the BIS. There is so much hate and death spreading across Europe and this must be stopped!" Karl was once again reverting to his military training.

The drive to Baldock was uneventful, neither of them really spoke they had their own agendas. After passing through Stevenge Karl started giving directions to get to the bungalow in Baldock. "Well old boy here you are, remember to follow the instructions we gave you, only take those pain tablets if you really need them alright. Let me also add, what you free Europeans are contributing to this war effort inspires all of us here in England, thank you Lieutenant." Karl opened the car door reaching over the bench seat for his overnight case then slide out to the open arms of his mother and sister Freida. "Goodbye sir, thanks to you for saving my life I promise to use it wisely." Karl saluted Doctor Mills as he backed out of the driveway, their paths would cross again when life and death would once again hang in the balance!

On Karl's first day home he relaxed outside continuing his recovery. Ronny called the following morning tension in the sound of his voice. "Karl I'm heading home to drop off the Austin and pack a bag. As of 1600 hrs today, everyone will be restricted to the base something big is expected to start within days, need I say more?" Ronny arrived home quickly packed a bag then asked to talk to Karl alone in the garden. "Karl, our intelligence is reporting an unusual buildup of aircraft along the coast of France, we now believe the attack we have been bracing for is about to start. It will be up to you to take care of Mama, Freida and Franchot if it looks like bombing could be in this direction, get them into a shelter right away." Ronny kissed and hugged the family then jumped into the waiting staff car, a quick wave and he was gone. "Mama, Freida Ronny asked me to explain what is going on as you saw he was very much in hurry." Over coffee Karl explained what could happen and what precautions they would start immediately. "Mama you and Frieda go to the shops, use up all your ration books we must be ready in case Baldock gets hit even though it's highly unlikely, we are close to military air bases, so it's possible a stray bomber might drop one in our general vicinity so let's not take any chances. I am going to call my base in Slough to see if they can provide me with more current information." Karl now was thanking his lucky star that he would be home in Baldock to take care of the family. "Clive its Karl what is going on can you share any information with me." Asked Karl hoping for a better understanding of what is expected to commence. "Karl, we have been expecting a raid on our airfields the Germans are going to try and soften us up before launching a land-based attack. We believe our new radar system along the southern coast will give us an advantage to where those raids are coming from and an estimate of how large their formations could be. The Hun has no idea what those towers are for. We believe nothing will happen for a few more days so don't go crazy just yet, I'll call you in the morning with an update try to act normal no need just yet to upset your mother. Bye for now." Clive hung up the phone thinking this is going to be very difficult for Karl.

The following morning Karl went for a walk through the old streets of Baldock he decided to stop at the George and Dragon for a pint, sitting in the lounge he imaged the beautiful Kitty seating beside him, starring at her engagement ring remembering those times would continue to hold his heart till he could stand in front of her grave and return her letter to him containing the pressed petal. This farewell letter would remain in his safety deposit box at Lloyds Bank here in Baldock till that time came. Karl also spent some solitary time thinking about Hazel and the roller coaster relationship they found themselves on. The final day before she left on that dangerous mission back into occupied Europe. He thought deeply about how he had committed to loving her did he really mean that or was it a good intention to ease her pain? Hazel, in a heated moment had insinuated that there were three in their relationship, was that still true? On the way home he stopped to seat on a bench near the park, he milled over all these thoughts as they collided in his mind. Yes, he did believe that he in a peculiar manner could love the sweet Hazel but not the way he loved Kitty, something else in his head kept repeating Karl you are happiest when you out at sea, life always seemed uncomplicated out there. When this crazy war is finally over, I would like to return to my first love as an officer in the merchant service! With that course firmly established in his brain, he stood up adjusted his cap to one side and set off back to the bungalow about three miles away, his walking cane was now a thing of the past so he simple deposited it in the collection box at the church *of St Mary the Virgin*, from here on he would walk tall, the limp becoming less of a problem with ever step.

On July 8th, Ronny called from his base at Duxford, "Karl although we are on a secure line, what I'm going to tell you is still highly confidential. Yesterday we intercepted a communique from the western command of the Luftwaffe, we are now confident the Germans will attack within the next several days. Karl you must prepare, have a bag ready to go to the air raid shelter up the road and keep the radio tuned to the BBC for the latest updates. Must go now and remember if you hear the air raid siren go immediately to the shelter, unfortunately I am confined to the base, so Karl I am relying on you to take care of the family.

On July 10th Karl was listening to the BBC radio when an announcement came on. We interrupt this program to bring the following news. "Less than an hour ago a large formation of aircraft has been detected crossing over the French coast their direction has been plotted to cross the South coast of England. You are instructed to seek shelter immediately. Karl sat up this was no surprise to him he and everyone in the BIS had been bracing for this day, the phony war had come to an end. Later in the morning a sizable formation of *Stuka 87 dive bombers* crossed the coast the first wave to attack, their targets to bomb the radar installations along the coast. From that day on all the newspapers along with the BBC would provide the latest casualties reports on aircraft shot down or damaged on both sides, the numbers were staggering, how long can we defend ourselves like this thought Karl.

By the beginning of August, the concern was, could the RAF continue to hold the Luftwaffe at bay, their numbers growing to as many as 750 bombers on each raid. The bombers were mainly *Heinkel 111* and the *Dornier 17* in smaller formations protected by *Messerschmitt 109* and *Messerschmitt 110's* fighters. Day after day The RAF scrambled their *Hurricanes* and *Spitfires* their young pilots continuously throwing themselves at a sky black with hostel aircraft. Throughout the aerial attacks the RAF relied on the advanced guidance of the radar to locate the formations, each wave of attacking aircraft always intercepted by the deadly fighters spitting hot lead into their formation. By early August most RAF squadrons had no reserve aircraft to replace the ones damaged or lost, England was almost on its knees. Then a blunder by the German high command gave England the opportunity it so desperately needed to recover and rebuild. The aerial bombardment of English airfields was abandoned in favor of a revised night operations by the relentless bombing of London and other major cities throughout England, this change in tactics would cost Germany the invasion of England known as *Operation Sea Lion*. Now the RAF could rebuild its decimated air force and once again rebuild its reserve of aircraft.

On August 20th, the BBC aired a recorded public message from Prime Minster, Winston Churchill to the people of England.
"For many days and weeks, the German Luftwaffe has thrown the might of its air force against our island to no avail. The seabed of the English Channel and the fields of England are littered with crashed German aircraft. Without the vital air superiority over the channel and England there can be no way a successful invasion can take place. It is the belief by the war department and this government that **Operation Sealion** has been postponed until further notice. Churchill finished the broadcast by saying.

"Never in the field of human conflict was so much owed by so many to so few."

"The battle of Britain is over. The battle to protect London and other major cities had just begun. God Save The King." Every person in England sighed with relief and sorrow for the cities in England that continued to be bombed nightly.

Chapter: Eight
Return to Duty

On his last day in Baldock the family had lunch together before Karl got picked up by a returning staff car heading back from Cambridge to the camp in Slough. "Mama I would feel so much better knowing the fate of my Father and three brothers, it's this constant worrying about them that is bothering me like this, I can only imagine how the two of you are handling this." Karl could always tell when Mama or Freida were hiding something with no intent of sharing. "Karl they are in Italy the problem is that same craziness that overran Austria is now spreading through Italy. Your Fathers has relatives in the mountains that are hiding them, so right now they are safe, those mountains are of no interest to the Fascists, they are more intent on taking over the factories and major cities. The downside is receiving mail from those remote locations is almost nonexistent. Karl, pray they remain safe in their mountain hideout till this terrible war comes to an end." Mama sat back in her chair the look on her face was painting a grimmer picture that Karl could see through.

The sound of a car door closing in the driveway told Karl his ride had arrived. "Well Mama and Freida it's time for me to return to work my driver is at the front door. Promise me you will not worry unnecessarily you have bigger problems than worrying about me. I will write as often as I can probably call you on the phone though, but there will be times when sending letters or calling could be difficult. You have enough spies at my camp that are keeping you updated so I don't see that changing any time soon." Karl laughing loudly saying this. Putting his tunic and cap on he kissed them both then picked up Franchot giving him a kiss on the forehead and a hug before heading to the door. As he got into the car, he wound down the window yelling, "Goodbye, stay safe and remember not to worry." This would be the last time Karl would see them and Baldock for many long months.

Karl was getting used to this drive back to Slough the convoys congesting the roads around Watford was the only delay they experienced. Approaching the main gate, the driver rolled down his window to show his I.D. then Karl did the same. The guard recognized the driver as well as Karl saying, "Welcome back sir, did everything go as planned." The guard making small talk as he examined their passes then waved them through. "Drop me off at building B-3 will you." Asked Karl as he buttoned his tunic and reached for his suitcase. "Thanks Charlie that was not a bad drive at all." Karl liked this driver, a real Scotsman that had driven Karl on many occasions. Smartly getting out of the car Charlie walks around to the passenger side to open the door. "Have a great rest of the day sir, hope to see you again soon." Said Charlie saluting as Karl got out taking in the all too familiar surroundings. Looking up at the main door and those dreaded steps, Karl thought well let me tackle them one at a time, surprising himself he walked up the steps with no difficulty and entered the lobby. "Well will you look who has arrived back here." Said Julie from behind her reception desk. "I can see you are on the mend, wonderful to see you sir." Julie had worked for Karl before being assigned to the clerical staff that also manned the reception desk. "I'll announce myself Julie thanks for the warm welcome." Remarked Karl as he started down the hallway that led to his cubical. "Chaps look what the wind just blew in its Karl Vita, welcome home old man." Yelled good friend Bill Lowes. Karl felt at home with the people in the room he had worked with them for over two years now. Hearing Bill announce Karl, Clive stood up from his desk opened the half-closed door to his office and entered the operations room, a beaming smile across his face, so pleased to see his friend almost back too normal. "You, old bugger I thought I told you to call before leaving Baldock, you crazy bloody Austrian we have all been worried about you, it looks like the surgery went well otherwise we would be sending flowers about now." Said Clive, he could not be happier to have Karl back in operations. "What's the news from Delta-1. Where are they, have they uncovered anything worthwhile yet?" Typical Vita, he's been back less than five minutes and already going a hundred miles an hour, slow down you maniac. The latest communication from Delta-1 came late last night, it said they had made their way down to *Saint-Nazaire,* there appears to be substantial amount of German construction equipment on the road south. They advised that once they know that heavy equipment has reached its destination, would we send a marine architect or someone that can access what the intent is for such heavy equipment. The last part of the communication said the weather tomorrow looks '*better*' for getting a closer look." Clive stopped talking looking at Karl smiling. He was thinking, there's that word again '*better*' thank God she is safe. "I should plan on getting over there maybe after the Christmas Holidays or maybe before if it looks like they are moving faster with their final plan. Clive, you agree?" Asked Karl. "Not in your present condition you're not, I have already asked the Navy for a marine architect to rendezvous with them in about four or five weeks. Your job starting tomorrow is to analyze all the communications coming in from all the Delta teams, something is going on down the entire Atlantic seaboard of France and we need to know what the hell those bugger's are up to, right now, you're the best man for this job, and stop looking at me like a scolded schoolboy. Your turn will come soon enough."

Clive always had a problem with Karl working behind a desk, once he regained his strength there would be no way he could keep him tied to that desk, but for now his ability to understand these communiques were just as important as the work of field agents. "I'm buying," came a voice from the back of the office, Bill was putting his tunic on ready to blow off steam in the officer's lounge. "Sounds good to me," said Karl. "I've got to check into the officer's quarters first. Doc Mills want me to stay there for a while. I'll catch up with you in a little while alright?" Before leaving Karl walked over to the radio operators station saying. "When are you next scheduled for a communication from Delta-1." "Will have a receiving band open at 2130 hrs tonight." Answered the operator. "When you acknowledge that transmission add this somewhere in the message," Karl wrote down on a pad. *All good with Mother.* "Sir I'm not sure I'm authorized to do that." Said the confused operator. "As of tomorrow morning, you will be reporting to me so just do it." Karl throwing his weight around in front of the operator. "You're the boss can you just initial that note you handed me so I can put it in the outgoing file." Asked the operator. Entering the lounge, the laughter and saucy jokes were in full swing, "Come over here you, old bugger," said Bill pulling a spare chair towards the table. "Did you blokes welcome back Vita yet? As of tomorrow morning, our good Austrian friend here will be directing the communication support for all the Delta teams so wish him luck he will be putting in long hours in that job. Karl what did you do with your walking cane?" Concluded Bill knowing full well that Karl was already pushing for another field assignment. "Thanks, Bill, your always so generous with those back handed complements, with any luck it won't be for too long, never did like pushing papers around a desk." Karl was throwing it back at his good friend. "And as for the walking cane, well I deposited into the church donation box back in Baldock," Karl saying that immediately regretted saying that as Bill still needed his walking cane to support his deformed leg, wounded years back escaping the Gestapo in Germany. After about forty-five minutes Clive entered the lounge with someone Karl did not recognize in a French uniform, must be a visitor, thought Karl. "Hey, you noisy bunch I would like you all to welcome our newest member, Captain *Jean Yves Jerva* of the *French 1st Light Cavalry Division*. Jean Yves will be our liaison officer on assignment from the Free French Forces station here in England. His primarily function will be to support the Delta Teams operating in Southern France, Karl you two will be working together later." Said Clive his eyes firmly fixed on Karl as he said this. Clive always had a way of finding the best people for his beloved BIS. "Bill, Karl please join us for dinner tonight it will be good time to get to know our new member, how do you feel about that Jean Yves?" As usual Clive was getting the introductions squared away before proceeding, he then steered the small group to a quiet table tucked away from the rest of the officers in the lounge. Karl sat across from the Jean Yves, not speaking until the drink orders had been taken then asked in his fluent French. "Tell me Jean Yves were you one of the Dunkirk evacuees?" Speaking in English with a strong accent the French officer replied. "Yes, I was. The Major here tells me you were injured in that operation, too many good men were lost and so many are now prisoners of war. It breaks my heart to see what happened, I never, never expected to see my beloved France fall to the Germans. Major Knight told me about your ship I am so sorry to hear it was a casualty of Dunkirk. On the positive side, now I have met you I am enthusiastic about working together. When the time comes for you and I to return to France, I can assure you I will do my best to be the operative you will come to rely on. Major, will it be tomorrow I join Karl, or do you have other plans for me?" Asked the French Captain. "Jean Yves I'm afraid It will be quite a while before you start working in the Delta support group. The BIS requires all agents to go through a condensed orientation program before you can be phased into any operating unit, poor Karl here went through many months of training just before the outbreak of the war. I can assure you I will do my best to keep that as short as possible, we really need you up and running as soon as possible." Replied Clive, recognizing that both these Europeans were anxious to get involved planning to disrupt the German expansion into French ports and supply lines. "Jean Yves, would you mind if I just call you Jean, it will make things much easier." Asked Karl. "Of course, that will be fine." Replied Jean Yves. "From your rank I'm assuming you're a good learner, so please get back here fast, you haven't even started yet but I'm already missing you!" Karl saying that got everybody laughing and by the look on Jean's face a new friend that would watch his back when they ventured into harm's way.

Karl threw himself into the new job, even finding out he liked the constant intrigue that was a daily occurrence. The months zoomed by into late autumn, the Christmas season was now upon them however manning the support group had to continue. Karl along with John and Peggy volunteered to remain behind to man the support for the Delta Teams. Without most of its personnel in the camp it felt more like a morgue than the busy military camp of only yesterday. Most of its personnel now with their family and love ones spending the Christmas holiday together, the thought of war being the furthest thing from their minds. On most evenings Karl would sit alone in the lounge sipping his mild and bitter pint of beer, not a good time to be remembering a Christmas only a few years ago in the cold of a Scottish winter. Those times when he and Kitty would take Clive's big Humber to a remote location for an evening of passion escaping the threats of a war yet to start. These images would forever burn in his mind. Kitty would never celebrate or share the joys of Christmas again it was that image that blocked him from freely committing to a lasting romance with Hazel. New Year came and went with a grand party in the lounge, Karl attended but unlike his normal boisterous self he was very withdrawn saddened by those haunting memories. Looking at each other, Clive and Bill knew the reason for his sadness, Clive reached over to him putting his hand on Karl's shoulder, "My dear friend we know what's going through your mind about now, you must try to let go of those memories or they will continue to eat you alive." Clive talking in a very concerned tone of voice. "You are right as usual," replied Karl fighting again with that following storm cloud in his mind. "I feel like another beer you blokes care to join me," Karl was trying to make this a good start to 1941. Excusing himself Karl wondered over to the operations to see if any new communiques had been received. "Only one tonight sir got this only a few minutes ago. Not sure what it means though, take a look sir? see if you can make head or tails of it." Said the confused operator, the message read. This next year it will be the '*Best*'. A smile came across Karl's face. "Send this reply will you. *All good with Mother*." Once again Karl could feel those clouds of despair rolling away. 1941 would be full of changes and danger for Karl and those around him.

By now the Delta-1 Team had the naval marine architect working on analyzing the reports and photographs that had been taken of activities in the very early stages of construction in *Saint-Nazaire*. "Sir this communication arrived late last night from Delta-1 they are pretty convinced those new structures could well be fortified docks for U-Boats." Said John the wireless operator. "Looks like the Huns are going to group their bigger *Mark-VII U-Boats* along the Atlantic seaboard. Operating from those new bases the U-Boats will dramatically reduce the time it takes to get out into the Atlantic shipping lanes extending their range by using less fuel." The time was now 0900 hrs, Karl leaning against his desk the communication still in his hand mulling around in his head the Delta-1 communique his brain in overload thinking, but why so much material for building concrete docks? Could it be those structures are not just reinforced docks but? Like a lightning bolt the answer came to him, Karl stood upright a light going off in his head, he knew exactly what the Germans were up to. "My God they are building bunkers to protect the boats from air attack. Those bugger's are masters at building massive structures like this, find Major Knight for me straight away." Said Karl as he studied the big wall map studying the many harbors along the coast with deep water access to support the needs of such submarine bases. Clive entered the room with Bill hobbling along besides him. "What's the big flap about Lieutenant." Clive knew if Karl had sent for him there must be something very wrong. "Come over here to the wall map, see these French ports." Pointing to the ports of, **Brest, Bordeaux, La Rochelle and Saint-Nazaire.** "Now let me read to you a communique that came in last night from Delta-1." Karl pointing to each of the ports as he read the communique. "At first, I thought all that material being taken to those ports would be used to build new docks, however there was something fundamentally wrong with that thought. The more I studied the wall chart the more I realized what they were up to, they are going to construct reinforced submarine pens, when finished they will protect the U-Boats from aerial bombardment by the RAF. These subs when operational in the North Atlantic, will deliver untold havoc to our conveys crossing to England from America and Canada. Gentleman our main supply lines are in danger of being severed. Germany is planning to starve this Island into submission, need I say more?" Karl watched the expressions of Clive and Bill faces and others that had gathered in the operations office to listen to Karl's assessment of what was happening. They all studied the wall map intently as Karl circled each port with a red grease pencil. "Lieutenant Vita, we have long suspected that once the Germans had control of France, they would reposition many of their Atlantic U-Boats to these western ports of France but this soon? God almighty, it's only been a little over six months since Dunkirk!" Said Clive loudly obviously shaken by what Karl had discovered. After a few minutes Karl spoke, "Sir we must get the RAF to start daily reconnaissance flights over these ports, then follow them up with bombing raids. Our strategy should be to disrupt the construction at every phase, create as many delay's in delivering construction materials whatever it takes, we must throw roadblocks up to slow down the completion of the submarine pens. I can assure you I have seen firsthand how effective German civil engineers can be in building structures such as these. When they are operational, there is not a bomber currently available in the RAF that could deliver a big enough bomb to penetrate those fortifications. As I just said and to repeat, the Germans are masters at projects like this, gentlemen time is not on our side." Karl stopped talking while the gravity of what was happening sunk into the small group gathered around the big map of Europe. In silence they stood waiting for Major Knight to respond. "Lieutenant, can you be ready tomorrow morning to accompany me to the minister of defense for a meeting with all heads of each branch of the services. Captain Lowes even though Captain Jerva is still in orientation and training, get hold of the base commander and have Jerva brought here today, he must be available to accompany us tomorrow morning, better still have the RAF boys fly him down that's the quickest way. I am calling the French minister in London to have him available for that meeting as well. Lieutenant your understanding of engineering has identified what those Huns are up to, well done." Clive the ever-professional soldier turned and headed for the door saying, "Captain Lowes accompany me we have work to do." Karl sat on the corner of his desk pondering what steps he would recommend to all the ministers and top brass tomorrow in London. "Excuse me sir did I do something wrong." Asked John. "On the contrary You did an excellent job by bring this to my attention." Karl looking back at John asking. "John, do we have another big map like this one that I can take with me tomorrow. Could you also make a file for me with the last six intelligence reports from Delta-1," John hurried off to the supply room to find the wall map then collect the field communications Karl asked for. "You are in luck Gov," said John waving a rolled-up map in front of Karl. "Oops, sorry sir for a minute I thought I was back in my civvy job." Said John trying not to blush at his remark. "That's alright John you can call me that if you prefer." Karl walked over to the big plotting table then spread out the large map. "John get some weights to hold the corners down, then bring over some of those grease pencils." Karl marked up the areas of interest then created a legend with approximate distances to each target, next he marked the present locations for Delta-1, 2 and 3 Teams and their proximity to each of the ports. "John, could you find one of those tubes we use for storing maps, then better call over to the typing pool for an assistant, make sure they send someone that knows how to type very quickly?" Karl spent the rest of the day working feverishly till about 1730 hrs with the assistance of the young corporal from the typing pool, compiling multiple copies of various documents that would go into each package. A loud rap on the door made them look up to see Bill and Jean standing in the doorway. "Mind if we join you, old boy," asked Bill. "Please do we're almost done, Peggy here has been a tremendous help, she stayed on when John left to go home, thanks again Peggy for staying late could not have done this without your assistance." Said Karl as he finished the last package. "Jean told me walking down the hallway he is in the mood for some English fish and chips, so we are heading into Slough. Please join us Peggy this boss of yours has been working you to hard." Said Bill looking for approval from Karl and Jean. "Personally, I would enjoy some female company this evening, so please come with us corporal or may I also call you Peggy." Asked the tall Frenchman. "Well sirs, I was going to go back to my quarters and probably do something with the other girls, but how often does a girl get to go out with three handsome officers, count me in." Peggy was young bubbly fair skinned redhead from Bradford in the Midlands, since joining the ATS she had worked in the typing pool always with an eye on working her way up to a permanent position as an assistant in one of the BIS groups. "All ready?" asked Bill. "Let's get going shall we. *The Bull* will still be serving so if we hurry, we'll be alright." Yelled Bill as he hurried the other three out the door and into the waiting staff car. The drive took all of fifteen minutes, Bill sat in the front passenger seat, Peggy sandwiched in between Jean and Karl in the back seat. "Well, I did not expect to be the lady in the middle tonight?" Said Peggy loving every minute of being squeezed tightly between two warm blooded foreigners. The Bull was busy but still had tables available. "Charlie are we still in time for fish and chips?" yelled Bill as they trooped into the lounge. "Be with ya in half a mo' gaffer, shall I put an order in for four fish and chips then?" As he wheeled two big mugs of frothy beer towards two air force privates sitting at the bar. Once they sat down Karl asked if he could buy the first round. "What would you like Peggy." "Could I have a pink gin sir." Of course, you can and please call me Karl, we're off duty now and amongst friends in this wonderful old Inn. Bill, Jean will you join me in a pint of mild and bitter." Asked Karl remembering another time several years back when a beautiful lady by the name of Kitty asked him the same question, would he like a pint of mild and bitter a term he had never heard before. That dark cloud was trying to move in and spoil this nice evening. "Hey Karl, did you hear me, we said yes to that beer order, looks like your drifting away, still thinking about that problem we have are you?" Bill saying that found himself thinking along the same lines, he was the last person to see Kitty alive!

This break, away from the office was what they all needed, a brief escape from the dangers lying in wait only a few months into the future. With dinner and drinks over the four headed for the door. "Night Charlie see ya soon yelled Bill as they walked out into the evening air. "Karl, I have to sign Jean into the officer's quarters, do you mind awfully taking Peggy back to the camp in a taxi, I did not realize the late hour? There's a taxi rank at the next corner, really sorry for doing this, hope you will forgive me Peggy." Said Bill as they waited for the staff car to turn around in front of The Bull. "No problem, I love the idea of being along in the back seat of a taxi with Peggy, what do you think Peggy?" Karl trying to be his old self even if it was said in jest. "I must say you blokes are showering me with all sorts of complements tonight." Replied a tipsy Peggy. The staff car drove off and Karl and Peggy walked slowly to the next corner to find a taxi. "The air tonight makes me think of my home in Bradford, although right now its feels like a million miles away, I can only imagine how you feel Sir, sorry meant Karl." Peggy in the dime light of the moon reminded Karl so much of Hazel and maybe a little of Kitty must be the uniform he thought. "We live in troubled times our todays may never be repeated, all our tomorrows are a gift, living for today maybe is all we have?" Replied Karl as he opened the taxi for Peggy. "Thank you, kind sir." Said Peggy as she slides into the taxi giving Karl a wonderful view of her nicely shaped legs as she did so. Not tonight you're not thought Karl as he slid in besides her. They made small talk driving back, each of them playing a what if scenario in their heads as they talked. "Karl I'm much younger than you and far less worldly in fact Slough is the furthest I've ever been away from Bradford guess you could say I'm somewhat naïve about so many things. Over dinner I listened to you three talking about the many places you all have seen and things you have done, makes me feel quite sheltered. Like you just said, this war makes all of us and especially me realize there may be no tomorrow. It would sadden me to think of all I have missed should something happen that might end it for me?" The alcohol was making Peggy a little more open and melancholy than she normally would be in the company of a senior officer, and Karl knew exactly where her mind was taking her. "Peggy you should not be talking like this, you have a lifetime ahead of you, there will be time for good and not so good adventures, there will be time for new romances and one day a lucky someone will be your lasting love." Karl was trying to give her advice about the ups and downs of surviving in this war. The lecture he was giving Peggy resonating in his own head, practice what you preach, he concluded was not working for himself. The taxi came to stop in front of the base guardhouse, Karl got out first noticing once again Peggy's shapely legs as she slid across the seat to get out. Karl paid the driver then the two walked up to the guard house producing their Identification cards for the guard. Karl the gentleman walked Peggy to the entrance of the female quarters. "Well young lady here you are, safe and sound hope you had a nice time this evening and again thanks for staying late to help me. Peggy your work ethics have really impressed me, you would make someone the perfect assistant." Karl stopped short letting an idea process in his brain. "Peggy, would you consider coming to work for me if I can swing it? Today was my first day in the department all that work has made me realized I can't do it all without help so what do you say Corporal Townsend?" Karl in the dime light studied her face for a sign that she would consider his offer. "Would I consider it, God you are making a perfect end to this day sir, damn it, I did it again calling you sir. Karl, I promise you, this will be the best decision you have made on your first day as head of the communication department. Your, out tomorrow can I expect your request for my transfer by weeks end?" Asked a very excited Peggy. "By weeks end, hell no you will start the day after tomorrow." Answered Karl enjoying the excitement Peggy was displaying. "Thank you so much see you soon, good night." Peggy had been given her wish opening the door she smiled and cheekily blew Karl a kiss.

Chapter Nine
Operation Free Land

The sky was still dark as Karl walked from the officer's quarters to his department in the main building, enjoying the cool morning air, thinking it's so quiet this early in the morning, even my limp is getting better hardly any pain not like last week anyway. First stop was to the cafeteria for a big cup of coffee then on to his office to gather the materials he would need for the meeting today. With time to spare he sat down at his desk to write an interservice transfer request to his department for Corporal Peggy Townsend. He elaborated on how her efficiency the evening before helping him prepare documentation for a very important meeting, he concludes by asking that this request be expedited with a start day for the following day. Folding the request, he sealed it into an inter-department envelope. Karl walked down to the reception desk manned during the off-duty hours by a guard from the military police. "Morning would you make sure this gets to the supervisor in charge of the clerical staffing first thing this morning. Thank you." Walking back to his office, Karl decided to stop for a coffee refill before returning to his desk. As he sat sipping the hot coffee, he started to formulate a convincing proposal he would present to Clive and his operations advisory staff. His proposal would be to authorize a mission for Jean Vyes and himself to be dropped into Southern France to observe firsthand the extent of construction going on. Furthermore, and if possible, to gain access to German plans for what type of submarines and how many would be based along the Atlantic seaboard. I can't for the life of me see how they would deny this request it's probably the most aggressive fact-finding mission proposed to date. Yes, Clive will make excuses about my injuries. He will argue they should utilize the Delta teams already operating in that region, I need to be ready for that question with a compelling answer? I need to give that more thought driving up to London. Without realizing it Karl had been back in his office for the best part of an hour. "Morning Sir," said John as he removed his tunic and beret hanging them on the hook by the door. "What did I miss after I left last night?" asked John sitting down across from Karl with his hot mug of tea. "Well, it worked out really good, see that stack of folders over there, thanks to Peggy we managed to finish what you and I started earlier in the day. As for Peggy, I offered her a permanent position working with us, what do you think to that John? Hope you approve because you will interface with her more than me." Enquired Karl looking for approval. "Well, if my opinion matters, I think she will be a welcome addition to the team and very easy on the eyes I must say." John was grinning at the last part of that statement. Karl simply grinned then chuckled in agreement. Karl looked at his watch well I guess I should get going as he entered his office to put on his tunic then carefully buttoned his top button of his blouse, straightening his tie, not too tightly though because of the dressing around his neck. The last thing he done was to put on his *'Sam'* leather belt with its diagonal shoulder strap. Walking over to the file cabinet he retrieved his forage cap placing it on his head to one side, old marine habits don't fad away! I'm now ready for those boffins in London he thought as he walked out into the office. The small staff was happy to see their new boss ready to take on the big brass. "Sir you have a call from the clerical department." Said, one of the office staff. "Thank you, Sargent. "Lieutenant Vita here." Replied Karl as he put the receiver to his ear. "Morning Lieutenant your request for Corporal Townsend to be transferred has been approved, she is on her way right now, is there anything else I can help you with?" Said *Susan McCabe* the senior officer at the other end. "Thank you so much I did not expect to see her till tomorrow, no problem though we are overloaded with work." Karl hung up the phone turned towards John beaming a big smile saying. "John, Peggy is heading over here, she is starting right away. I'm leaving for that meeting in London, could you please give her the rundown on how things work around here that should keep her busy till I return tomorrow morning." Karl was feeling good about how this day was starting out. "John you will have to help me carry all those packages to the car." As Karl was asking John, a reply came from behind him. "Let me help you sir with those packages! Where do I put my things in the meantime?" asked Peggy carrying a cardboard box. "That will be your desk over there corporal." Said John with a look of approval across his face. "Right, I'll carry this pile if you can carry the reminder Sir, be right back Sarg! Care for more tea on my way back, anyone else need some." asked Peggy walking confidently towards the door which Karl was holding open. Three others in the department responded, "Yes please, milk and sugar if you don't mind." Walking down the hall Karl spoke first, "Well Peggy you just jump right in, don't you? I like that, did not expect to see you this morning though." Remarked Karl. "Well sir my supervisor told me that opportunities like this are few and far between and if I liked the idea go right away just in case someone else beats me to it. She also said that the new department head is a smashing looking bloke." Peggy was cheeky with her answer and Karl being Karl loved her boldness.

"See you tomorrow," said Karl climbing into the back seat of the staff car giving a cheerful wave to Corporal Townsend. "It looks like you have bought along everything except the kitchen sink." Laughed Clive sitting in the rear facing seat.

The big staff car had room for five in its double row interior. Seating next to Clive was Bill and across from them sat Jean Vyes, the stack of folders placed between Karl and Jean. "Well chaps hope you're ready for today, everyone attending has voiced concern at the latest findings. I talked last night to a couple of chaps that were in the Kriegsmarine before the war broke out, they concur with your findings, in fact they both felt that the best opportunity for the German Navy would be an offensive from U-Boats stationed on the Atlantic seaboard, moving those boats would also mean increased exposure to aerial attack, so concrete reinforced bunkers would make absolute sense, did not expect them to move this fast though." Clive was watching the eye play between Karl and Jean, how well he knew his friend. "There is something on your mind Karl I can tell you want to discuss something is that correct?" Clive saying that now left the door open for Karl to speak. "Well seeing as you know me so well, I might as well share my thoughts with you three before we arrive at the defense department. For the record Jean here has not heard this before, sorry about that Jean this plan I have was only conceived yesterday Major would you make sure that privacy window is closed before I outline my plan." Over the next forty plus minutes Karl explained the main points of his plan and how Jean and himself would go undercover posing as an officer in the Kriegsmarine and Jean would pose as a Vichy French Naval Officer assigned to assist in the occupation of French port facilities. Their cover assignment would be to coordinate munitions and spare parts for the four submarine bases being built. Karl finished his proposal then sat back waiting for the backlash he knew would follow. "First let me say this plan is a brilliant, very ambitious but also a very dangerous one. I would however ask you why one of the Delta teams could not do this? They are already imbedded in France and very familiar with German activities in and around those ports, why not use them instead of the you two? As Karl was about to speak, Jean butt in saying, "Sorry Karl may I add to this discussion. Karl's plan is aggressive yes, but let's face it who better to go undercover that two officers that know their way around ships and ports in Southern France than the two of us working together. If this plan gets approved, we should be given the opportunity to participate, it's our countries that have been overrun when all said and done isn't that right Karl?" Jean had made up his mind that he and Karl should be the ones on this mission. "Well looks like you two have already made up your minds, Karl remember you are still recovering from those Dunkirk injuries and have you considered the very high risk of not coming back from a mission such as this?" Clive could see the determination in both their faces. Clive looking up at the roof of the car thinking, they will never give this up or have someone else do it, it's their lives that are in danger. "Have you given any thought to, if your captured what then?" Clive throwing another roadblock at them. "Remember Bill here has already seen and felt the cruelty of the Gestapo why don't you ask him what's that like? You need to understand being a tough guy doesn't matter much in the hands of the Gestapo." Clive now asking Bill to interject. "Clive is correct the Gestapo doesn't give a dam about the Geneva Convention or in fact any form of humanitarian rights, they have one objective to break you and drain every last piece of information from you after which they more than likely will shoot you." Bill remembering his time with the dreaded Gestapo and the daring escape planned by local freedom fighters, ramming the van transporting Kitty and himself to Gestapo headquarters a few years back. His leg was badly injured in that crash, but poor Kitty was killed instantly. Karl sat without saying a word. "Well Karl any more thoughts on this plan of yours?" Asked Clive. "Yes, sir I do. Jean and I have a lot of training and research to do when we arrive back tonight, is that right Jean?" Karl with that defiant smile put out his hand to Jean who grabbed it saying, *"Viva la France."*

Arriving at the very impressive Ministry of Defense Offices in London, they got out of the car, Clive telling the driver it could be a long meeting so go get something to eat but stay in the building in case I need you. Karl and Jean with the help of Bill carried the packages down a long hallway at the end they were asked for their identification cards. The elevator stopped at the third floor and once again an MP looked at their ID's, after which he asked them to follow him to the meeting room. The room was large with a long conference table running down the length of the room. The left wall was all windows the other three were clad in dark walnut paneling with impressive large pictures to enhance the look of the room, at the head of the room to one side of the presentation board hung the biggest picture in the room. *King George VI* prominently displayed in his Royal Naval uniform. "Gentleman please come in and have a seat at the front if you please," Said the *Right Honorable Winston Churchill.* The Prime Minister of England had appointed himself Minister of Defense May 10th, 1940 and would remain so throughout the war. Present at the meeting were ten high ranking officers from each of the British services along with eight cabinet ministers. Also, in attendance French Government officials with staff members from the Free French Army and another from the French Navy. "Would you take your seats, coffee and tea is available at the rear of the room, but please refrain from moving about or talking while these Gentlemen present their report." Requested a, high ranking English Naval Attaché.

Clive approached the front of the room, thanking the Prime Minister and each of the services for making themselves available this morning. "Yesterday Lieutenant Karl Vita received information that he immediately brought to my attention and that is the purpose for this meeting this morning. Since the fall of France, we have speculated that the Germans would move quickly to utilize the Atlantic ports for their U-Boat fleet, however we did not consider they would immediately start the construction of heavily reinforced pens for those boats. Lieutenant Vita was a former Maritime Officer and Structural Engineer he has extensive knowledge of German Civil Engineering capabilities. During the evacuation of Dunkirk, he volunteered to command an armed trawler, during that operation Lieutenant Vita was badly injured. His command was sunk by aerial attack during their second return trip. We are very lucky to have him here today not fully recovered yet but very determined to present his finding at this meeting. Lieutenant please take it from here." Concluded Clive as he returned to his seat. Karl stood up approaching the presentation board which now had the wall map attached to it. He was about to speak when the Prime Minister rose and started clapping followed by everyone else. "Young man we commend your actions, Austria can be proud of its son and we in England bless our good fortune that you are on our side, now please proceed." Everyone sat down turning their attention to Karl and his big map. Jean and Bill passed out the packages to everyone thanking God, Karl had made more than they anticipated would be needed. Over the next two plus hours Karl made the presentation making sure that everyone was in total agreement to the severity of what the Germans were doing. Clive lent over to Bill and whispered, "He always makes a compelling presentation, every point clearly discussed, never leaves a stone uncovered we better hope this bunch don't try to steal him away from us!"

Karl concluded by adding, "I propose that Captain Jean Vyes Jerva and myself investigate further by going undercover in Southern France." Karl had once again usurped Major Knight from assigning the mission to others in the BIS. Karl now detailed how the mission could be undertaken and what resources would be needed to prepare for such a complicated undertaking. The Prime Minister turned to the French Minister asking him if he approved of one of his officers taking part in a mission such as this. "Of course, the Captain is an excellent officer I'm sure if he can play a part in disrupting the German advancements, he will be doing it for Mother France, how can we assist?" Concluded the Minister making a saluting gesture to Jean Yves. "Well, that's settled, Major Knight you will spearhead this operation through the BIS any resources you need will receive the full backing of this office, as for you Lieutenant Vita thank you again for an excellent presentation. If I was Major Knight, I would be putting your name in for a well-deserved promotion. Once again we thank you for your brave contribution bringing our boys home." The Prime Minister rose and once he did that everyone else did the same filing out into the hallway. "Well let's gather our stuff and head home shall we, it's been a hell of a day so far." Concluded Bill with a smile. The drive back was a little busy with work traffic and the convoys head in and out of London. Clive broke the ice first by saying. "Nice job Karl, think you got across the gravity of what is happening over there very nicely. As for you bugger's heading over to the Continent, well I can assure you I will not challenge my boss *Winy*! Tomorrow morning, we will meet to start laying out this plan shall we, if that's alright with you Jean? Say 0830 hrs is that good for everyone. Now let's get a pint in the lounge shall we, I believe the new *Captain Vita* is buying? I'm only following orders from the top so don't thank me thank Churchill, a nice follow up letter would be nice also." Clive could not be more pleased to make this commendation. Their friendship had been through so much and Karl never stopped impressing him with his planning abilities and a driving commitment to set Europe free once more. Arriving back at the camp they all filed into Karl's work area to find that everyone had left except John and Peggy, they were rearranging the filing system that had been overdue for some time. "Well did not expect to see you two here at this time of the day, I can see there is some house cleaning going on, is that right?" remarked Karl putting the map tube down on the planning table. "John, I need this file to be stored in the safe can you do that for me." Asked Karl. "Peggy, I'm assuming you have met these officers already, haven't you?" Karl was engaging Peggy to strike up some dialogue. "Yes, I have Sir but thanks for asking me." Peggy was standing at attention with very senior officers present. "At ease corporal its after hours and your boss is not a big one for strict enforcement of military protocol so relax will you, now tell me how you like working for Lieutenant Vita, he will be working you very hard, he's known for that." Said Clive thinking too much saluting gets me tired. "Well sir this is my first full day on the job I think it will be challenging and that I like, if your done with me I will head out, promised to meet up with my room mates for a pint." Peggy was still a little uncomfortable around such senior officers. "Please remember young lady in the BIS mums always the word?" Clive was making sure whatever happens in this office stays in this office. Peggy and John headed for the coat rack at the back of the room, putting their tunics, caps and their shoulder bags containing the mandatory gas mask and steel helmet. "Goodnight sirs see you tomorrow." "Is that the new girl you hired earlier today?" Asked Clive obviously taken by her looks. "Way too young for you, your randy old bugger, she would probably kill you if you ever got that far," Said Karl laughing and very pleased to see his friend taken by the new corporal. "Alright enough of this standing around let's wander down to the lounge shall we. Karl, you did agree to buy the first round, did you not?" said Clive walking ahead of the others. "Why don't you chaps go on ahead and get a table, I'll be along shortly." Said Karl as he walked over to the night wireless operator's station. "Any important messages that I need to be aware of corporal." Karl really wanted to see if Hazel had sent news. "Nothing of real importance, this one came in earlier today from Delta-3." Said the operator. After reading the communication Karl gave it back to be filed in the daily log. Walking down the hall to the lounge he started thinking about agents he would recommend for consideration on the upcoming mission and their cover story. Wonder if we can meet up with the Delta-1 team? Jean would like to work with those agents that's a given, the advantage is they are already in Southern France? Hazel is part of that team, that could create difficulties, Gunther would agree with me on this logic. Karl stopped his planning as he entered the lounge. "Over here Karl, yelled Bill over the noisy bar crowd. "My God, this is a very noisy place tonight, guess we will put aside any business-related talk for tonight anyway." Said Karl loudly so everyone could hear him.

The following morning the team gathered in meeting room # 3 along with Sheryl and Peggy taking the meeting notes. "Gentleman this first meeting is to organize the strategy and assets for *Operation Free Land.* Captain William Lowes will be the operation director once the plan has been cast in stone, he along with the support team yet to be assigned will back up Captain Jerva and Captain Vita while they are in Southern France. Now let's begin by having Captain Vita bring us up to date on the plan, shall we." Clive now turned the floor over to Karl and the stack of support documents they would all study repeatedly till there was no chance of a slip up or mistake that could derail the operation. This intense training and coordination continued daily for five days heavily charged with role playing and rehearsing the parts Karl and Jean would play, their stories had to be exact and traceable should their identities be questioned or challenged, that part yet had to be formulated. A timetable of sequences was also to be documented. Planning who would join them in the field, timing events, a list of French Resistance Fighters that could be trusted with the plan. Jean and several fellow French Officers also present at the meeting would take charge of organizing these contacts and exploring suitable parts that he and Karl would play in the operation. The final detail would be the date and place for their extraction assuming they would be coming home at the completion of the mission. At the end of each day all the support plans, charts, photograph's and mountains of other vital documentation would be stored in a very large safe that had been installed in M-3 the room itself had military police inside as well as outside the entrance, securing it till the following morning then taking station at the entrance through the day. Karl and Jean got fitted for their uniforms then photographs were taken ready to insert into their forged documents. Their uniforms were altered from originals issue, they had to be very convincing even their watches, cigarette lighter, cigarettes and side arms had to fool proof nothing was left to chance. The drop was changed from parachuting into France, to be flown in by a Royal Airforce *Lysander* aircraft further North, then by road into Southern France. The German driver loyal to the free French had disclosed that two officers would be traveling to port facilities down the Atlantic coast compiling information on the construction planning. Jean seeing this report said, "Here is our perfect cover story we will take their places, modify their documents that can be forged ready for new photograph by the partisans, once this was done no one will suspect us." By taking their places Jean and Karl had the perfect cover story. Two officers would have to lose their lives making this happen and the partisan group had no problem in sending these unlucky chaps to their maker. Once in Southern France they would commence their new rolls as inspectors for the German Supply Corp. The German officer would be accompanied by a Vichy French Naval Officer. The same German driver would now be driving Karl and Jean along the same route in the same Kubelwagen, their story was close to be ironclad.

Wednesday morning the day was drizzling rain but perfect for the evening drop into occupied France. "Guess this is where I say thank you for all the hard work you have done, *au revoir* as we French would say," Jean putting his raincoat and cap on then picking up his canvas carry bag headed for the door. "I'll be along in a minute Captain. I need just a few minutes with my people before we head out alright?" Karl wanted to speak privately to his hard-working staff. "I can't believe it's time for us to head out God willing we will be back amongst you once our work is completed. Please think of us and look for those communications on our progress, thank you all again." Karl reach for his raincoat that hid the German uniform until they were on board the aircraft. In the lobby Clive and Bill waited to say their goodbyes, neither one wishing to say more, this mission was very dangerous and with that came the high probability this would be the last time one or both would return to Slough. The drive to RAF *Tangmere* was uneventful neither one of them really wanted to talk. Their thoughts were of family, loved ones and that this could well be the last operation they would participate in. It was dark when they finally arrived at the base and home for the 161 Squadron. The lorry rumbled out over the grass to the waiting Lysander aircraft stopping at its tail. Three uniformed RAF Privates approached the lorry, saluted then took the luggage, the only acknowledgment they made was, "Evening Gents your pilot this evening will be *Lieutenant Ronald Cooke,* the aircraft is warmed up and ready to depart. Cooke yelled from the cockpit, "Evening Chaps climb aboard, then I need to review with you both what you need to know about this night flight and especially the very quick turnaround once we land. Now climb up that ladder behind me, mind those boxes and bags we are also delivering tonight. Once we land it will be your job to hand down those bags and boxes to the blokes waiting below on the field. The time on the ground will be less than three minutes so move smartly. Now, once we are in the air, I will be wave hopping over the channel at approximately 50 or so feet till we reach the French coast then tree hop till we get to the designated landing field a little over an hour away. Now, when we reach the landing area I will circle the field flashing a coded recognition signal using a signal light on the underside of the fuselage which I operate with my left foot, if we get a return signal they will put out fire buckets to aluminate the landing strip. Try to get comfortable, strap in and let's be off." Captain Cooke fired up the big Bristol Mercury radial engine its nine-cylinder engine producing a cloud of exhaust smoke as it thundered into life sending vibrations throughout the aircraft and its crew. Releasing the brakes, the Lysander moved forward then with the right brake squealing it turn towards the grass runway. Captain Cooke standing on the brakes brought the engine up to full power, releasing the brakes the big single engine aircraft leapt forward in less than nine hundred feet it left the grass runway climbing into the velvet blackness of the night sky. The time to the coast was short followed by a fast drop down to fifty feet as they headed towards the French coast. Captain Cooke called back, "I will be flying at this height till I have the French coast in sight, then I'll climb only enough to clear the cliffs and the line of trees, enjoy this wild ride gents." In the very noisy rear cockpit talking was almost out of the question, Karl moved close to Jean's ear yelling, "This flight is quite nerve racking a little exciting though, these pilots have nerves of steel, don't you agree." Jean simply nodded his head in agreement before turning towards the plexiglass canopy watching the white caps of the channel fly by. Karl's legs were wedged between two big sacks and a long wooden crate, this flight was not about passenger comfort, he too was watching the breaking white caps that seemed to be reaching up to capture the Lysander as it flew by at over two hundred miles per hour. Through the half moon and clouds Captain Cooke could see the coast rapidly approaching. "Chaps we are almost over the French coast won't be long now." From here on the pilot would be watching for higher trees, telegraph poles, wires, towers, and other high structures such as the occasional church steeple. After about twenty minutes the pilot climbed then throttled back banking to the left in a big circle. From the ground a flashing signal lamp tapped out a Morse code recognition signal as the plane flew overhead. On the next pass Captain Cooke responded with the aircrafts signal lamp on the underside of the fuselage. "That's it chaps, get ready we need to be moving very quickly once our wheel touch down." Captain Cooke looked at his watch it was 2212 hrs thinking I need to airborne no later than 2220 hrs. The field completely black only a minute ago now blazed a path for the Lysander to touch down in safely. The big wheels shook the aircraft as they bounded through the uneven grass to a stop in less than three hundred and fifty feet. Turning the aircraft around Captain Cooke taxied back down the field to where the signal lamp was flashing. Applying the brakes, he came to a full stop throwing the plexiglass canopy up against its stop. "Alright you two out you go, hand those bags and boxes down first, please be safe out there I look forward to maybe seeing you on your return trip." Captain Cooke kept the big radial engine idling ready to depart within minutes. Karl climbed down behind Jean jumping the last two runs of the ladder, not a wise thing to do considering his right leg. Two men moved quickly up the boarding ladder past Karl and Jean making a silent gesture of good luck. Once inside the new passengers knew the drill pulling down and locking the canopy. With a wave from his cockpit Captain Cooke gunned the engine speeding off down the makeshift grass runway, the French partisans dowsing the fire buckets as the aircraft went by then carrying them off to the waiting lorry, any evidence that a plane had been there only minutes before was now gone. Karl And Jean remained besides the bags and boxes until a man approached them whispering in French, "We, must get away from here please move quickly, you never know if the *Bosh* is close by. My name is *Albert* we can talk in the lorry now let's get going shall we, the other men will carry these supplies you brought with you to the lorry." Walking fast half running they reached the old *Citroen* parked between a clump of trees and bushes. Two men helped them climb up the tailgate into the canvas covered cargo bed, the supplies being handed up behind them. "Good now we can leave, welcome home Captain and to you also Sir. Your mission code names we already have, which one of you is the Vichy French Officer." Asked Albert. "That would be me in this light it's hard to see our faces and uniforms so yes that's me Lieutenant *Claude Marceau* and this is the Kreigsmarine

Officer *Lieutenant Herbert* Krause, very pleased to meet you all." Replied Claude speaking once again in his native French and using his assigned mission name. "The identities for the two officers you are masquerading as, where shot only yesterday. We are not merciless killers they could have given you away if they were to escape knowing our plans. We could not take that chance these are not the kindest of times I'm sure you will agree. Now you know why we told your people in Slough to use those names." Albert stopped talking momentarily allowing the two intelligence officers to process the cover story. "Once we arrive at the safe house you will meet your driver Sergeant *Rudy Muller*, a loyal German to the allies, he is the one that drove those two officers down yesterday from *Rennes* in their Kubelwagen, starting tomorrow this will be your transport for the time you are here in Southern France. A little over a week ago we discovered we had found our perfect cover for you two. Those unsuspecting officers were heading to Saint-Nazaire on a fact-finding mission, we were fortunate to intersect that communique for this particular trip, swapping their driver for Muller before they set off from Rennes, this could have not worked out better." Concluded Albert now passing around a bottle of French wine with some bread and cheese saying. "This should keep you going till we reach the safe house. Wine is easier to come by these days than water." Albert and the others in the lorry started laughing, it was a good introduction for the two weary travelers.

The lorry turned into a narrow lane slowed to cross a stream then turn again into a long driveway, stopping to flash its headlights as it approached the old barn waiting for a return signal before it proceeded into the farmyard, momentarily waiting for doors to swing open. Inside the partisans moved quickly to hide the supplies unloaded from the lorry into a room hidden by a haystack its door ingeniously concealed with hay. Inside the old farmhouse kitchen, the partisans gathered around to greet the new arrivals. Albert once again passed around several bottles of wine before they all sat down at the table waiting for the rabbit stew still steaming on the blackened wood stove. "Gentleman tomorrow morning you will start your mission, the first stop will be the docks where construction is moving very quickly. Many of the French civilian dock workers are loyal to our course, however with that said there are some that will report you for a reward, hunger for their families makes them turn to becoming stool pigeons for the Bosh. Our people on the docks will do their best to shield you from these traitors however you yourselves must be acutely aware of those around you." Albert stopped talking as the hot stew was passed around the table. The next two hours was spent on the refining the plan to gather information and copies of blueprints if the opportunity presents itself with the miniature camera brought by Claude. "Gentleman we should adjourn for today, try to rest tonight tomorrow will be very taxing." Albert terminating the planning for that evening. Herbert in the upstairs room laid on top of the squeaky old bed tossing and turning, sleep would not come easy this night. In his mind he kept asking himself the same question, if my cover is blown will I be strong enough to withstand the brutal methods used by the Gestapo. If it becomes too much that I cannot maintain my silence I am prepared to use the cyanide capsule wedged at the back of my mouth between my molars. These thoughts weighed heavily on his mind however sleep eventually overcame him in the early hour's past midnight. A voice awoke him saying, "need to get up and get ready Herbert its almost 0600 hrs." Quietly said Albert gently pushing him back into consciousness. "Thanks Albert, I will be right down," Herbert felt the chill in the air, he opened the bedroom door and walked down to the small closet where the commode was kept. As he opened the door the intense smell made him gag, I better get used to that perfumed aroma, I guess. Back in his room he crossed over to the table that had a jug of water and a basin on it for him to have a painfully cold shave, next he made sure his uniform was properly adorned with its insignia's, in the correct location. Feeling much warmer now he was dressed, he stood in front of the cracked wall mirror to make sure one more time he would pass any scrutiny by Germans at the base. Must admit these Kreigsmarine uniforms are very smart, pity they are worn by the wrong side. Downstair Claude was drinking hot coffee standing against the sink his brown knee-high boots shining in the morning light, other familiar faces in the kitchen were doing the same drinking strong hot coffee with the addition of one new face dressed in a German Wehrmacht uniform. "You must be Muller is that correct?" asked Herbert speaking German. "Yes, I am sir glad to make your acquaintance. And a fine good morning to the rest of you," said Herb in a cheerful French voice, "Hope you all slept well last night, let me get some coffee then we can coordinate today's plan."

Convinced their plan was watertight the partisans retrieved their weapons from the hiding place behind the stove then filled out the door to the waiting lorry. "Muller are you ready my friend," said Herbert speaking in German to the driver. "I am sir," Standing up straightening his uniform he was a tall figure of a proud German soldier. The three walked over to the barn the doors already open with the Kubelwagen facing out in front of the Citroën lorry. "Shall I leave the canvas top down Sir or would you rather I put it up?" Asked Muller. "No leave it down, let's look the part shall we." Said Claude climbing into the back seat ahead of Herbert. "The drive will take about fifty minutes. I will stay to the main roads just in case other partisan's squads see us and decide we should be killed." Said Muller laughing. The roads were very busy with convoys of heavy equipment heading towards Saint-Nazaire and the other French ports. "When the Germans decide to undertake a new construction project, they are a force to be reckoned with?" said Herbert. "Muller before you drive us to the port, swing by the *Hotel Lutetia* so we can check in I'm assuming you know the directions to the *Boulevard Raspail*, after that you can drive us right into the dock area, we must act the arrogant German part. At the port entrance they stopped at the guard house to show their credentials asking directions to the headquarters for the construction offices. Muller pulled up in front of the building, ran around to the passenger door saluted the two officers as they stood to exit the vehicle, saluting as they did so. "Park close by, not sure what will happen in there. If you suspect something is going south, leave and return to the safe house don't attempt to find us, is that clear Muller." Said Herbert. Inside the building they looked for the construction or engineering office, finding a sign hanging over an office marked project engineering about halfway down the hall. "Here we go are you ready," said Claude. Opening the door, they entered to find rows of desks and drafting tables lining both sides of the sizable area. An officer wearing the regular grey uniform of a Captain in the Wehrmacht approached them asking, "State your business." As he raised his arm in a Sieg Heil salute. "We are here to inspect the progress being made on the new submarine pens, here are our orders." Said Herbert in an arrogant sounding voice. The officer inspected their identification cards and then reviewed the orders issued by the office of *Admiral Donitz.* "This document instructs this office to give you full access to all areas, what would you like to review first." Said *Captain Max Meyer,* now showing a friendlier side to his personality. "Gentlemen before we continue would you excuse me while I verify your being here, just a formality I'm sure you understand." Meyer picked up a desk phone, instructing the operator to put him through to Headquarters. "Major Schneider, Meyer here, the two officers you sent down have arrived just confirming the orders they presented Sir." Meyer stood up and with a scared tone answered. "Of course, I will show them every courtesy Major thank you." Meyer's attitude had done an about face after getting an earful from his superior officer. Turning he approached Herbert and Claude saying. "Gentlemen thank you for your understanding, I think we should start by reviewing the routing schedule and corresponding time schedules followed by a review of the current construction blueprints, I'm sure there will be many changes before the project is completed. The construction has not really started then, we are still clearing the site of old building and equipment." Explained Captain Meyer. "So, I'm assuming there has not been any progress such as cement slurries or steel forms and footings forms is that correct?" Asked Herbert not taking his gaze off Meyer. "Captain Meyer, if the schedule I handed you is expectable we can proceed." Herbert seizing the opportunity to get the upper hand. "Captain Marceau would like a tour of the port facilities, so while I do my due diligence here in the office you can escort the Captain on that tour, this way we will be out of your hair that much sooner." Herbert was pushing the envelope but there again this was the nature of being an agent in the BIS. "I will leave Sergeant Grucker to assist you in your review and for the security of all documents, Said Captain Meyer giving Herbert a questioning look. "Captain Marceau shall we get started?" Said Captain Meyer directing the Vichy French officer to the door. Grucker lets start by reviewing the layout schematic followed by the material requirement shall we." Commanded Herbert. The documentation was extensive, like most German military documentation, the files are extremely well prepared, thought Herbert as he started his review. How can I take pictures of these prints with that Grucker breathing over my shoulder, the other two will be back in an hour or two so whatever I need to do must be very soon, Herbert mind racing for an answer? Over the next thirty-minute Herbert reviewed the files making mental notes of which ones need copying. Once he was ready Herbert broke out into a coughing fit, attempting to clear his throat as part of the act. "Grucker, can you find me some pain tablets and some water I have been fighting a sore throat for most of the week also a mug of hot coffee would be appreciated." Herbert was silently praying the Corporal would oblige his request. "Would you like milk and sugar with that coffee Sir." Once Grucker had left, Herbert sprang into action reached inside his uniform for the miniature camera, time was against him would he be able to copy all the documents in such a short time? As Herbert got to the last blueprint, he heard the door at the far end of the office open, slamming the camera shut he quickly returned the camera to the concealed pocket inside his tunic then resumed his masquerade of pondering the document in front of him, continuing the cover story by coughing. "That does not sound good Sir maybe you should continue this tomorrow, here are the tablets and water, I also brought you a pot of coffee in case you would like more than one cup. Grucker showing concern for the Captain. He really is a nice considerate chap pity he is on the wrong side. Thought Herbert as he down the pain medication with the glass of water. "I thought the medication I took earlier this morning would last for most of the day guess I miss judged, should have brought more with me, hopefully these tablets you just gave me will carry me for the rest of the day," concluded

Herbert. For the next forty-five minutes Herbert continued his construction review, when suddenly he stumbled onto a file labeled structural specifications update. The document inside clearly described how thick the roof of the bunkers would be along with the extent of the steel rod reinforcements to be used. Herbert looked around to see where Grucker was, luckily, he was returning the blueprints to a flat storage draw where they were kept. Herbert reached inside his briefcase and removed a small pad and a pencil, he started to scribble down the most pertinent information. The reinforced roof would be a minimum thickness of over eight metres (*twenty-six feet*). Total number of sub pens fourteen, eight of which were dry docks. Each pen could accommodate two U-Boats, other details included, sixty-two workshops, one hundred and fifty offices, ninety-two dormitories for sub crews, four kitchens, two bakeries, two power stations, a hospital, and a restaurant. As he took down this information, he kept looked over his shoulder to see what Grucker was doing. Returning the pad and pencil to his case he returned to reviewing additional files for the build schedule. The actual construction would not commence till February 1941 only a week away. The file had a routing schedule with a projected completion date of June 1942. One last document had the overall Dimension which were approximately three hundred metres (*nine hundred and eighty- five feet long*) by one hundred thirty metres wide (*four hundred and twenty-six feet*). This is a very ambitious construction plan, thought Herbert, considering the other ports involved in this project I am thinking the Germans will use forced labor from other European countries as well as those here in France. The office door opened and in walked Captain Meyer with Claude behind him. "Well said Meyer are you satisfied with the extent of the documentation we have on file. Asked Meyer as he pointed towards a small table at the side of the room. "Yes, very impressed with how the extent of the detail and very precise the routing sheets are, well done Captain. Must also complement you on how accommodating Corporal Grucker has been, I had a coughing episode earlier, thanks to the corporal he found me some tablets, water, and a pot of coffee. Took two tablets this morning thought they would last all day that was a mistake, feeling much better now thank God." Herbert was eyeballing Claude as he explained the incident to Meyer, he was also sending him a signal he had successfully photographed most of the files they needed. He also removed any doubt Meyer might have finding out he was alone for a while when Grucker left the office. "Well do you need anything else while you have my attention." Asked Meyer really wanting to get rid of these two empire builders. "Only one request and you may have already covered this on your tour earlier, I would like to observe the actual construction site if that's not too much trouble. "Not at all, will you both be accompanying me?" Asked Meyer standing up to ready to leave. "Captain Marceau I would like you to accompany us as well." Said Herbert again looking at his partner in this deception. The three walked outside to Meyers Mercedes staff car. "One moment please let me tell our driver we won't be much longer. Poor fellow has been standing around all morning. Muller why don't you get yourself some coffee will be back shortly." Herbert was acting very much like a considerate Austrian, but there again he was! Arriving at the construction site Herbert walked confidently around the site, stopping at the bulkhead he looked over to the narrow entrance and the lock gates that lead to the outer harbor. I wonder if these arrogant Huns have considered that lock to be a potential choke point if it was bombed. "Captain there is one observation I have, that lock, if bombed could stop any coming or going of submarines what contingency are there in place if this lock was indeed blown up." asked Herbert using the same tactic he used back in 1938 in Kiel when he gave the ship builders an observation adding extra shielding on the incomplete aircraft carrier *Graff Zepplin*. Giving useful advice can sometimes work if it made a real contribution to the project. This tactic generated a higher level of confidence and this time was no different as Herbert confidently pointed to the locks. "Very good observation Captain I can see you are already looking at the downfall of this harbor and you are absolutely correct. When we first considered this location that entrance nearly made us reconsider its viability. The newly revised blueprints which unfortunately I do not have here, detail the construction of a reinforced roof like the submarine pens, this addition will prevent any aerial attack from happening." Meyer had a big smile on his face, pleased to see these visitors were volunteering constructive criticism to this monumental project. "Gentlemen what are your plans for tomorrow, your orders said to give you the time you needed before you move on to your next location at *La Rochelle* is that correct." Asked Meyer. "No that's being handled by another group, our next stop will be in *Bordeaux*." Replied Herbert thinking that bloke is trying to trick me. "Oh, that's correct, sorry got my ports mixed up." Replied Meyer his smile more like a smirk as he acknowledged his mistake. "I believe we have most of what we need, we can always return if we need more clarity wouldn't you agree Captain Marceau." Asked Herbert in perfect French, just to irritate Meyer. "Oh, I'm sorry Captain I forgot you don't speak any French. Herbert was deliberately intimidating the German officer speaking in French. Back at the main building they thanked Captain Meyer for his time and help before climbing back into the Kubelwagen they turned raising their arms with a hail Hitler Salute then sat down. "Drive on Muller" Said Herbert in a loud voice. Well that went well don't you think." said Claude. "Yes, and maybe no, I'm willing to bet that bloody Meyer will be calling around about our visit." Replied Herbert. "Why did he not do that while we were there." Asked Claude. "Those types are sneaky they will not do that in front of you, they are concerned about reprisals should they say something wrong or put themselves into a compromising position, gutless swine." Answered Herbert. They drove out of the harbor, out of harm's way for a while anyway. "Let's go to the hotel shall we, time for a cocktail what do you say chaps. Muller why don't you change into civilian clothes and join us in the lounge no need for you to be alone tonight, before you do that take this film and give it to Albert's men waiting at the hotel, pull over while I take a picture of my, hand written notes then you can pass it on." Herbert feeling so much better than he did this morning.

Upstairs Herbert opened the door to his room placing his bag on the bed, thinking tonight I will sleep well. Herbert returned to the lobby, not finding Claude he strolled over to the lounge and found him waiting at a secluded table in an alcove off the restaurant, "This will do just fine, let's sit here and wait for Muller shall we." Said Claude pleased with this very secure table. "I think we obtained some real meaningful information today. Don't you agree? That Meyer fellow is a typical arrogant representation and attitude of the German officer corp." Herbert displaying his continued dislike for the new German military. "Not all Germans are evil, look at Muller he wore the uniform until he saw what the Nazi Party was doing to his country, he was one of the few that decided to do something about it by joining the resistance fighters. From the top down there are thousands of Germans that secretly are scared to speak up or act against the Brown Shirts, the Gestapo and S.S officers. they refrain from making their opinions public in fear of painful reprisal, their families safety come first and it's that fear that make them subservient. It's simply amazes me that just a few power hungry evil bastards can control the masses using brutality and the control it generates." Remarked Claude a Frenchman that refused to surrender to the victorious Germans or the traitorous Vichy French puppet Government. Muller entered the lounge looked around then crossed over to their table. "Sorry for taking so long, my quarters are all the way at the back of the Hotel. I also took care of that matter you asked me to do for you Captain." Muller confirming the transfer of the roll of film to one of Alberts men. "Let's get our drink orders shall we then decide if we have enough information from this first day, or do we need to return tomorrow morning? "Herbert putting the question out to the other two for their input. "Well why you two were with that pig Meyer I managed to strike up a conversation with some of the lower ranking military fellows, quite amazing what you can gather with useless gossip. One of the drivers was from Hamburg he told me that before the war started, he had a wood working shop, he really had no choice he was required to enlist he also said quietly to me that most of his neighbors were deeply concerned that Germany was taking on more than it could handle and what did I think? I of course evaded giving him a response in case he was a plant. He went on to tell me that most of the present labor used in the port were rounded up from French towns and villages surrounding the Saint-Nazaire but due to extent of the project they were shipping additional labor down from Poland and other countries that were now under German occupation, this included prisoners from the POW camps. The fear some of the Germans have with this is how much sabotage will there be from those workers?" Muller had found out a very important piece of information. Could the BIS and Free French recruit from this new labor pool? "Nice work Muller that can help us down the road," said Claude thinking these POW's, could also be a good source for new recruits for Albert's partisan group. "Claude, how did you tour of the docks and work areas go. "Asked Herbert. "What I expected most of the docks and piers are in bad shape, some you can see were deliberately smashed in a hurry with whatever means the dock workers could find once they knew France was lost. I also gathered many of these workers were here before the war and from the way they looked at my uniform I would say they would willingly strike a blow for Mother France given the opportunity. There are others I gathered would sell you out for a few francs, you could see the hate in their eyes. As for the dock equipment the larger derricks and rail mules for the most part are operable, but in desperate need of servicing. If you look in one of those schedules, there is substantial amount of documentation on the condition of existing equipment." The discussion went on for about an hour longer before Herbert said. "I'm calling it quits for tonight, we can decide in the morning if we are moving on to the next location or remain here in Saint-Nazaire, good night chaps and thank you for a job well done." Herbert stood up and left the table, tomorrow would be another hectic day of deception.

Herbert rose at 0530 hrs, put his trousers and shirt on, picked up his toilet pouch not forgetting his briefcase then headed down the hall to the bathroom. At that time of the morning there was no one around another reason to claim the bathroom before anyone else could beat him to it. Back in his room he packed the small suitcase then headed down to the lobby, gave a waitress a coffee order then settled in on the couch to wait for Claude. This Hotel must be the one the Germans have a contract with, to many military uniforms not to. Thought Herbert as he sat drinking his coffee watching the traffic in the lobby. After about twenty minutes Claude entered the lobby, "Fancy breakfast or are you fine with just coffee?" Asked Herbert. "Coffee will be fine for me." Answered Claude. "Herbert, I think we should move on I have a funny feeling about going back down to those docks. It almost like a voice in the back of my head is telling me that someone down there could recognize one of us and turn us in for a reward and that thought concerns me. I may be overreacting, but my sixth sense is telling me we should leave this morning." Claude was showing Herbert a side of himself he did not expect to see. "Claude we really don't have a reason to stay we have almost everything we came for, so your right best not to push our luck drink up and let's check out do you have your voucher for last night." Herbert after listening to Claude was starting to feel relieved that they were leaving Saint-Nazaire. At the reception desk Herbert asked to use a telephone, "Please connect me to the operator at the port." Herbert waited for the call to go through, then asked for Captain Meyer's extension. A voice at the other end replied Captain Meyer's office. "Morning Captain Krause here could you locate Captain Meyer for me." Asked Herbert. Meyer picked up the phone and in a friendly voice answered." Captain, I was just wondering what time I would see you this morning." "Well, we have decided to move on to our next stop, last night we reviewed what you showed us and felt there is really no reason to return this morning we would be wasting your time, thank you so very much for the assistance you gave us it was appreciated, we will be in touch very soon. Again, thank you." Herbert hung up the phone feeling so much better about their decision. Meyer said goodbye, then sat thinking about his visitors from yesterday, there is something that does not feel right. I just might call the base commander in Bordeaux and convey my thoughts that I'm suspecting they may not be who they say they are, need to think about that carefully though!

After checking out they walked out of the Hotel looking for Muller they found him talking to several other drivers waiting by their vehicles. "Good morning sirs, did you sleep well? Will we be returning to the port this morning?" Muller could sense from the expressions on their faces that the answer would be no. "No Muller we are heading to our next stop in Bordeaux instead, let's get going shall we." Replied Claude stepping into the rear passenger seat of the Kubelwagen followed by Herbert. "When I spoke to Meyer, a little while ago he sounded almost relieved to hear we would not be returning this morning. I also got the feeling he was not totally convinced our visit was not above board, just a feeling I was having." Said Herbert now having doubts about the next port inspection.

Chapter Ten
Prisoners of the Gestapo

The drive to Bordeaux took over four hours, little was said they had their own reasons to question what they were doing it was war and this was their job. Herbert broke the silence saying. "The forged documents we are using are the same in every respect as the originals other than the ID picture and country of origin is that correct Muller?" Asked Herbert. "Yes, sir they have been printed on the same paper, the same ink, the same typeset and page size, the seals are copied from Donitz own stamp, everything is exactly the same, why do you ask?" Replied Muller. "I was just contemplating if Meyer decided to investigate further into our visit could he uncover anything or trace that these documents are forged if he decided to investigate further?" Herbert speaking like this was starting to concern the other two. "Are you suggesting we should call this mission off, I thought we were doing very well in our roll playing yesterday." Asked Claude now questioning Herbert's statement. "As an intelligence office it is always best to proceed with extreme caution, sometimes when you think you have the perfect cover is when someone will try to trick you. So, if I am sending caution signals to you both its because yesterday Meyer tried a couple of times to test me, luckily, I was on to him, he realizing I was not playing his game. I believe that by now he has called the base Commander in Bordeaux to give a head's up and perhaps even the Headquarters of Admiral Donitz? Think more about this, when we decided not to return probably triggered Meyer's instinct that we could well be foreign agents." Concluded Herbert. "So, what's your thoughts right now, are we in harm's way? Shall we continue, perhaps we could consider modifying our cover story. *Karl* you're the leader on this mission tell us what is going on in your head at this point?" Concluded Claude. "When we get to our Hotel, I am going to call Meyer's office, I will tell him once we have completed our inspection of the progress in Bordeaux, we intend to return to Saint-Nazaire to make one last inspection before we conclude our finding and return to our headquarters." Herbert had a new plan in his head that would create fear in Meyer head. "Chaps, we must plant in Meyer's thick head that as part of our inspection tour we will be submitting a progress comparison on both commands at each facility. Making this call could well put Meyer on the offensive and perhaps make him think twice about pursuing any further investigation into who we could be. That gentlemen is our story lets pray it works how long to the Hotel Muller?" Concluded Herbert. "Should be there in about thirty minutes, sir." Replied Muller.

Arriving at the Hotel Herbert immediately called Meyer's office. "Captain Meyer so glad I got through to you this afternoon. After we have completed our inspection tomorrow, we will be returning to Saint-Nazaire for one more visit. Please make yourself available, sorry for such short notice we just received additional instructions only an hour ago. Have a nice evening." Herbert hung up the phone thinking I hope that worked. The following morning, they met early to rehearse their cover story, then proceeded to the dining room for a light breakfast. Muller drove them to the main entrance present his ID card to the gate guards the guards then moved to the rear of the Kubelwagen saying. "Your papers Captains and your purpose for being here." The guards were business like with no intent of being polite to the occupants of the Kubelwagen. One of the guards took all three sets of documents into the guard house, from their seats they watched him as he made a telephone call. As the guard listened, he kept nodding his head agreeing with whoever was on the opposite end of that telephone. The guard returned saying. "Corporal, once I open the barrier pass through and park over there next to that black Mercedes, stay in your car till your escort arrives." The guard stepped back snapping his arm upwards in a Heil Hitler salute. "Not a friendly sort is he." Said Claude as they waited patiently for their escort to arrive. Herbert was becoming nervous that sixth sense was telling him that something was not right. "Muller turn the car around and exit the gate, I will tell the guards we will be back very soon, I have forgotten some very important documents in the Hotel safe, do it now." Muller turned the Kubelwagen around then approached the gate. Herbert lent forward to tell the guards why they were leaving. "Remain here said the guard as a grey Mercedes car screeched to a halt blocking the exit as this was happened that Black Mercedes did the same behind them, they were completely block in. Four armed guards from the front car and three more from the rear car sprinted over to them with their weapons at the ready. "Hands up and get out of the car do not attempt to reach for your sidearms, we are ordered to shoot if you attempt that." The Lieutenant in charge walked up to them saying. "You are all under arrest for spying and impersonating German military personnel, guards take them to Major Siegler's office." Herbert looked at Claude and Muller then slapped each of them on the shoulder saying. "Be brave you two, God willing we will see each other soon. Unbeknown to Herbert and Claude a dock worker that was a plant for the local resistance group witnessed the incident, when he finished his shift, he would report what happened to his leader. Inside a large office a German Major sat at his desk signing some documents. The Lieutenant lead the three captives into the office, snapping his boots and saluting he yelled, "Remain standing till the

Major is ready for you." The minutes ticked by slowly the eerie silence only broken by the sound of paper being turned. "Relax gentlemen my young lieutenant gets carried away with events like this, sit please, would you care for coffee?" Major Siegler was an older officer in his late fifties or early sixties wearing a regular German army uniform. Herbert thinking this chap was probably some bank manager or businessman before the war, he is just doing his job and not interested in integrating English spies. "So, you are wondering why you are under arrest, are you not? This morning we received a call from a Captain Meyer at the Saint-Nazaire facilities, he said we should investigate two officers that had toured his base yesterday. He strongly suggested you could be imposters masquerading as an Austrian Naval officer and a Vichy French army officer, so we investigated and was convinced his observations were wrong until we heard from a dock hand that the Austrian naval officer was in fact an officer for the Langstaff shipping company who disappeared from his ship when it was docked in Marseille back in 1936. Finding this out we immediately contacted the Vichy French authorities to find out about the Captain here. According to the description they gave us you have either grown very quickly in the last year or you must be an impersonator, so which one are you." The mild mannered Major Siegler was very deliberate, he was trying to manipulate the integration being nice to see who would fold first. "Corporal Muller am I on track with this line of questioning? Are you a conspirator to this deception? As it turns out you have a clean record with the army, so explain to me why you are driving two impersonators around France. Could it be that you are also spying for the English?" Yelling he walked over to Muller, face to face he slapped him hard across the face. "Look at me when I'm talking to you, do you all take me for a fool, do you really think you could get away with this, guards take them away let them ponder in their cells till tomorrow when the Gestapo arrive to interrogate them more, I want no part of this." Yelled Siegler as he sat back down waving his hand to the guards to take them away. Three guards pushed them down the dimly light hallway. Another guard unlocked the prison style door to the overnight holding cell, pushing them in before locking the cell door again. Muller went to speak but Herbert putting his finger across his lips and with his left hand pointed to his ear. Herbert moved in close to Muller and beckoned Claude to do the same, in a whisper he said. "This cell is probable bugged with microphones so only speak up when there is something you want them to hear. I think we are in for a rough time with the Gestapo, only tell them useless information like, we were instructed to see what was going on with the new docks. How big a force would man the facilities once it is finished. Under no circumstances mention or imply we took pictures if that comes up simply state we were always with guards or military personnel." Herbert was avoiding the question that would be next. "We will be tortured for certain, but do you think we will be shot as spies. Going to a prison of war camp does not look like it's in our future, does it?" Whispered Claude reaching out for the hands of his companions. Laying down on the wooden cot Herbert could not conceive of sleep his mind was racing thinking of the torture training they had received years ago in Scotland. The Gestapo had a reputation for torture methods that most governments would never endorse but here they were only hours away from experiencing such atrocities. Muller would be slapped around, but more than likely because he was merely the driver would be sent to a hard labor prison camp. Claude on the other hand faced torture before being turned over to the Vichy French for prosecution. As for me I will not go through all of that I will break that cydnid capsule and free myself once and forever of this black cloud that has followed me for so many years. Sweet Hazel, I have let you down I hope when you return to England if you make it back that is? You'll find a nice young man that will give you a good life, you and I never really had a chance to start a long-term relationship, did we? Whatever time I have left I will be thinking of you, I love you Hazel. Karl let all these memories and thoughts run through his mind while he still had one to use. Sleep eventually overtook the fatigue he was trying to avoid.

Before dawn Herbert was awakened by a guard carrying some old clothes. "Remove your uniform now and put these on". The stale smell on the old wool trousers and a shirt that at one time was white now a stained rage, gave Herbert an insight to what would be coming, his polished shoes replaced with wooden clogs. Standing up he looked through the barred window, the dawn changing from a dark grey sky to a fiery shade of blue and orange. The wind had not picked up yet, all was peaceful as he stood there thinking, this could be a perfect day to leave this troubled world behind. A rattling noise from down below made him strain to look down at what was going on. Three armed guards along with a shackled Muller walked slowly across the forecourt to the very same Kubelwagen they had been using. Karl watched as Muller was pushed into the back seat by one of the guards, turning around the Kubelwagen headed for the main entrance, Muller turned around in his seat and with both hands shacked tried to wave towards the holding cells on the second floor. God keep him safe thought Karl, will we ever meet again I don't believe so, he continued watching till the car was out of sight then sat down again on his cot.

The sound of a key being put into the lock made him stand up to face the guards as they entered, telling him to put his arms out so the shackles could be put on his wrist. Shuffling down the hallway he could see Jean and two guards ahead of him wearing the same shabby clothes and shackles. The big steel door was unlocked for both prisoners with their guards to pass through into the main building. The first door on the right opened into the same office they were in the day before, Major Siegler was leaning against his desk one leg hanging across its corner, arms crossed across his chest. "Gentlemen sit down and have some coffee with me, last night I hope you took the time to consider your limited options because if you haven't decided to cooperate with us, I will have no alternative but to call Gestapo headquarters to pick up both of you. Realize that If I make that call, they will arrive here in less than hour. Help me keep you out of their hands, I'm told their methods are extremely painful, you can be assured you will be praying for death sooner than later. Again, once the call is made there will be no turning back that van will arrive to take you both to the Gestapo interrogation center. I deplore such violence, war is not the answer, but the English must realize we cannot be stopped. Europe once united will be a better place believe me. Now why don't you tell me why you were sent to spy on our facilities, let's stop this foolishness right now and save you both from unnecessary pain and suffering." Major Siegler stopped talking walked around his desk and sat down looking at both the men in front of him. The silence between them and the lack of any body movement convinced the Major he was wasting his time. Slowly shaking his head, he was thinking that did not work let me make that call. "Lieutenant Gerber please get me Gestapo Headquarters will you." The phone rang, the Major lifted the receiver putting his hand over the voice piece in a last-ditch attempt to get the prisoners in front of him to talk, those ten or so seconds felt like hours as Karl and Jean waiting in silence not moving a muscle. "Major Siegler here, the two prisoners we discussed yesterday are ready for you, I'll have them brought down to you. Their driver was picked up early this morning by now he is on a train back to Munich, I am told he will be sent to a hard labor camp, Heil Hitler." Major Siegler hung up the phone stood up saying. "Well now you know that I was sincerely trying to keep you out of Gestapo hands, I apologize for deceiving you the Gestapo is already downstairs the call was made to a Gestapo Captain waiting in the lobby. I suggest you drink that coffee it may be the last you will have for a very long time. Guards take the prisoners down to that waiting van." Karl stood then spoke controlling his tone. "You have played your little game on us Major and may I say well-acted. You are right if we told you a story whatever that story may be, it would be an easiest our way out for us, however that would be the cowardly way out and may I remind you we did not start this war. Before we part let me conclude by saying, Herr Hitler cannot dictate or enforce his Nazi criminal ways on the good people of Europe. There will come a day when all of you will be forced to pay for the atrocities you are committing upon others. No war can survive forever and like the dictators before Hitler this regime will also crumble and fail. Freedom cannot be chained forever Germans will pay the price one day." Karl turned to Jean saying, "I believe we have an appointment no need to keep these guards waiting shall we go?"

From the upstairs landing they could look down on the two Gestapo Officers and the four guards waiting to escort them to the interrogation center. Negotiating the stairs was difficult and clumsy due to the leg shackles, "Are you alright?" Jean asked Karl as they reached the final steps. "One more step," Said Karl again. Major Siegler following them down to the lobby. "Captain please sign for the two prisoners then you can take them away." Siegler turned to address Karl and Jean. "You are very foolish you should have cooperated with me because whatever your concealing will now be forcibly taken from you by this officer." The Major turned away and climbed the stairs turning his back on the fate of these two perpetrators. "Get into the van yelled the younger Lieutenant slapping Jean in the back of the head. The four guards climbed in behind them their black uniforms and helmets making them look so menacing. In silence they drove approximately an hour to the Gestapo Headquarters. The van stopped briefly at the guard house to show documents then proceeded to the main entrance, as the van turned in front of the entrance Karl and Jean could see on either side two enormous red banners with an equally large black swastika on a white circle slowly waving in the breeze. The doors swung open followed by the guards jumping out ready to escort their new interns inside. "Move you treacherous pigs hitting Jean on the back of the head with the butt of his submachine gun." Said one of the guards. Pushing and almost dragging the two prisoners into the building, "You go into this interrogation room and you go into that one. Split them up." Yelled the guard. "Jean you must stay strong." Karl yelled out to his friend as they parted. Inside the dimly lit room Karl was pushed into a wooden chair, other than the chair he was seating in there appeared to be only a makeshift desk and an array of devices against the wall on a stand. The guards stationed themselves on either side of the door remaining perfectly still, Karl could hear loud voices from the room right next door, whoever was yelling was doing so in French not German, Karl could just make out what was being screamed at Jean, "You are a traitor an English collaborator tell me right now what was primary objective spying on our facilities or suffer the consequences, I don't have time to waste on traitors like you." A brief period of silence came from next door, then a spine-chilling scream of pain erupted as the interrogator slammed his fist into Jeans face repeatedly followed by more demands. As Karl sat in his chair imagining the horror taking place just a few feet away on the opposite side of the wall. The door opened and in walked two muscular Gestapo henchmen that by their appearance took great delight in administering pain to defenseless prisoners. Behind them a Major entered the room saying, "Your French accomplice has passed out that's alright the eltro-shock treatment to his testicles will bring him round very quickly, don't think he will be much good to the ladies after that. Now lets you and I get to know each other shall we. My name is *Major Becker,* and your name is Captain Karl Vita of the British Intelligence Service. I must say you have had a colorful history so far, pity to spoil it starting right now. Tell me why I should not order these two animals to turn your beautiful face into a bloody pulp, there again we could introduce you to some water games seeing as you were a maritime officer before the war. Yes Vita, we know all about you so why don't you start telling me what your orders were." The Major from his accent is probably from upper Bavaria thought Karl, would not expect a Bavarian to be associated with a torture squad like this one though. "You're not talking Vita you're from Wien (Vienna) is that correct such a nice city, I attended University there for a brief period back in thirty-five. Pity we are not on the same side right now we could exchange wonderful stories about that charming city. Karl remand very quiet staring right at the pompas officer in front of him. Still no response from Karl, the Major silently waiting realized that would not be forthcoming, he assessed his next move, this strong-willed Austrian will not break that easy, time to let these animals loose on him, pity. Becker stood up and addressed the two soldiers saying, "Call me when he's ready to talk." Karl braced himself getting ready for the punishment that would start within minutes. One of the soldiers moved forward putting on a pair of black leather gloves then stood less than a foot from Karl, again Karl braced his teeth together waiting for the facial blows to commence, that did not happen instead a powerful smashing blow to his abdomen took his breath away and in doing so made him scream out in pain releasing his clenched teeth, before he could catch his breath that gloved fist slammed into his face sending his jaw to one side. Again, the same treatment was administered left to the abdomen right to the jaw. Karl was in total agony his mind however was processing how the punishment would proceed. After about thirty minutes the agent was tiring so the next agent took over at this point Karl could barely open his left eye which was badly swollen and the right one was close to becoming the same. Karl's top lip was split open blood freely flowing down his face, somewhere in between this merciless punishment Karl somehow continue to think about what they would try next he did not have to wait long. The straps that bound his arms and legs to the chair were removed allowing Karl to fall to the floor. One of the guards moved forward to throw a bucket of cold water on his face. The two soldiers moved to the desk sitting on top freely swinging their legs as they enjoyed a cigarette break, laughing at the workout they were getting using this prisoner as a punching bag. Karl trying to handle the pain just lay there thinking. Got this far that water sport Becker mentioned may be too much for me to handle perhaps I should consider cracking that cyanide capsule lodged in the back of my mouth, kind of surprised that beating did not dislodge it already in which case I would already be dead? A crooked smile crossed his broken lips, Hazel would be looking for another boyfriend if she could see me right now. Karl forced his brain to take him to other places where the pain could be tolerated easier. The two sadistic muscle men returned looking down at the disfigured face lying against the cold floor. "Shall we call the Major back in, or are you having too much fun to talk to him yet? Why don't you take a few more minutes to consider your answer?" The guards walking out of the room. Karl took this time to listen for a sign of activity from next door, but all was quiet. His eyesight was now severely impaired as the left eye was completely closed and caked in dried blood. The two animals returned stopping in front of Karl's body on the floor and once again asked him if he was ready to talk. Karl did not make a sound or move a muscle defying his captures. "Right let's get you ready for a bath shall we," said one of the animals with a big grin on his face. From across the room Karl could hear running water and the movement of what looked like a big wooden water barrel being positioned by a low long bench. "You two pick him up and bring him over here." Ordered one of the soldiers. "So you were a sailor is that right? Well, you are not going to like this too much. Put him face down on that board then strap him tightly onto it. One last time are you ready to talk to the Major?" Asked the soldier again, not one word left Karl's shattered lips. The two guards lifted the board so Karl's head could be pushed into the barrel up to his shoulders. "Ready asked the senior soldier, give me two and half minutes on the first dunking, alright push him in and I will hold his head down." Karl once again braced himself for this water torture, as his head entered the icy cold water it was hard for him to keep his mouth shut and hold his breath the water was that cold, but he did. All those years swimming with his sister as a boy in the *Danube* and jumping into the *Donakanal* from the bridges that circled Wien, would now help him hold his breath, even though it would be so much easier to just let the water end all this pain and torture but that would never be the case with Karl Vita! The only way they have left is to shoot me, if I can get my hands on a gun, I will gladly shoot these barbarians they are less than humans. His mind kept him from gaging or choking but his lungs were saying something else. "Pull him out," yelled one of the agents. "What is it with this pig, we beat him to within inches of his life with no reaction and now with water torture still nothing? Dunk him again this time for three minutes if we can't break him with that, I'm telling the Major we're getting nowhere so he can decide make the next move." The second dunking would take Karl within inches of losing his life and that would have been fine with him at this point. Once again, the ice-cold water was taking all this concentration to resist opening his mouth, his lung screaming out for fresh air, the pain of holding whatever air he had not released was about to give into the cold water. "Pull him out?" said the same soldier. "The Major has made it clear we cannot use electro- torture on this one so let's call it a day. You two guards drag him to a cell, tomorrows another day that's if he doesn't die on us during the night." The two animals walked out of the room leaving Karl close to death on the floor. "The youngest of the two guards finally spoke up, "I can't believe what they have just done to this poor fellow, I did not sign on for this kind of inhumane treatment, yes we are at war but there is a certain conduct that we all should be abiding by don't you agree?" The other guard was bending down carefully lifting Karl up trying to give him a glass of water. Barely able to speak Karl managed to say, "Thank you, don't you think I've had enough water for one day?" The words hard to form as he said that, vehemently holding on to his sense of humor. The two guards took one arm each and walked him, half dragged him through the door down the hall to his cell, placing him on a cot for the night. Karl lay there in the dim light the pain was all over his body, I think I have a cracked rib or two maybe a broken nose as well best not to dwell on it. Karl now willed his mind into a more pleasant place as a younger man he would call on his girlfriend *Annie Lourie* at her parent's house in Wien (Vienna). Those long walks through the *Stadtpark* and afternoons at the *Spanish Riding School* watching the *Lipizzaner Stallions* rehearsing was amongst his fondest memories. I always believed Annie and I would eventually get married, wonder if she still lives with her family in Switzerland? the last time I heard from her she had a new love in her life and so did I, my sweet Kitty. Stay safe Annie, I will always think of you fondly. Karl continued to drive his thoughts to events, people and places that would forever remain part of his memories. Poor Kitty she also became a prisoner of the Gestapo, thank God that was before the declaration of war in 1939, she died on her way to a Gestapo interrogation center, a blessing in disguise. Sleep was overcoming him even though he tried to resist but to no avail he simple did not have the energy to fight sleep.

Loud sounds from a door opening then slamming minutes later woke him up just as dawn was breaking. The pain immediately returning as he lifted himself up on the cot. Voices in the hall made him wonder if Jean was being returned to the interrogation room, please God no more he thought out loud. Down in the courtyard armed soldier were forming in a line facing the wall. Karl dragged himself to the windows holding onto the bars to support himself. Looking down it took milliseconds to realize what was about to happen. Two guards were dragging Jean's blood-spattered body towards the wall. God please not after all he has been through, where is your mercy? Karl could feel himself shaking and crying simultaneously his head in a spin as he continued to watch. He was almost at that point, about to give up and crack that cyanide capsule in the back of his mouth. Suddenly a tremendous explosion followed by another seconds later rocked the building, the execution squad taken by complete surprise were falling in all directions as a hail of machine gun bullets shredded their uniform sending blood and body fragments in all directions. The Gestapo Captain was running for cover but not sure where to find it, shooting blindly in the direction of the gunfire. Another hail of gunfire sent him into a sickening spin as the bullets kept coming, he was dead before he hit the ground. The two guards holding Jean had put their hands in the air a little too late as three partisans took them down with knives. Jean having no strength left fell to the ground. The partisans lifted him up by his arms half running out of the courtyard to the waiting vehicles at the front of the building. Karl's attention was now directed to the loud gunfire in the hall outside his cell door, he could hear the bullets ricocheting off the walls and his cell door. The shooting finally stopped, French voices were yelling to get all the cell doors open and help the prisoners that could not walk out of the building. "Get them all down to the vans quickly." yelled the leader. Karl's energy miraculously returning from God knows where spurred him to the door and the friendly face of a partisan, "Quickly we must go, the Germans will be sending more troops very shortly." At the end of the hall four partisans had the two animals that had tortured Karl standing with their arms behind their heads. "Wait yelled Karl, someone give me a pistol we cannot leave until I give these barbarians a taste of their own medicine." Karl's anger was consuming him, giving him a surge of energy, he would rather die than leave without his revenge on the two barbarians. Someone gave Karl a revolver saying, "Whatever you're going to do make it quick we are out of time."

Speaking German Karl pushed them against the wall, one started to cry the other pleading for forgiveness. Karl pointed his gun directly at the one animal crying, lowering the gun in line with his crouch saying, "Death is too quick for you, I want you to remember this to your dying day. A loud bang followed by a sickening scream sent that soldier to the floor blood spreading over his trousers. The second agents now in hysterics as he watched, pleaded for Karl to show some mercy. Karl laughed at him as he triggered the gun and watched as this coward fell screaming to the floor. "We must go right now sir please." Karl half running down the stairs assisted by the strong arm of a resistance fighter out the main entrance and into the waiting van. "Karl, thank God your alive," came a very weak voice from the front of the van, there in the corner supported by two men was Jean. "Though I was almost to the pearly gates back there everything happened so fast, somebody must like us up there." Said Jean barely able to finish the sentence. "You could be right Jean however it took him long enough to come to that conclusion though." Karl was feeling the release of freedom pain or no pain he would enjoy this moment as he looked out the rear window at the Gestapo Headquarters burning with one side already collapsing into the courtyard, hopefully never again to operate as a torture center.

Chapter Eleven
Returning home to England

The three vehicles bouncing through the farm lanes at high speed, they needed to put as much distance between themselves and Bordeaux as possible. By now the Gestapo headquarters would be swarming with storm troopers. In the dim light one of the partisans spoke up saying. "Remember me," Karl strained through his one good eye to see who was talking to him, "Albert, oh my God so good to see you again was it you that organized this break out? Jean and I will be forever in your debt and to all of you that took on this extremely dangerous rescue, thank you will never be enough." The small talk continued till the van slowed to cross the forge over the lane and into the farmyard. "By the sound of it we have arrived back at the safe house, good luck is on your side this day as the Brigade Commander sent us a doctor and nurse to take care of our wounded, they arrived yesterday just in time for their first patients." Said Albert as he climbed over legs to the rear of the van.

The doors of the van opened strong arms helping Jean and Karl out and into the farmhouse. The other two vans had their injured men helped by their friends into the safety of the farmhouse. "Bring those two in here my nurse will start dressing their wounds while I care for these chaps with bullet wounds first." Said *Doctor Bernard Dubois*. Karl's energy was almost depleted, Jean was about the same lying on an old couch his legs hanging over the arm. Laying on the makeshift examination table Karl's left eye was becoming infected his vision from it was barely a blurred imagine at best. The pressure from that eye was giving him a severe headache. The nurse after taking care of Jean's wounds came over to the battered face of Karl. "Oh my God it's you I can't believe this it's been over four years since I said goodbye to you in the café parking lot. You can't remember or have I changed that much, please lay back and let me start dressing your wounds the doctor will be in soon to examine that left eye, I'm sure when you're feeling better you may remember me." Whispered the nurse moving closer to Karl left ear. Laying there while she tended to his wound's he started processing the information she had given him, four year ago in a French café, I must have still been in my maritime uniform, in a parking lot that means I was driving my Opel Kadet. His brain may have been fuzzy, but his memory was able to link the events together and the memory of that night on the road to Austria came back clear as a bell, he remembered! "My God *Monica*, can this be you from a waitress to a nurse I can't believe this, how fortunate am I today." Karl was trying to smile but his face

hurt too much for that. "Karl please don't move to much I believe you have two fractured ribs your nose is a mess but does not appear to be broken. The Doctor can make that assessment shortly. I would know you anywhere I often wonder what became of you after you left me hanging that night, I must have appeared to be a lovesick schoolgirl making a real fool of myself like that. If you would have stayed that night, I can assure you, you would not have forgotten it that quickly." Monica now had a very big smile on her face as she continued cleaning the blood off Karl's face. Karl being Karl simple answered, "Well it's never too late." It was now completely dark when the doctor entered the kitchen, Karl was snoozing, so he moved over to where Jean was lying on the couch. "Let's take a closer look at those wounds shall we, it looks like you have a badly bruised rib cage but no apparent fractured bones. Your nose appears to be broken, Jean reacting as the doctor gently apply pressure to the sides of his nostrils. "Monica I am going to strap his rib cage come and give me a hand will you. I need to reset his nose so I will give him a local anesthetic to reduce the pain, would you prepare a syringe for me." Asked Doctor Dubois. While that anesthetic numbs around your nose let's get you seating upright, Monica cut away his shirt then wash his upper body, once you have dried him off you can strap his rib cage. While you are doing that, I'm going to look at Karl's eye." Said the Doctor as he moved over to the limp form
 of Karl. "Sorry to wake you, young man, but I need to look at that eye of yours, can you try opening it for me." Karl tried to open the left eye, but dried blood had caked it closed again. "Alright let me wash it out with this eye cup then clean and medicate it with a swab, should be able to roll it open after that. If it's becomes too painful just squeeze my arm or tell me to stop. I'm sorry to put you through this but I must examine your eye wide open. I realize this is painful for you, there it's almost open." Dr. Dubois covered all around Karl's eye then with a small penlight looking at the eyeball which was completely bloodshot. "Monica get me that vial from over there, I'll put some ointment into his eye to ease the pain as well as lubricating it, but this is really bad Monica. Fetch Albert for me right away, this man needs a hospital and an eye surgeon as soon as we can air lift him back to England. The right eye is bruised but should heel fine, I'll put ointment in that one as well," next he addressed Karl's ribs and nose after which the doctor asked Karl. "I think we should also remove that cyanide capsule, can you open your mouth wide for me so I can pry it out." The doctor help Karl lay down again then returned to administer the same ointment to Jeans eyes although badly bruised with time they would recover nicely he would however be left with a permeant scare over the right eye. Monica sat holding Karl's hand while the medication took hold. "So,

you're a nurse now Monica," Asked Karl trying to remain perfectly still as instructed by the Doctor. "Well, I did not quite make it to getting my nursing diploma, Herr Hitler spoiled that for me, nevertheless I am totally qualified to perform all nursing duties." Monica keeping close watch on Karl's left eye which the doctor did not want to cover until he was certain the medication was working. Karl holding still with a firm grip on Monica's hand started to drift off into a deep sleep all the tension and excitement was catching up to him. Once she was certain he was sleeping Monica carefully released the grip he had on her hand, standing up she went into another room coming back with a blanket to cover up the battered form of Karl Vita. Satisfied he was as comfortable as she could make him, she walked out into the large room where many of the partisans were sitting quietly talking so as not to disturb the nine injured sleeping in the other rooms on makeshift cots. "Jean looks in better shape than Karl does, those two took a hell of a beating. The two that tortured poor old Karl will probably bleed to death unless they are given immediate medical attention and that seems highly unlikely." Said Monica repeating the story she was given by Karl a just ending to those bastards in the Gestapo. "Albert, did you manage to get off that wireless message concerning the urgency of air lifting Karl back to England." Asked Doctor Dubois. "Yes, we did they are requesting if he is in such a bad way, we should consider sending a medic to escort him back to England, no telling what could happen from pressure differences once airborne." Explained Albert. The doctor sat pondering what he should do next. "When will that plane be arriving to pick him up and where will that pickup be?" Asked the doctor. "All going well it will be close to here, they never tell us exactly till the last minute as a precaution, probably tomorrow night if the weather holds up, they will also be delivering another shipment of arms at the same time." Replied Albert wondering where this line of questioning was going. Turning his attention to Monica, he asked her, "Ever been to England in a plane?" Monica with a look of surprise simply answered. "No to England and no to ever flying in a plane, Doctor?" Monica was now feeling somewhat excitement at this line of questioning. "In that case you will accompany Karl back to England. Once you have turned him over to the medical people at the airdrome. I need you to meet with their medical supply people and deliver this list of medical supplies we are so desperately in need of. Whenever the next supply drop is planned you will return with those supplies, you're the only one we can spare even though it's only a few days I need you back here as quickly as possible, Monica are you alright doing this for me." Asked the Doctor. "If that's what you want me to do sir the answer is yes." She replied. Monica returned to the sleeping patients in the other room, quietly checking each one to make sure all is well before she climbed the stairs to her small area in the attic. The morning was already sunny, waking Jean with its brightness, feeling so much better than the day before Jean moved to stand up but those deep bruises reminded him, he would be in recovery for a long time, those sharp pains stopped him from standing upright, bent over he quietly moved towards the old kitchen door. "Morning." Said Albert standing up from the table to make room for Jean at the table. "What's the prognosis on Karl's eye can it treated here, or will he need surgery, it looked really swollen as I walked by a few minutes ago?" Asked Jean his own appearance looking pretty beaten up as well, he would recover with time unlike Karl. "We are sending him back to England tonight, Monica will accompany him on the flight then return on the next available flight with desperately needed medical supplies." Answered the Doctor. "As for you Jean, I'm holding you back here until you are fit enough to travel back to your command in England." Dr. Dubois noticed a look on Jeans face that would indicate he would not accept the Doctor's explanation. "I am relieved to hear you are sending Karl back to England best not to take a chance with that eye of his, as for myself I am going to request from my brigade commander that I remain here where I can best serve the needs of France. Albert, can you arrange that wire for me? I'll write down what to send if you give me some paper and a pencil." Albert looked at the Doctor before answering Jean. "Are you sure about this request, joining the partisans is extremely dangerous with a very good chance you will land right back in the hands of the Gestapo have you thought about that?" Asked Albert as he slid the writing pad over to Jean. "I came within minutes of being shot so facing death has given me a completely different perspective on combating oppression, I'm staying and that's that."

For most of the day Karl was out of it sleeping deeply, so desperately needed to regain his energy. Monica would tip toe into the room on a regular basis to check on his eye which remained very red and swollen. "Doctor, what instructions do you have for me tonight and what should I be prepared for in case that eye becomes a problem?" Monica would be alone in that plane if things went wrong with Karl's eye, this concerned her greatly, would her nursing skills be enough during that dark night flight. About two in the afternoon the Doctor asked her to wake Karl so he could determine whether to proceed with lancing the corner of his eyelid to relieve the pressure, this he really did not want to do but battlefield medicine was not always a perfect science. Entering the room Monica found Karl awake his head still lying straight on the pillow. Speaking in an almost whisper Monica asked Karl how he was feeling and to inform him that Doctor Dubois would be in momentarily to relieve some of the pressure on his eye. The Doctor entered the room carrying a bowl of warm water and medical instruments on a tray covered with a towel. "Good afternoon Karl, glad you slept, you were near total exhaustion yesterday, let me examine that eye of yours, then we can decide whether to proceed with relieving some of that pressure. Let me also bring you up to date with what we have planned for you later today. Albert and some of the partisans will be transporting you along with Monica to a location about forty minutes from here. Karl, I have come to a decision, that eye of your need's expert surgical attention sooner than later, so tonight you will be flying back to England. I have decided to send Monica with you just in case a problem arises from altitude and pressure, Albert will instruct the pilot to fly as low as possible to reduce the possibility of this from happening. Once you're on the ground Monica will leave you to meet up with our medical supply contacts, returning back with much needed supplies on the next available Lysander." The Doctor could see that Karl was about to protest but quickly stumped him by adding. "Captain there is no negotiating on this matter my decision is final, now let me attend to that eye, Monica please thoroughly clean around his eye for me." The Doctor laid clean clothes over Karl's face then injected his cheek to deaden the area. With precision he lanced the eyelid splattering congealed blood onto his gloved hand. "There that should make you a little more comfortable for that flight home, Monica your help please, I need to suture that incision keep his head very still and apply very light pressure to the opposite side of the lid." With a very steady hand he inserted two sutures into his eyelid. The final thing Doctor Dubois did was to bandage Karl's eye with a gauze pad placing a bandage around his head to hold it in place. Now let's get you sitting upright shall we, I'll help you if you need me to. A big bowl of hot soup will help you regain some of that lost energy." Karl being Karl stood up on his own thanking the Doctor and Monica for the excellent attention they had administered, he also mentioned he was feeling much better now that pressure had been reduced. In the kitchen Karl sat next to Jean the friends obviously pleased to see each other. Several other partisans sat devouring their soup and fresh baked bread at the long farm style table. "That is the best meal I have had in a long time." Said Karl, wiping the bowl clean with bread. In the meantime, Jean did not say too much allowing Karl to dominate the conversion. "Jean you have not said anything about returning to England? I know Monica and I will be going tonight but when will you return?" Karl did not expect the answer that came back at him from Jean. "Karl, I have requested that I be allowed to remain in France, I believe I can serve my Country so much more effectively by doing so, I will very much miss working with you, God willing we will meet again." Jean looking straight at his friend's face waiting for an argument that did not happen. "In the time we have worked together I have grown to trust the decisions we have made together and this one is no difference, of course I'm disappointed you're not returning with us, but your love of Country is one I will never challenge. There is never a day when I do not think about my homeland of Austria and the family members I left behind." Karl showing Jean his support for this decision he had made.

The daylight was fading almost time to depart for the landing field, Dr. Dubois took another look at Karl's eye applying additional ointment to the corners one more time, satisfied he had done the best with the limited resources available to him, carefully he replaced the dressing over Karl's eye securing it with a bandage around his head. "Time to go you two, this fresh application and dressing should get you back to England, Karl you need to tell Monica if that sever pain returns to your eye, don't try to be a martyr tell her alright?" Dr. Dubois was showing his concern about sending them off on this flight to England. "I guess this is where we part company old friend, please take care of yourself remember Rome was not built in a day and this war will last a lot longer than that so please be careful, till we meet again." Jean stepped forward giving Karl a big French hug with a kiss on either cheek. "Tell Peggy I look forward one day to buying her fish and chips along with a pint of mild and bitter." As the two friends parted, Karl walked over to the Doctor standing next to the lorry, thanking him again for the excellent care he exhibited with the care of his eye. Jean followed walking over to Monica embracing her with the kiss on either cheek then asking her to take good care of his friend. Speaking out loud so everyone could hear, Jean said, "Monica, you know those rear cockpits in the Lysanders are really tight they also bounce quite a lot during flight, if I were you, I would not sit on Karl's lap never know what could happen?" Everyone started laughing the tension was broken from departing comrades in arms. "Really you men are such pigs, if there is not much room in that plane well it's not the worst thing that could happen isn't that right Captain Vita?" Replied Monica in a very jovial voice. Albert helped Monica and Karl climbed into the covered lorry along with six other armed partisans. Once everyone was aboard the lorry rumbled down the lane leaving Jean and the Doctor standing silently watching until they were out of sight. The drive through the backroads was uneventful Karl was thinking about the many dangers Jean would face in the months ahead, showing such strength and conviction to free his Country. It makes me wonder how a large military force like the French had collapsed so quickly to a smaller military like the Germans, arrogance probably! The lorry slowed as it approached the landing field turning its lights off it moved very slowly to the edge of the clearing. Ahead of them images of other men running stealthily to take up defensive positions around the field. The quiet was deafening as they waited patiently for the sound of an aircraft. After about fifteen minutes an overhead sound announced the arrival of the aircraft everyone looking skywards straining to see the morse code recognition signal. The black shape of an aircraft made a second pass this time flashing the code for that night's operation. The return signal from Albert put the team of men into motion running out of the bushes with their pots of flammable material to aluminate the landing strip. "Alright let's make this fast," whispered Albert as he led the two passengers out to the edge of the strip. At the far end they could hear the Lysanders big radial engine throttling back as it made its approach, bouncing just once as it contacted the rough terrain of the field stopping almost immediately. Moving quickly the group approached the left side of the aircraft and the permanently attached board ladder to the rear cockpit. One of the partisans jumped onto the ladder opening the canopy then climbed inside to remove the boxes of supplies and munitions, handing them down to the others waiting below. "I say down there just want to confirm Captain Vita is one of the two returning with me tonight is that correct," whispered, Captain Cooke from the cockpit. Karl turned to Albert thanking him again for putting their lives on the line rescuing them from certain death. "One day I hope our paths will cross again when Europe is again free." Karl saying this turned to Monica saying, "Let me go first as I know the cockpit arrangement." Albert as a parting gesture replied. "You know he means let me get in first, so you have no alternative but to sit on his lap." The group quietly chuckled as Karl climbed up the ladder saying. "Nice to see you Cooke will this be a champagne flight," Karl was showing signs of relief knowing he was heading home. "Up you come Nurse let me help you settle in, I told you it would be tight did I not." Remarked Karl as the canopy closed. The whole operation landing, unloading, and reloading took less than six minutes, by the time the Lysander left the ground the fire pots were doused returning the field once more to darkness. "Captain Vita when we land there will be an ambulance waiting for you, as for you miss a car will take you straight to the Free French Headquarter. This flight will be quite bumpy as I have been instructed to fly as low as possible because of your injury, sorry for this but orders are orders." Yelled the pilot over the noise of the engine. Monica looked at Karl as they both broke out laughing.

Thirty or so minutes into the flight, Monica took out a penlight from her pocket saying, "I need to look at that left eye Karl, are you in any pain right now." Slowly she unwound the bandage holding the dressing in place over his eye saying. "The light from this penlight may course some discomfort just try to remain as still as possible, guess that might be difficult the way this plane is moving around sorry for that." Said Monica as she removed the dressing. "In that case stop bouncing on my lap like that I can't do two things simultaneously, must say I prefer the bouncing though." Laughed Karl trying to make light of the pain. A quick response came back at him, "As I said earlier men are such pigs, but I will not squeal if you bounce me again." Monica was acutely aware he was fighting tremendous pain so whatever she could do to take his mind off the splitting pain in his head was alright with her. Apart from this when she looked at Karl, she still saw the dashing maritime officer she had served dinner to at the roadside café back in 1936 if only he would look at her in the same way but that will never happen will it? As difficult as it was Monica managed to apply ointment to both side of his eye before replacing a fresh pad and bandage. Monica felt quite fatigued after holding on to the side of the cockpit as she replaced the dressing, "There it's done, what a struggle it's taken most of my energy. I feel like all my strength has been drained." Said Monica looking for a way to stretch out and get some sleep. "Lean back against my chest and put your head on my shoulder I think you will find it to be much more comfortable." Karl thinking this brave lady has not stopped since we returned from our mission now it's my turn to take care of her as he placed his hand on the side of her face to stop her head from rolling off his shoulder. Karl was also starting to feel the strain of the days excitement he could feel the waves of sleep rolling over him, within minutes he surrendered also falling asleep.

"I say you two back there, time to rise and shine we are over the English coast and only minutes from landing, make sure your wedge in tight for touchdown will you please." Instructed Captain Cooke. The Lysander touch down in a remarkable short amount of runway then taxied to the dispersal area, spun around by revving up the engine and applying the right brake once in place the pilot shut down the engine and silence returned to the evening what was left of it that is. An RAF private jumped up onto the ladder and swung open the canopy latching it securely to the top. "Welcome home," Said the smiling private as he helped Monica climb down the ladder backwards. "Your next sir, are you carrying any luggage tonight?" "No corporal, we are it for this trip anyway." Replied Karl as he proceeded to navigate down the ladder backwards. On the ground Karl looked towards the front of the aircraft to finally face the pilot, "Captain Cooke I presume." Laughed Karl using a line from English maritime history. "You are correct, sorry for a turbulent flight old man flying that low can be hair raising," as he wiped salt off the aircrafts wheel spat with his finger in a sign of believe it or not, we were that low tonight!

"Glad it was me old boy they selected to pick you up tonight, we were told you have a badly injured eye and altitude could be a problem I have a reputation for wave hopping so that's how you got to fly with me twice, hope all goes well for you in surgery, must be off now." Captain Cooke made a casual salute picked up his bag and walked off towards the hanger. Although the area in front of the hunger was dimly lit Karl could make out the form of Major Knight. "Karl over here, thank God you made it home I can only image what you have been through." Said Clive shaking Karl hand. "Major Knight, may I introduce you to Monica my French nurse. Believe or not we first met one night in a French café back in 36, oh my goodness Monica, after all these years forgive me, I don't know your surname?" Karl feeling somewhat embarrassed, Its *Thompson* sir my grandfather was in the First World War although he was in the British Flying Corp he returned to France after the war to reunite with my Grandmother and never returned to England." Monica looked at Karl seeing his jaw drop in disbelief. "See Captain Vita, you're not the only one with a good story." Monica had a smug look on her face and was loving every minute of it. "No wonder your English is that good, some intelligence officer I turned out to be." Karl was still dumfounded as they all walked towards the waiting vehicles. "Major, would you mind awfully if I take a few minutes with Monica, she has done so much for me I really would like to thank her privately." Karl's brain was racing to find the correct words to say knowing when they part it could be the last time, but there again he thought that once before? Karl took Monica's hand and lead her back towards the aircraft, stopping he reached out for her hands then started speaking. "Monica words cannot express my thanks for what you have done for me, this is the second time we have said goodbye and quite honestly I find myself asking why?" Would you consider coming to see me before you depart back to France? Suddenly I want to say so much, I suppose in a way we are back in front of that café only the rolls have been reversed, haven't they?" The flood of emotions were consuming Karl's head making him very confuse and vulnerable, he sensed by the look on her face she was looking for that kiss never given so many years ago. "Oh, to hell with it, Monica come here let's make this a memorable farewell." Said Karl as he swooped her into his waiting arms. Monica's reply said it all. "Took you long enough, didn't it?" As she eagerly responded thinking make it last it probably will be the first and last time, I get to kiss him. Over by the vehicles Clive stood smiling slowly shaking his head thinking here we go again. The attending Doctor walked over to Clive saying, "we must get Captain Vita to the hospital sir, don't want to break up the goodbyes but his injury needs immediate attention. Said the Doctor, concerned about his new patient. "Give them a few more minutes they have been through a lot together five more minutes will not make a big difference." Clive knew his friend so well and when a situation like this occurs it's best to let it play out. Monica slowly pulled away from Karl placing both hands on his cheeks, "Karl, you dear man how I have imagined kissing you like that, we never will have the time to make it more than this once will we?" Tears welled up in her beautiful dark brown eyes before she spoke again. "Karl when we leave here, I will be going to the Free French Headquarter and you will go on to the hospital, you will need this pile box to give to your Commanding Officer over there, or had you forgot about the film it contains." Karl's head snapped back hearing this, "I thought that film had already been sent You have had it all along but why you?" Karl was dumfounded once again. "Because Albert thought it would be safer returning with you, so he instructed me to only give it to you as we parted here in England." Monica, open her medical bag withdrawing a pile box then pressing it into Karl's hand saying. "You nearly gave your life for this Karl make it pave the way for a free France." Monica held his hand for a moment, lifting she pressed it again her cheek then kissed the back of it, turning she walked over towards the waiting French officer standing by the vehicle. Speaking out loud as she walked away, saying, "Karl don't forget me I will always have a place in my heart for you, but I'm sure you already knew that didn't you and please make sure they send me the results of your surgery." Monica refrained from looking back as she walked that short distance to the car, tears slowly rolling down her face. The French officer kissed her on both cheeks then opened the rear door saying, "I hope those tears are tears of joy young lady." Monica simple replied, "They are tears of goodbye sir." As she entered the back seat she turned once more throwing Karl a kiss before the door was closed by the officer also waving goodbye. The car's engine started, the driver making a wide turn away from them as they sped off towards the main gate out onto the road leading to London. "Karl, we must get going right now." Clive was out of time waiting around for Karl. "Clive one quick question, did you ever get the microfilm I took?" Asked Karl thinking here is that BIS secret stuff again. "No Karl we received another film from another group, we were told it would be better to send it with the agent who took it, so do you want to give it to me now? Clive waiting for Karl response. "The bloody BIS secrets at it again, you knew all along that it would be on that plane didn't you. "Yes" was the only response he got from Clive. "Karl I'll stop by tomorrow if I can, to check up on your progress." Shaking hands Karl's looked at Clive with a concerned expression on his face, Clive's parting words were, "Captain Vita, this has been a dangerous year for you so far, if cats have nine lives you probable only have four or five left, now go and get that eye taken care of will you." Clive was smiling knowing that within a week or two this strong-willed Austrian with his driving convictions would be hounding him for a new assignment anywhere on the Continent. Thank God he is not on Hitlers side thought Clive as he broke out into a chuckle.

Dr. Phillips climbed into the ambulance and introducing himself to Karl, "it's going to take the best part of an hour to reach *Saint Vincent's Hospital*, once we arrive, I'll accompany you into the surgical suite. I need to take a closer look at that eye before we can determine any type of procedure, hopefully it's going to be something we can take care of relatively easily. So, while we are enroute let me look at that left eye to make sure we don't have an emergency on our hands alright." Doctor Phillips carefully removed the head dressing then with a very steady hand he removed the gauze pad covering his eye. The male nurse in the ambulance held a diffused light, shining it directly into Karl's eye. "Sorry if this light gives you some discomfort I need to see as much of your eye as I can. I am going to roll your eyelid up with this wooden pin so I can see the upper eye clearer. I say that French Doctor and that Nurse traveling with you did a splendid job of containing the problem, from what I can see I would say there may be blood vessels that have ruptured, there may be more once we remove your eyeball." Doctor Phillips lowered the eyelid applying a new dressing with tape instead of a bandage. "Remove my eyeball," asked Karl not sure of what would be involved with this procedure. "Don't get alarmed Captain it sounds a lot worse than it really is, you would be amazed at how quickly I can remove an eyeball. The reason they asked me to meet your plane is I'm the resident Ophthalmologist at the Hospital. The wireless message received at the BIS was vague to say the least. I'm told, Captain Vita you're a very important member of that service, is that correct? Let me put your concerns to rest, this eye problem can be taken care of rather quickly. That French Doctor made the right call if it was left for another three or four days you may have run the risk of permanent damage. My suggestion is if you ever get to see him again you need to thank him for making the right decision, now lay back and relax we are almost there." Dr. Phillips moving over to the opposite side of the ambulance so Karl could spread out.

"Here we are let's get you taken care of shall we." said the Doctor standing up to help Karl out the back. A hospital attendant pushed a wheelchair up to the back of the ambulance for Karl. "Won't need that thing but thanks for assuming I'm not capable of walking, it's my eye not my bloody legs that's the problem, alright Doctor lead the way." Karl feeling a little guilty about how he had spoken to the old timer trying to help. Karl stopped by the main door turning to face the attendant.

"That was a bloody stupid thing to say, I'm really sorry for saying that you must think I'm an arrogant sod, sorry." The old timer merely smiled and waved a signal that no harm done. Inside the surgical area a male nurse handed Karl a hospital gown to put on with instructions to climb into the bed once he had undressed. "I'm going to give you a close shave then shave the left side of your head don't worry, I'm not going to scalp you just need to make sure there is no hair close to the surgical area. First, I will need you to have a shower in that shower stall over there, make sure you wash your hair thoroughly with this medicated shampoo." Instructed the nurse. Karl complying with the instruction added jovially, "Have not had a real hot shower in quite a while, guess you sensed that right." They both chuckled at that remark as Karl entered the shower stall the hot water cascading down his body. Feeling so much better he returned to the bed, waiting patiently for the nurse to return with a tray containing a straight razor, shaving brush, and shaving cream for that close shave and partial scalping. Laying there in that bed he drifted back to another surgery earlier in the year, that one was much more intense than this one he thought. The surgical nurse entered the room saying. "Hello, I'm *Helen* your nurse, I'm here to get you ready. First, I'm going to cover around your eye followed by medication to make you feel sleepy. Once we enter the surgical suite the anesthesiologist will be administering the medication to put you under, any questions." Asked Helen. About ten minutes later Karl started to feel drowsy, the feeling of being calm for the first time in so many weeks was almost therapeutic, so he let it take him into the twilight. Inside the theatre Dr Phillips along with his assistant gave him a brief overview to what he was going to do, followed by the anesthesiologist placed the face mask over his mouth instructing him to breathe deeply. Ninety minutes later he was in the recovery area a nurse hovering over him saying. "Welcome back Captain that did not take long, did it? Let me prop you up then I'll get you some tea and biscuits, back in a minute." As she turned to leave a drowsy Karl asked. "Nurse could you make that coffee instead, I'm not ready for tea just yet." Asked Karl. "Of course, you can no problem back in a jiffy." As the nurse hurried off down the ward Dr Phillips and his assistant entered both with big smiles on their faces. "Well, my good man you are a very lucky individual the surgery was not only successful but nowhere near what we were expecting after we removed your eyeball." Karl could see from their faces that they were pleased. "What exactly was the problem Doctor, can you describe it for me." Asked Karl anxiously. "Well as I said once we removed your eyeball, we found an accumulation of dried blood in the Anterior Chamber that's the space between the Cornea and the Iris. You also had numerous ruptured blood vessels which caused the leakage into the white part of the eye that resulted in a *Subconjunctival Hemorrhage*. Under normal circumstances this would have taken care of itself but seeing as we already had your eyeball out, we cleaned that out also. Because the injury was severe the supporting muscles and ligaments to the eyelid were damaged quite badly, however they will recover with time. Now the good news, we are only keeping you overnight so Major Knight will be here to pick you up in the morning at 1000 hrs. Now there is an inconvenience you will have to live with for about two months that could be less or more depending on how well you obey instructions, something according to Major Knight you are not good at following. The patch over your eye must be kept on during the daytime and only removed when you go to bed. The eye drops I have prescribed for you must be applied first thing in the morning and last thing at night, do not forget to do this alright. Now can I rely on you to keep this regiment up?" Asked Dr. Phillips. "Your directions will be followed as instructed," Laughed Karl delighted at the outcome.

Karl ate a hardy supper feeling truly happy for the first time in weeks. Tomorrow I can return to running my department, looking forward to seeing John and Peggy again and the rest of the gang. I wonder how many wires were received from the Delta-1 team, it's been so long since I heard or seen Hazel, hope she is safe? For the first time in months Karl slept soundly throughout the night, no bad dreams or storm cloud to wake him up in the middle of the night in that cold sweat which had been the case for so long. A gentle touch on his shoulder made him jump with visions of the two Gestapo interrogators about to start beating him merciless. "Sorry sir did not mean to startle you like that but its 0630 hrs, time for you to shower and get yourself dressed. Once you have done that, I'll clean and replace that dressing for you. The Doctor will be along about 0800 hrs to take another look at your eye, how does it feel this morning?" I understand you'll be leaving us this morning at 1000 hrs is that correct?" Asked Helen as she handed him a hospital dressing gown. Karl as he stood up, thought about what she had just asked him. "Helen, I don't have a headache or any pain just a little twinge of soreness when I move my eyes, you chaps are the best thank you, thank you." Karl enjoying this feeling of freedom from relying on others. "Back soon won't take me long in the bathroom, hope you have breakfast ready for me I'm famished." The time flew by, the Doctor met with Karl for an examination, pleased with the condition of the eye he parted by saying." Well old chap I would say you're on the way back to having normal eyesight. I will need to see back here in a week's time other than that just follow the instructions I gave you, bye for now." With that Dr. Phillips walked out into the hall.

Good old Clive arrived punctually at 0950 hrs to find Karl waiting in the hospital lobby his smile needed no further explanation. "Morning Clive I am so ready to be back at the camp, hope you're ready to put up with me again?" The old Karl was showing through and Clive simply gave Karl's arm a two-handed shake indicating that all was well. "Clive when we reach the camp, I would first like to retrieve my stuff from long term storage then head over to my apartment to change and unpack before returning to camp, would that be alright with you?" Karl's mind was already going a hundred miles an hour, almost his old self again.

In his apartment Karl got himself squared away, instead of calling for a staff car to pick him up him elected to get back into his old habit of taking the bus to work. Walked to the corner of the street he queued up waiting for the #5 bus that would make a stop at the main gate in front of the camp. Other than a few soldiers saluting him as they got off the bus traffic was relatively light, he enjoyed the bus ride immensely, whoever would think riding a bus could be so enjoyable looking at all those faces, each with a different story to tell. The conductor announced the next stop as *Hammond Circle*, Karl stood up and moved to the open platform at the rear of the bus. Those squealing brakes and sudden slowing down announced they were stopping. Approaching the main gate, the MP saluted him then looked at his ID card then said. "Pass through sir nice to see you." The tall MP had passed Karl through this gate so many times before, however he would never say 'welcome back' just in case someone was listening. Karl walked up to the main entrance the patch on his eye made him look more like a pirate than a Captain in the British Intelligence Service, he was home.

Chapter Twelve
Espionage Operations.

Karl entered the lobby of the BIS headquarters and was about to say, glad to see you to the attendant when he was usurped by a group of army and air force personnel from the secretarial pool. "Welcome back Captain Vita we are so pleased to see you back amongst us, with that patch eye over your left eye makes you look more like a rusty old pirate, very appropriate If you don't mind our humor, we will address you as Captain Cooke the famous Pirate!" said First Lieutenant *Susan McCabe*, the department director as she laughingly made the welcome back speech, clapping along with the other ladies. Karl smiling at the welcome back reception he was given. "You can call me anything you like but never call me late for a big hug from each and every one of you." Karl was always the favorite amongst the ladies in that department. "We aim to please, now ladies remember he is recovering from combat wounds so be gentle." One by one each of the twelve girls walked up to Karl kissing him on the cheek before returning to their department, two of the junior clerks cheekily preferred to take advantage of the welcome back event by planting a big kiss right on his lips even though they were still a little sore from the beating. Karl thinking, I am so fortunate to work with these wonderful ladies if they only knew how close I was to never seeing them again! "Lieutenant how on earth did you know I was about to enter the lobby?" asked Karl. "Well old Harry down at the gate called us as soon as he passed you through. We had heard from Major Knight that you would be here later in the day, so I asked Harry to call as soon as you arrived, we are so thankful to know your home safe and sound sir. By the look of that patch over your eye you had a rough time wherever you were, no need to answer that question its none of my business? All of us have been praying for you sir, again welcome back." Susan stood back saluted then like a flash gave Karl a big kiss saying. "I have wanted to do that for a long time, apologies for taking advantage like that." Susan was blushing as she looked at the lipstick on both of Karl's cheeks. "Well lieutenant I could put you on report unless you have a good enough reason for me not to?" Asked Karl trying to keep a straight face. "Well sir, if you let me buy you a pint tonight, I could try to persuade you not to do that, so what do you say? How does the *Ships Knees* sound after work say at 1730 hrs?" Karl's response was what Susan wanted to hear. "Well, if I may call you Susan, I think that would be a wonderful way to spend my first evening back in Slough, I will meet you there, are we in or out of uniform? if we are out, make it 1830 hrs so I can change at my flat before meeting up with you. Question, do you live here on base or do you have your own digs off base?" Asked Karl. "I live close by to the pub so that time will be great, see you later." She saluted again then turned to return to her department her face beaming with a wonderful smile. Karl remained standing in the lobby thinking what the hell are you doing? Only home two days and you are already excepting a date for tonight, oh to hell with it, I've looked death in the eye twice so far this year so I'm not going to get a guilty conscience over a pint of beer, especially when it's being bought by a very charming lady. Laughing out loud, he thought I have a thing for ladies in uniforms as he turned to pick up his bag. Karl walked down the hall to his department, opening the door, once again he was mobbed by members of his small staff so thrilled to have their boss back safe and sound. Peggy was the first to speak, "Sir when we heard about your eye from Major Knight, we decided to buy you an appropriate gift hope you like it," as she brought her hand from behind her back holding a brightly colored giftwrapped box then continued speaking. "John, let me take off for a few hours earlier today and Major Knight kindly allowed me to borrow his staff car to go and find this gift." Peggy handed Karl the box just as Clive entered the department barking. "And who gave you all permission to stop working just because this bloke arrived back here today. Even though it's against regulations I think we all need to welcome him back properly don't you all agree." Clive opened the door and in came his sergeant pushing a cart which had rows of glassed and two champagne bottles in ice buckets along with a welcome home frosted cake made it feel more like a birthday party than a welcome back party. "Now we can welcome this old bugger back properly." Clive as usual had thought of everything. While two of the office clerks poured the Champagne, Karl ripped off the paper from the box then with a look of total surprise started laughing out loud. "How appropriate you people are the best." Inside the box were two beautifully stitched leather eye patches, one in brown and one in black. Clive had mentioned that Karl would be wearing an ugly hospital patch for at least two or more months hearing that gave Peggy the idea to visit the leather accessories shop in Slough confident they could provide such an item for her. "Allow me, to put the brown one on for you sir." Asked Peggy as she carefully placed it over the gauze patch and tied it at the back of his head. "Now that looks so sexy you will have all the ladies around here following you." Peggy had not intended to say that, but she did, and everyone was getting a big laugh from it. "Not if I can help it young lady this chap gives me enough problems without all the female in this building going

giddy over his patch." Clive was enjoying this small gathering finding something good to celebrate during these strenuous times in a war that was forced upon them, this was the medicine they all could enjoy. As he stood watching the merrymaking, he thought more about how he knew his friend so very well and the painful reality they came close to losing him, so let him enjoy this attention. The welcome back gathering finally came to an end, Karl thanked everyone then proceed to his small office saying, "John would you bring me all the latest wires from all the Delta groups and any correspondence that needs my attention, one other thing, make sure I leave by 1600 hrs I need to go over to my flat and change out of this uniform got a dinner engagement that I don't want to be late for." Said Karl as he dived into the pile of communicates on his desk. "Will do sir, so good to see you back behind that desk." John was showing his admiration for his commanding office. Karl separated all the Delta teams then started reading the ones from the Delta-1 team, skimming through each communication carefully looking for that word '*better*' that would tell him Hazel was safe, there it was in many of the wires until he got to the last two that simple stated. We are moving to a new location stop. Getting too hot to stay in present location stop. Could be several weeks until we transmit again. out. Karl sat behind his desk, not moving the last communication still in his hand. I hope they are going to be alright, sounds so much like what happened to Kitty's group back in 1937. John walked in and advised him it was time to leave. "Thanks John see you tomorrow have a nice evening," replied Karl as he closed the door to his office walking out into the hallway, wishing everyone still at their stations the same good evening. Karl stopped at Clive's empty office to retrieve his bag closing the light as he left. At the bus stop he waited patiently in a short queue for the # 5 bus to arrive. Around the corner came the familiar green double decker bus leaning to the right as the driver wheeled it around the left-handed corner. The queue moved quickly once the passengers getting off had done so. On-board Karl found an empty seat towards the rear near the open platform, looking out the window he thought how drab all the building looked most having tape across their windows in an X pattern. An announcement brought him back to the surrounding of the bus,
"*White Chapel Lane* next stop," Said the bus conductor in a very loud voice. Karl stood up and stepped down onto the platform waiting for the familiar squeaky brakes to announce its arrival at his stop, with a lurch the bus came to a full stop. Karl got off and started walking down the road till he arrived at his apartment building, it had been a while since Karl had been here, as he opened the gate to the small garden, he started to tremble those feeling and painful memories

flooding back into his subconscious mind. His left hand started shaking on the doorknob while the other fumbled uncontrollable for the key slot. Karl, get a hold of yourself you are far away from that Gestapo headquarters now. Start thinking about your date for this evening block those ugly thoughts that will unglue you, do it right now or you will not be able to cope. What seemed a long time was only seconds as Karl stood there with his hand on the doorknob allowing his brain to take control of his emotional being. Feeling the waves of anguish subsiding he opened the door and carefully climbed the stairs to his flat. Feeling so much better now, he opened the door entering the small efficiency unit. Inside he unpacked the travel bag undressed hanging his uniform up in the wardrobe, put on his bathrobe and went down the hall to the bathroom for a bath and shave. Due to war time regulations the use of hot water was limited he did not care what water he had in the bathtub it was refreshing. Back in his room he took out a white shirt, grey trousers, and a double breasted dark blue blazer from the wardrobe, hanging them on the open door, he crossed over to a chest of draws and chose a pair of grey socks and a black leather belt, smiling he changed the brown eye patch for the black one. Standing there he pondered whether to wear a tie, it's a pub I'm meeting Susan at, guess we will have a drink then have dinner so maybe I will wear that tie after all. Thinking again about what had just happened by the front door, he willed himself to take charge of future emotions, I will have to start being aware of when an attack could flare up and what brings it on, I don't want to take the risk of being sent to a sanatorium for therapy, if that was to happen at the office I would be in trouble, now I'm aware of its symptoms I should be able to control them, well I pray to God I can? Karl walked down the stairs stopping momentarily to glance into the hallway mirror when a voice behind him made him jump, "Mrs. *Mann* you made me jump," Karl saying that turned to address his landlady. Sorry to startle ya Captain, cor' don't ya look smashing haven't seen ya in months." Mrs. Mann was a typical Londoner, short and stocky, rollers in her hair most of the time but tough as nails with a big heart. Her facial expressions gave her away, she was so pleased to see Karl back home, it was war, and he was in the intelligence service which meant he would be in harm's way most of the time, she never asked him where he had been because she also knew he would not tell her or take the easy way out by lying. "Well, it is so good to see you too, it's been quite a while so glad to be back here, done a stint in hospital months back after Dunkirk then done a very stupid thing a couple of weeks ago in a training accident landed up bashing my eye which needed surgery, all's well though the patch should be off in a couple of months." Karl feeling good about his cover story. Mrs. Mann however was not sure which part of his story she would believe, maybe the one about Dunkirk! Karl wished his landlady a good evening and promised to have tea with her in a couple of days then walked out into the deserted street. At the corner bus stop he waited for the bus that would take him to the town center in Slough. The directions Susan had given him to the *Ships Knees* would take him about ten plus minutes to walk. The evening was quiet with clear skies, Karl walking reasonably fast he kept thinking it's amazing how good my leg feels. Now if I can get my eyesight back in the left eye, I'll be as good as new. Fourteen minutes later he saw the sign for the Ships Knees dimly lit due to the blackout regulations. Opening the door, he was surprised at how large the lounge was, charming with its low beamed ceiling and heavy dark oak furniture, very nice he thought as his one good eye focused on the patrons sitting at the bar and a few more sitting in booths. Susan does not appear to be here yet guess I'll seat in that booth at the back of the lounge till she arrives. The proprietor came over asking if he would like to order a drink and will there be anyone else joining him. "Yes, I'm expecting a young lady shortly, in the meantime I'll have a mild and bitter if you please." Replied Karl. The beer arrived and Karl took a long first sip enjoying the taste as it went down his throat. He started to relax enjoying this time alone with his beer. A voice behind him said softly, "So sorry to keep you waiting sir, got delayed leaving the base earlier, how long have you been waiting?" Susan looking a little flustered as she slid into the bench seat opposite Karl. "Please no apologies I have been enjoying this quiet time alone with my beer, what can I get you to drink." Karl waving his arm to get the proprietors attention. "Miss Susan so nice to see you in civilian attire, you look really smashing, don't you think sir." Said Ben, the proprietor. "I would totally agree with you, she also looks really smart in a uniform." Karl was looking at Susan in a whole different way, even with his one eye he could see the dark blue fitted suite made her look completely different, I'm such a lucky chap when it comes to meeting and dating the ladies he thought. "So tonight, we will not talk shop, nor will you keep calling me sir agreed!" Karl was looking to have a nice evening alone with a brand-new lady friend, there would be no guilty feelings this evening, in his mind having looked death in the face more than once he reconfirmed there may not be a tomorrow, war had a way of changing your prospectus on life. "Well Susan what's our game plan for this evening, shall we stay here in this nice lounge for dinner, or did you have some other plan?" Asked Karl as he watched her fidget in her seat moving her sherry glass from side to side, no longer the cocky, overconfident army officer hiding behind that uniform anymore. "Susan you're surprising me, you have always impressed me as being a very confident young lady, take you out of that uniform and you become a very shy and may I say very attractive lady." Karl was smiling enjoying how he was affecting the lady opposite him. "Karl, you have no idea how the girls in my department talk about you and the relationship you have with Lieutenant Collings it's a little intimidating seating here knowing you could be out with any one of the single girls at the base. I also realize your only here this evening because I was goating you on to have a drink with me. Lieutenant Collings has been on assignment for many months, am I to assume when she returns." "If she returns," interjected Karl as he listened to her speak. "That you will become a couple once again." Concluded Susan looking so much calmer now she had got that off her chest. "Susan, I have had this discussion a few times before and now I'm find myself doing it once again, so let me clarify this right now for you. We are at war there could be no tomorrow, especially for chaps like me that find themselves in harm's way all too often. My forward vision for next week, next month, next year is, I probably won't see another year so no matter what the scuttle butt is about Lieutenant Collings and myself, I intend to live for today and nothing beyond that, does that answer your questions." Karl could feel his temper trying to overcome him, taking a large swig of his beer he quickly regained his composure. "Sorry for that outburst Susan I had no right to unload on you like that, again my apologies." Said Karl not really feeling good about his actions. "It's me who should be apologizing I started this so can we start again Karl." Asked Susan trying to reset the mood. Over dinner they both shared stories laughing about things they both did growing up and the path that brought them together this evening. "Well, that was an excellent dinner thank you for recommending it." Said Karl as he drank the last of his beer, looking at her watch Susan calmly asking what time is your last bus it's still early yet? There again we could go back together in the morning?" Susan was exploring to see if there was an opportunity for romance when they left the Ships Knees. "Well, we could do that but I'm in civilian attire that may be a little too much first thing in the morning." Karl was being diplomatic to get out of Susan's invitation. "Tonight, was wonderful maybe we can do it again when I have two good eyes shall we?" Karl could see by her facial expression the disappointment of the evening coming to an end. Ben brough over the bill placing it between them on the table. Susan went to pick it up but a strong hand on her arm stopped her. "Tonight, is my treat young lady, I have had a wonderful time so please it's my pleasure to do this." Said Karl as he retrieved some cash from his wallet. "You do realize I was trying my best to seduce you into staying with me tonight don't you." Said Susan as she reaches over to grasp Karl's hand. "Susan I am flattered to think you would like to make love to me but right now is not the time for such thoughts as much as I will regret it in the morning. Let's see how things go in a few days maybe we can take a weekend out in the country what do you think to that." Karl had already made up his mind if no news comes from Hazel, then he would peruse a romantic weekend away with this charming lady. "Can I at least walk you to the bus stop." Asked Susan as Karl paid the bill. "Of course, you can maybe we can find a quiet spot to have a good night kiss, I would like that what do you think?" Karl stood first reaching out for her hand as she slides across the seat, the material on the cushion made it difficult to slide holding her skirt in place providing Karl with a view of her thighs, hum I'll willing to bet she did that intentionally! Outside the air seemed a little cooler so Susan looped her arms tightly around Karl's left arm as they started walking towards the bus stop. The blackout created a challenge for pedestrians with no streetlights to show the way, just the occasional torch in someone's hand as they passed them by. "This is ridicules Susan, let me walk you home then I'll go catch the bus. It would concern me allowing you to walk home on your own, it's not the gentlemanly thing to do." Karl was also thinking it's his way out of an impossible situation. "Karl you are such a gentleman, no wonder I have a crush on you." Susan once again fortifying how she felt about this charismatic Austrian, sending him another message she was trying to persuade him to stay overnight. "Karl my house is over there, and the park is here on the left, let's sit for a while on the bench before you leave, shall we?" Susan would give it one more chance to convince Karl to change his mind about spending the night. The benches were not completely in the dark, dim lights gave just enough light to show the path. They sat in the middle of one of the benches, Susan making sure she was right next to him. "Now handsome how about that good night kiss you promised me earlier?" She was wasting no time as she turned in towards Karl putting her arm around his neck, Karl reciprocated put his arm around her waist pulling her in closer. In the dim light Karl could see and feel her tensing in anticipation of that contact. She did not waste any more time with moist lips she found his mouth and kissed him deeply, momentarily they parted looking at each other without uttering a sound. Karl placed his hand on her cheek she responded by leaning her head to one side trapping his hand between her shoulder and cheek. Once again, they kissed this time Susan opened her mouth, her tongue forcing Karl's mouth open and connected with his, that kiss was exciting her to no ends she wanted Karl so desperately. Susan pulled away breathing heavily. "Karl if I can't persuade you to stay with me tonight would you please touch me, I want you so much." Karl hearing this pulled away from her holding her hands to calm her down she was totally out of control. The alcohol had removed any inhibitions she may have had up to this point. "Susan, I can sense you are emotionally aroused maybe a little too much, so I've delivered on that kiss and now lady you need to sleep off that wildness those drinks have put you into, so up you get and let's cross the road to your house shall we." At the front door Karl hugged her and gently kiss her cheek saying. "Thank you this was a wonderful evening see you tomorrow morning, don't be late." Susan started to turn towards the door then stopped saying. "You realize because of you I'll probably not sleep a wink tonight if that happens, you will owe me big time and I will collect on that next time, see you tomorrow you sexy man." Giggling at what she had just said, Karl simply laughed out loud, walking away into the night. Walking the ten minutes back to the bus stop, gave him time to digest the evening and the events that kept him laughing as he walked. I think this one is wild out of uniform, not to be handled lightly. I can't believe what a few drinks could turn her into. Of all the women I have known or dated she is without doubt the wildest, God help the chap she eventually lands up with. Must admit I prefer women that have strong convictions and go after whatever it is their after. Thinking this made him laugh again as he arrived at the bus stop. The following morning Karl got an early start had a quick cup of tea with his landlady, "Don't be late tonight Karl remember you are still recovering from that eye wound." Said his Mrs. Mann more of a mother to Karl than his landlady. "Will do Mum." Replied Karl as he got to the front door, instinctively he reached for his umbrella normally kept in the hallway stand, then remembered he had given it to that pretty Sargent Gwen Phillips on another rainy morning. "Mrs. Mann, can I borrow one of your umbrellas must have left mine in the office." He did not elaborate any further. "Go right ahead my boy." Replied Mrs. Mann. Walking to the bus stop, Karl started thinking, why do I continue to take the bus, on my salary I can easily afford a little car, the petrol ration books I will receive will be more than enough for driving locally around here. When I go to Baldock to see Mama and the family I can still use the train that way I'll never run out of petrol stamps. With a new objective in his head Karl started to think about all the freedoms a car will give him. On the crowded bus a businessman seating next to Karl said. "I'm getting off at the next stop old man care to take a gander at the *Daily Mail*." As he stood ready to exit at the next stop, "I'm all done with it so be my guest." Karl thanked him and immediately started scanning the classifieds. After four more stops the conductor announced, "Next stop *Hampton Lane*," Karl hearing this announcement folded the paper and made his way to the rear platform. Like so many times before the bus squealed and shuddered as it slowed to the next stop, Karl stepped off the platform before the bus came to a complete stop tucking the newspaper into his briefcase then walked briskly towards the camp entrance. At the gatehouse the guards took a quick look at his ID, then waved him through. Entering his department Peggy smiled handing him a pile of folders for his review saying, "Good morning Sir, last night communications are in the sealed pouch on your desk, why don't you start reviewing them while I get your morning coffee." Karl smiled back his immediate thoughts turning to the contents of that pouch. "Thanks Peggy, be a dear and include a buttered roll with that coffee, feeling a little nippiest this morning, take some money from my cash box in the top draw buy yourself something as well." Peggy opened the draw and took four shillings from the box then walked out. That girl is becoming my right arm she is so efficient at everything she does thought Karl. Taking the key chain from his pocket he opened the dispatch pouch removing its contents onto the desk. The dispatches were separated by elastic bands. He opened the Delta-1 batch first to see if Hazel had included their code word. Out of the four communiques, the very last one contained that special word, it read. Enroute to meet up with southern partisan's cell, Stop. They will guide us over the Pyrenees mountain into Spain, *better* for us right now, stop. Hun has been one stop behind us for last twenty days, stop. Getting too dangerous to stay, stop. Believe we have a mole operating amongst us, stop. Better not to use radio until we are secure again, stop. Karl sat back in his chair the communique in his hand, thinking thank God they are safe but for how long? He turned his attention back to reading the remaining communiques however he found it hard not to continue thinking about the Delta-1 team. The more he thought about that communique the more he realized they needed to act on this information right away. Karl stood up from his desk and headed for the door saying, "John, when Peggy returns tell her I've gone to see Major Knight, have her bring the Delta-1 personnel file as quickly as she can." Walking down the hall he noticed Susan coming in the opposite direction. "Captain Vita may I have a moment of your time please." Asked Susan with a timid tone in her voice. "Would love to talk to you Lieutenant but right now we have a code red condition, let me take care of this then I'll come find you, had a very nice time last night, bye for now." Karl was not wasting precious time talking to Susan, telling her he had a nice time would settle her frayed nerves for a while anyway.

Karl arriving at Major Knights office, asked his secretary if he was in his office? "Yes, Captain Vita, he's on the phone with London right now, please take a seat and I'll let him know your waiting." Said Mrs. *Mary Evans* expecting Karl to take a seat. "No time for that." said Karl as he knocked loudly on Clive's office door then walked right in. "Captain Vita you can't do that, please close the door and take a seat," pleaded Mrs. Evans. Karl closed the door alright once he was inside. "General can you hold one minute please one of my officers has just entered and by the look on his face there is trouble afoot, may I call you back in about an hour, thank you sir and sorry for ending this call so abruptly." Concluded Clive. "Alright Karl you have that look of anger on your face, what the bloody hell is it now." Clive was rattled as well, concerned that Karl would not do this unless something was drastically wrong. "Read this latest wire from the Delta-1 team we received this morning." Karl placed the wire down in front of Clive's, then sat quietly facing his Commanding officer as he read the wire. "Karl, you did the right thing bringing this immediately to my attention, a little less theatrics next time please! If this is correct their locations and radio traffic has been compromised, but who could that mole be? They are in severe danger and there is nothing the BIS can do to help them, from here anyway." Karl sat back in his chair saying, "Is there anyone over there that could join them and help identify the whistle blower?" Karl was racking his brains who in that handpicked team would betray their movements. A knock on the door Peggy entered carrying personnel folders for the Delta-1 team. "Here are the files you asked for Sir, I have also taken the liberty of bring you your coffee and roll as well, we all know how you get when your, on a mission!" Peggy placed the files in front of them, placed the roll and coffee to one side of the desk saying, "Is there anything else I can do for you sir before I return to the office." Clive looked at Karl with a frown on his face. "Thank, you Peggy, that will be all tell John if any more communiques come in, especially from Delta-1 team bring them straight to me, find me if you have to." Karl and Clive started spreading the files out to review starting with the team leader Gunther. "Is there anything that would sway Gunther to provide information to the Germans?" Asked Clive studying his file. "Don't be ridicules Clive I would trust Gunther with my life." Replied Karl. Clive his arms folded behind his head as he ran through all the scenarios that would force a man like Gunther to turn on his team members. "Gunther has family in Hamburg is that correct?" Asked Clive. "Yes, but they may have been evacuated to another part of Germany by now why, do you ask?" Karl answering with a concerned expression on his face and anger in his voice. "Let's create a scenario as an exercise, let's say the Gestapo or S.S. got word to him by some means that they knew he had returned to the Continent, then threatened to torture and perhaps kill his family members if he did not cooperate with them? That's one avenue we should be investigating further, don't you agree?" Asked Clive knowing full well he was hitting a nerve when it came to the trust and loyalty of Gunther. "He would never betray his team, nor would he cooperate with the Germans in anyway even if it meant putting his family in harm's way and let's not forget that is a big concern to us when screening new agents that still have relatives on the Continent correct? In the unlikely event they discovered he had returned as an English agent, a capture or kill order would become high priority. As much as this line of investigation angers me, we must pursue it further for everyone in that team and every other team, Delta or otherwise currently deployed, this could well be the weak link in our security screening? Get Peggy back here to help us further with each of the agents that have family on the Continent." Clive stood up and proceeded to the office door saying. "Karl be a good chap gather those files and follow me to meeting room A-1, we need to spread out and tell Peggy that she and John should plan on going home very late tonight, let's go." Clive and Karl walked down the hall towards the meeting room approaching they noticed all the lights were on and a meeting was in progress, Clive pulling rank instructed those in the room to hold their meeting someplace else as he was taking this room for the foreseeable future. "Yes, sir said one of the junior officers with a hint of sarcasm in his voice." Karl picked up the wall phone and dialed his department extension. "Who's this," asked Karl. "Its private Ann Watts sir, what can I do for you?" Karl responding, "Tell John and Peggy to pull up the Delta team files. "Yes, sir, Ann would you also tell them they should plan on being here very late tonight and hurry up with those files, thank you." Karl hung up then returned to the conference room table. "When the other two get here we can start by identifying each group by nationality, then we can start background checks and current locations of family members." Said Clive as he removed his tunic and unbuttoned the top button to his shirt, "Might as well get comfortable, it's going to be a long night. Karl, call my office and tell them to bring down some hot coffee in thermoses, include some biscuits with that request as well." Asked Clive as he started into the first folder. Shortly thereafter John and Peggy arrived pushing a trolley piled high with personnel files. "Blimey this is going to take a long time to weed through all these files?" Said Clive as he stared at the pile of files on the conference table, John arranging the files by Delta team numbers. Karl explained the plan to John and Peggy then told them to get comfortable by removing their tunics and loosening their ties. Peggy started spreading the files out down the length of the table, with so many files to review they took up its entire length. To make things easier, John moved all the chairs away from the table other than the four being used. "Alright we are ready, Karl you and Peggy start isolating the foreign members of each team placing each folder to one side. John and I will do the same on the opposite side of the table. Once we have separated them, we can start the real work of reviewing and taking notes on what we find out about their families, are their parents still alive? Are their husband or wife still over there or are they in a safe place like here in England? Have we missed any updates? That sort of stuff alright? Do they have siblings still alive if so where are they residing? If that information is not available in the folder make a note to have one of our agents investigate to confirm? We must not leave any stone unturn? Children don't forget to note how old they are? Who do they live with? Maybe it's a wife, husband, brother, sister, grandparent? People we are looking for a needle in a haystack so don't assume anything if there's a question flag it in your notes." With those instruction Clive started to take apart his first folder. The only sound in that room was the shuffling of papers and quiet discussions between them. After an hour the coffee arrived with biscuits and a large plate of assorted sandwiches.

"I took the liberty of ordering sandwiches for you all, the tea is labeled just in case one of you doesn't drink coffee. The cafeteria said they will check in with you before they close at 2000 hrs just in case you need refills." Said *Nancy* as she removed everything from the trolley. The hours clicked by with no real concrete information until Peggy found a link between the Delta-1 and Delta-3 teams. "Sirs I think this may be worth investigating further, these two teams have been operating together for over three months, for the most part they are traveling together only hours apart. Now here is the interesting part in the D-3 there is a Polish agent by name of *Jakub Czeslaw*. He was living and working in Berlin before the war. His wife and daughter are still there according to this file. His wife's brother is in the German Army stationed in Southern France. The initial BIS interrogation report does not mention the German brother-in-law anywhere, this could be our first big break." Peggy was feeling really pleased with herself over her discovery. "Well done Peggy but we still have to go through all of the other files, great start though, now let's take that coffee break shall we." Said Clive as he stood stretching his back. The four of them sat drinking coffee and devouring the sandwiches. Clive looking at his watch then with a look that suggested he had a question, asking John. "Are we in a transmit mode right now." John also looked at his watch saying. "Got another twenty minutes left sir, what are you thinking?" Clive stood up pacing back and forward as he spoke. "Karl why don't we have John wire Gunther to contact us. John the message to read, Mole close by Stop. Get to secure location with H' wireless Stop. Will wait for your call signal, confirm, Out. Go over to your wireless station and send that right now. I will join you once they confirm they are ready to transmitting/receive. "I always thought our background checks were very thorough, how could something so obvious slip through like this. I remember so very well my interrogation and the lengths you people put me through to make sure I wasn't a German spy." As Karl spoke, he started to formulate a new procedure for the BIS to follow for all existing agents and all new prospects entering the BIS.

The wall phone started ringing, "That must be John, Peggy you continue to review those folders, Karl you come with me to the radio room." Commanded Clive as he picked up a pad of paper walking towards the door. Entering the radio room, they found John taping out a signal with his Morse Code key. "Sir we are going to make this call an audio transmission in about fifteen minutes, they are setting the equipment up as we speak." John was showing signs of excitement knowing they could talk instead of Morse Coding, "Remember three minutes or less we can't take a chance on the Germans getting a radio fix." Reminded John. The three sat around jotting down talking points, time was of the essence when using audio communications. "Our code name for this call is 'Overlook' and theirs is 'Willow'. Said John as he arranged the microphone in front of all three. "Let's go over how to address this call, Karl let me see your notes and compare them to mine, damn it Karl there in German couldn't you have written your questions in English?" Sorry Sir have a habit of doing that when it's for my own use. "Too late now, good thing I read German I suppose." Clive settling down again. A crackling sound came over the speaker a female voice quietly asking, Overlook, this is Willow over. Overlook receiving you loud and clear, stand by. "Go ahead sir the line is ready said John to Clive. "Willow we suspect you are being compromised by a leak from your Polish agent giving the Hun your ongoing activities. Take whatever action is necessary to neutralize agent immediately. Send wire when it's done, over." An intense brief silence made the seconds of waiting more like minutes till the answer came back. "Overlook, drastic measure but if this is a command it will be done as instructed immediately, is there any other instructions before signing off." The female voice came back on saying, "We have one last message to pass along, tell Grandmother she is the best, over and out!" The line went dead Clive turned to look at John saying, "what the hell was that last statement meant to imply?" John lowered his head trying to hide a smile, Karl quietly doing the same. Clive watched the eye play then sternly replied. "Alright I got what's going on, can we all remember that every second those people are over there, their voice transmissions are in extreme danger, now let's go back to work." As Clive stood to walk out the door Karl and John saw him chucking to himself, all was forgiven. Back in the conference room they returned to the job of screening each agent operating in the Delta teams,

Peggy identifying three more that could become a problem in the future a result of the leak from the Polish agent. At 2300 hrs the last folder was closed, all four seating back with relief to completing their purge of the BIS foreign agents. "John when you transmit to D-4 and D-2 send the same transmission as we used earlier using the code names for these three, add this at the end. Make arrangement to recover agent immediately. Might as well fire up the receiver, isn't it about that time to make contact?" Asked Clive. "Will do sir, maybe there is an answer from D-1, I will tell the night wireless operator to get himself some tea while I do that." Replied John as he walked towards the door. "Alright young lady, Karl and I can return all these files, you look really tired so thank you for staying this evening and a real big thank you for being so astute at identifying the leak, now off you go." Said Clive looking at Peggy. "Nonsense sir, I always finish what I start, now let me get the cart over here and we can start loading the files." Peggy was not about to bail out just yet. Well in that case let's get started after that if your so inclined we can all have a whisky chaser in my office before heading home. By the way Peggy your boss here will not expect you till at least 1000 hrs tomorrow morning, isn't that right Captain." Said Clive looking at Karl for approval. "Could not of put it better myself Major." Replied Karl as he walked in the vanguard behind Clive and Peggy. In Clive's office they sat enjoying some vintage single malt whiskey as they waited for John to return with an update. "Peggy while we wait for John to join us, tell me about yourself and how come Captain Vita managed to have you join his department thinking he pulled one over on me, ever thought of becoming an analyst here in the BIS?" Clive was not making small talk he meant every word. "Girls like me rarely get those opportunities sir." replied Peggy her heart pounding as the Commander in Chief of BIS operations was asking her if she would consider this opportunity. "I can make that happen Peggy, you would have to go through extensive training no easy task may I add, it will be your call, sleep on it and let me know in a day or so, any objections Captain?" Clive turning to Karl looking for his approval, "none what so ever glad you see what I saw in Peggy's abilities, so I think you should jump at this Peggy while there's an offer on the table." Responded Karl swigging down the last of his Whisky. The office door swung open and in walked John a solemn look on his face. "Got a wire back from D-1 sir, it reads. Have eliminated problem did not like doing it though. Stop. I also dispatched to the other groups your directive about those other agents. "Thanks John, now how about that glass of whiskey?" Asked Clive as John pulled up a chair. Clive went around refilling everyone's glass then toasted them by saying. "Today we eliminated a problem as painful as that may be, we have safeguarded our agents out there in harm's way, thank you for making that happen." Clive gulped down his whiskey then said. "Alright you two, lets head for home. Karl, do you need a ride or are you planning on staying here at the camp tonight? How about you Peggy are your quarters here on the base? John how about you its late how will you get home?" John answered, I have my motorbike so I'm fine, sir. Peggy answered next I'm only two building over in the female quarters so don't worry about me." Peggy went to stand up when Karl spoke up. "Well young lady I will not allow you to go unescorted, so allow me to do that." Karl had decided to get a spare shirt and toilet bag from his office and stay at the officer's quarters for tonight. Well shall we adjourn, again thank you for an outstanding job, well done. Karl stopped at his office picked up his shirt, underwear, socks, and a travel toilet bag and headed for the lobby to wait for Peggy to join him, he did not have to wait long the door swung open and out walked Peggy looking like she had stopped at the powder room to freshen her makeup. "Ready said Karl as he opened the main door for Peggy, the evening was a little chilly, English weather had a tendency, to be damp this time of year and tonight was no difference. "You must be feeling quite weary about now sir." Asked Peggy as she walked out the door. "Got my second wind how about you?" Answered Karl. "I'm feeling really good about now, we worked hard as a team and managed to plug the leak in our intelligence, so today was a success." Peggy feeling proud that she was the one that found the culprit. Karl agreed but felt sorry that a husband and father had panicked acting recklessly in defense of this family, unfortunately that decision cost him his life not that many hours ago. "Peggy, we lost a good man tonight, our training let him down. An agent should never believe they can make a deal for the safety of family members by leaking information to the enemy. We are trained to always confide in our own leaders if there's a way to extract them, they will find a way. Betraying your own team members will never be the right way, it will cost you your life which was the case this evening." Karl was trying to justify why a man had lost his life in a gallant move to save his family without pouring cold water on Peggy's achievement. Reaching the female quarters, they stopped in front of the entrance Peggy parting words. "Think we have done this before! Thank you for escorting me to my quarters, I think your explanation is well taken good night Karl, see you after 1000 hrs tomorrow. Walking over to the officer's quarters he made a decision I'm going home to Baldock this weekend I have a family that has not seen me in a long time, God tomorrow is Friday better asked Clive first thing for a pass. Checking into the room reserved for officers in Clive's division Karl felt the wave of fatigue taking over as he stripped and climbed into bed falling asleep almost immediately.

Chapter Thirteen
His Final Love

The following morning Karl made his way to his building while it was still dark, first stop was to buy a large container of coffee before proceeding to office. At his desk he sat feet up mulling over the tragic events of yesterday, he did not like himself or the others involved with taking another agents life, right or wrong it would be insensitive not to show some remorse for this action. Changing his thoughts, he lightly touched the leather patch over his left eye thinking it is feeling so much better having only one eye makes it harder to focus on things, still have a month and a half to go before I can remove it completely. Better stick my head into Clive's office then wonder over to the medical building to have the dressing changed. Think I will call Mama and tell her to start cooking the Goulash, she will be ecstatic to hear I will be there tomorrow, I will also talk to Ronny about buying a car once this patch comes off. Walking towards Clive's office he remembered the brief meeting in the hall with Susan and how nervous and embarrassed she was, better stop over there as well. "Morning Clive hope you slept well after that long day yesterday?" Asked Karl as he plonked himself down on the couch. "Not really, kept thinking about having to eliminate poor old Jakub, he must have been really desperate to fall into that trap, surely he realized it would end badly?" Said Clive. "Clive, I have an idea on how we can address that moving forward. With so many agents involved it will be no easy task but let me ask you this first. Would you mind awfully if I went home to Baldock this weekend?" Karl already knew Clive would not object. "Of course not, you deserve some time off, report back on Tuesday morning alright." Replied Clive as he filled out the travel pass. "Now tell me about your thoughts on how we can add another layer of screening to field agent's security, or would you like to work on that plan in Baldock?" Asked Clive knowing full well what the answer would be. "I'll have it on your desk on Tuesday, alright." Karl stood up and headed for the door a spring in his step. "Don't do anything crazy?" yelled Clive as he watched his friend leave the office. Entering his department, he could see everyone was hard at work heads down with only the sounds of typewriters and shuffling papers. "Peggy, John could you join me in my office please." Karl wanted to bounce his idea off them on improving security when it came to their foreign agents with families still on the Continent. Seating around Karl's small conference table he started by saying "Yesterday Major Knight was faced with a horrible decision by condemning Jakub to death, a trusted agent that in his mind had no choice by put family first. Moving forward we need to consider whether we can continue using foreign agents that have similar situations. For security reasons if we cannot deploy them, we could be severely handicapping our intelligence operations. We need to overhaul the existing requirement, changing them to protect these agents if a similar situation happens again and we must assume this may already be happening! I have been racking my brains with what we can come up with to address this in a revised training program to combat the blackmail tactic being used by the bloody Gestapo and S.S Bastards. What I would like to do is propose to Major Knight, when I return from seeing my Mother this weekend is to have the counterintelligence boys join us in exploring an effective plan to counter blackmail incidents in the field. Don't be surprise if they suggest recalling all our foreign agents immediately, can't see Clive going along with that idea?" Karl stopped talking waiting for a response. John spoke first saying. "Sir that type of planning and recommendation is way above Peggy and my pay grade, if it was my decision to make, I would recall all of them!" Peggy holding her hands together on the table simply nodded with her agreement. Karl started to realize that there was no easy way around this problem and maybe this disruptive move was the only way to go. Well, I'm starting to think you two are right, lets address this on Tuesday. Peggy while I'm away draft a memo to Major Knight with a copy to Colonel Jacks that I would like to schedule a meeting next week to discuss this glaring weak link. Another thing you can assemble for me while I'm away, can you compile all the agents in the field that have families on the Continent. Then list all the single ones. Finally purge the trainees in the same way, I think their way to close to that weak link. Now, I must be off, or I will miss my train, see you on Tuesday you know how to reach me if it's important, Peggy be a dear and call my mother and tell her I shall arrive by 1650 hrs." Karl walked out into the fresh air, walking quickly to catch the #5 bus back to his apartment. He had laid out what he was taking with him which was little as he had most of his civilian clothes and accessories already were at the bungalow. His case packed he headed back to catch the bus that would let him off at the train station.

Like the times before he changed train in London catching the Baldock train from Kings Cross. When the train pulled out of the Letchworth station Karl took his case from the overhead rack and watched the countryside go by for the fifteen minutes it took to arrive in Baldock. Karl could feel the excitement building it was always so good to unwind back here. After all he had been through recently this would be the medicine he needed. The train slowed to a complete stop, opening the carriage door he stepped down into the smoke and steam drifting down the length of the platform creating a familiar sight in Karl's mind. Something made him look back hoping in his mind to see the lovely Kitty walking to meet him, that image was as clear today as it was years back when she arrived to meet the family and consent to becoming his wife. Instead of shaking off that vision he embraced it for a few extra minutes, thinking, how close we came to having that perfect life together. Could he ever really open his heart to Hazel? In the depths of his heart, he knew that probably will not come to pass. Standing there he also started to realize if this was what he really thought he was not being fair to lovely Hazel. She would always feel that a ghost existed between them condemning any future to failure, shaking his head he headed to the familiar tunnel that ran under the tracks to the small entrance at the front of the station. The evening temperature was not too bad, so he decided to walk the two miles to the bungalow. Walking through the town center he passed the George and Dragon thinking I will go there tomorrow maybe with Freida and Ronny for a pint that would be nice. Arriving at the bungalow, he walked up the driveway the curtains parting and the image of his mother looking out, excited to see her youngest son approaching the front door. The door swung open and out came Mama followed by Freida holding Franchot in her arms with the windup car Karl had bought for him last Christmas. "I'm home and you are the medicine I need right now come give me a big hug, mind my eye though." Said Karl feeling so much happier to be back with family. Mama had supper already, the wonderful aroma coming from the kitchen was making him quite hungry. "Karl how is your eye doing?" Asked Freida as he took his coat and cap off. "It really feels good can't wait to remove this patch though. The people in my department had two leather patches made for me, very thoughtful on their part." Karl changing the subject away from his injury. Over a wonderful dinner Karl devouring everything on his plate then asked for seconds saying. "Mama you have no idea how I miss your cooking, now you know why I lost so much weight." After dinner Mama made hot coffee and the three sat talking about Papa and his brothers still in hiding in the Italian mountains. Karl could see the look on their faces, they wanted to know more about where he had been and what or who had hurt his eye but knew he couldn't say too much. "Mama, Freida what I'm about to tell you is highly classified so I need your promise to respect its secrecy, if you mention it to anyone and that's including Ronny, I could face a court martial or worst. The reason I'm doing this is to put your minds at ease for a little while anyway. The injury to my eye is the outcome of a severe beating by thugs in the Gestapo and yes, I was on the Continent the countries and places I will not tell you however I feel you should know what it is I am doing currently in the BIS. As of this last deployment I was a field operative and now the department director for field agent support. At this point my days of going back to being a field agent are over. The injures I have sustained over this past year have eliminated me from doing what I do best and that is field operations. Mama let me put your mind to rest from here on I will be in Slough operating my department. Other than a stray bomb landing on the camp I will be out of direct danger. The upside to all this is I am going to try and schedule most of my weekend to be here with you all. Having been that close to leaving this earth on several occasions has made me aware I need to be with my family more frequently, something that I have not been too good at doing." Karl stopped talking, waiting for a response. "My darling brother I have suspected your lack of writing and calling could be associated with the work you have been doing. This year has been terrible for us here not knowing if you were hurt or somewhere you could be in jeopardy has kept us on a mental roller coaster. Each time you come home you always looked worn out, underweight those black shadows under your eyes are a dead giveaway. Are we surprised at what you have just told us not really, when we landed that first time in Dover Mama had said with your background you would be in high demand and from what you have just told us she was right? This news you have just given us is wonderful, knowing that from here on you will be stuck behind a desk, even though my wonderful brother you will hate being tied down in an office like that." Freida had spoken something she had wanted to say for several years. "Now for some good news!" That perked up Karl needing to change the subject. "When Ronny comes home, I want him to help me buy a car, I'm getting tired of taking the bus to work every day I can afford it so why not." Karl reached over to grasp his mother's and sister's hands knowing they would rest easier with the information he had just given them.

The sun was shining through Karl's bedroom window wispy clouds floating by. Karl put his dressing gown on and walked into the kitchen, Mama was already cooking for the day, the smell of strong coffee filling the air. Karl walked up behind her and put his arms around her waist. Speaking in German he wished her good morning, kissing her cheeks as he did so. "Today's a wonderful day Frau Vita lets you and I have coffee together in the living room shall we." Said Karl feeling comfortable about being home. Ronny was next to enter the living room, wearing a shirt, trousers and in bare feet. "Karl so good to have you home, sorry I did not get to see you last night it was really early morning by the time I arrived home. You can't imagine how worried we have been about you and that patched up eye of yours, how you got it is none of my business, I can only imagine though?"

Remarked a concerned Ronny seating down next to Mama. "Ronny, I have been given an office assignment in charge of a communications department, from now on I will be home more often." In his mind he was thinking my spying days could well be over, well for now anyway. "Ronny, I have a favor to ask I need your help finding a car to buy." Asked Karl. "Glad to help, when do you want to start looking?" Hearing Karl talk like this was a welcomed relief, seeing the strained look on his wife's and mother in law's face each day was hard to live with day after day, then again, they were also worrying about the rest of the family hiding in the mountains somewhere in Italy. Ronny never said much about his own family living and growing up in the North of England. His two older brothers were both in the Navy stationed in Portsmouth, secure in maintenance positions. Both his parents had passed on before the war hard working people that lived long enough to see their three lads grow up with the same work ethic as they had. "Good question Ronny, I'm in no rush until this left eye is better and I can see normally again. I thought over this weekend I could start looking, need to get an idea on how much I need to spend for something decent does that garage on the high street still have used cars for sale, *Quimby's* I believe is their name?" Asked Karl. "The problem right now is used cars are mostly available from people that have lost a loved one in the war. Other people have stored their cars until this war is over, whenever that is. New cars are not being manufactured for private use so that's out. We can start at Quimby's and go from there. Here's the classified from our local newspaper while I'm in the bathroom why don't you start scanning the classified for private sales." Ronny stood up and headed to the kitchen for his second cup of coffee taking it with him to the bathroom. Karl eagerly looked at the limited offering from garages in Baldock and Letchworth finding nothing of interest he started circling cars of interest in the classified. I'm a single chap why am I looking at family cars? He thought, not sure how long I'll be around, so let's look at something sporty that's more my style. He did not have to look too much further, a new listing in Hitchin described a *1935 MG-PB* for sale, reason for sale husband died flying during the Battle of Britain. Will not negotiate price 185.00 pounds. Please call Hitchin 4569. Karl sat back thinking tragic to lose your husband and now faced with having to sell his car. Ronny came back in dressed in casual attire saying. "Find anything of interest?" Karl gave him the paper said. "How about an open MG sports car, perfect for a chap like me, what do you think?" Ronny taking the paper let out a very loud belly laugh, "Karl it is definitely you, God help the ladies at your camp when they see you drive up in a spiffy little gem like that, let's call and find out if we can go and see it this morning." Ronny still laughing went back into the kitchen to get a cup of coffee for Freida who was still sleeping. After bathing and shaving Karl dressed in grey trousers, dark blue vee neck pullover and black socks and shoes. Ronny was already on the telephone getting details. "Got it thank you *Claire*, we should be there in about an hour." Ronny beaming turned to Karl saying, "Lets head to Lloyds and get some money out of your account. We need to move fast though, Claire the owner told me, she has had three calls on the car so far this morning, by the sound of it we are the closest to her, so let's get going." Ronny was moving fast grabbing a light jacket he headed for the front door Karl right behind him. At the front door they both yelled, be back later wish us luck. First stop was at Lloyds Bank where Karl withdrew 220 pounds then driving quickly Ronny headed for Hitchen, Claire's direction said to look for *St Michaels College* on the right then take the very next street on the left which will be *Hemmings Way,* her house number was #46. "Almost there," said Ronny excited to be out looking at cars. Number 46 was a detached home with a single garage at the end of the driveway. The brass door knocker was very unusual it represented a *Hawker Hurricane fighter* in flight. "Poor devil, hope he did not suffer too much." Remarked Ronny as he used the Hurricane to knock three times. The door opened and there was the smiling face of Claire, dressed in a tweed skirt and a sky-blue jumper set, with shiny brown brough shoes, she was what Ronny expected a true fair skinned English rose. "You must be Ronny and you must be his brother-in-law Karl is that correct? Gentlemen, please come in, may I offer you some refreshments before we go out to the garage." Karl with a smile on his face answering. "That's very kind of you but would you mind awfully, if we look at the car first?" Claire reached for the keys hanging on a peg by the front door smiling at seeing the schoolboy smile on Karl's face, it reminded her how her husband looked when they visited the MG dealership in Luton before the war. As Claire unlocked the garage door Karl asked. "Excuse me for asking but haven't you thought about keeping and using the car yourself?" Claire shook her head the tears freely rolling down her face. Karl instantly knew he should not have asked that of a woman that had lost her husband. "Forgive me Claire that was not appropriate I was not thinking straight I should know better." Karl was now feeling angry with himself his mind thinking rapidly how to correct that stupid statement. Claire pulled the two garage doors open and there sat the beautiful low-slung MG-PB in flawless British Racing Green. Standing back her arms crossed across her chest Claire had recovered from her moment of sadness and now was enjoying watching Karl fall in love with his soon to be new car. Claire handed Karl the ignition key saying. "Well why don't you start it up and see how you like it." Claire was thinking Patrick would be pleased to see this knowing his baby would be going to someone that really enjoys this type of sports car. "Can we give it a quick run up and down the road," asked Karl. "Of course, we can, but I will have to go with you alright." Claire was starting to enjoy this transaction very much and riding in the MG again with a man besides her after a very long time was healthy medicine for her frame of mind. Ronny went back out into the driveway backing his Austin into the street, Karl and Claire waiting while he did that. "Karl, forgive me for asking but what is that accent I'm hearing?" Claire was hoping it was not German because if that was the case the deal would be off immediately. "I was wondering how long it would be before you asked me that and quite honestly, I should have brought that to your attention right up front in case you would preferred to slam the door in my face. I'm Austrian from Vienna now serving as a Captain in the British Intelligence Service. Prior to escaping to England in 1936 I was the First Officer on a German registered merchant ship. Would you like me to shut off the engine now and leave?" Karl waited to see Claire's reaction he didn't have to wait long. "You will not Captain your taking me for a drive." Claire was thrilled that whatever apprehensions she had a few minutes ago were gone thinking. This bloke is one of those spy people you hear about, God I'm stupid. "Claire before we leave can we settle up on the bill of sale, you know I'm going to take it don't you, your asking price is extremely fare so what I'd like to do is pay you in full and I'm hoping you will allow me to add another 50.00 pounds for you to donate to the RAF benevolent lost airman's fund. Will this be alright with you? Claire turned to face Karl those tears back in her eyes saying. "Karl you are so thoughtful, but don't you think that's a little too generous." Karl quietly answering her "Your husband gave his life for this country 50.00 pounds is the least I can do." Karl sat motionless watching her. Claire sat pondering then opened the door saying "I have an idea wait here while I get the logbook and the bill of sale. Walking briskly down the driveway Claire approached Ronny's car then leaning into the open window started telling him something. Karl was becoming confused, thinking what is she up to? Claire stepped back waving as Ronny drove off also waving goodbye. Karl was now thinking, alright I'm really mixed up now what just happened? Claire returned after going back into the house. She came back with a scarf in her hand wearing a tweed three quarter length jacket. Opening the door again she slid into the cockpit besides Karl. "Could you tell me what just happened and where is Ronny going?" asked Karl. "Ronny is heading home we will drive there later, then Ronny can take me home later today. Right Captain, I am going to buy you lunch at the *Fox Pub* in the village of *William*." Claire had a strange smile on her face saying that. "Over lunch we can finalize the sale alright." Claire for the first time in a very long time was feeling alive again, she had mourned to long, the last time she saw Patrick he made her promise if he did not make it, that she would not become an old maid, your too young and full of life please don't let that flame die out, live life please promise me that so I can go off to fight knowing I need not worry about you. "Claire, you realize I'm only using one eye right now don't you." Said Karl as he started up the car. "I won't tell anyone if you don't?" Replied Clair. "Turn right then left we will take the back road you will enjoy them more as they are made for a sports car like this." The drive to the Fox was delightful winding country lanes that made them both enjoy the wind blowing through their hair and over their faces, the exhilarating sounds coming from the exhaust pipe made for a perfect day. "Here we are Karl think you will enjoy this haven't been here in a while, let's say far too long." Karl could see in her eyes she was remembering another time when Patrick was driving the little MG. "Shall we eat outside it's such a beautiful day." Claire was coming alive in just a few hours she had transformed herself from a grieving widow to a young lady full of life even though that could change in moment. Over lunch she turned over the logbook and bill of sale to Karl who then gave her an envelope containing the cash. Claire thanked him placing the unopened envelope into her handbag. "Don't you think you should count it first?" asked Karl as he put his paperwork into his inside pocket. Claire simple smiled saying, "I trust you Captain. Now tell me all about yourself excluding the classified parts, looking at that eye patch I'm assuming you will not be able to tell me how you got it, is that correct?" Karl smiled back at her then started from that fateful day in Marseilles, holding nothing back about his dangerous drive across Europe the wonderful ladies he has met and the one that died taking his heart with her. "Claire, I have tried to bury that lost love, the relationship I'm in right now will not go any further that lady is far away right now, I must be man enough to end it when she returns it's really not fair to her trying to put a round peg into a square hole. Believe me I have tried so hard to convince myself I love her but that has been nothing wishful thinking, that ghost is still between us. I'm not sure how to move forward Claire other than becoming a monk maybe." They both laughed at his last statement. Now tell me all about Claire, leaving none of the juicy parts out." Karl felt comfortable with Claire she was not like anyone else he had met before, but there again he had said that before hadn't he! That isn't true a bell sounding loudly in his head. She is so much like Kitty why did I not see that right away. In the back of his mind a quiet voice was saying thank you lord, thank you. "Well, let me see, I have a professional position in a law firm in Hitchen which has been my saving grace through the dark time after Patrick's death. Karl, I have lost a very special man, from what you have told me we have so much in common and I can see Kitty is still very much a part of you. Life sometimes has a way of dashing your chances for a rewarding future and when all looks lost someone else enters your life to change that. I have known you just a few short hours, but I will not lie to you Karl I hope this is the start of a new chapter for both of us. Think I have just overstepped my boundary though, sorry about that." Claire sat eyes fixed on Karl waiting for his response. "Claire I'm lost for words we are definitely thinking along the same lines can't believe we are talking like this, should have thought about buying your MG sooner." Karl's humor was kicking in at just the right time. "How long is your leave for Karl?" asked Claire. "I have to report back on Tuesday so only have three days left, why do you ask?" Karl could feel Claire was about to propose spending time together till then and he was right. "Have you ever toured Cambridge?" Asked Claire as she slowly reached over to take his hand. "Only on work related visits why do you ask?" Answered Karl. "I was just thinking it's been a long time since I have been on a field trip, going on my own is not for me. Going together could be so much fun." Claire was a little nervous asking this stranger to accompany her. "Count me in, you will have to drive though, is that alright with you?" Asked Karl wondering what will come next. "Not a problem, love driving that car but never wanted to do that on my own though." Replied Claire. "Let me get the bill and we can go meet my family, can't believe I went out this morning looking for a car, found one and now driving it home with a brand new, girlfriend." Karl started shaking his head quietly chuckling to himself as he stood up to pay the bill. "I said this was going to be my treat put your money away and that's an order Captain." Karl loved the way she started giving orders, those memories were flooding back only this time there was no clouds to spoil the feeling of happiness. "Claire maybe its best you drive to my mother's she will go through the roof if she sees me driving with this one eye." Remarked Karl as they walked back to the car. "Alright where am I going?" Answered Claire. "Go right and head towards Baldock we will be there in about fifteen minutes." Karl's head was in a spin could it really be true that he found a loving soulmate at a time when he least expected it to happen. Karl with his one eye stared at Claire as she shifted gears. "Claire you are making this such a wonderful day for me even though it scares me somewhat." Claire smiled at him taking her eye off the road momentarily answering him her hand reaching for his. "I feel the same Karl." Turning into the driveway Karl could feel himself tensing up. Claire sensing this reaching over again to take his hand saying, "We are going be fine stop worrying darling." Karl sat there thinking she just called me darling, still can't believe this is going so incredibly fast, but it feels so right, can this really be happening? Karl got out and walked around the car to open Claire's door, by then Ronny, Freida and Mama had come out to see the car. "Wow, will you look at this baby," said Freida running her hand down its side. Mama, Freida let me introduce you to *Claire McGivern* she is the lady I just bought the car from." Karl wanted to say so much more but felt he should not rush this first meeting. "So very nice to make your acquaintance young lady I see you are married." Said Mama looking at her left hand. "Was." Came the cold response from Claire. "My late husband was a pilot in the RAF and gave his life during the Battle of Britain, his parting words before leaving on his last patrol was for me to live life to the fullest and that I have not done till now. Does that answer your question Mrs. Vita?" Claire was a strong woman and Mama loved that. "I did not intend to hit a nerve forgive me if I gave you that impression, welcome to our home I can tell there is a bond already starting between you and my Karl, if it's meant to be, I will be thankful that Karl has found what he has been missing for so long." Karl was still in a strange place his mother and Claire were already comfortable with each other. "Let's go inside and find out more about each other shall we." Said Mama thinking that by accident Karl may just of found his life mate. Ronny approached Karl saying, "That is an incredible women Karl, when she approached me at her house, she simple said, "Ronny, go home I need to spend time with Karl, he will give me directions to your house." Ronny could not believe what had just happened it was like the first time Kitty had visited them. For the next three hours they all shared stories some funny some so very sad. Ronny looking at his watch then said, "Claire I think I should be getting you home." Claire looked at Karl then said in response. "Thank you, Ronny but Karl and I are having a day out in Cambridge tomorrow so maybe the best thing is for him to return home with me, unless any of you object to that? Karl why don't you get some things together for tonight and tomorrow." Claire had taken complete control, and no one had any objection. Karl packed a small bag along with a garment bag then return to the living room where Mama and Claire were sitting on the couch laughing and holding hands. Freida and Ronny sitting on the opposite couch enjoying the small talk that was going on. "Karl let's think about leaving we should put the top up on the car it could be quite chilly driving home in the dark." Karl the calculating Intelligence officer was lost for words, Claire had moved in and stacked her claim. War has a way of making relationships happen that much faster, Karl always had a habit of saying. There may not be a tomorrow!

"Good night Mama we will stop by after we leave Cambridge tomorrow afternoon to see you. That little MG has brought us all together don't worry about

Karl I intend to take care of him and that you can be sure of." Claire hugged Mama then Freida and finally Ronny concluding, "well Ronny it has been an interesting day has it not, never thought when you called me this morning, we would be saying good night like this, I guess you could say fate played a big part in this. I'm so very thankful Ronny you made that call this morning. War is strange it brings people together, so much quicker, don't you think?" Claire slid in behind the wheel Karl getting into the passenger seat still not sure what was happening. "Ready darling won't take too long." Claire still controlling.

Chapter Fourteen
New Beings

Turning into the driveway, Claire asked Karl to open the garage doors for her. Karl was feeling very strange as she led him through the back door into the kitchen. Everything inside was completely tidy nothing out of place. "Would you like a drink before we go to bed asked Claire, realizing Karl had not processed that they would be sleeping together. "Claire this affair is spinning me off my feet I can't believe this is happening so fast and my mother appears to be alright with this, please excuse me but is this really happening?" Karl felt out of his comfort zone with a woman that was still a virtual stranger to him but totally committed to making this a lifetime commitment. "Let's take it nice and easy tonight we need to feel comfortable with each other before becoming intermate don't you agree." Claire knew she had come on fast and strong and decided she needed to take one step at a time. Karl swigged down the whiskey Claire had poured for him then excepting her hand she led him upstairs to her bedroom. Karl undressed putting pajama bottoms on then pulling back the bedcovers laying there, excited at being in bed with a woman that had every intention of being the last love of his life, this thought was still consuming him with anxiety. The bathroom door opened and there was Claire standing in a pink nightdress that simply took Karl breath away. "Darling forgive me if I'm nervous but I have not been with another man since Patrick, I want this to be perfect for both of us I know we are meant to be together so for as long it takes, I want this to work." Claire climbed into bed reaching for Karl's arm pulling it around her. Feeling the warmth of her body Karl responded lifting her head towards his. Their first kiss was so much more than Karl expected it felt so natural, could this be happening just like this? As he kissed her softly surrendering to the beautiful Claire. "Karl tonight I know I will sleep so much better probably for the first time in I can't remember when, hold me tightly until I fall sleep will you?" Claire looking at him again asking, "Am I disappointing you? Were you expecting to make love tonight? As much as I really want to commit to you completely, I can't bring myself to being intimate just yet. Karl it may take a while to reach that point, I am so afraid I could lose you please forgive me. This morning was just another gloomy day for me feeling lost and alone it's being alone that depresses me so. Now here I am not many hours later, lying next to a man that could make my life whole again, is any of this making sense to you Karl." Claire said as she snuggled even closer, maturity could have something to do with this, she thought I hope we can have a life together that is based on love, truth, understanding and lasting devotion to one another's needs?" would Karl be alright with all of this? Right now, I'm feeling I'm risking too much, maybe I'm better off acting out the part of a lover with few feelings for the act itself! While she lay there pondering these thoughts, she was brought back by Karl saying, "Claire, please don't beat yourself up over this, it just may be a better way to start this new relationship? You are nothing like I've ever experienced before. I won't lie to you, I have always had my way with the ladies, but something is changing within me, I find myself embracing a different feeling and one that is changing me completely. Maybe I'm finally growing up and need more than just making love to make it feel real. Claire, take whatever time you need I'm not going anywhere other than back to work on Tuesday. Now there is one thing you must promise me, and I do mean promise?" Karl was about to add a little humor to this otherwise serious conversation. "And what is that darling?" Asked Claire rapping herself around her new love. "Well, I'm sure you did not really give much thought about coming out of the bathroom in that very sheer nightgown with the light shining through it, it has left little to my imagination, that act could of well reverted back to the old Karl Vita." First there was a brief silence, then Claire pulled the bedcovers up to her neck this made them both start laughing, "Oh, I'm so sorry I should have thought about that first. However, one day in the future I will repeat that and you, kind sir will take appropriate action is that clear?" Claire was now becoming comfortable with her new beau, Karl simply laughed still holding her tightly. "Good night handsome." Was the last thing Claire said before falling asleep still holding his arm tightly. Claire, woke up about 7:30 am, rolling over she momentarily panicked patting Karl's side of the bed only to find he was not there. Jumping out of bed she grabbed a bathrobe took a quick look into the other two bedrooms before heading down stair. Stopping at the bottom, her look of fear turning to relief and a big smile. In the kitchen there he was in one of her old housecoats he found in the bathroom. Seating with his feet up on the counter Karl was reading yesterday's newspaper a steaming hot mug of coffee in his hand.

"I could strangle you Karl, you bugger!" Her beaming face gave her away though, you scared the life out of me I rolled over to kiss you good morning only to find you gone. For a moment I thought my frankness last night had made you bolt." Claire saying that thought it feels like we have been together for years, this feel is so right. "I'm sorry dear I am a very light sleeper so about 0500 hrs I found one of your house coats to put on, its way undersized for me so that's why I can't close the front." Said Karl in a very jovial voice. "Wait right there I'll be right back. Claire ran back upstairs returning with a box. "This will work, lover boy. From the box she removed a navy-blue man's bathrobe. "Here try this on." Claire had bought it several years back for her departed husband but never had a chance to give it to him. Karl stood up and tried it on, it fit perfectly, however there was a strange look on his face and Claire recognized a nerve had been hit so what did I do? "Claire are you sure about this." Asked Karl. "Of course, it's yours now and will always be hanging up next to mine in the bathroom. Karl, did I do or say something wrong a few minutes ago that hit a nerve from your past?" Claire wanted no secrets between them ever. "Claire its nothing really, thank you so much for making me feel right at home with this beautiful bathrobe." Karl had a telltale look on his face that gave him away and Claire picked up on it right away. "Karl don't give me that look, I thought we agreed good or bad we would not have secrets between us, now what did I bloody well say or do?" Claire the strong-willed woman would not let this go that easy. "Alright seeing as you will not let this go, Kitty had several pet nick names for me, lover boy was one of those names. There I told you it was no big thing." Karl just wanted to move on. "And what are the other ones so I can be aware of what not to call you," Claire was showing a little anger saying that. "Sailor was the other one now can we move on?" "I like that Karl do you think Kitty would mind if I also called you Sailor as well?" Claire was so much like Kitty in so many ways and Karl could relate to those head strong ways because of that. "You can call me that and anything else you like, but never call me late for a good morning kiss." Karl put his arms around her waist and pulled her into him then bent down to kiss her softly this time she responded by opening her mouth, her tongue met his in an electrifying moment. In Karl's mind he was thinking this beautiful lady when she finally decides the time is right to make love will be amazing, but as my father once told me, everything comes to those who wait, and I am prepared to wait for as long as it takes! "Alright how long do you need to get yourself ready?" asked Karl. "Give me forty minutes or so." Replied Claire. Karl had brought brown trousers a white shirt and a tweed light brown jacket. Brown shoes and a stripped beige tie making for a well-dressed gentleman. Karl walked down the driveway to retrieve the morning paper, the news was bleak to say the least tragedy was a daily occurrence these days. Back in the kitchen Karl made himself another cup of coffee seating down to read more of the paper when Claire entered. "Alright I'm ready how do I look, Sailor?" asked Claire entering the kitchen. Karl suppressed an emotional feeling hearing Claire calling him Sailor but that was quickly becoming a thing of the past. There she stood everything Karl could expect, Claire beaming with life happy in her newly found relationship. "You are truly a classy lady making it harder by the minute to keep my hands off you." Said Karl feeling he would like to take her right there in the kitchen which of course he would not do. Claire dressed comfortably for their day of exploring the ancient city of Cambridge. "We will have that time real soon my darling Karl today I feel wonderful about exploring as a couple it's something I have not done in so long. Summer is going by to quickly the war seems far away don't you think?" Asked Claire her arms around her new beau. "Today the war will not spoil our day, two days from now it will again consume all my available time. Karl in the back of his mind was thinking about all the horrors that had transpired since the start of 1941 and his own near-death experience at the hands of the Gestapo in one of their prison cells, despair had made him contemplate ending his life that morning, thank God, he never followed it through. "Come on we are getting too serious, nothing or no one will spoil our day." Said Claire as she put her jacket on and reaching for her handbag. Karl backed the MG out of the garage then proceeded to raise the convertible top as it would be chilly driving this early in the morning. "Don't forget your driving, where are the side curtains kept?" asked Karl. "Their hanging on a peg at the back of the garage, I'll be right out." Called Claire as she locked the back door to the house. Karl installed the curtains after figuring out how they are attached. Claire slid behind the steering wheel and started the engine. "We need to stop for some petrol, I have been hoarding ration coupons, so we don't have to worry." Called Claire over the sound of the engine.

The drive to Cambridge was enjoyable, Karl thinking with the top and side curtains installed made the cabin feel smaller, it was a sports car after all. Arriving in Cambridge finding a parking place was not a problem they found one on the main square in the center of town. People these days were refraining from using their vehicles conserving precious petrol coupons. "Feel like some tea and toast before we start exploring, don't believe getting eggs will be possible." Said Claire reaching for Karl's arm as they started walking towards the small Café on the square. "Darling this is the way I like it. I have never been a good solo how about you?" Claire was ready to start venturing out again now, she could share special times with her man. Inside the café their both ordered tea and shared a plate of piping hot toast with strawberry jam. Sitting there, drinking tea they took the time to find out more about each other and past loves that had left an impression on each of them. "Karl I am really enjoying hearing all of this, but what I would really

love to hear more about is Kitty, your mother told me I remind her of Kitty." Claire had listened intently to Karl's colorful past and the ladies that had left an impression on him, however she also recognized it was Kitty that took his heart with her to the grave. Karl poured his heart out telling everything right up to two days ago. "Well do you want to leave without me now after hearing all of that," Asked Karl a smirk across his face. "Now young lady I want all the details on your past including the sordid boyfriend parts, I need to feel jealous of them all." Karl was teasing her saying that and Claire loved the way his self-confidence allowed her to tell him everything. "Well, it's by far no way close to your past but here goes. I'm born and bred in Hitchin Hertfordshire so was my parents and sister. I attended a Catholic school also in Hitchen, this my mother insisted on for both her girls. My father was a founding partner, in the law firm of
McGivern, Tilbey & Morrison. I had a relatively sheltered life before going to University then on to law school. Here I met my first boyfriend, Daniel Bell, also studying to be a solicitor. We were together for about four years. He was the one that I lost my virginity to, a very stupid thing to do on my part because I became pregnant. We had talk about getting married however I could tell he would only do that to save face. Two and a half months into that pregnancy I lost the baby. Daniel bolted right after that, emigrating to Australia with another law student, he left me with a broken heart but so much the wiser. After that I dated a few fellows but never anyone I wanted to stay with. In 1937 I went to a dance with two other girlfriends in Bedford there I was swept off my feet by an RAF pilot who turned out incidentally to be my father's partner's son, what a strange coincident. I had not seen Patrick since he went off to the *RAF College at Cramwell.* Patrick and I were married right after I graduated from the Cambridge Law College. We honeymooned in *Looe Cornwell.* Right after that Patrick went off to train on Hurricane fighters and I joined my father's firm as an intern working up to a fully-fledged solicitor, I still work there to this day. There is only one of the partners still alive he retired last year, so right now I'm the senior partner with two junior partners to help me. The families decided to retain the original shingle out of respect for the founders. Our life was wonderful although Patrick only came home on weekends, we both accepted that is how it had to be. My life took a turn for the worst on May 28th 1940, when I received a Telegram from the War Department informing me that Patrick's plane was missing. Two days later two RAF officers came to the house to inform me that his body had been found still wearing his parachute and life vest in the English Channel. After he was given a military funeral, I thought my world had come to an end. My work has been my only

salvation until about a week ago when I open the garage door looked at the MG and decided it was time to sell it, I needed to move on. I had mourned enough and that is not the way Patrick would like me to continue living. Two days ago, I started to live again and it's all because of that little MG. Oh about the house that was my parent's house, my mother continued to live there after father past in April 1939. I moved in to keep her company. Mother only passed away, five months ago, so I bought my sister out, she lives with her husband and children in Oxford, we both agreed we did not want to sell the house we both grew up in. If your, wondering about my surname I kept McGivern for business purposes, adding Patrick's surname of *Bennett* when we married, after he died, I had it reversed now you know. There you have the complete Claire story up to date." Claire ordered another cup of tea then waited for Karl's questions she knew would follow. "Wow! Can't believe I've fallen for a brainchild that's also a solicitor. Claire I also noticed a beautiful upright piano in your living room, who play's that beauty?" Asked Karl. "My mother, my sister and I, love classical music have not been near it in years though." Again, Karl was somewhat surprise how Claire detailed everything. "Well, if we don't get going it will be too late to see the historic sites." Said Claire. Right replied Karl as he stood to pay the bill then helped Claire with her coat before headed out into the town square. The first stop they made was to visit the historic *Trinity Church* to see the famous and amazing pipe organ built and completed by *Metzlerin in 1735*. Karl had seen many such organs in Europe but when they started rehearsing, he just sat there mesmerized by the clarity of those tones coming out of the big pipes. The next stop they made was down by the river, Karl had always wanted to go punting down the *River Cam* after seeing pictures of it before the war. Claire looked at Karl she could see that twinkle in his eye. "You want to go boating, don't you? It warms my heart to watch your facial expressions. Let's go!" Karl bought two tickets, the guide smiled and said, "Not much business lately so I'm going to give you the deluxe tour." Karl stepped into the boat first then turned to help Claire step down into the boat. Karl looked up at Claire as she held his hand stepping down into the boat their eyes locked onto to each other as her skirt slide up her thighs revealing what Karl knew was a vision of times yet to come. Claire shook her head smiling as she realized what Karl was looking at. She sat down thinking it's going to be a long night tonight I know it and I can't wait. Punting down the river the guide gave them an excellent description of buildings and event that shaped English history however these two people were thinking of something more important and their own history yet to come! After the boat ride, they visited the places Claire had spent in her younger years as a student in this magnificent town. Several hours later while walking through the small shops and narrow streets Claire out of the blue said, "Karl what say we head back to see Mama and Frieda before we head home. Tuesday you will be leaving to return to your camp in Slough and I would like some private time with you before you leave. Lieutenant Vita you are not leaving without making love to me even though I told you it would be a while before that happened. Darling can't you see I've fallen completely in love with you!" There she had said it, Claire had surrendered to a decision that was *BEYOND ALL DOUBT*, evaporating any barriers that may remain between them. Those memories of her past life were now locked in a compartment in her mind. Karl the intelligence spy had noticed she was wrestling with mixed feeling all day and now he knew why. Claire had just openly made her intentions perfectly clear she was in love with the stranger from only two days ago, quickly becoming her life companion, could that really happen she continue to think? Karl replied to her distant look, "Of course darling let's head out, it's been a wonderful day so far, from what your, telling me the best is yet to come?" Karl pulled her in close, his arm around her waist as they walked back to the car there was no reasons to say more, they both knew their future starting from this moment on. Driving back Karl suggested they make a stop before seeing the family and return to Claire's house. "If that's what you would like to do Sailor? where is it that you would like to take me." Replied Claire more interested in returning to her home. "Why don't we have a cocktail at the George and Dragon before making that stop to see my mother. Claire, I need you to see and feel the emotional ties that have shackled me each time I have come close to making a commitment to someone. Claire, you can help me close that chapter, will you do this for me because when I leave tomorrow, I want to feel my return will be to you and you alone. The George is where I spent my last Boxing Day Holiday with Kitty. It would mean so much to me knowing you understand that I'm trying to say goodbye and in a strange way I want to feel her approval to the woman that I will share the rest of my life with." Karl saying that realizing he was asking for Claire's help to make that final goodbye to Kitty happen, if their magic had strength it would happen. "Karl, I really don't know what to say you could say I'm speechless. Most girls would probably take offense at such a request, I'm not most girls though, am I? If we are always to be open with each other, then I will do whatever is needed to help you make that closure happen. Don't forget I also am wrestling with my own demons and will lean on you to help me through them as well." Karl we could say we are both physical and emotional wrecks, now let's get that bloody drink I need one about now, might as well order one for Kitty and Patrick as well, if they can't drink them, we can do it for them." They looked at each other a smile of agreement crossing between them that led to laughter, another barrier had just crashed and burnt!

The George had not changed at all the same decor and staff had made time stand still Karl and Claire felt very comfortable in this old-world charm. Claire sat next to him by the big fireplace that was dark without those burning ember's throwing a warm glow in its large opening. Watching and listening to him, she sensed he was living out a vision of that last time he sat here with Kitty, "Darling tell me what you're feeling so I can become part of it as well." Claire was starting to read his expressions very well it must be that professional training that gave her this ability. "These are the very same chairs Kitty and I spent time together when she visited Baldock, the only difference is there is no fire in the fireplace today. You are sitting in the very same armchair she sat in on that last night." A cold chill crossed over Claire's face the more she embraced the feeling the more she felt Kitty's presence. It was if Kitty was sending her a message, he's yours now, love him the same way I did, convince him to let me go, the more she concentrated on that feeling, the more she could feel the strong will and personality of someone she would never meet, not in this lifetime anyway!

"Karl are you ready to let those feeling go or are those demons still with us?" He turned to her then replied with a wicked smile across his face. "If I were sitting here with Hazel or any other lady, I would be throwing a shield around myself and making all kinds of excuses about now, however with you I can honestly say there are no shadows, demons or dark clouds they simply are not there or will they ever be again. Claire back there you came right out and told me you were in love with me after only a couple of days, well my sweet lady when do you want to make that permanent? I have no more skeleton in my closet, for whatever its worth I'm yours. From here on I want us to plan a life together after this inhumane war is finally over." Karl had come full circle the womanizing and running from the truth was over from here on Claire would be his life. The biggest problem he faced now was how and when to confront Hazel when she finally returns to England?

"Karl, you have drifted off someplace let's settle up and stop by to see Mama before heading home, shall we? "Claire, something happened a few minutes back there, it's like you were someplace else, what a beautiful smile you had on your face and your eyes had tears in them, I decided you were making your goodbyes to Patrick, so I left you alone, was that the case?" Asked Karl cautiously, the look on Claire's face said something completely different. "It's alright Karl it's just girl talk." Karl looked around, thinking what girl talk there is no one else here? Claire paid the bill standing up she reached for Karl saying, "Everything is going to be just fine from here on, promise me this when the war is finally over, we will find Kitty's grave in Germany and give her a new headstone with her correct name on it, Lieutenant Kitty Johnson, that's the least we can do, correct?" Karl with tears welling up in his eyes, moisture seeping out below his eye patch felt a sense of relief, had Kitty in this place connected with Claire? If she did, she had never done that with anyone else and yes that includes her friend Hazel. I think Kitty somehow gave Claire her blessing, that would explain this feeling of relief I have right now looking up he only saw sunshine and blue skies that *'Following Storm'* had faded away it was all thanks to this complicated, loving lady in front of him she had made it happen, life is starting to have a real meaning for me now. There, were no need for words as they walked arm in arm back to the car. "Claire, what do you think about my surname do you like the way it sounds?" Asked Karl setting Claire up for the next question. "Yes, it's a fine name, why do you ask?" Claire started to tense up she was a trained professional that knew the power of suggested words! "Then you will have no trouble with having your surname changed from Claire McGivern to Claire Vita will you. Stopping in the middle of Church Street Karl reach for her hand. "Claire, will you consent to becoming my wife?" In his mind saying that he was also thinking this will be the last time I'll ever say this. "Karl I was praying and willing you to propose, yes I'm going to love being Mrs. Karl Vita, do you believe in love at first sight well I do because when I first laid eyes on you a strange feeling inside me told me, one day he will become your husband and here we are standing on Church Street making that very commitment, kiss me you crazy Austrian." Claire was changing her life away from all the sadness she had been living through. Karl with a frown on his face was thinking, why does everyone keep calling me a crazy Austrian, maybe I am. When we reach the bungalow, I must ask Mama privately if she will consent to me giving her ring to Claire at least she is not a field agent in the Intelligence Service that's a blessing and she lives and works close by will be a comfort to my Mother.

Claire was floating on a cloud her life from this moment on would become full of joy excluding those times when Karl would be called upon to undertake another mission disappearing for extended periods of time that would always be hanging over them. "Let's head back to the car shall we, said Karl. "I'm still in a state of shock I don't know what to say I'm lost for words you have made me a very happy woman. I still can't believe all this is happening to me, war is hell but at times like this it makes things move that much faster." Claire from now on would enjoy life waiting patiently for each weekend to reunite with her fiancée. Their next stop was back at the bungalow, Mama and Frieda where thrilled to hear about their announcement, maybe a little scared as well that something could happen to Karl, breaking yet another heart. At least this time Claire would not be going off to war like Kitty did.

After the congratulations Mama guided Claire to the couch saying. "He's a good boy so much like his father. I knew instinctively when we met that you were the one, so my new daughter when will we see you next? Living so close will be nice, we can see each other whenever you can make time." "Mama how about you and Frieda joining me for lunch at the George and Dragon this Thursday I'll pick you up at about 11:30am how does that sound." Karl came back into the living room with his luggage, "Here I go again see you next weekend don't believe I'll have a problem getting a weekend pass. Goodbye you two, love you both and give little Franchot a big hug when he wakes up. Mama was thrilled as she listened to Karl, her instincts were correct he would marry this charming lady. In her mind she thought, time does not play a part in how long it takes, falling in love does not happen with a clock it happens with feelings and chemistry. Earlier Mama had told Karl she would collect her engagement ring from his safety deposit box at the bank so when he arrived home the following weekend, they could all join in as Karl slide the ring onto Claire's finger. "Time to leave are you ready Claire," asked Karl as he pushed his case into the small space behind the front seats. "Thank God I'm traveling light. Goodbye will call you tomorrow from Slough, I have lots to do so be patient it may be later. Claire will be calling you anyway love you both." Said Karl. Claire backed the MG out of the driveway turning right onto the Letchworth Rd, as they drove back Claire looked over at Karl asking, "Guess you could say we've had a very full day, what shall we do about supper tonight are you very hungry darling?" asked Claire, Karl smiled answering back, "Fish and chips will do me fine, have other ideas about dessert though!" said Karl changing the subject. Hearing his last remark Claire simply smiled thinking, I know what's coming, life will always be interesting that's for sure being married to Karl when that happens? "Claire, will you help me medicate my eye I completely forgot to do that this morning my doctor will be giving me hell when I get back to Slough." Karl enjoyed being the passenger something he rarely did. "Karl what were you and your mother talking about back at the bungalow." Asked Claire sensing there was something afoot, stop acting like a solicitor he is allowed some privacy with his mother is he not, Claire was scolding herself thinking like that. They parked the car in front of the fish and chip shop, "Do you want to eat it here or take it home with us." Asked Claire. "I think we should eat here then head home for that dessert, how does that sound." Replied Karl getting an immediate response. "Karl, I got a feeling you are going to be a hand full, now behave yourself." They sat around the corner in a dimly lit booth side by side. Before digging into eat, Karl turned towards Claire teasing her by saying, "Did I tell you dessert comes first?" "What on earth are you talking about Karl, you are making no sense saying silly statements like that?" Claire a little nervous could tell from the look on his face the gears in his head were scheming something mischievous. "Karl your up to something and making me nervous doing it." Claire was becoming unhinged as she felt his one good eye burning through her. "Close your eyes for me Claire just for a minute, don't say a word just relax and take the feeling in, you are in my hands and you are very safe. Claire complied trying very hard to control her breathing. She felt a slow soft touch on her skirt, she remained very still even though she wanted to react to the sensation. Slowly with deliberate control Karl slide his hand under that skirt and moved with skill up her thigh. "Karl please, we are in a fish and chip shop and I work in this town now behave." As Claire was speaking her voice had a quiver to it. Karl looked into her eyes with a soft smile that calmed her fears. Continuing the movement up her thigh, this time Claire was surrendering to this inappropriate behavior and just like that all her fear and inhibitions faded as she closed her eyes again waiting for that touch from a man's hand she had not felt in so long. Karl looked around to make sure there was no one close by, the coast was clear, Karl continued to slide his hand slowly and deliberately to the top of her thigh then without stopping under her panties feeling her very wet and swollen, she is more than ready, he thought. With very light slow movement Karl massaged her till he felt her tense her thighs and putting her hand over her mouth suppressing any sound she could make as she experienced her first orgasm from her dashing beau. Karl held her softly as she trembled in his arms followed by warm tears as her tension melted away, loving every touch Karl made "God Karl you could of, warned me of your intent to explode my senses." Claire was recovering pulling her skirt down again and straightening her hair. "I did give you warning about dessert did I not?" Replied Karl. "Well, if you wanted to shock me you have succeeded. "Now let's eat up and head home shall we, I'm famished because of your shenanigans." Said Claire her face gave her away she was totally in love and feeling good about it. Karl was thinking how he liked finding the old mischievous fellow he had once been. Sweet Claire was that catalysis in making him feel like that again. "What time is your train tomorrow morning darling." Asked Claire as they walked back to the car. "I'm catching the 1130hrs train into Kings Cross then on to Slough from Paddington. Once I arrive, I will phone for a staff car to pick me up." Replied Karl a part of him already returning to the Intelligence Officer he would return to on Tuesday. "Darling we need to make a quick car change at my office its close by so won't take long." Said Claire as she drove the MG towards her office building on *Bandcroft Street*. "Car change? We're not going home in this car?" Asked Karl. "No darling I only brought the MG over after Ronny called me Saturday, I drove my Wolsey to the office garage to make the exchange. The MG is going back into storage till its new owner, drives it out maybe next weekend there again it may be when he has two eyes to drive with." You never told me you owned another car, Claire?" Well Karl it was my Mother's car, I just kept it because it's a roomy four door saloon so practical in my line of business. The MG is a fun car but not for everyday use, you can image pulling up in front of the courthouse in a car that low can be very embarrassing with all those Barristers gawking up my skirt when I go to get out. You took a few pictures of your own over the last several days, didn't you? You must think I didn't notice. There again how could you be sure it wasn't deliberate on my part? Here we are. I'll back out the Wolsey and you drive the MG in we must baby her she is what brought us together always remember that." Karl walked around getting behind the steering wheel backing the MG out of the way of Claire as she maneuvered the Wolsey around him, Karl thinking it's in great shape she is right it does look very business-like though, Karl turned the MG around backing it into the garage, retrieved his luggage from behind the front seats he closed and locked the garage doors giving the key to Claire. "Ready Sailor lets go home we have already had dessert, by the look on your face that's not really true is that correct?" Claire was playing with him thinking we have so much to learn about each other. I'm pretty certain though, Karl likes his sport of teasing and turning me into a babbling wreck, going to love being married to him, full of surprises she though. Turning into the driveway Karl took his garment bag and the small case as Claire put the Wolsey into the garage. In the kitchen Claire made coffee as they sat at the table Claire asked, "Karl when I take your Mother out on Thursday do you want me to bring your clothes and other things back here afterwards?" Claire thinking might as well get him use to calling this home. "Karl is there anything else I should be doing for you during the week. Those clothes you have been wearing I'll have them cleaned before you return home." Claire was making conversation to cover her nervousness thinking about the bedroom and having to see Karl off tomorrow morning. The thought of being alone again was not so bad he would be returning on Friday evening, so she had a lot to look forward to. "Why don't we retire to bed it's going to be a strenuously long day tomorrow." Karl could see she was feeling a little uncomfortable, why he could not understand maybe it was just sexual jitters. "Don't forget darling we have to medicate your eye before we go to bed, or you will be in trouble with the Doc. Karl had a quick bath then climbed into bed waiting for Claire to join him. What seemed like a very long time the bathroom door opened and out came Claire in that same pink night gown. In the doorway she stood teasing Karl with the way she postured herself against the door frame. "Claire you are deliberately trying to arouse me if you are well its working extremely well." Claire pulled back the bed sheet and slide into bed cuddling up to Karl, she wanted him with every ounce of her being, but that nervousness still gripped her, and Karl could feel it. "Claire, we have all the time in the world, relax we can take it slowly." Karl wanted her to need him but only when she was ready. "I'm alright Karl just a little nervous at being with you tonight." Claire reached over taking his cheek in her hand as her mouth found his tongue Karl reacting to the sensation, slowly he traced the shape of her body going over her breast he placed his index finger on her nipple making slow circles feeling them becoming erect to his touch. Claire reacting, becoming aroused to this touch. Moving down further his hand barely making contact, with the silk material of her nightgown. Claire arched her back for more, "Karl let me remove my nightgown, please don't stop it feels so wonderful and right now I want you inside me." Claire was finally ready to be intimate with her man. She moved her hand down circling Karl's erect penis stroking it, then with slow deliberate movements she moved her hand up and down taking delight in hearing him quietly moaning. Karl kissed her again moving over her, parting her legs as he did so. Slowly at first then deeper with each stroke he made love to her maintaining a steady rhythm till he felt her body going into an intense orgasm, this excited him to also climax with her. Laying on top of her without moving Claire slowly stroking his back until she said. "Darling we made it didn't we? I feel so relived and a little silly about being so nervous making love to you. It was beyond my expectation, from now on Sailor you will be on notice to perform as soon as you come through that door at the end of the week. God, I love you Karl let's have a repeat performance shall we. Their love making became more intense, more comfortable as they tumbled deeper into their love making. Spent they embraced each other closely as they drifted towards sleeping.

The alarm clock went off at 7:00 am waking Claire immediately, reaching over she felt the emptiness on the opposite side of the bed. That bugger she thought gets up so early guess I will have to adjust my sleeping habits from here on? She got up and made the bed thinking I should be washing the sheets, but not today. When I go to bed tonight alone, I want to smell his presence, I'll do that washing tomorrow. She put on her bathrobe and headed downstair expecting to see Karl in his new bathrobe. There at the kitchen table what she saw was the figure of a British Intelligence Officer in a very striking military uniform, drinking coffee and reading the morning paper. "Morning Claire I have a bad habit of rising early, sorry I tried to remain really quiet allowing you to continue sleeping, you looked so peaceful and so beautiful just lying there. Nearly changed my mind by ravaging you before you woke up." Karl was all smiles, a happy soldier in a new relationship. Claire answered him by saying, "Wishing you would of." My God Karl this is the first time I've seen you in uniform, you are gorgeous, I could devour you, right on that table." Claire was taking in the transformation of her man, sad at his leaving but so happy he would be returning Friday evening. As for her week, well it would start by announcing to her partners and employees that yesterday she had gotten engaged and consented to becoming Mrs. Karl Vita the date to be announced. "Darling I'm going upstairs to get ready, then we can have breakfast together before I take you to the station alright." Claire wanted Karl to have a hearty English breakfast, she knew eating would be the furthest thing from his mind once he boarded that train back to Slough, she was also thinking I've been down this road before. Karl was still reading an account of the German battleship *Bismark* sunk sinking in *Denmark Straights* earlier that year on May 26 and 27 approximately 350 miles west of *Brest, France.* Although it was a decisive action for the Royal Navy, there was sadness seeing another ship and its brave crew succumb to its wounds, ablaze and sinking by the stern. This action was not one sided, it cost the Royal Navy, the lost and pride of its Navy, the Battleship proudly known as the *Mighty Hood.* Several direct hits to her forward ammunition locker created a massive explosion breaking her in two, sending her to the bottom in less than 3 minutes. All but 3 of the 1,415 crew members went down with the ship. At her commissioning May15[th]1920 she was the largest battleship in the world. Karl briefly thought about the sailors on that vessel that would forever remain young at the bottom of the Denmark Straights. The article was questioning if these gigantic ships were quickly becoming Dinosaurs and ineffective as well as very costly to operate in a modern war where aircraft and the new aircraft carriers were becoming the new capital ships. Karl reading this remembered a report he wrote back in 1937 about this very topic after a covert mission into Germany to assess their ship building program. He also thought back to when he and Ronny had met three young sailors from the Hood having a pint in the Red Lion in Baldock, nice lads that had their future lives stolen from them in less an a few minutes by those shells fired from the Bismarck! He closed the paper when he heard Claire coming down the stairs very quickly. "Well let's have that breakfast said Claire all business like. "Wait one minute lady let me take a real hard look at this solicitor in front of me. What a transformation my goodness Claire you are such a classy lady in that business attire." Claire had changed into a bottle green suite and matching high heeled shoes a single strand of pearls tastefully adorned her neck. That beautiful auburn hair now tied back into a bun completed the look. "That's right we have never seen each other in business attire, we look good together, Sailor. Before we have breakfast can I please take a few photographs of you Karl I really would like a few for here and my desk. Oh, and here is a relatively recent one for your desk, make sure it's in a position that all those women around you can see it. The framed picture had a message diagonally across the right side it read. *To my loving Karl. Hurry home to your fiancé that loves you so very much, Love always, Claire.* The picture was taken sitting behind the wheel of their MG-PB. "Claire this really is beautiful it's almost like you are saying I'm waiting for you." Claire took her camera out from the sideboard draw then pushing Karl to the right place said, "Big smile Sailor this one is for me to brag about once its printed and framed and prominently displayed on my office desk, you can sign it when you return Friday." Karl was enjoying the high spirited Claire, then he remembered he had a print taken several weeks ago at the camp, I had brought it with me to give to Mama. Claire, wait one minute, can you find an 8"x 10" picture frame? Asked Karl as he ran upstairs to retrieve his case. Claire thinking don't tell me he has pictures stashed away in his case, there again you never know with Karl, do you? Karl came back down the stair two at a time beaming a big smile, "Just remembered I have had this picture inside by case for weeks to give to Mama completely forgot to give it to her so don't tell her I gave it to you when you see her on Thursday. We can give her one of the pictures you just took to give to her next weekend." Said Karl as he handed over the photograph. "My you look good with that wonderful smile of yours even that devilish look is there, perfect now take my pen and write something really nice for me, don't you write something saucy Karl." Claire didn't really care what he wrote so long as it said Love on it. Karl thought for a moment then wrote across the bottom. *To Claire The Lady that stole my heart and turned my dark clouds into sunshine, Love always, Karl.* "Now where is that picture frame?" Asked Karl not letting Claire see it until the picture was mounted into the frame. "Now you can look at it," said Karl proud as a peacock. Claire eager to see the final product snapped up the frame then read what Karl had wrote. Karl stood waiting for her to react, she just stood there then brushing the tears from her eyes she finally said. "Karl my sweet loving sensitive man, what did I do right to find you, I have been praying so long for this and now here I am with a man that is so much more than I hoped for. Karl you alone will always be the keeper of my heart, thank you darling. "Over breakfast they talked about all the things they should be doing and planning for in the next few months. "Tomorrow I will have the logbook for the MG changed as well as having my secretary notarized the bill of sale, sounds kind of silly really because the car will still be here." Said Claire making a to do list. Time was marching on and so was Karl's final few hours, he was far from ready to face the music on his return to the camp. "Claire before we leave, I need you to apply my medication in my eye, I'm going to catch hell if the doc sees it dried up in the corners like this." Karl flipped his leather patch up away from the bright sunshine coming through the window. "When do you have to return to London to see the surgeon?" asked Claire. "Not sure think it's the beginning of the following week?" replied Karl why do you ask. "Because St Luke's Hospital is only about fifty minutes from here if you can use that slick tongue of yours to convince your superiors to change the appointment to a Monday, I can drive you up there for that appointment then you can arrange for a car to return you to Slough, how about that for a plan." Said Claire pleased that it could buy her more time with Karl. "I've got a better plan that you may like. You drive down to Slough and stay overnight, this way I can show you off to everyone in my department, later we can have dinner with my Commanding Officer and his wife and other members of the general staff that are also my friends. Claire, they will love you shall I mention that to Clive later today?" Karl always the planner was also thinking if everyone finds out that my fiancé is visiting it will stop any further advances from women like Susan and a few other. The biggest problem is how to handle Hazel when she returns not to excited about that meeting, he thought. One thing is for certain someone up there is giving me another chance and from now on unless its concerning Claire I'm not interested. Claire responding by saying, "That could work also, I would really enjoy meeting some other spy people from Slough and get to meet some of those young ladies in uniform that think fishing is a big sport." Claire took his hand brushing it against her cheek with tears welling up in her eyes, she quietly said. "Time for us to head out to the station, now check your wallet again to make sure you have this telephone number and my private one at the office. Darling please call me at home once you are back in the camp." Claire was putting on a brave face, well until his train has departed. Claire drove to the train station all of six minutes away, parking the car she got out and waited for Karl as he took his small case from the back seat. "Here we are, time for us to part my darling, have a good week and don't forget to put that picture on your desk. Will call you once I'm back, I don't think it will be the same from here on. Before it was all about hitting back at the enemy nothing else other than getting drunk and womanizing away the empty moments. I will do my job and anything else the BIS requires of me but know this, my sweet, beautiful Claire, my heart will remain here with you." Karl could feel those emotional words were bringing home that empty feeling, he was saying goodbye with the comfort of knowing she would be going to work far away from the horrors of the war he was forced to deal with, she would remain safe till he returned to her. Claire was holding this moment back as they walked hand in hand to the ticket counter. "One return ticket to Slough please. Is it on time today?" asked Karl. The conductor punched out the ticket clipping the Victory Station stop saying. "Should be arriving in about five or six minutes Gov just time for one more smooch." They walked up to the platform buying just a few more minutes. Claire had both her arms around Karl's left arm her head resting against his shoulder, they didn't say much all of that was done earlier. Off in the distance they could hear the train approaching, a large column of smoke trailing behind it. "Claire why don't you leave there's no sense getting yourself upset for only a few more minutes." Karl was feeling the tension of separation. Claire looked up at him with a smirk on her face, "Not a chance Sailor, I'm standing right here till that bloody train is no more than a distant smoke stream." That remark broke the tension by this toughie standing next to him. Karl with only a minute or two left turned to her his strong arms around her kissing her tenderly till the train pulled into the station. Karl separated himself from Claire then said loudly for all to hear. "Claire, I love you, miss me till next Friday." With that he moved quickly to the first open compartment. Placing his case on the overhead rack he returned to the compartment door lowering the glass window using the leather strap that held it closed. Leaning out Claire rushed over to grab his hand kissing the back of it with tears flowing from her checks she yelled. "Karl please be extra careful, no more dangerous assignments please now I've found you, please do that for me or I'll ring Churchill's bloody neck." Claire walking along side as the train slowly pulled away from the platform finally releasing Karl's hand. His last sight was seeing her standing and waving on the platform. As her image got smaller, he yelled on impulse. "Mrs. Vita, I love you." Claire watched till the train was no more than a small image with smoke marking its location. "I love you to Sailor." She said under her breath. Claire returning to her car, inside she took a moment to regain her composure, fixing her hair and makeup, satisfied with the results she started the car putting it into gear then headed down the driveway towards Bandcroft Street and her office.

Within minutes she was parking the car in the company's courtyard. Claire stopped at the entrance thinking I should make an announcement right away its better that way. She opened the door and walked into the busy office. Inside people were already at work and genuinely happy to see their boss. "Good morning everyone nice to see you smiling faces." Claire entered her office and immediately took Karl picture from her briefcase. She stood there reading what Karl had written only a few hours ago then lifted the picture to her lips thinking I love you, Karl. Beverly her secretary entered carrying a mug of hot tea for her. "Have a nice extended weekend, did you manage to sell the MG on Saturday? Asked Beverly. "Yes, I did, for a much better deal than you could ever imagine, have a seat and let me tell you what has just happened because of that MG. Over the next twenty minutes or so Claire gave Beverly a condensed version of what transpired right up to one hour ago when she saw Karl off. "Is that a picture of your young man Claire, may I take a look?" Asked Beverly. "Yes, it is, isn't he handsome?" Claire was smiling as her secretary continued to stare at the picture. Claire you are going to make an announcement, I'll cover the switchboard while you do so. You owe it to all of us, they will all be elated knowing the grief you have been carrying for so long is behind you. I'm so happy for you and what an amazing story to tell your kids when you start a family that is. Beverly went out into the main office and in a commanding voice said. "May I have your attention please! Claire has an announcement she wishes to share with everyone. I will cover the switchboard during this announcement." Beverly walked off to the switchboard "Thank you Bev, Yesterday I became engaged to Captain Karl Vita an Austrian in the British Intelligence Service. I know what you must be thinking how come I didn't mention this last week or even before that? Well before Saturday I did not know Karl, in fact I only met him when he came to look at my MG, you know the car I keep in the garage, Claire making light of selling the MG. There is a long story attached to this but now we have work to do, thank you for your attention." The buzz in the office after hearing this news was amazing with everyone crowding around her to give their congratulations and best wishes for a long and happy future. Returning to her office she dived into her workload sipping her tea waiting for the two junior partners to join her.

Arriving at Kings Cross station, Karl made his way to the underground that would take him to Paddington station and from there the train back to Slough. Sitting by the window he watched the city streets fly by thinking, I will have to confront Clive first thing, then my staff. This is going to be very interesting. Clive's first reaction will be, here we go again. It's going to be difficult to convince everybody this is really happening. Back in 1936 Gunther had warned me, you alone must correct the mess you have created with your lady friends and now it's happening again, think I cried wolf to many times. The train started to slow down as it approached the station, Karl reached up to remove his case from overhead rack then waited by the carriage door. Outside the station Karl decided the bus would take too long so he elected to splurge by taking a taxi instead. Paying the taxi driver, he presented his ID to the guard, "Good morning Sir you are clear to pass. Approaching the steps that led up to the entrance Karl smiled thinking it doesn't seem that long ago that these steps would be a big challenge to me, taking them now two at a time was proof that his leg was almost completely recovered. "Good morning Captain Vita did you have an enjoyable extended weekend?" Said *Janis* as she spun the registry around for him to sign in. "Very much so corporal you could say it's probably one I will always remember." Replied Karl as he headed down the hall towards his department. Stopping before making an entrance he took a deep breath thinking, well here I go, think I'll wait till later to announce the engagement, I'm pretty sure I already know what the answer will be, here he goes again. I have developed somewhat of a reputation around here. Entering the office, he made himself heard by saying "Good morning all, nice to see your smiling faces. John, have you put the communication pouch on my desk yet?" Sally, where is Peggy this morning? Have you seen her yet?" Karl was firing question to the staff covering up his apprehension to making the bomb shell announcement about the engagement. "She is with Major Knight at a meeting till 1100 hrs Sir." Replied Sally. Looks like Clive acted on his offer to move her into operation analysis, good for you Peggy he thought, will miss having you working for me I will keep that promise to not stand in your way. "Sally please could you get me a big mug of strong coffee." Asked Karl. Walking around to the opposite side of his desk he sat down removing Claire's picture from his case placing it at an angle facing him running his finger over the caption at the bottom. Time to go to work was his next thought as he removed the communication files noticing on the routing sheet Clive had already signed each one that he had reviewed. You can always rely on Clive to stay on top of things like this he thought proceeding to the Delta-1 file first. Sally entered placing the steaming mug of coffee on the desk mat, from the corner of her eye she noticed the new picture on the desk, "I say is that a new picture and what a striking lady at the wheel of that sports car." Yes Sally, that's the MG-PB I just purchased Saturday pretty snazzy don't you think?" Said Karl hoping her next question would open the door to who is the lady? "As for the lady well, she is the lady I bought it from and as of yesterday is now my fiancé." Karl did not elaborate expecting additional questions to come and they did. "Is this someone you have known a while sir?" Sally was discreetly reading the caption at the bottom of the picture. Karl the Intelligence Officer was keeping his eye on her as she did so. "No Sally, I never laid eyes on her before last Saturday morning. "Cor blimey sir! Talk about a whirlwind romance you only get to see these in the moving pictures and here in our office we have one going on right in front of us. Sir do you mind if I share this with the other girls you know this sort of thing gets everyone excited and feeling good. Congratulations Captain Vita! She is a very lucky girl." Sally was enjoying this. "Why don't you gather everyone together and I will make an announcement." That's a good way of making this announcement I suppose smiled Karl. Sally in a loud voice said, "Ladies and gents can I get your attention for a minute Captain Vita would like to make an announcement please gather around." "Thank you Sally for that. I had planned on making this announcement later today, but this is as good a time as any to tell you all about my extended weekend, as of yesterday I became engaged to a wonderful lady from Hitchin. When I left here last week, I had no prior knowledge of Claire McGivern in fact all I was going to do was buy a sport car which I did and got the owner to boot. My reputation has never been that lilywhite, but I can assure you from now on you will see a big difference in how I conduct myself, sometimes events like this happen, I am fortune enough that it happened to me. Claire more than likely will pay us a visit within the next few weeks. I told her what a great bunch of people I work with, thank you for your attention." Karl saying that felt a sense of relief. Like a cannon going off one of the girls yelled, "Three cheers for our Captain Vita." Their loud applause could be heard all the way down the hall. Captain Lowes came out of his office halfway down the hall swearing, "What the bloody hell is all that hullabaloo about this is not a public house, I'm on the bloody telephone with the war department I can only imagine what they are thinking. Mary, hold down the fort I'll be right back." Bill was fuming as he hobbled down towards the communication center. Entering he said in an angry tone, "Who the hell is responsible for this outbreak." Standing with his hand on his hips came a reply. "I am," said Karl as he approached his friend, "Karl, for God's sake control your staff will you, I was on the telephone with the bloody war department what do you think old *Campbell* was thinking hearing that hullabaloo in the background." Bill was cooling off now he knew it was Karl that they were cheering for. "Bill got a few minutes to spare there is something and someone I need to share with you." Karl guided Bill into his office then closed the door behind them saying. "Sally, hold all calls for a while unless you get a call from Claire McGivern or maybe the bloody Prime Minister." Said Karl also adding a little sarcasm to that request. Inside Bill sat down and immediately shifted his gaze to the picture prominently positioned on the desk. Karl sat quietly while Bill read the caption. "Karl don't tell me you have another one. What happened to Hazel or is she last year's flavor, God I can't keep up with your romances. Is that what the noise was all about? Now you have my undivided attention why don't you tell me all about this one, I think there is still some room left on your page for one more." Bills, sarcasm was coming through. Over the next forty minutes Karl told the story to his now tentative friend who sat there listening and occasionally shaking his head. "Well, Bill there you have it. I hope I can rely on your support you have always been a trusted friend and over the next few months I will call on that friendship." Said Karl as he stood up to walk Bill out into the office. Everyone was hard at work keeping their heads down in case Captain Lowes exploded again. At the door Bill turned around and said calmly, "Sorry for the outbreak do me favor next time wait till after hours then invite me, I can make more noise than all of you put together." Bill left returning to his own office saying, "See you at six Captain Vita usual table at the lounge." Karl returned to his office and the stack of paperwork still to be reviewed. The communication from Delta-1 indicated by eliminating the mole appeared to have cured the problem of the Germans being one step behind them. They would remain in the present safe house for maybe the next several months.

Before heading down to the lounge Karl picked up the telephone getting an outside line then dialing Hitchin 4567 the phone at the other end ringing four or five times before hearing the sweet sound of her voice, "Hitchin 4567." Claire's heart skipped a beat it was Karl. "Claire my gorgeous woman, do you miss me as much as I miss you?" asked Karl. Claire's tone suddenly changed to that of a woman totally in love replying, "Do I ever, how's it going getting a lot of flak over that picture on your desk. My bunch are over the top with excitement promised to have them all over the house very soon. Mary told me if I throw you away can she please have you." Claire was laughing saying this. "My situation is a lot more difficult old habits and past girl friends are making it difficult, guess you could call it pay back. My friend, Captain Bill Lowes, is an understanding sort but still a little skeptical. Major Clive Knight, you know the one I told you about will join Bill and I in the officer's lounge after I hang up with you. These two are like brothers to me, they are the ones that met me on the ship when I first arrived in England, we have been close friends ever since. I was thinking on the train about asking Bill to be my best man when that time comes. Darling, are you still having lunch with Mama and Freida on Thursday hope you have a nice time with them this will be a real treat as they are stuck in that house way too much." Asked Karl feeling saddened being apart from Claire in his mind he was already thinking I'm a field agent, I can't put Claire through another lose if I fall in action, this feeling will hang over me till this bloody war comes to an end. "Well darling have a nice evening will call you tomorrow with an update on how it goes tonight, love you sweetheart, bye for now." Claire could sense that Karl was struggling so she simple closed by saying. "No matter what happens, what obstacles we may have to face darling, we will lean on each other and face those times together I think our love can weather any storm even the one that constantly follows you around, good night darling remember you have a lady that loves you so very much." With that she hung up the phone headed upstairs to that empty bed.

Karl entered the lounge looking around he saw Bill and Clive at their favorite table. "Karl, you're the bad boy so beers are on you." said Clive. Karl waved off the sarcastic remark bringing back three mugs of beer then sat down next to Clive slapping him on the back. "So, what's this Bill is telling me you are on to another lady? Tell me that's not so." Clive was clearing the way for Karl to tell him about this new Lady. Over the next hour Karl told Clive all about buying the MG and how Claire had entered his life because of that car. The uncanny likeness she had to Kitty. How his mother and sister took to Claire immediately. "Clive, I know you think I'm a complete lunatic when it comes to relationships but think back to another time not so long ago, when I was totally committed to marrying Kitty and would have been the model husband, but we all know that was dashed by her sudden death. Since then, I have been on so many dates even went as far trying to make a go of it with Hazel, Clive I would run from any relationship and nearly did before Hazel left on that mission. Claire is the woman I want to share my life with no more trying to make it fit. This war is far from over, Claire and I are willing to take the chance that I make it through to the end. The commitment I made to the BIS will never change you can bank on that. Do I have your support? When you meet Claire, you will understand." Karl had said his peace, in silence they drank their beers. "Alright you say she is meeting you here a week today and staying the weekend before driving you to your eye appointment on the following Monday correct, well then let's plan on a special evening at the *Charter Arm in Slough*. You know *Julie* has not seen you in over eight months, I will tell her to arrange for a babysitter for the girls, should not be a problem. Bill that Monday all right with you?" Clive saying that changed it to an order. "One week from this Saturday you and Dorothy will be our guest to celebrate Karl and Claire's engagement, that my friend is a direct order." Clive had a way with him when it came to an event like this. "You want this to be your treat that's not right don't you think we should split the bill?" replied Bill. "OK you can buy the cocktails and wine! Gentlemen we have a dinner plan, now let's talk shop shall we. Karl has Bill shared with you that I intend to recall the Delta-1 team next month? they are overdue for some rest and recuperation. You will need to have your story straight about how you are going to handle the Hazel situation it's not going to be easy she is expecting you to greet her with open arms. The team on arriving back will be debrief at the *Hammersley Barracks* in Aldershot before returning back here." Clive was rattled by the messy Hazel affair but something inside him was willing to stand by Karl, once again hopefully this would be the last time.

Before returning to his flat Karl made another stop to his office to check the incoming wires for that evening seeing nothing of interest, he headed out catching the #5 bus back to his flat. The week was going by so very quickly Karl was buried in paperwork which he hated more with each passing day, but he did promise Clive to run this department efficiently and that he would do. Sally entered his office happily announcing, "Your fiancée is holding on line two sir." Karl thanked Sally, marking the page he was reviewing. "Claire so nice to get a midday call from you is everything alright?" He asked. "Yes, and no? I'm sitting here with Mama and Frieda about to leave for the George and Dragon, we want to know did you put your eye drops in this morning don't lie to me Karl you forgot again didn't you?" In the background he could hear Mama and Frieda laughing enjoying how Claire pushed him around just like an old married couple. "When I hang up you will go and put them in, the doctor warned you what could happen if you kept forgetting, did he not? Oh, did you confirm if the eye appointment is this coming Monday or is it the following week? Don't forget to confirm it's a Monday." Claire said laughing. "I have already confirmed that it's going to be a week Monday." Answered Karl glad she had jogged his memory. "In that case before you leave tomorrow call me, so I know what time to pick you up at the Hitchin station. On Saturday I told Mama we would be over in the afternoon she is going to give me my first Austrian cooking lesson, really looking forward to that, she also mentioned you are also a pretty good cook yourself, my man of many talents. Well, we're off to lunch hurry home to me darling this lady is missing her man, love you." Claire hung up the phone, Karl on the other hand was processing some ideas in his mind still on the telephone without realizing the line at the other end had gone dead.

His little flat had been his sanctuary away from everyone and at times everything. As much as I have enjoyed that flat it really doesn't make sense keeping it up anymore, think I will check with housing about availability in the new wing of the officer's quarters sometime next week. Apart from that when I work late it's a pain getting home and even worse when it's raining. So much for buying a car to eliminate doing that, thinking this he smiled laughing on the inside. Picking up several files he headed down the hall to Clive's office. "Major, I have the files I need to review with you, think we need to make a decision on how to handle those German submarine blokes before they are carted off to a POW camp. Over lunch let me map out a plan of action for you." The files Karl was carrying pertained to recently captured German naval officers being held in *Bedford* for interrogation. The more Karl examined the files the more he felt they could have valuable information about the submarine pens that nearly cost him his life not that long ago. The German Submarine Service was not about to part with any information unless they get tricked into sharing. Finding a private corner table Karl mapped out a plan to put an agent into their holding area disguised as a survivor from a German surface naval vessel someone they would not be aware of. The mission could only be a week at best to gather information any longer would be taking a chance that agent being found out, we know what the outcome of that could be, another dead agent. "As usual Karl this is when your mind is razor sharp, great plan but who do we have that is German with a Naval background," Asked Clive already thinking here he goes again but this time I'm putting my foot down the plan can work but not with Karl Vita as the plant anyway. "We have a few agents that fit the bill but not as knowledgeable about submarine pens as me." Said Karl aware he could be devastating a future with Claire. "No Karl I'm putting my foot down we have only recently got you back and that was almost in a body bag, you have gone above and beyond the call of duty, that's an order do you understand me." Said Clive still admiring this officer that always put duty first no matter what the consequences could be. "Clive if you won't let me take on this operation then at least let me train whoever it is we send in, I will need to give him firsthand knowledge of the designs and construction details and what we are trying to find out, at least let me do that." Karl although at first was disappointed at not being the agent he was on the other hand relieved by Clive's decision. It was as if Clive was protecting Claire's future. How well my boss knows me, Claire is going to love my friends. "Karl you and Bill will be on sight in Bedford throughout this mission is that understood you crazy Austrian." Clive always enjoyed calling Karl a crazy Austrian. "Yes boss! When can I start recruiting, are you going to bring Bill up to speed or would you like me to do it?" Asked Karl. "No get on the interoffice phone and tell Bill we need him to join us over here and on the double." Clive was already putting his own contribution to this plan together in his mind. The biggest hurdle could be justification. Over the next two hours they tried to formulate a plan spending much of that time discussing what qualifications should their pick of agents be. Bill suddenly through up his arm saying. "Why are we only thinking of one agent why don't we consider two it would look more believable to our German chaps, what do you think Karl?" Bill asked, believing he had come up with a safer more believable plan of action. "Clive stroking his chin followed by. "Brilliant idea Bill, now what's the cover story Karl?" Karl eyes fixed in thought finally said. "The submarine arm of the Kriegsmarine is a very close-knit group, so we can't use that approach but what if our agents were from a surface ship, say based in Norway that got attacked and sunk then rescued by an RAF air sea rescue craft, that could work. We need to find out if any German surface craft have been lost in the last six weeks or so." Karl's brain in overdrive as he formulated this web of deception. "Gentlemen we have an outline of a plan, Karl your part is to interview agents for this plot, Bill you research what ships were sunk recently and I will write the request documentation needed for the operation. "Karl what time is your train tomorrow? You may want to leave a little earlier there's a lady in Hitchin that would love to see you earlier than later. "Well, I was planning on taking the 1645 train, changing in London would get me into Hitchin around 2130 or maybe a little later." Karl was hoping to hear Clive throw him out by lunch time and he did. "Chaps no need to tell you mums the word on this operation alright." Clive saying that thought that's a stupid thing to say these two are front line spoofs. "As much as I would love to stay here with you two, I have a lot of work to do before leaving tomorrow, by the way from the bottom of my heart, thank you for believing in me even though you still think I'm a 'Crazy Austrian, good night chaps." Karl stood up gathering the files he would return to the office, tonight would be a long one for sure. "As much as Karl may be off the wall when it comes to women, he is a wizard when it comes to intelligence and field operations. The least we can do right now is support him, he relies on us two to always be there to prop him up. Bill, I don't know about you, but I have a gut feeling this time may really be different." Clive was starting to believe Karl had found his soul mate. "Think your absolutely right Clive." Answered Bill.

Karl walked into his office then called the motor pool to order a staff car for 1130 hrs to take him back to the flat. Next, he placed the call to Claire's house the phone ringing until he heard her voice. "Karl how are you darling did you have a productive day?" Claire stepping lightly as she knew what he did for a living was very hush, hush. "Yes, sweetheart I did, can't tell you much but what I did was very productive, really fun driving a lorry." Karl laughing out loud saying that. "Karl, I swear to God your humor is sometimes hard to follow, what time should I plan on picking you up at the station tomorrow night?" she asked. "Want some good news, Clive is taking pity on me he is throwing me out lunch time so plan on picking me up at 1600 hrs, sorry that 4:00pm to you civilians. Saturday morning when we go to pick up the MG, why don't you show me around, I want to ravish the boss at her desk. Karl was in a wonderful mood enjoying his work and loving his new lease on life, no cloud anywhere to be felt or seen. "Karl really you come out with the most idiotic things to say, no you will not use my office as your own love parlor and that's that." Claire was trying to control him on the phone thinking he's capable of turning this phone call into a long distant love fest. There again life with Karl would always be a combination of tenderness, caring and yes off the wall moments. "Night darling, see you tomorrow don't stay all night at the office, use your lorry to take you back to the flat and Karl put those eyedrops in tonight you hear me." She deliberately said flat not home because home was now with her in Hitchin! Karl hung up the phone thinking its feels so good Claire bossing me around it's like we are old married people and just think it's only about a week since we met, God does move in mysterious way I suppose? Karl returned to the stack of documents on his desk, time would not stand still tonight. A knock at his office door brought him back from planning that mission. "Excuse me sir, your car has arrived shall I tell the driver you will be along shortly?" Asked the night MP. "Yes, please do I need to secure these folders in the overnight safe first." Replied Karl. The car ride back to the flat was reasonably short at this time of night. Karl thanked the driver and entered the front door. In his little room Karl could not surrender to sleep he kept tossing and turning, he had too much going on in his head. To force his mind away from intelligence matters starting to think of what things had to be done this weekend those thoughts calmed him down falling asleep after 0200 hrs. At 0630 hrs he hit the bathroom put some items in his small carry case, made the bed and quietly slipped out the front door into the cool morning air. At the bus stop he waited for the #5 bus to arrive. The day was cloudy not that uncommon in England this time of year. Like a programmed robot Karl stopped at the cafeteria for his large coffee and a powdered scrabbled egg sandwich. Back in his office he could hear staffers arriving cheerfully cracking jokes and telling tales. "Morning, you noisy bunch is that happiness contagious if so spread some my way. Sally I will be leaving at lunch time inform the motor pool to have a car ready outside at 1200 hrs thank you." Karl smiling returned to his office continuing the work from the previous evening. "John would you and Sally pull all the files we have on German speaking agents presently here in England, no older than forty- five years old. John brought the first batch of files into Karl's office overwhelming him with how many they had. "This is not going to work John, it's like what we just went through a few weeks ago. Have two of those collapsible table brought in and set them by the file cabinets, we can work right there." Karl gave instructions what they were looking for. "We need to weed out any agents that was in the navy or merchant service, men that worked as a marine architecture as well, in that order. Next, we want to know where they are presently. I shall be leaving at noon, I can't for the life of me believe this will be done by Monday morning, so have Peggy help you as well. Keep her and John on it till it's done. Major Knight gave me the green light should we need this extra help." Noon found them all busily separating files with no agents that qualify yet. Sally, seeing Karl engrossed in piles of papers was reluctant to disturb him, his time was up to catch the train. "Sir it's time for you to leave don't worry about this we will stay on top of it and be assured it will be ready when you return Monday." "Have a nice weekend everybody, see you Monday." Said Karl as he retrieved his case and headed for the door. Arriving at Kings Cross he boarded the train to Cambridge one of the stops being Hitchin. He found a compartment to stretch out in for the short trip. Leaving Stevenage Karl put his tunic jacket and cap back on excitement building at the thought of seeing Claire. The train slowing entering the Hitchin station its bumpers banging at each carriage. Karl looked out the open window familiar smoke and steam floating back along the length of the train. Karl out of habit searched into the smoke looking for a lady from his past instead he saw a striking lady in a blue business suite her hair flowing over her shoulders jumping up and down with excitement. Karl did not wait for the train to come to a full stop, flinging the door open his boots slide on the concrete, running up to Claire sweeping her off her feet as he swung her around several times. That smoke and steam had a different meaning from now on, that haunting image had left and would never return, his thoughts from now on would be only about Claire. "Darling your home it feels like an eternity since I saw you off last Monday." Said Claire her excitement becoming contagious to Karl. "I told Mama and Freida I can't wait to become another, Mrs.Vita, they both just laughed hugging me tightly, by the way she also mentioned you have something to give me tomorrow? Karl I am praying it's what I think it is." Claire so wanted to make this permanent and marriage would give her that closure. "Yes, sweetheart I do but remember it's only been a week can we at least agree on a couple of months before setting an actual wedding date." Said Karl laughing out loud thinking we are going to do this it's time for me to become Claire's husband and I am more than ready to make that happen. Back at the house Claire took him upstairs into the bedroom, beaming she open the wardrobe on the opposite side of the room to hers there neatly arranged were all of Karl's hanging clothes then she showed him the chest of draws with all his other things also neatly arranged. "What do you think darling, Freida and I moved all your thinks over on Wednesday afternoon while Mama took care of Franchot. "Claire you are moving faster than an express train, thank you." Karl was a little nervous but really delighted to how thinks were taking place. "Let's stay home tonight it will do you good to wind down after your hectic week. I hope you are up for beef stew, its quick and very tasty, why don't you relax in the living room while I set the table." Said Claire so very happy to be a couple once again. Over supper they enjoyed small talk with a bottle of white wine that they finished in the living room. Sitting very close on the couch, Karl had his arm around her shoulder. Claire still talking could tell Karl was changing his gaze, he moved with stealth to the top button of her blouse still without saying a word. Claire a little nervous to how Karl could arouse her sexual desires so easily. Talking was no longer necessary, Karl was controlling the inevitable. His hand slide inside her bra this very movement took her breath away turning towards his face and surrendering to his touch and kiss. Claire stood up and removed her blouse then her skirt leaving her underwear and nylons to Karl's view. Sitting back down she started undoing his trouser thinking two can play at this game. "You are a big tease tonight, that friend of yours will be my dessert." Karl laid back as Claire performed her magic on him for the first time thinking this lady is no amateur thank God. With a slow and deliberate motion Claire would bring him to the brink then stop, this teasing was driving Karl over the top, she felt his tension mounting continuous throbbing, looking up she smiled then lowered her head again as Karl asked. "Claire this is too much teasing," With that she felt his eruption followed by Karl totally relaxing. Claire raised her head with a big smile of success saying. "You needed that sailor tonight's dessert was way overdue was it not?" Claire reached over the back of the couch, grabbing a throw blanket then wrapping it over them. She said almost in a whisper. "Let's lay here quietly for a while, you need this rest darling." Karl responding almost asleep by saying. "What about you Claire I need to take care of you." Karl could hardly keep his one eye open. Claire kissed him softly on his forehead replying. "Tonight, was wonderful, as for me I have a lifetime to make love to you so don't worry I'll still be here in the morning." Claire did not need anything else she had everything she needed right here in their place exhausted they fell asleep safe in each other arms. Karl woke first looking at his watch it was past midnight softly he whispered into Claire's ear, "Honey its after midnight lets go up to bed shall we." Claire responding by saying, "Goodness Karl I guess we needed that nap we have to get up early in the morning so yes let's head upstairs, we've both had a long day.

Around 2:30am, Claire woke Karl up he was thrashing around in a nightmare. "Karl, Karl it's alright whatever your dreaming can't hurt you anymore, come here let me hold you till you fall back to sleep." Claire's heart was pounding thinking, what did they do to you Karl, was it so bad that you considered taking your own life? Still holding his head on her chest, she fell back to sleep for the few hours before the alarm clock went off. Claire moved Karl to his pillow then rolled over to silence the alarm clock putting on her bathrobe she went downstairs to make the coffee. Last night episode had shocked her to her very core. I wonder how long these nightmares have been going on. We need to get help for him before they get any worst. Without a sound she felt those strong arms enfolding her, "Good morning darling did not mean to scare you like that." Karl thinking, now she knows I nearly took my own life out of despair. I must have yelled that out when she woke me up during the night. Taking their coffee to the kitchen table Karl reached over taking Claire's hand before saying. "Claire that should never of happened its only occurred a few times before. I am so very sorry to scare you like that please except my apologies." Asked Karl looking at her fear written across her face. "Karl, you poor man, I feel so stupid not having the foresight to see you have been wrestling with this for God knows how long, share it with me Karl it's too much of a burden to carry it all on your own? Please darling let me remind you we promised to never have secrets between us." Claire was pleading with him to share this nightmare of horror and by doing so help him face that trauma. "Claire what I am about to tell you can never be repeated so put your solicitor's wig on, which will bind you to client confidentiality is that right?" Asked Karl. "That is absolutely correct Captain Vita." Claire was thinking this is one time that I'm glad to be his solicitor. Taking over an hour and a half he told her everything leaving nothing out. As he spoke the look on her face was one of complete horror and shock. "Am I the only one that knows this outside the military." Asked Claire. "No darling my Mother and Freida know as well, I had to tell them, my mother would see right through that lie." Claire responding by saying, "Karl, we must get you help you cannot handle this on your own. It's our problem now so who should we contact?" Karl getting concerned responded by saying, "Claire it can't be military, that could cost me my commission so whatever I do, I can't include any military help, are we clear on that, no military whatsoever." Claire with that legal look on her face said, "I understand Karl I will work on that right away we have very good contacts at the Lister Hospital, Father knew doctors that handle cases like yours, we'll find someone we can trust my darling. Are you up for breakfast yet I really would like to arrive at Mama's no later than lunchtime?" Claire the very professional women would diplomatically look for the help Karl needed. He had been through so much during the year keeping it locked up inside like this was now surfacing in those nightmares. "Claire let's take the MG it's a nice day and I would like to clean and polish it while Mama gives you those cooking lessons." Whenever Karl returned home to Wien on leave from his ship the Tristian, he always found cleaning his little Amilcar to be so relaxing it was almost a ritual and today he was on leave so cleaning the MG was the therapy he needed. "Of course, we can Sailor, if I get finish with Mama before you're done, I'll help you clean the inside." Claire had cleaned that little car so many times before with Patrick, today however she would look at that car in a whole new way.

Arriving at the bungalow Karl removed the polish and leather cleaner Charlie from motor pool had given him to take with him. The drive through the back roads to Baldock was the relaxing medicine Karl needed, Claire could see the look on his face, it was one she could see would help him by blowing the ugly thoughts out of his mind, maybe not today but for sure one day in the future. Turning into the driveway she reached over to pull up the handbrake, her heart skipped a beat looking at Karl's face as he sat there a big smile on his face enjoying the warm sunshine. "*Servus*, where is everybody," yelled Karl." Servus, what does that mean is it like saying hello? "Asked Claire thinking must be an Austrian slang word. In the living room they all sat around drinking strong coffee and some of Mama's homemade strudel she had made for Karl. "Claire this is the first thing you need to learn to cook and of course Mama's Goulash." Karl was happier today than he had been all week. What could be better, family, a new fiancée and his beautiful little MG. Mama kept looking at Karl in such a way to remind him while they were all together this should be the time to bring out the red leather box? Karl smiled back at his mother, nodding his head in agreement. Ronny, Freida and Franchot sat on one couch, Mama sitting next to Claire on the opposite couch. Karl left the room returning moments later. "Claire darling now we are all together I have something to give you, although it's been my Mother's for so many years, she would like you to be its new custodian, that's if of course you care to wear it on your wedding finger! Claire, in a little over a week you have won my heart and whatever I am and what I may become in the future, I will be faithfully yours." Karl stepped forward kneeling down on one knee he opened the box containing Mama's engagement ring gleaming in the light streaming in from the window. Taking Claire's hand with tears in his eyes he asked. "Claire McGivern, will you consent to becoming my wife?" Karl was having such a hard time holding back the tears and the emotion held back for so long. Mama for the second time was gaining a daughter, Freida and Ronny were reliving their own engagement. "Karl Vita, I married you in my heart the day I first met you, to wear Mama's ring from this day forward will be my honor and pride always with love for you and my new family. Karl what are you waiting for are you going to put the ring on my finger or not?" Claire laughing with tears of joy rolling down her face was enjoying this moment of humor. Karl slipped the ring onto her finger, it fit perfectly. Mama looked at Karl their eye contact confirming what they were both thinking, it was originally sized for Kitty! Claire was so much like Kitty it's like she was giving them her final blessing. Karl from this day forward would stop the crazy life he had been living. The image of Kitty in his mind was softly fading into a distant memory always fondly remembered never forgotten. He continued to hold Claire's hand as she stared at her ring. The last act Claire did was to whisper something into Mama's ear they both embraced each other holding hands and smiling at each other Claire saying, "Mama we should start our cooking lesson and Freida can you help me learn German while we do that, no correct that, show me how to speak like a *Weiner*." Karl stood up starring at Claire she would be a wonderful wife and one day an amazing mother. Claire Vita! had a real nice sound to it.

The weekend flew by Karl and Claire spent the rest of Saturday with the family then a nice Sunday down by the river in *St. Neots*. Claire had packed a lunch and a bottle of wine along with a blanket to spread out on. The sun was warm Karl laid back closing his eye drifting off into a restful sleep. Claire had her arm under his head as a pillow perfectly happy reading a novel she wanted to finish for such a long time. The following morning Claire took Karl to the station at 0630 hrs as he wanted to get to the office no later than 1100 hrs. "Claire, now remember to book a room for us at the Charter Arms in Slough, let me know as soon as you are checked into the hotel alright. Clive will arrange for a pass to be issued in your name so remember to take the directions to the camp I gave you last night, try to be there by 1600 hrs if you can, so I can show you off and Claire remember to wear your engagement ring alright?" Karl started laughing. As he said that, there was no way that ring would ever leave her finger. "Karl you are such an idiot at times you know full well that will never happen." Claire was enjoying the bantering till the conductor yelled "All aboard!" Claire hugged Karl tightly, "I won't sleep well till Friday evening at the Charter Arms and Karl keep applying those eyedrops or you will be in real trouble with your future wife." Claire standing back from the door as the train slowly pulled away. Karl as usual stood by the window waving and starring at Claire as she held up her left hand wiggling her engagement finger. Karl settled down for the quick ride to Kings Cross station opening his brief case he took out the morning paper. The headline news where yet again bleak, the people of Norway were band from having a radio in their houses! Changing trains in Paddington station Karl placed a call to the motor pool to have a car meet him at the station in Slough this would save time getting to the office. Outside the station Karl spotted his car and driver waiting by the entrance, "Morning Charlie did you have a nice weekend? The car dropped him off at the main entrance Karl thanked Charlie for the ride then proceeded to scaling the steps two steps at a time. Entered the building he wished the ATS girl on duty a pleasant day then walked down the hall to his department. Karl was in a marvelous mood, entering he gave a jolly greeting to his staff followed by a request, "John do I have the wires on my desk yet." He asked firing orders in all directions. Bill walked in with a binder under his arm containing the biography on the U-Boat prisoners. "Morning you old bugger, well did you put that magnificent ring on Claire's finger over the weekend?" Asked Bill with an edge of sarcasm in his voice. "Here is the binder that Clive generated over the weekend, I think Sally and John with the additional help of Peggy did a superb job of identifying potential Germans officers we can consider using for the mole operation. Their effort made it possible to have these files ready for you this morning, don't forget to thank them for doing this?" Said Bill sitting down in front of the desk. "Who asked them to do that, I had no idea they would volunteer to do this." Asked Karl somewhat embarrassed he did not stay to help them. Karl excused himself going out into the office saying loudly. "John, Sally thank you so very much for the hard work you both did, I'm somewhat embarrassed that I did not have the forethought to stay and help you." John from his desk stood and responded. "Sir we knew you needed those files for Monday so after you left on Friday, we decided to pool our resources to have them ready for you. Glad we could make that happen. Excuse me for asking sir, are we allowed to brag about your engagement yet?" John and Sally beaming with the praise they were getting. "I'll stop by the analyses department to thank Peggy on my way down to the meeting room, thanks again." Karl and Bill walked down the hall stopping in to also thank Peggy. Karl was always the gentleman and Peggy was so happy he had included her in his thanks, she especially liked this because it was in front of her fellow workmates. At the end of the hall, they entered meeting room M-3, Clive and several other officers from the general staff sat waiting with two clerical ATS girls that would be recording the meeting. "Morning all," said Bill taking his seat alongside Karl. "I'm assuming you have all read the brief on this operation, so we all know what we are attempting to accomplish over the next couple of days correct?" Said Clive looking around the room at their faces standing up and walking over to the big board at the head of the room, with a pointer he tapped on the harbors they wanted to collect additional information on.

"St Nazaire was the one Captain's Vita and Jerva visited, in his report Captain Vita stressed that if we could immobilize those lock gates, it would deny access to transient submarine entering or leaving these pens. "So, how do we disable those gates?" asked Clive turning his attention to Karl he said, "Captain please take it from here. Karl stood thanking Major Knight. "Bombing, could cause delays but not for very long. Germans by nature are masters at building and repairing large structures. But Major, we are not here to talk about specific French harbors, we are here to review candidates we can train to be inserted in with the surviving sailors from the U-Boat, are we not? Do we even know if there are others being held in other POW camps we could interrogate using the same approach, I really believe ordinary seamen could also be another excellent source of information so sir, don't lets overlook these in our review process, all day long they hammered out a profile for the perfect candidates each file being scrutinized many times over till the list was narrowing down to just five then eventually down to two." "Make arrangements to have those two brought here, if their stationed up North fly them down we don't have time to waste on this operation, are we clear on this, we will reconvene once those agents are here. Gentleman, thank you for putting this together so quickly." commanded Major Knight. Karl quickly spoke up correcting Clive who really put these files together last Saturday, it wasn't Captain Lowes or himself, it was members of my team Sally and John with the help Peggy, we are so lucky to have conscientious people here in the BIS that gave of their own time to make this happen. The time was now 1700 hrs walking out of the meeting room Clive asked. "Up for a pint or two or do you have other plans turning to Karl saying that. I'm game said Bill followed by Karl saying, "Hope you don't mind must make a quick call first?" Clive and Bill looked at each other, Bill laughed by saying, "Isn't love grand," Clive joining in by adding, "Tell Claire we are all looking forward to meeting her this weekend. Oh, before I forget Julie asked me to have Claire call her anytime, over the next couple of days you have our home number, don't you?" concluded Clive. "Will do responded Karl as he hurried off to his department. Entering the department Karl said to Sally and John, "Major Knight sends his thanks for a job well done." Seating down Karl looked at his watch then placed the call to Claire. "Darling is that you, I have been waiting for your call all day. How did your day go I understand you have been at meetings all day so you must be exhausted?

Everyone at the office could not believe how magnificent my ring is Karl I keep looking at it and pinching myself in disbelief. I'm sorry I'm rambling on and you haven't said one word yet or are you all talked out?" Claire stopped talking her enthusiasm was getting the best of her. "Claire, I'm fine so much for working on a secure military base you know what I'm doing every minute of the day." Karl was laughing saying that. "Sorry Karl I called this morning to tell you we are booked into the Charter Arms for three nights, now don't get mad at me I booked their best suite, only the best for my man. Anyway, that nice Sally on your staff told me you would be tied up all day and could not be disturbed till after 5:00pm so that's how I knew you were unavailable." Claire saying that thought, I guess my excitement is getting the best of me, need to slow it down. "Claire that's wonderful when you get excited it's like medicine, please never change. By the way before I forget, write this telephone number down, when time permits Clive's wife Julie wants you to call her, you will love her, she is a real sweetheart. Time to go darling, the chaps are waiting for me in the lounge, sleep tight only four nights left till I see you, hope you are ready for dessert Friday night?" Karl laughing hung up the phone then headed down to the lounge thinking so much to do and not enough time between now and Friday.

As expected, the rest of week did not have enough hours to achieve the elimination process. Karl still believing he was the best candidate for this operation however Clive would have no part of it. Karl got up early Friday packed his case then went down to have morning tea with his landlady. "Morning Mrs. Mann, sadly I need to inform you that I will be moving out at the end of the month. Right now, it makes more sense to move back into the officer's quarters. I am working longer hours sometimes late into the evening so I think this will be for the best, would you like me to post my flat in the officer's lounge? Really don't think there will be a problem in leasing it." Karl could tell Mrs. Mann was saddened by hearing this but understood in his line of work would require more of his time. "Sorry to see you go Captain, I totally understand though, if you could post the flat It would be greatly appreciated. Hope you can stop by for a cupper when you can to brighten up my day with that big smile of yours." Mrs. Mann would miss having Karl as her tenant but understood completely his need to be closer to the duties at the camp.

Chapter Fifteen
Claire in Slough

The workload continued to pile up on Karl's desk no matter how diligently he pursued each project. "Sir you have a call on two, think it's your fiancé." Said Sally sticking her head into his office. "Claire don't tell me your already at the hotel, are you?" Karl looking at his watch in shock, where did the day go? "Yes, I am dear decided to get an early start, well that's not totally true Beverly threw me out, what time should I come over?" Answered Claire her excitement building at the thought of meeting Karl's staff and fellow officers. "Clive suggested you plan on about 1630 hrs alright, make sure you have the directions and instructions for getting the pass at the gate any problems have the guard give me a call, see you real soon, bye darling." Karl hung up the phone then called Sally to come to his office. "Sally, that call was from Claire she will be here in about forty minute or so. Please make sure that all sensitive documents are covered up or put away before she gets here." Asked Karl thinking she may be my future wife but everything in here is highly classified. Next, he called Clive then Bill advising them Claire was on her way over. "Is everything secure in your department?" Asked Clive knowing full well that when it came to security he never had to worry about Karl. At 1645 hrs the guard house called requesting permission to issue a pass and parking ticket for a Claire McGivern, the guard asked for someone to meet her in the lobby. "Sally stuck her head into Karl's office. "Sir, I'm going down to the lobby to escort Miss McGivern back here to the office, be right back." Sally with a cheeky smile on her face turned and marched out to meet their guest. Claire signed in at the reception desk receiving a badge to clip onto her suite jacket then sat down to wait for her escort to arrive. "Miss, someone is on their way down to escort you, shouldn't be too long." Said the receptionist. Sally entered the lobby looking around at the visitors waiting there, her gaze falling on Claire. "Miss McGivern pleased to meet you my name is Sally I'm here to escort you to Captain Vita's office." Sally, putting her hand out to shake Claire's saying. "We have all been waiting to meet you this way please." Said Sally as she held the lobby door open for Claire. Karl put his files and documents into a desk draw then put his tunic back on before sitting back down at his desk to wait. Out in the main office Karl could hear people talking boisterously as they introduced themselves to his future wife. Karl walked to the door, opening he could see Claire making friendly introductions and winning over everyone. Standing there he was thinking she is a real solicitor, look at her winning over these people. In her peripheral vision Claire court sight of Karl leaning against the door frame his arms crossed with an uncontrollable smile that gave him away. In a loud voice he yelled, "Who let this civilian in here?" Karl loved how his staff were enjoying meeting Claire and it was obvious she felt the same. Claire turned towards Karl answering him. "Private McGivern reporting for duty, Captain Vita." Karl laughing loudly walked over to the group putting his arm around Claire's waist then kissing her on the cheek. As the head of the department, he needed to show restraint at times like this. "Well now you met my bunch let's take a walk down to Major Knights office shall we, Sally would you please call his office to inform him we are on our way down, also call Captain Lowes office and let him know to meet him there also, thank you." Karl turning Claire towards his office before heading out. With the door closed he turned Claire towards him kissing her passionately before saying, "What an artist you are must be that solicitor training, they all loved you, am I surprised, no?" Waving goodbye Claire linked her arm through Karl's as they walked towards Clive's office. "Claire so very pleased to meet you," said Clive extending his hand to Claire followed by Bill giving Claire a kiss on the cheek. "Please have a seat can we get you some tea or has this Austrian got you converted to coffee?" Clive being the perfect English gentleman was giving Claire every courtesy. "Either one is fine Major, or may I call you Clive and is that alright with you also Bill? I'm so please you allowed me to visit your facilities, Karl is so proud of everyone here especially when it comes to you two. Meeting you both face to face is the only way I know to distill any doubts that may still be lingering in your minds about Karl and myself. Until this meeting you may be thinking I'm another one of his flings, which by the way I can't blame you for thinking that. Karl and your charming wife Julie have told me all about his wild romancing the ladies so let me categorically deny I am not one of those ladies, enough said for the time being, really it's a real pleasure being here." Claire saying that was thinking I believe that preemptive opening may be what is needed to set our intentions on firm ground. Karl sat there with that big grin on his face staring at Clive and Bill thinking God she gets right to the point and in such a diplomatic fashion, glad she is my solicitor not one suing me. Clive was the first to speak, "Miss McGivern or may I from now on refer to you as Claire, how delighted Bill and I are to finally meet the lady that will keep our friend in line. We think very highly of him, and may I say he is one of the best officers I have had the privilege of serving with, so if we initially appeared cautious it's because we have been with Karl from his first day when he arrived in England wearing the uniform of a merchant marine officers. If we created the wrong impression, it's still a little hard to comprehend that in less than a week you two have become engaged Bill and I are now willing to admit we are looking forward to seeing Karl slide that wedding ring on behind that beautiful engagement ring." Clive and Bill knew that ring so very well when Kitty Johnson wore it. Clive excused himself picking up the intercom and telling his secretary to hold all calls except for his wife and his Commanding Officer. Turning to the cabinet behind his desk he took out a decanter and four glasses saying. "Claire, I believe we have something really special to celebrate and may I add it's been a long time coming." Clive pored four healthy glasses of Scott then with a raise glass said, "I give you the future Mrs. Karl Vita, an English Rose if there ever was one. Now I know it may be premature to ask but when should Bill and I have our Dress Uniforms made ready for the wedding. You must also consider we are fighting a war so when you plan that you must remember to keep me in the loop in case it interferes with the plans of the war department," that comment had them all laughing. Clive asked Claire if he could show her around the places not in a secure location though. Clive took great delight in introducing Claire to each department Bill and Karl, walking behind them. Bill whispered to Karl, "Wow, she is such a catch, would marry her myself and may I also say quite the looker, you lucky bugger you." Bill was noticing the form fitting dark red suite and walking behind her was enjoying that view. Karl excused himself while he got his suitcase and briefcase from his office telling them he would meet them in the lobby, walking fast he swung open the lobby door saying, "Seeing you at Charter Arms at six Saturday evening, have a nice evening." Said Karl as he guided Claire to the lobby entrance. Clive and Bill watched them leave saying nothing till they were back in hallway, Clive spoke first saying, "Well Bill what do you think, quite the woman you agree? smart as hell! Old Karl will have to stay on his toes around her," Bill sarcastically remarking. "I would venture to say she is built for comfort and lots of speed hope old Karl still has the stamina to handle that one." Clive just shook his head thinking Bill will never change.

Claire opened the door to the suite then walked Karl right behind her. Claire had already unpacked putting everything away except the new silk negligee and matching light blue sheer robe hanging from the door of the armoire. Karl just looked at it then back to Claire saying. "Darling Is that the dessert wrapping." Claire approached him sliding her arms around his waist saying. "If that's what you want it to be? But we could be wasting time doing that, I had the hotel deliver Champagne while I was at the camp this afternoon. Are you ready for some now or would you like to wait till later?" Claire crossed the room pulling down the bedsheets while Karl just stood there watching her. Next, she removed her jacket followed by her skirt and slip but remove nothing else. Karl was in ore, of her poise her deliberate actions and how she did not take her gaze from him, a mysterious fixed smile across her face. Crossing back to where Karl was standing still wearing her black high heel shoes thinking, if this doesn't get him going, I need to go back to school? Standing closely in front of him in her alluring black lingerie, she was sending Karl a very strong message. She was not leaving this room till he had made love to her. Karl just stood there playing her teasing game waiting for her next move. Claire reached up removing his tunic then his shirt, kissing his chest as she opened each button, fumbling with his military web belt not sure how it unclipped, quickly she figured it out. With confidence she pushed him down onto the love seat behind him, removing his boots and socks. The silence continued amplifying the sexual charged desire Claire was generating. She continued by unbuttoning his trousers giving them a strong tug to slide them down. Parting Karl's legs she placed her left hand on his cheek kissing him slowly her tongue mingling with his. Karl's eye closed felt the sensation of her hands pulling down his underwear. Karl went to speak, Claire simply put a finger across his lips not to say a word. With deliberate slow movement she allowed her hand to stroke his skin all the way down to his erection. In his mind he was following her every move and he knew where she was going! Caressed him further with her hand she softly encircling him with her warm moist mouth. Karl remaining perfectly still thinking, something has happened to Claire to act like this, not that I'm objecting but there is a reason she is acting this way. She stood up bending over him passionately kissing him again and in an almost whisper said, "Karl, I love you so much let me make all the moves alright." Karl slowly nodded not wanting to break her magic. Claire pulled back from him still starring at his one good eye then removed her underwear stroking his chest with them before she lowered herself onto to his erection. Karl could not believe what was happening. This very proper English woman acting like he could never of imagined. His mind was scrambling in this web of magic she was creating. Claire quietly moaning as she increased the depth of motion. As much as Karl tried to hold back it was becoming harder to contain himself. Feeling Claire starting to shake, her moaning increasing she looked at Karl's face crying out, "Oh God Karl." She never finished the sentence as they both gave into a magical orgasm. For the longest time Claire remained perfectly still straddling Karl lap, her head on his shoulder, both mingling in sweat. Claire after a few minutes said, "Karl once we are married promise me, we can make a baby and to hell with waiting for this damn war to end, promise me that Karl, if anything should happen to you, God forbid, I will have you in that baby Karl please make me that promise right now while you are still inside me." Claire had just made her intention very clear. Her hormones were racing and only he could satisfy that maternal desire. Karl holding her tightly was processing what she had just asked of him. So, this amazing sexual display Claire just gave me was leading up to that question and she was looking for an answer right now? Claire kissed him on the cheek as she climbed off the spell now broken, saying. "How was that lover boy." At first Karl clenched his teeth as Claire hit a nerve by saying that, but that tension quickly melted away as he looked at this beautiful woman in front of him. "Let's talk about what you just asked me over dinner alright." Claire shook her head in agreement kissing him on the forehead, then walked towards the bathroom saying quietly. "I hope you realize I meant ever word of that Karl?"

Karl locked the door behind them as they walked downstairs for dinner feeling refreshed after a nice hot bath. Claire had changed into a fitted bottle green dress with a standing collar, a wide matching belt finishing the look. Claire had put up her hair in a French Twist so the single strand of pearls adorning her neck would not be covered. Karl in a tweed jacket with dark blue trouser, instead of a tie he elected to wear a stripped cravat. Entering the restaurant, the *maître D,* commented on how handsome a couple they looked. Karl held the chair out for Claire kissed her on the neck complementing her on how attractive and very sexy she appeared. "Did I tell you I'm head over heels in love with you, instead of seating across from you I'm going to sit right next to you, it will be more romantic that way." Karl wanted to hold her hand when the question of a baby came up again as he knew it would. The menu was limited due to rationing but what they had was very tasty. After dinner they moved to the lounge for a glass of port. Sitting on a couch the baby question coming up again. "Karl, I know what must be going through your head and I need to apologize for allowing it to come out that way. We have both lost someone special, my darling Karl I can honestly say I have never met or wanted to make love to anyone like I wanted you today. I didn't mean to surprise you by acting like I did, something inside me eliminated any reservations about make love to you like that I just gave into that sexual desire by the way I may have discovered another side to Claire?" She Concluded.
"Well darling anytime you want to reenact that style of love making count me in." Karl kissed her again on the neck before bluntly asking the real question. Talk to me Claire about having a baby, where did that come from?" Asked Karl. Claire was blushing she really didn't want to address that tonight, so she answered by saying. "Karl we are going to become man and wife, what scares me the most and darling forgive me for putting it this way. When Patrick died there was little left of that

wonderful bond between us but memories, some more painful than others. Which brings me to us, we are both intelligent and mature enough to except you are an intelligence agent and could be killed in your line of work before this war is over, guess you can say such is the life of a spy. Karl I can't face this twice in a row. The love we share is strong enough to weather that storm, I pray that day will never come but if it does, I will have a part of you living and breathing at home with me a testament to what we made together out of love, does any of this make sense to you darling." Claire sat quietly as Karl gathered his thoughts before answering. "Claire, were you trying to trick me into becoming pregnant earlier?" Claire responded right away. "Today I was, it's something I want us to share together?" Karl still holding her hand answered, "If it is meant to be, we will cherish that child with all the love we can muster, would be nice to get married first don't you agree?" Karl trying to make light of what his new wife would want first after the wedding. They retired to bed content and secure that their relationship had just taken another step into becoming a real family and Karl was alright with that.

Up early the following day they drove to Great Windsor to explore the sights of this historic city. Arriving back at the hotel they had an afternoon nap safe in each other's arms. Karl woke to the room phone ringing, "Yes," he answered. "Did I wake you or were you doing something I don't need to know about," Asked Clive laughing at what he had just said. "Clive you can be such an idiot at times didn't you figure that was the first thing on the agenda when we entered the room, now what's on your mind," Asked Karl. "We will be there at 1800 hrs shall we meet you at the bar or should we go straight to the table?" Asked Clive. "Why don't we get Claire comfortable by meeting at the bar alright?" Karl saying that, thought Claire was a very confident lady in any new crowd. "By the way old man, Julie can't wait to meet Claire face to face she said they talked about so much yesterday and if you are wondering they did discuss you, imagine that?" Clive enjoying the ribbing he was giving Karl, see you later Casanova." Karl sat there on the edge of the bed thinking, what did these girls talk about? Claire must have been wearing her solicitors, hat again I can only imagine that discussion. Karl looked back at Claire still sleeping soundly he moved over to kiss her forehead gently and in a soft voice said. "Claire, honey time to get up and get ready for tonight." Karl hated to wake her, she looked so serenely secure in having her man next to her. "Come on sleepy head the gang will be here at 6:00pm including your new pal' Julie?" Claire rolled over rubbing her eyes she turned to Karl lifting her head she kissed him on the cheek saying. "Sounds like Clive has been telling you about our ladies chat on

Friday?" Karl got dressed in his dress uniform which Clive had requested the three men wear for this special occasion. Karl was getting very fidgety thinking about tonight and the long wait for Claire to come out of the bathroom, finally the door opened and out came Claire. "Wow!" was all that Karl could say. Claire answering him by asking, "So sailor, how does your fiancé look for tonight's celebration?" Claire had on a form fitting black dress that showed off her figure off so very well, the wide off the shoulder neckline made the single strand of pearls stand out in a very classic look. Once again, her hair was up in a French Twist to finish off that look of a very classy, elegant lady. Flashing her engagement ring in front of Karl she was enjoying the attention he was showering her with. Karl with his arm around her waist whispered in her ear, "I think we should make them wait, I feel like ravishing you right here against the door." Claire was getting Karl's juices going again and she loved every minute of it. "Down tiger, everything comes to those that wait." Claire saying that had triggered a fond memory Karl had of his Father saying that. "Claire what you just said is an expression I have used so many times in the past. Hearing you say that convinces me we are somehow on the same wave band. God, I love you Claire, now do I rough you up or will that be later?" Karl his arms around her held her tightly, no more words were necessary they had what they both needed.

Walking down the stairs they entered the lounge, looking around Karl saw Bill's arm waving at them. Clive and Julie were seating on one couch, Bill, and Dorothy opposite on two armchairs. "Show time you, sexy creature, are you ready?" asked Karl holding her arm. "As ready as I'll ever be," Replied Claire. Clive stood greeting Claire with a kiss on the cheek, then introduced Dorothy and finally Julie who came round to greet Claire putting her arm around her giving her a cheek to cheek embarrass. "Claire so nice to finally meet you, enjoyed a talk on Friday afternoon feel like I already know you so well." Julie patting to the couch for Claire to sit next to her and Dorothy. Clive seating opposite with his fellow officer. "Dorothy you are such a Gem, hope Bill appreciate what he has got and Julie it's hard to believe you have daughters five and seven years old, you look so young, quite the figure too for being a mother. These three blokes are lucky men, wouldn't you agree ladies." Claire the diplomate had won over two ladies that would quickly become her close friends as the dangers of war increased for the BIS and its agents. They would lean on one another when their men went into harm's way but not tonight anyway.

Over dinner they all enjoyed the bantering, so much to talk about. Clive eventually stood up with a glass in hand asking for silence and for those at the table to raise their glasses. "Tonight, we come together as friends to celebrate the engagement of our close friend Karl to his new fiancé, Claire. We have only just got to know you, if the term love at first sight can be used, we are all guilty. When Karl announced he had bought an MG sports car, I could not imagine that also included its owner as well and may I add a true English Rose. Claire and Karl may your lives together be full of love, health and may your lives always be fortified with the hopes and dreams you both aspire to reach for one another." Clive sat down as they all clinked glasses. Claire asked, "May I also add to that wonderful toast, a few weeks back I was sad and very lonely lady, then on a Saturday morning a dashing intelligence officer changed my life forever. Yesterday, I started making new and lasting friends, tonight I can honestly say this may be one of the best times Karl and I will ever have. Thank you again for this special evening." Claire hugged them all then wrapped her arms around Karl neck saying, "Ladies he's all mine, you have my permission to slap him if you see his eyes looking in the wrong direction. Clive and Bill if he gets out of line just call me, I know what gets his attention real fast." Claire and Karl started laughing, it had been a wonderful celebration.

Sunday Karl and Claire were invited to Clive and Julie's home to meet their daughters and enjoy a wonderful lunch. Driving back to the hotel there was silence in the car until they parked. "Claire tomorrow God willing I will get good news about my eye and you will be heading home to Hitchin. Darling I must tell you I'm working on an operation that will keep me in Bedford for a couple of weeks. When I return home on Friday, I will use the MG to drive to Bedford, don't believe I will have any problems driving with one eye. With any luck I may be able to sneak an evening or two during those weeks, how does that sound to you." Karl was careful about what not to say. "Karl, are you doing something dangerous on that spy operation?" Asked Claire knowing full well what he did in the BIS. "Not really, as for tomorrow when you drop me off you can take my case home with you alright." Karl guiding her away from her pointed question. That night they had a quiet dinner neither in the mood to make conversation it had been a wonderful few day's all they wanted to do now was retire to bed in the comfort of each other's arms. Monday morning, they left early to drive to hospital, the traffic as expected was heavy, arriving at the entrance Claire turned to Karl saying, "Darling let me come in with you otherwise I'll worry till you call me." Claire could not bring herself to say goodbye, not just yet anyway. "Claire, we talked about this last night, did we not? It serves no purpose, waiting around this hospital, and lets also remember you have a responsibility to your practice, now be off with you don't worry I'll call you as soon as the doctor has finished with me." Karl holding her arms tightly looking into her face, reach over to kiss her passionately before opening the car door. "Drive carefully and don't fret about me alright?" Karl stood on the pavement smiling throwing kisses as she drove off, entering the lobby he registered with the receptionist, then made his way to the waiting room. A nurse came out of the examination area calling, "Captain Karl Vita." Karl stood up then followed her into the room. "Have a seat Captain, while I take a look at your eye and get it ready for the doctor to look at it." Instructed the nurse as she carefully removed the gauze from under his leather patch. "Nice job Captain taking care of your eye it's looks very clean other than the ointment in the corners." Karl responded by saying. "I can't take credit for that it's mainly my fiancé that changes the dressing and applies the ointment. When she is not with me, she hounds me anyway." Karl making light of her question. The middle door opened and in walked Dr. Phillips. "Well old man let's get a look at that eye shall we, I'm going to recline you then pull that incandescent light up close." Dr Phillips rolled his eye lid up telling Karl to look up then down and finally from left to right. "Well Captain you are doing better than I expected, I'm going to raise the lights a little higher, then I'm going to ask you to look straight ahead and tell me what you see. On the opposite side of the room the nurse was slowly waving a round target. "What do you see now with your left eye only," Asked Dr. Phillips. Karl being his usual self, answered. "A white ring with two red stars on opposite sides being waived by a charming nurse. "That's really good I believe your vision will improve as it continues to strengthen and as long as you continue to clean it daily. I'm satisfied the doctor at the camp can take care of you from this point on unless something goes dramatically wrong. In the next couple of weeks that nice patch can be returned to its box hopefully it will not be needed in the future?" Dr. Phillips shook Karl's hand saying, "Goodbye Captain Vita take care of yourself doing that undercover stuff, Nurse would you replace the dressing before the Captain is released." Dr. Phillips marching off to the next patient. "I didn't even have time to thank him nurse." Said Karl as he stood up from the examination chair. "He knows how thankful you are, getting better is all the thanks he needs. Answered the nurse as she escorted him back to the lobby. "Goodbye Captain, God bless you for what you do please stay safe." Karl walked outside in the dismal morning drizzle not caring at all about the weather, there was sunshine in his heart. Looking around he saw Charlie standing next to the big Humber with an umbrella already opened at the rear passenger door. "Everything go alright Sir?" Asked the friendly driver. "Yes, Charlie we are on the mend, have you been waiting long?" Karl always liked this Londoner his questions were truly sincere. "No really Gov only about forty-five minutes.

Returning to the camp Karl went right to wireless room asking, "What came in that needs my attention?" Karl was back in intelligence mode. "Only got six sir they are in the locked pouch on your desk, Major Knight reviewed them before I locked them up." Answered the operator. Back in his office Karl opened the pouch then read each one of the transmissions, one of them court his attention, its closing line read, has grandmother passed on? Karl kept looking at it before he put it in with the other wires. This is not going to be easy when Hazel returns. Peggy entered saying well sir, how did it go this morning, you are looking very concerned? By the way we all think Miss McGivern is really smashing. Captain Lowes asked for you meet him in his office at your earliest convenience" Sally taking the pouch from his hand as she said that. Karl grabbed his agent file from the locked draw in his desk, thanked Sally and headed for Bill office. "Afternoon Bill, are we going to finalize our pick of agents today?" Asked Karl. "Yes, we are but first how did you make out this morning with the eye exam?" Bill the ever loyal, friend needed to know his status. "Better than Dr. Phillips expected so I'm on the mend, thank God." Answered Karl as he opened his file to continue with the planning of the operation.

Claire had gone right to her practice, throwing herself into the pile of folders on her desk. Beverly entered asking her how the weekend went, her gaze not leaving the ring. "Oh, Bev it was wonderful everyone in Karl staff made such a warm fuss I felt like a princess. As for Karl friends they also gave us a marvelous time Saturday evening then Sunday at Clive and Julie's house for lunch she has two beautiful girls so well behaved. It could not have gone any better, think I have made lasting friends in Julie and Dorothy, crazy Bill's girlfriend. "By the way, your sister called looking for you, she said to remind you she has not heard from you in a long time, and it must be that army chap your over the moon about." Beverly giving a little chuckle saying that last part. Oh God, Bev' I usually call her every weekend she must be really angry at me right now, willing to bet she's more interested in all the juicy stuff, she always was the nosy one." Claire shaking her head as she said that. Claire got home a little after six o'clock to an empty house. The first thing she did was call Karl at the camp, the operator asking to hold while he located him. "Karl darling, what did the doctor say this morning is he pleased with your progress? Said Claire her brain going at a hundred miles an hour. "Everything is better than expected, Dr. Phillips, told me there's no real need to see him again unless something goes wrong, the camp Doc can take over from here on, isn't that great news. Karl could tell she needed to talk so he kept it brief. "I Just got home a little while ago, I'm so bogged down with file reviews I think I'm going to start real early tomorrow morning, so I'll have an early night tonight. Karl while I was driving home this morning, I had time to relax and reflect on how I have changed in just a few weeks. When I was married to Patrick, we had a good marriage, our love making was comfortable but never over the top, if you are following me. Friday evening before going out something came over me making me someone else, someone who was forceful and daring in her teasing and God knows leaving high heels on during love making is something I would never do, till I met you I was more the flannel nightgown type. I swear to God Karl it's being with you that's turning me into nymphomaniac and that scares the heck out of me, you must be thinking what on earth am I getting into with this sex starved woman." Claire saying all that thought, oh my goodness I've said too much haven't I. Karl on the other end of the phone was trying hard not to burst out laughing. "Claire you are so adorable in the innocent way you just described yourself. Darling it was always there you just suppressed those feelings holding them back maybe too scared or even to aloof to let yourself go and be the person you secretly dreamed of being when you love someone with all your being. You do understand if I ever see you in a flannel nightgown, I will burn it don't you? What a wonderful, complexed, intelligent and the sexiest solicitor you are. Claire when I come home you realize I want and will get a repeat performance of Friday night, don't you? Claire what happened is something you have always wanted to do, I simple opened that door you have always been too scared to pass through." Karl was becoming serious, realizing that this proper English lady had scared herself and maybe a little afraid the confident upper lip had been slightly altered. Whatever happened she knew there was no going back nor would Karl allow her to. "Darling must call my sister Caroline, she called my office wondering why I haven't called her she must be really mad at me about now. I'm willing to bet she wants to come meet you what are we doing this weekend other than scaring me half to death?" Claire now returning to her composed self. "Nothing as far as I know, I'll let you know my schedule tomorrow, good night Claire you make each day a delight, never change." Karl hung up the phone then went back into Bill's office to continue were they left off.

Claire dialed her sister's number hearing her sister's voice she said, "Caroline are you mad at me, I'm so sorry it's been a whirlwind weekend. I drove to Slough to meet up with the people that work for Karl, his close friends gave us an engagement party at this swanky hotel and restaurant called the Charter Arms, what a night. Caroline I can't wait for you to meet your new brother-in-Law, I know you will love him, his personality is so contagious. When I'm with him I find myself becoming daring in so many ways." Over the next ninety minute she told her sister everything leaving nothing out, their bond of sisterhood was such they always told each other everything and this phone call was no different. After Claire had finished, she quietly asked, "Well what do you think to your big sister now?" There was a pause before Caroline yelled out in laughter. "Claire, you're such a slut what happened to my stuffy, stuck up sister always proper in whatever she does and say's. Tell me again about Friday Night and what you did to him." Caroline was loving this new side of her big sister. "Now let's stop laughing and be serious shall we, I was thinking of inviting myself for the weekend. I have cleared it with *David* he is alright taking care of the kids in fact he told me last night, don't you think you should visit your sister and especially now she is engaged to that Intelligence chap. So, should I plan on it?" Asked Caroline. "Yes, yes, yes my little sister that would be wonderful. Karl usually arrives Friday late afternoon, he catches the train from Kings Cross which arrives here in Hitchin about 6:30pm. If you plan it right, you could meet up there then take the same train, that would be so much easier picking you both up at the same time." Claire the organizer was excited to finally have Karl meet her younger sister. Feeling really tired she made herself a sandwich then went upstairs to bed. Undressing she went to put on her night gown, stopping she broke out laughing, from now on I'll have to hide this one on Fridays before Karl arrives home.

Tuesday morning, Karl and Bill sat in the small meeting room waiting for the German candidate to arrive. The door swung open and in walked four uniformed BIS agents. "Gentlemen please take a seat," asked Bill. The four agents took seats across from Bill and Karl, "Your files are very impressive as former seamen for the Kreigsmarine. This morning we will interview each one of you separately before deciding which two fit the requirements we are looking for. Do you have any questions to ask before we start the process? The four German all said no they wanted to know the details before going any further. Over the next five hours each agent was asked the same question, then cross questioned until Bill and Karl zeroed in on two. "Bring, "Fredrick and Walter back in," asked Bill to the MP stationed at the door. "Gentleman please have a seat sorry it's been a long day for you so far, the mission we are asking you to undertake is right here in England, we need you both to masquerade as shipwrecked German sailor. Your mission is to gain their confidence and by doing so get them to disclose certain facts about U-boat activities, their numbers, strengths and how they are directed to attack allied convoys in the North Atlantic. This mission will be very dangerous for both of you, it could cost you your lives, are you prepared to undertake a mission like this?" Asked Bill staring at them both. "How do you propose we go about doing this assuming we can gain their trust?" asked the one that had been a senior office on a destroyer based in Norway. Bill turned to Karl asking him to take over the meeting, describing the details of the plan. Speaking German Karl proceeded, the look on their faces when they discovered he was a maritime officer for a German shipping company was amusing to both Karl and Bill.

The German agents after hearing the plan agreed they were eager to undertake the mission asking, "When are we going to do this and where are these prisoners being held right now." Karl pulled the thick files out of his briefcase spreading them out on each prisoner then said, "Alright let's get to work, shall we?" Over the next two and a half days they refined the plan and their cover stories. At 2345 hrs Wednesday evening the plot was finished the four of them could do no more they were so tired. "Alright chaps let's call it a night, tomorrow you two will be transported to the Bedford facilities in an armed lorry we will be arriving later masquerading as interrogators, remember we have never seen you before so act the part of being rebellious German prisoners of war. "Have a good night sleep tomorrow, will be a long one." Said Karl walking towards the door.

The following morning Karl and Bill met early at the *NAAFI* for hot tea and a sandwich before driving to Bedford, Bill doing the driving. Their interrogation cover would commence Monday morning only the camp commander had knowledge of what was happening. Fredrick and Walter would be driving to holding cells at the camp they both would occupy a cell together till Monday that would give the rumor mill time to spread the news that two more sailors had been brought to the Interrogation Center. Arriving at the camp Bill and Karl spent the afternoon with *Major Warren Biggles* the camp commander who later invited them to join him for supper in a very posh officer club. "Gentlemen what role would you like me and my chaps to play in this masquerade of yours?" Asked the Major. Once again, they explained their web of deceit. Major Biggles hearing the plot and how it would play out sat back saying. "Bloody marvelous idea who did it come from?" Bill looking at Karl said, "from Karl." "So tomorrow you two will start your interrogation of all the German sailors correct, will there be any roughing them up or will that be later? "We will have to play that one by ear, our two moles may have to go along with that idea if it brings credence to them being loyal German Kriegsmarine sailors. The Major walked them over to the visiting officer's quarters before wishing them good evening. "Hope you have a relaxing evening chaps see you in the morning."

Karl was tired he needed to get an early night. Bill was feeling the same so they both headed to their own rooms, Karl decided it wasn't that late to call Claire, so he walked back to the operations area. "Excuse me Sargent where can I use a private phone?" The Sargent pointed to an officer across the hall replying. "Right over there, Sir, dial the operator for an outside line." Karl went in closing the door behind him, sitting down he placed the call, "Hitchin 4567 answered Claire, without asking she knew it was Karl. "Darling I was wondering if you would call me tonight, are you in that other place tonight." Claire careful not to mention locations. "Yes, I am Claire will be home tomorrow early evening, now where do I meet your sister in Kings Cross Station? And what will she be wearing?" Karl took his pocket pad and pen out to write down the information. "Remember on Monday morning I will be leaving at the crack of dawn, Sunday I need to park the MG at the house, that will work out nicely, then on the following Friday I can drive back home again. Now Miss McGivern, I need to know, do you miss me terribly?" Karl already knew her answer. "You tease why do you say things like that, I can't wait to devour you tomorrow, sister or no sister. By the way we are having Goulash for supper tomorrow. I have invited the family over to meet my baby sister should be fun. I'm picking Mama, Freida and Franchot up about 2:00 pm she wants to help me make dinner, should be interesting. Karl how are you sleeping any bad dreams I should know about?" Asked Claire. "Not really, I think talking about it like we did, has help me tremendously. See you Friday, by then your sister will have spill the beans on your younger days. Good night darling." Karl hung up the phone and headed back to his room. The following morning Karl and Bill reviewed the plan with Fredrick and Walter making sure they had studied the plot over and over till it was engraved into their brains. Both agents were using their cover names even when Karl shot a question at Fredrick in German using his real name he answered, "I'm sorry I don't know a Fredrick is he a POW in this camp as well?" The plot was as bullet proof as it could be. Bill satisfied with the readiness of the two agents turned to Karl saying, "Time for us to hit the road Captain, any last minute advise you would like to pass on before we leave?" "Only this, weigh each and every word carefully before you speak, they will be feeling you out at first so that's the most dangerous part of this plot." Karl and Bill stood up shaking their hands then left, in the lobby they said goodbye to the camp commander saying they will arrive back on Monday morning before 1030 hrs. The drive back to Slough was surprisingly quick, with no traffic delays. Bill took Karl straight to the station, "See you Monday looking forward to seeing the MG, no speeding with only one eye." Bill driving off laughing about his last statement.

Karl standing under the arrivals and departure board in Kings Cross Station kept looking for a younger version of Claire in a *Harris Tweed* suit. Looking repeatedly at his watch, he was thinking she's cutting this really close? Almost ready to head to the platform on his own, Karl spotted an attractive woman walking fast, almost in a jog and waving as she approached yelling, "Karl, hold on I'm here so sorry for making you wait are we going to miss the train?" Caroline had made it thank God she was only looking for a military officer wearing a brown eye patch to identify him. "Caroline I was almost going to leave without you, come on we can make formal introductions once we are on the train. Here give me your suitcase and grab my arm we will have to move fast how strong are your legs?" Karl laughing as Caroline tried to keep up with him. The ticket conductor punched their tickets saying jump into the first available compartment the train is leaving right now. Karl opened the first empty door half lifting and pushing Caroline into the compartment saying, "almost out of breath," Caroline yelling back at Karl as he shut the door. "Bugger that was close, what a way to meet my new brother-in-law thank God for the eye patch, I would probably missed you amongst all those uniforms? Now come here and give me a hug and a big kiss on the cheek." Caroline excited to meet Claire's future husband. "Karl I must say Claire picked a smashing bloke to marry, I can see how she fell for you in such a big way, quite the Lover Boy from what Claire has told me." Caroline looked so much like her big sister, but their personalities were so different, she had a devilish side to her which Karl enjoyed. "Caroline, I must say you are a very attractive bubbly lady." Caroline with a big smile on her face answered. "Thank you kindly, sir glad you approve now wait a minute we need to celebrate before we get into Hitchen." From her hand luggage she retrieved two metal cups and a hip flask containing Whiskey. Karl watching her was laughing at what she was doing as she handed Karl a very full cup and one for herself, linking arms she looked up at Karl saying, "Welcome to the family Karl, Claire loves you so very much, please don't get yourself killed she has been down that road once already, now drink up we have enough for one more refill." Caroline the younger sister was so outgoing and very cheeky other than looks the two sisters were completely different. "Next stop is ours, let me get your case down ready," Said Karl putting his tunic back on, the trains brakes squealing in protest as it entered the station, there on the platform was Claire along with Freida looking at the passengers getting off. "Freida, there they are behind that porter Karl, Caroline over here!" yelled Freida as they all came together on that crowded platform. Claire introduced her sister to Freida then turned quickly to face her one, eyed soldier. "Claire kiss him or I'll do it for you?" Said an excited Caroline. Karl put down their cases then with open arms rapped them around Claire quietly saying, "I'm home," with that he kissed her first on the lips then on her neck. "Freida so nice to see you coming to welcome us," Karl hugged his younger sister asking where is Ronny? "He'll be along after 6:30pm he's driving straight here from the base. Back at the house Mama hugged her son then did the same to Caroline. Karl's nostrils were catching the familiar aroma of Goulash wafting from the kitchen. "Karl you should be proud of Claire she made our supper all by herself," Said Mama. "That's not completely true Mama and Freida guided me on some of the steps." Claire was excited having her sister there to finally meet her new family. Seating in the lounge waiting for Ronny to arrive Caroline picked up Claire's hand saying, "I say sis that's a smashing engagement ring your wearing quite an unusual design?" Caroline knowing full well its origins. Ronny arrived on time to join them all for dinner, Claire with Freida help served dinner, Karl and Ronny enjoying the large portion they were given of tasty Goulash finishing it off with bread. Ronny turned to Claire saying to her "Have to wait for Karl to come home to get this treat, come home more often, will you?" Ronny loved it when they all came together like this, with Karl and himself in uniform a normal life was out of the question.

The weekend was delightful Claire and Karl took Caroline to Cambridge stopping on the way back in Baldock to have cocktail at the George and Dragon. Their final stop was at the Bungalow for cake and coffee with the family before returning home to Hitchen. That evening Claire and Caroline told tales of growing up in this house with their parents. "Caroline before you had children what did you do for work, did you also work for your father?" Asked Karl. "No, I did not I was a Science teacher in *Watford* that's where I met my husband David, the rest is history. We moved to Oxford after our first child was born, we decided it was the perfect place to raise a family, wish you both could be closer though, putting her arm around Claire's shoulder. "Tomorrow is Sunday so what shall we do?" asked Karl wondering what to do with these two beautiful ladies. "How do you feel about going to church you both have much to be thankful for?" suggested Caroline eyeballing Claire then starring at Karl. "Why not you are absolutely correct hope the roof doesn't cave in when I walk in though?" Said Karl trying not to laugh. The two sisters dressed in their Sunday best and Karl wore his dress uniform. The old church built in the late 1600's had a musty smell to it, probably from all those candles burning at the back by the entrance. Karl in an almost whisper said, "so far so good," Claire answering, "Vita, behave yourself." After mass Claire introduced Karl to the priest. Karl surprised them by telling tales of when he was an altar boy in Vienna. "Father thank you we will see you on Sundays from now on?" said Claire as they returned to the car. Caroline adding, "Well, I thought if it remains nice and sunny, we could go walking around the streets of Hitchin, we must be boring Karl to death with our stories of growing up in this old town and doing things proper young ladies should not be doing." Caroline enjoying embarrassing her sister in front of her fiancé. "Well, if we do, we can stop at your office on the way back to pick up the MG, got to be on the road early tomorrow morning if I'm to arrive back at the camp by 0900 hrs. How does that sound to you two ladies?" replied Karl enjoying the horseplay between the sisters. Another wonderful day was spent walking around the old historic farming town, Claire and Caroline explaining the history of the old building as they walked alone, Karl enjoyed it immensely, stopping in at the *Bull* Public House for a plowman's lunch, before leaving Caroline asked Claire, "May I use the Wolsey later, I would like to stop by to see *Pearl* my old school friend while I'm here in Hitchin, you don't mind, do you?" Caroline knew Claire wanted some private time with Karl before he left in the morning and this would be a good way of excusing herself. Karl looked at Claire a twinkle in his eye as Caroline said that, leaning over he kissed Caroline on her cheek saying, "Thank you that's such a sweet lie." Arriving at the office Karl backed the MG out of the garage Claire locking behind him. "Alright let's head home Karl park the MG to one side of the driveway so Caroline can put the Wolsey back in the garage when she returns home later today."

The house seemed very quiet once Caroline had left to see her friend, Claire asked, "Well now you have me all to yourself Sailor, what do you want to do with me?" Claire pulling him closer to her. Karl answering with his unique Austrian humor. "Well seeing as I'm leaving early tomorrow morning, I seem to be experiencing some separation tension, I know you could treat that with those wonderful lips of yours, a good way to start off the evening would it not?" Karl giving Claire that stare that unhinged her each time he did that. Claire knew what he was thinking. Leading him into the living room she guided him to the couch saying almost in a whisper, lay back darling, close your eyes and think only of me, I know exactly how to treat that tension." Claire kissed him her hand unbuttoning his shirt and then his trousers. To arouse him further she removed her jumper and slacks allowing her soft skin to arouse those feelings within him. Claire's lips kissed him all the way down then her mouth encircling him. Karl fully aroused turned Claire over onto the couch removed her underwear and spread her legs to reciprocate with his tongue, Claire was on a cloud Karl had a way of eliminating her inhibitions letting herself go in a way she never done before. Claire's breathing was becoming intense she was at the bring, of exploding Karl pulled back and immediately entered her to feel her orgasm that triggered his. Karl laying on top of her without moving softly kissing her as she still quivered totally spent. Claire finally regained her composure saying. "Karl you continue to bring something new out in me, I have never felt this type of intensity from anyone else unfortunately that includes dear Patrick. Darling you know, as much as I love us being this close there is a part of me that is scared to death of losing what we have. In your line of work there will always be a part of you that needs to be out doing spy things and it's that part that scares me so, I would never ask you to change positions in the military that would be selfish to do that to you, all I can ask of you is try not to be a hero will you do that much for me?" Claire needed Karl to know in her heart she knew he would return to the dangerous missions someplace not so safe. Karl looked at her before he answered her. "Claire, you know I will try to be careful I can't promise you more at this time, now let's get dressed again so Caroline doesn't get a shock when she walks back into the house. Claire smiled answering, "Nothing you could do, or say, or what we are not wearing would phase Caroline in anyway, whatever your thinking, she has probably done many times over." Claire somewhat serious saying that. Caroline returned home at 9:15pm entering the living room she cheerfully announced, "That was so nice to spend time with Pearl and her family for a couple of hours, expected to see your bedroom door closed." Claire hearing that looked at Karl before they both started laughing Claire eventually saying, "Caroline for once, you are too late." In the middle of a world war three people were taking the time to enjoying themselves but for how much longer?

The following morning Karl dressing in his everyday field uniform, kissed Claire then Caroline on both cheeks giving her a big hug saying, "Caroline I am so please to have met you next time Claire and I will come to Oxford to meet your family, that's if you want us to?" Karl gave Claire a last kiss and hugged her like he would never see her again. Backing out of the driveway he took a last look at Claire and Caroline, thinking someone up there has given me a second chance and I will not take this lightly, thank you Lord, he thought as he put the MG into gear driving away back into the intelligence world, he lived and survived in.

Chapter Sixteen
1941 A Time of Change

Claire had given Karl the direction the night before, although her direction would direct him to Bedford's City Center, realizing his final destination could be some secret location, he could not divulge to her. Claire indicated the secondary roads would be better that early in the morning, she told him to look for signs that would take him through the villages of *Arlesy* then *Shefford* and close to *Amphill*, when he crosses the A-421 he would arrive at the outskirts of Bedford. "It's only about twenty-five or so miles so it shouldn't take you to long," Indicated Claire with a puzzled look on her face, Caroline interrupted by blurted out, "If that's where he's actually going? I'm willing to bet he's going to *RAF Cardington*, no need to answer that Karl, I know you won't tell us anyway if that's the case. When you get to the A-421 you need to head North East the camp is not too far after you turn right assuming that's where you are really going?" Caroline remembering some years back when she was dating an RAF warrant officer stationed at Cardington the electrifying evening, she had experienced in the back seat of a Hillman staff car. Karl had his Intelligence face on as he listened to Caroline that had just given him the true directions to his location. Karl kissed them both goodbye then climbed into the cramped cockpit of the MG with a final wave goodbye he was on his way. Driving through the town of Shefford, Karl was enjoying shifting the gears of his little MG, loving how nifty it handled on these winding roads wishing it could be nicer weather to drive with the roof down, maybe on the way back he could do just that. Turning right on the A-421, he noticed the volume of traffic increasing with mainly military vehicles heading east to who knows were? Getting closer to the camp he noticed several silver colored Barrage Balloons hovering about fifty feet off the ground in front of an enormous hanger their massive sizes looking more like giant tear drops. At the gate he presented his credentials to the guards then followed a jeep that led him to the building the BIS was using for their interrogation activities. Pulling up to the entrance, Karl parked the car close to the big Humber being used by Bill thinking, he's already here, not surprised. Entering the lobby Karl registered then proceeded to the room that had been secured for the next several days. "Bill good morning, did you arrive last night or did you drive up this morning," inquired Karl. Bill answering, "Karl did you drive the new MG here this morning? let's go take a quick look before we get serious about our task for this morning shall we." Bill slapping Karl on the shoulder as they went back outside. Bill took one look at the gleaming little sports car, then asked Karl, "So this is the culprit that made you and Claire the success story for 1941?" Bill was belated with joy to see the look of pride Karl had on his face. Getting behind the steering wheel was a challenge for Bill his leg injury received back in 1937 was still giving him problems. "Karl, you will let me drive it before you head back to Baldock won't you? By the way Clive asked me to have you call him as soon as you can, he did not want to spoil your time with Claire calling you over the weekend? why don't you make that call before we start our interrogation session?"

Back inside Karl asked for a quiet office with a secure phone, the pretty WRAF rating escorted him to an empty office telling him, "Dial the operator for that secure line by dialing #871, she will secure the line for you." Karl sat down taking out a small pad and a pen. The phone rang through to Clive's office, Mary, Clive secretary answering, "Major Knights extension who is calling please." Karl replying. "Good morning Mary it's me Captain Vita is the boss in his office?" Mary knew instantly it was Karl by his distinctive accent, "Morning Captain yes he is, nice to hear from you, hope all is well and how is that sweetheart of yours, Claire?" She inquired. "Thank you for asking Mary, we are all fine should be back at HQ soon." Concluded Karl not wanting to give an exact date. "Hold one minute Captain I'll get him for you." Clive picked up the phone answering in that controlled voice of his. "Karl good to hear your voice, are you on a secure extension?" Clive making sure their conversion would not be compromised. "When you arrive back, come see me right away, I have some exciting news for you, oh, by the way you will need to pack for ten days? We are sending you to Scotland, remember that camp up there? Well, you will be returning to it." Karl stopping him mid-sentence asking, "Why?" is all he could say. "Well Karl you are to be promoted to the rank of Major as the Commanding Officer of a brand new Special Intelligence Division, that promotion by the way is a battlefield commission, I'm confident that will be made permanent at some later date, we did this because it was the quickest way to get your rank bumped up, by the way this was not my idea, although I am delighted to know you are one rank below my new rank of Lieutenant-Colonel! As of this coming Friday, I have excepted a position on General Jacks Staff." Explained Clive, knowing all these changes would rattle Karl who never embraced changes that well. "So, if your being promoted out of this Commander, who will be its new C.O?" Asked Karl now suspecting another bomb to be dropped on him. "Another new Major by the name of William Lowes?" Clive could not contain himself he loved it when Karl got rattled. "You are pulling my leg so when Bill returned to Slough last Friday all of this happened over the weekend?" Asked Karl thinking here we go again with all that secret BIS stuff? Clive simple answered, "Yes, I took it upon myself to wait till you arrived this morning to tell you about the changes that are happening, so don't yell at Bill to much after hanging up the phone, he is your friend remember that." Clive as he spoke was also deciding whether to tell him that he had spoken to Claire earlier this morning?" "Karl there is something else I need to share with you this morning after you had left Hitchin, I took it upon myself to call Claire to inform her that you have been promoted to Major. Karl she was so excited, it made me feel really good, one last thing considering you will be out of town for a while I told Bill earlier to send you home earlier probable Wednesday afternoon, so you and Claire can celebrate your promotion together. Karl are you still there?" Asked Clive not sure if he had lost him. "Yes, Clive I'm still here, I'm trying to wrap my mind around all the changes taking place right now. Thank you for making this happen old friend, that was so considerate of you to include Claire, I can't thank you enough, if you don't mind, I'm going to give her a quick call before becoming a devious Intelligence officer for the next three day." Karl hung up the phone looking at his watch to make sure he still had enough time to make that call. Calling Claire's office, he greeted Beverly saying, "Morning Bev, is Claire busy this is Karl," Beverly answering cheerfully "Never too busy to talk to you Major Vita, I'll put you through," Claire picked up the phone, "Karl darling isn't this marvelous news, please don't be mad at Clive he is so proud of you and wanted to tell me right away, darling you're a flashy new Major when do you think you'll receive your new insignia bars? Hopefully before you arrive home on Wednesday evening." Claire being so excited had told everyone in the office about his promotion, however she had no knowledge of the dangers associated with this promotion! Karl had been usurped by his boss Clive, being the last to receive the news on his new assignment and promotion. Just think one of these days I will be the one to surprise everyone with some breaking news? thought Karl.

Walking back towards the meeting room Karl could see five German POW's being escorted down the hall from the opposite direction by four armed Military Police guards. As they shuffled closer, he heard one of the U-Boat officers speaking in a shushed voice to the officer behind him, Karl recognizing his insignias and white cap to be the Captain, "Look at this pompas ass thinks he has the upper hand pity the S.S weren't here he would be shitting himself to death?" Karl walked right in front of him poking his finger against the Germans chest, standing there he glared at him face to face hate and anger in his one good eye. Pointing at his patch he screamed at him in German, "You conceded pompous idiot, who do you think you are, this eye was the work of those gutter scums in the Gestapo maybe I should be doing the same to you how does that appeal to your sense of survival you idiot you are looking at one of your interrogators, yes that's me? I was forced to leave Austria because of pig headed maniacs like you that bulled their way into my country, stand at attention, while I'm talking to you and deciding your fate." Karl had lost his composure over this sailor and now was regretting it however this sailor was visibly scared at what Karl might do to him. The Captain came forward and politely saluted Karl asking his forgiveness for the insolence behavior exhibited by his junior officer. Hearing the screaming Bill came out into the corridor saying, "What on earth is going on out here. Captain Vita, please explain." Bill was worried that their strategy may have been compromised. "It's alright now the Captain here has apologized for the insolence shown by this classless officer, I really expected more from the U-Boat Service." Said Karl as he elbowed his way passed the offending sailor.

Lining the five prisoners up in front of the table, Bill asked the clerk to record their names, rank and serial numbers starting with the U-Boat Captain then on to the next who was the big mouth in the corridor somewhat less arrogant than earlier. The third did the same very politely answering in English to the surprise of Karl and Bill. The two moles were next expressing they were not from the U-Boat Service but served on a fast E-Boat. "So, you are telling us you did not serve together in the U-Boat service? Well, that changes things." Said Bill working up to their cover plot. Over the next three hours they skillfully laid their trap focusing on the big mouth to be the one that would spill his guts to the two E-Boat sailors. "Guards we're done for the day take them away and bring them back at 0700 hrs tomorrow morning." Said Bill as he stood up, Karl on the other hand walked up to the big mouth saying in German, "I will have my time with you count on it now get out of my sight." Pointing to his patched eye, Karl was laying a trap and needed the sailor to think about what his future would hold for him. Walking back to the lounge Karl congratulated Bill and Bill did the same to Karl on their new promotions and postings, Bill adding "Karl, Clive will be moving to General Jacks headquarters thank goodness he will not have to move the family, the new offices are only twelve miles away, so he is tickled pink about that. As for you, your new division will be formed at our present location unless you request another location?" Bill looking at his friend for an answer. "Bill, I have a lot to understand about what will be expected of me, I'm assuming there will be an in-depth indoctrination on our return to Slough next week, correct?" Inquired Karl. Bill stopping him in the corridor by answering, "Karl its counter espionage, not that different from what you have been doing for us all along you're the best at this sort of thing, that's why you, over anyone else was selected to lead this new division.

The following morning Bill and Karl sat once again at the table ready to interrogate the prisoners on an individual basis this time looking for a weak link to focus on. The Captain as expected was a polite but totally uncooperative when it came to providing information. "Guard put the Captain in isolation cell #03 till we need him further. Bring in Lieutenant *Wartburg* next. "Come in and sit down," Bill directing the German to take the seat directly in front of them, Karl glaring at him, not taking his eye off him, "Now we have heard from other POW's you did not want to follow your Captains orders when leaving Brest to attack a British destroyer squadron operating in the channel is that right?" asked Bill. "I follow orders whatever my Captain tells me, I do, I know nothing about challenging those orders. When we left Brest, it was to attack a convoy nearing the Lizard off the South West tip of England, I repeat I know nothing about attacking a destroyer squadron?" Wartburg had a confused look on his face wondering where this was going. "Guard take this prisoner to cell #2 until we need him further. Once Wartburg was out of the room Karl turned to Bill saying, "Now our moles can commence their fact finding, let's now repeat this on the Captain with the other mole." Over the next two days they gathered snippets of information that when pieced together would create a harvest of data how the Germans were directing U-Boat patrol in specifically defined numbered grid patterns and more importantly their encrypted communications to those vessels using an encryption device known as the *Enigma*. Wednesday Bill pulled the two moles out of their holding cells their work had been done successfully and a new method of none-aggressive interrogation has been created. "Karl, you asked why are you being given command of this new division? Look at what you have just done with this new head game of yours it worked, did it not? I'll report back to HQ on our initial findings. Tomorrow those prisoners will be dispersed to new and different POW camps never to see each other again till this blasted war is over anyway, good job Karl." That afternoon Bill and Karl drafted revisions to this new procedure for future interrogation sessions. Their work complete, Bill walked Karl out to his car saying, "Enjoy your four days off old man. Monday you are scheduled for an early morning flight to Scotland, are you getting excited yet?" Bill was laughing at the look on Karl's face. "I got a feeling you and Clive are behind all of this?" Said Karl, see you on Monday, climbing into his little MG. "Hold on Karl, I nearly forgot something, you must come back inside with me I promised Clive, I would change your rank insignias before you left today, come on follow me." Said Bill angry at himself for nearly allowing Karl to leave. Entering the supply area, they waited while a WRAF sergeant replaced the badges on his tunic and issuing his new Identification cards. "Now you can go home Major and give Claire a big kiss and hug for me." "Will do Bill but I'll decide were those kisses go." Laughed Karl as he drove off with the roof down. The traffic was heavier considering the time of day but that did not deter Karl from enjoying the drive back to Hitchin.

Karl parked the car to one side of the garage, removing his house key he unlocked the door and entered the kitchen to find Claire was not home yet. Draping his tunic over the kitchen chair he made himself a pot of coffee then removed several folders from his brief case and went into the living room to get some work done. He did not get far before the heavy feeling of sleep overcame him, giving in to that feeling he removed his boots to lay on the couch surrendering to that feeling. Claire arriving home becoming excited to see the MG back in the driveway, entering the kitchen she sensed the lack of sound, tiptoeing into the living room she saw Karl stretched out fast asleep. He's probably exhausted best not to disturb him. Claire climbed the stair to get out of her business suite and have a relaxing bath. Feeling so much better she dressed in a casual pair of slacks and a loose fitted jumper, before going back downstairs. Karl was still sleeping so she went back into the kitchen to make herself a cup of tea, returning to the living room she placed her brief case to one side of the desk then started working. A little after 7:00pm the telephone rung loudly, Claire thinking oh God that will wake him up for sure. "Hitchen 4567, who's calling please." Asked Claire upset about the loud ringtone. "Claire how are you doing its Clive did Karl make it home yet?" Claire quietly started to answer him by saying, "He's still sleeping on the couch." when Karl's surprised her his lips kissing her cheek saying, "Sounds like it's for me, is it?" Claire turned to kiss him back saying, "Its Clive darling so sorry I was going to let you sleep you looked so relaxed." Karl took the phone from her hand tapping her on the backside and pointing to the coffee pot gesturing for another cup. "Clive old man good to hear from you, guess Bill filled you in on our little scheme, won't say any more till I see you on Monday." Clive listening to him felt bad that he was cutting his time with Claire short. "Karl, I hate to do this to you, but we have been told to report on Sunday for a general staff meeting, please adjust your plans accordingly, by the way I'm having a secure separate telephone being installed Friday morning, I've cleared it with Claire she understands completely, guess you haven't had time to talk about it yet. See you Saturday afternoon, by the way, Julie is inviting you and Bill for dinner about

1800 hrs, sorry to wake you up, cheers." Karl hung up the phone thinking what is going on for the big wigs to call for staff meeting this Sunday. "Claire, we have a change of plans, I have to return to Slough Saturday instead of Sunday afternoon, sounds like something really important is happening." Karl saddened that instead of ten days away from Claire would now be twelve or maybe more? Thursday Claire went off to the office so Karl drove to see his family in Baldock. Mama prepared a wonderful lunch for her son the new Major while Karl fixed a hinge on the bathroom door. In the afternoon Karl, Freida, and Franchot took a walk up the street to the pasture to see Tug, the big draft horse. This time alone gave them time to talk about Papa and his brothers, Hazel and how to handle that glaring problem. Finally, the question of wedding plans came up, where would it be held? Probably in the church Claire attends services at. Sitting on the fence Karl spoke up by saying. "Claire told me earlier with all that is going on right now, next June would probably be a good time to plan the wedding, she also thought we could have a small reception at the *Letchworth Hall Hotel*. The problem is going to be my work that could take me away with little to no notice, so we need to give that a lot of thought, she has already told me we should not let this war interfere with our wedding plans." Karl, on the other hand would prefer to wait till they knew more about which way the pendulum of this war could swing, but if Claire needed that security, he would be for it. Back at the bungalow the afternoon was fading fast and the time to return home to Hitchin had arrived, kissing them goodbye he told them he would be going up North for a couple of weeks to coordinate his new command his parting words being, "See you when I return, stay safe," as he drove off up the Letchworth Rd back to Hitchin. Claire hearing the car pulling into the driveway walked outside throwing her arms around his neck saying, "Corporal McGivern reporting for duty Major." Karl could not help laughing at this line she was using. "Darling we have been invited to meet up with my partners and their wife's later at the *Crown and Castle*, I told them we would love that, is that alright with you darling?" Claire knew he would not object he was that type of a fellow. The Crown and Castle was a quant historic public house that had weathered many an uprising since the late 1600's. Karl opened the door for Claire then followed her into the lounge. "Over here," called *Jeffrey* standing and waving his arms. Karl looking at Claire's two junior partners thinking, wonder who they know to keep them out of military service? "Nice to see you again our last meeting was short and chaotic, so pleased you could join us this evening." Said *David,* moving over to make room for Claire and Karl. To his surprise Karl found himself enjoying this gathering, however that question was still in the back of his head, the British military needed more young men wonder what their story could be?

Friday morning Karl alone at home waited for the telephone service people to arrive along with a military security chap that would program the encryption for the new telephone. Claire arrived home after 6:00pm carrying a large document case, "Darling did you miss me, haven't heard from you all day?" Claire could see he had been working as well then noticed the green phone on the desk saying jovially, "Is this the only color available? I would prefer a white or dark blue, only pulling your leg you sensitive chap." Claire being amused by his facial expression. "I'm going upstairs to get out of this suite and have a quick bath, care to join me?" Claire thinking he's in that BIS mode again, I can see he's already thinking about tomorrow. Claire came back downstairs saying, "I'm going to start supper will you be ready in half an hour? Karl was still writing directions placing them into each folder. "Almost done corporal McGivern," replied Karl. After supper they sat in the living room listening to classical music and enjoying their quiet time together before Karl left Saturday morning. "Let's have an early night shall we, I'm really tired I did not stop all day." Said Claire hoping Karl did not want or expect more this evening? Lying in bed they had that quiet time in each other arms both thinking about Karl's new responsibilities and the dangers that surely lay ahead? Rising early Karl got his things together then joined Claire downstairs for breakfast at 0730 hrs. Karl in his duty uniform could tell Claire was acting fidgety probably because he was going North to Scotland on Monday, but what will he be doing? She thought. In the living room they sat together on the couch continuing their small talk that eventually came around to scheduling their wedding, Karl on the other hand was only going through the motions his mind already in Scotland. "Time to go darling, what will you do after you have dropped me off?" asked Karl as he put his tunic on. "I'm going to pick up Freida for a girl's day out she really does need some time away from her daily chores and the baby." Replied Claire. From the garage she backed out the Wolsey, Karl putting his things on the backseat then climbed into the passenger seat. "Ready lover boy or should I get you into trouble by jumping you right there in that seat." Claire laughing tried to make light of saying that. The train was scheduled to arrive from Cambridge at 1045 hrs. Claire insisted she walk him to the platform, her arm firmly locked around his. The smoking train slowed to a stop discharging and boarding passenger heading to London, Karl turned to Claire saying, "Claire I'm sorry I was not the best company last night or this morning please forgive me, you know how I hate goodbyes, Claire my sweet adorable, lady I already miss you." Karl pulling her into his arms kissed her passionately before picking up his luggage. Three sailors walking by, yelled back at them, "Sir maybe you should take the next train?" The sailors waving and laughing as they walked down to the third-class section of the train. "Karl, you know how I miss you please don't do anything silly, in just a very short time you have become my world so keep that in mind when you are playing hero." Said Claire that worried look showing through. "Darling I'm only going to meet my men and start classroom training, now take that worried look off your face, see you in a couple of weeks." As Karl said that the PA announced the departure of his train on track number four. "That's mine, darling, now give me a big wet kiss it's got to last me awhile." Karl turning towards his compartment waving as he did so. Claire yelled to him. "I rather do something else with that big wet kiss Lover Boy." Claire watched as the train chugged slowly out of the station, she remained there till it was clear of the station taking a big part of her heart with it.

Waiting in Paddington station Karl called the camp motor pool from a telephone box on the platform to give them the train number and arrival time. This second train was always the quickest, in an hour he was walking down the pavement in front of the station to the waiting staff car. "Afternoon sir, are we going to the camp or to your flat?" Asked corporal Adams. "To the camp Charlie, I gave up my flat, please drop me off at the new officer quarters alright." Karl looked at his watch I have a little over an hour before Bill picks me up so plenty of time. In his room he freshened up then changed into civilian clothes before walking outside to see Bill already waiting. "Bill good to see you, how are thinks in the BIS since I left?" Asked Karl making small talk. The ride to Clive and Julie's home took twenty- five minutes, Bill pulled into the driveway parking next to Clive's staff car, the front door opened and out came Clive saying. "Welcome you two come on in Julie managed to have her mother take the girls for the evening thought you two would prefer no children running around while we have dinner." Concluded Clive. "Welcome you two good looking chaps, what's your poison to start off with?" Asked Julie as she came out of the kitchen, "I thought we could have cocktails before dinner is ready, do you chaps feel like those cocktails outside in the garden seeing as its still nice enough. Oh Karl, Claire said for you to call her either tonight or early tomorrow morning before you boys start your meeting, you can use Clive's office if you would like to make that call tonight while you're still here?" Julie and Claire along with Dorothy had quickly formed a lasting bond of friendship all three of them would lean on that bond in the coming years leading up to the climactic end to WW2. "Claire called you Julie?" inquired Karl. "No Karl, I called her just before you arrived, she was having super with your mother and family." Replied Julie. Clive changed the subject by bringing up BIS stuff, "Karl all of us here are very close friends these bonds are what we lean on during difficult times so keep that in mind? While you two were in Bedford, oh by the way superb job of extracting that information from those German POW's, well done chaps. Now back to what I started to say Major Vita. I attended a debriefing of the Delta-1 team in Aldershot at the Hammersley Barracks and yes Karl, Hazel was there. She and I had a drink together after the first day's debriefing she came right out and asked me where the rumors true about Karl's involvement with someone else. Karl, I had no choice I had to tell her it was true. The look on her face was one of defeat and maybe despair. Karl the following morning she gave me this letter to give you and told me to tell you she wishes you both a wonderful life." Clive went over to his desk returning with Hazel's letter. "Here you go Karl put it in your jacket, I think after you have read it you should write back to her or if you're up to it call her." Clive returned to the whiskey decanter asking, "You two, ready for a refill yet?" Asked Clive. Karl standing with the letter in his hand felt terrible knowing he had broken Hazel's heart, to come back to this after all she had been through. "Clive is she still here?" Karl thinking, he would prefer to confront her to explain how sorry he was that it happened like this. "She left right after the debrief to return to her parent's home, she has also put in a request to be transferred to another branch after her leave is over." Clive was looking at the pain in Karl's face realizing it was a slam to his gut. "Alright you blokes hope you are hungry," Said Julie as she came out into the garden. After a wonderful dinner they adjourned to the living room, Karl excused himself to call Claire. "Hitchen 4567," answered Claire knowing it would be Karl at the other end. "Darling, are you still at the Knight's house talked to Julie earlier she said you would call from their house, are you having a nice evening? Everyone here sends their best, I will be thinking of you tomorrow don't volunteer for something dangerous darling, I know how you get?" Claire was fishing for something, but what did Julie tell her? "Yes, darling its nice spending time reminiscing about the old times, tomorrow we will find out more about changes and new assignments. Just wanted to say hello and how much I miss you, I love you Claire, will call you tomorrow evening, bye for now." Karl hung up the phone thinking I'm willing to bet Julie has told her about Hazel being back in England? Sitting back down next to Bill, Clive gave Karl a questioning glance as if to say, what did Julie tell her? Bill stood up and kissed Julie on the cheek saying, "This was a wonderful evening, but our Austrian friend and I should think about leaving, Sunday will be a long repetitious day of what if's?" said Bill looking at Clive for support. "Julie let me add to Bill's thanks, how you got that beef is beyond me, who said you can't find things with ration books?" Karl laughing at his sarcasm. "Oh Karl, you can always count on you for a knife edge complement." With that they gave Julie a goodbye hug, shook Clive's hand and a man hug before stepping out into the black of night. Bill dropped off Karl in front of his quarters then headed out back to Dorothy's flat, Karl walked slowly up the steps into his building. In the corridor he felt his jacket to make sure the letter from Hazel was in his inside pocket, he opened the door. Inside he poured a glass of whiskey placing it on the nightstand, next he took off his shoes and hung up his jacket. Laying on the bed he stared at the envelope in his hand, aching at the pain he was responsible for. Removing the letter from its envelope he unfolded it and started to read.

My Dearest Karl,
First let me congratulate you on your engagement does she know how lucky she is to be the one that will finally be your wife? That same thought kept me going all those months away from you, how I yearned for that time when I would finally arrive back in England, you waiting to sweep me off my feet. Karl every hour of every day I prayed for that and to finally wear your engagement ring. All the things we would be planning for our wedding after this crazy war comes to an end, but now that will never happen!

When I arrived back in Aldershot, I was so excited that I would see you in a couple of days, Clive could see my excitement and decided he should be the one to break the news to me. Over a drink he diplomatically gave me the shattering news that has devastated my world. Clive told me he had sent you and Bill on a field missions, good old Clive always making the right decisions when they are most needed? Darling by the time you read this letter I will be home with my parents, I have an extended leave coming to me, so I'm taking this time to apply for an overseas posting maybe America or perhaps as far away as Australia. Will we meet again? Maybe but more than likely not, I don't believe I'm strong enough for that. So, my crazy Austrian lover boy, my heart will always have a very special place in it for you, securely locked away. Wish me luck and please stay away from those dangerous missions, that last one nearly cost you your life.
I will always remain truly yours,
Hazel Collins

Karl kept reading it over then over again tears cascading down his cheeks, what have I done, how could I hurt her so badly. The day she left on that mission she had told me how scared she was about losing each other. She was correct in thinking there would always be three in that relationship, two of us and Kitty's memory. Every time I looked at Hazel, I was really seeing Kitty, why did I allow that to continue it was doomed from the very start. Once I'm in Scotland I will write to her I owe her that and probably much more, taking the last swig of whiskey he undressed and went to bed completely exhausted.

Sunday morning Karl and Bill had a quick breakfast at the NAAFI, Bill asking had read Hazel's letter, yet? "Yes, Bill I have and at this particular time I really don't like myself, I feel like all I do is break hearts as Gunther once told me I need to take responsibility for the damage I create." Karl his head hung low as he poured his heart out. "Karl let's hope that you have finally released Kitty and given Hazel a chance for happiness while she is young enough to make a new start, that is all you can do right now. Clive and I have been your loyal friends from day one, we both share the same opinion that, Claire is strong enough to give you that wonderful life, she loves you that much, maybe you should consider giving Hazel a call I know she would prefer that to a letter, consider doing that my friend now drink up we have a war to win." Bill, feeling his guilt was trying to give him a way to help Hazel through her pain. Leaving the NAAFI, they headed down to the meeting room it was now 0730 hrs. Entering the meeting room, they were surprised to find about twenty officers of higher rank all milling around with mugs of tea in their hands. Clive came over to welcome them then surprised Karl by saying, "Before we start why don't you both welcome back your old friends over there with General Jacks?" Clive, thinking maybe it would have been a better idea to mention this last night? that Gunther and Herbert would be also attending this meeting. Glad I decided a relaxing evening with these two would be more appropriate, Sunday would come soon enough to mend broken bridges! "My God so pleased to see you two again safe in these surroundings, surprised Clive did not mention it last night, that both of you would be attending." Karl delighted to be reunited with his old friends, looked at Bill, he instantly knew Bill already knew! "Nice to see you to Karl, I understand congratulations are in order, must admit I was under the impression it would be Hazel that we would be congratulating on getting engaged?" Gunther on one hand was pleased to see his old friend but inside he was seething at seeing Hazel coming apart after Clive broke the news to her about Karl's engagement. "Karl, I understand you got that wound to your eye from Gestapo thugs, is that right?" Asked Herbert trying to get Gunther away from the fire storm brewing inside him. "That is correct if it wasn't for the French partisan's attacking the Gestapo Headquarters, I was within minutes of cracking that cyanide capsule and ending it all." Replied Karl still looking at Gunther like the good German officer he was he simple shook his head listening to what Karl had just told them. Moving to Karl's side he placed his arm around his shoulder, composing himself before responding. "Karl you crazy Austrian, I was ready to give you a piece of my mind then hearing you were that close to taking your own life made me realize your loyal friendship takes precedents over my anger, even though I feel like banging your head again for what you keep doing." Gunther expressing their friendship meant more. "When do we get to meet this new lady of yours?" concluded Gunther.

"Gentlemen please take a seat we have much to cover today and let me apologize for taking away from your weekend but getting you all together like this is very difficult so that why it's a Sunday meeting, Colonel Knight would you first take the roll call." Asked General Jacks. After getting all the trivia out of the way Clive asked them to refer to the folders in front of them. "Each one of you is here because of your unique abilities that enabled our intelligence service to continuously infiltrate the highest levels of Nazi Party. This war is so much more than military equipment and armed forces Its about infiltrating their highest levels of secret scientific developments. Today we will formulate how we can improve and accomplish those objectives. During this meeting we will call on some of you to describe your most recent missions and how you met or exceeding those objectives behind enemy lines." Clive asked Gunther and Herbert to describe their recent mission, how effective were the Delta teams in obtaining information on military movements in the occupied countries. Gunther was the perfect officer to answer that question describing the many obstacles they faced daily and how they were nearly compromised by one of their own agents that collaborated with the Germans to save his family, a good agent that placed family over duty. This situation opened a whole discussion on screening more effectively European agents. Clive asked Karl to describe further how he made that discovery of such a glaring problem brought up another question, should they continue using agents that still had family ties in Europe that could be blackmailed into becoming a double agent? Another officer, asked Karl to take them through his experience, masquerading as a Kreigsmarine Officer and what went so terribly wrong that it nearly cost him his life? One by one they told their stories of espionage and how in so many cases the partisans proved to be an invaluable underground force that saved their lives, including Karl's own life. It was agreed that moving forward partisan's support in all operations should be paramount providing, additional training and assistance in the use of munitions, better field medical supplies and better distribution of funding so desperately needed to expand their disruption of the German war machine. Other programs that would be given a higher priority were to embed BIS agents into larger partisan groups providing better utilization of newer radio equipment and their operators effective immediately. General Jacks asked the question how to improve prisoner interrogation methods now that more POW's, were arriving in England. The biggest problem they faced was how to weed out the lies and deception that constantly provided erroneous results. Karl and Bill gave an outline of their recent success interrogating three U-Boat prisoners by imbedding German members of the free European brigade in with these POW's. Also stressed was the need to expand how many agents could be trained as interpreters capable of determining a prisoner's origin by listening to their language and dialect. Major Knight explained further, a concerted effort was underway to recruit and train agents with these abilities to fill that gap. He explained further that Major Vita's new division was already getting survival training in Scotland before training as interpreters began in Slough then Aldershot. The meeting concluded at 1900 hrs everyone mentally drained. Clive was heading home so Gunther, Bill and Herbert and decided to treat Karl to a hardy fish and chip supper at a local pub, they refrained from discuss the meeting to many ears around them to do that. Herbert asked Karl how he found his MG-PB and captured the heart of its owner Claire. Gunther making light of the small talk continued by asking, "When are we being invited to Hitchen to drive the MG and meet Claire, do you have a photograph we can see?" Asked Gunther grinning. Karl removed his wallet from his inside pocket, removing a color photograph of Claire, passing it around he got a chuckle out of them as he watched their faces with remarks like, "Wow what a beauty and will you look at the gams on her." Karl feeling good about the acceptance of his friends. Quietly he said "When I return from Scotland, we can arrange a weekend in Hitchen to meet Claire and then Baldock to meet my family. Gunther looked at the others as if to say I think this is it, but there again he had said that before? Bill finally spoke up by saying, "Dorothy and I had the pleasure of spending an evening with Claire, Julie and Clive not that long ago. She is not only an elegant lady but an accomplished solicitor in her own practice. Karl should never get out of line with this one she is way too quick for Karl here." Bill broke out into laughter at that last line. "Seriously it would be very hard not to adore Claire, we all did and do." Concluded Bill. About 2000 hrs the party broke up, each heading off in different directions. "Karl the car will be waiting to take you to the airstrip at 0730 hrs, if I don't see you before you leave, I'll be anxiously awaiting your evaluation report on your return." Said Bill as he let them all off back at the camp.

Karl like a clock was at the curbside promptly at 0730 hrs, he had a topcoat over his arm as he waited, remembering the taxing weather conditions at the training camp just North of *Glen Nevis* and the five-hour drive, from the City of Edinburgh. Karl was thinking about the first time they all went to that bleak outpost when he was a mere first lieutenant, the journey to Edinburgh on a train followed by a coach ride to the camp which added another five hours making for a real long day. Today it was different, he would be taken to the airstrip in a staff car then by plane to *RAF Kirknewton* just outside Edinburgh and from there to Glen Nevis in a staff car, how things have changed in just a few short years. The car arrived at 0740 hrs the driver apologizing for not being on time. The flight was noisy but so much quicker than a train. At the airbase a staff car was waiting to drive him to the camp, four hours later the car turned into that familiar driveway stopping at the gate the driver telling the guard, "I have Major Vita reporting." The MP walked back to the open window saluting he asked, "Your ID sir and welcome to camp Nevis." They drove up the hill arriving in front of main building, Karl feeling a little tense looking at these drab building that were flooding his mind with memories of Kitty but no black clouds just fond memories. Entering the lobby Karl registered with a burly MP behind the desk. "We have been waiting for your arrival sir, I'll call your second in command Captain Meyers, that you have arrived," said the guard. "That's alright sergeant I know my way around this camp I'll head down to the officers lounge have my bags delivered to my quarters then bring me the key," said Karl feeling better than the last time he was here as a trainee. Opening the familiar swinging door to the lounge, head turning to see who was entering, someone yelled, "Attention," Karl was not ready for these junior officers to stand at attention for him. "Please, no need for this pomp, this is a training camp not a parade ground, no need to stand on ceremony for me. A tall officer in his early thirty's approached Karl saying, "Major Vita so pleased to see you again after so long, remember me *Captain Hardy Meyers* your second in command, may I be the first to congratulate you on this new command and please may I buy you a cocktail." Asked Meyers, "Thought you would never ask and of course I remember you, we will get on famously." replied Karl already feeling at ease. Over supper they discussed their strategy for molding the new trainees into Intelligence interpreters for the BIS.

At 0630 hrs Karl entered training room M-3 his swagger stick under his arm, Meyer at the front of the room yelled, "Attention," Karl approached the stage turned next to Meyer then asked everyone to be seated, "Gentlemen good morning, my name is Major Karl Vita, it wasn't that many years ago that I sat where you are sitting this morning, more than likely thinking the same as you are doing right now, wonder what type of bloke this one will be like? Well, let me put your minds at ease if we all work together and abide by the rules, things will go smoothly. If you cross the line, I will throw the book at you is that perfectly understood, this is a new division in the Intelligence service your life could well depend on the individual by your side so pay attention. As new recruits you have never been exposed nor have any idea how brutal the enemy can be. I have firsthand experience to their barbaric torture methods." Karl pointing to his patched eye adding, "This was a gift of the Gestapo. The training you have been undertaking these last few months is to prepare you for field operations. This new division will more than likely not be put into those dangerous situations. Our primary function is to provide interrogation support. We are processing more POW's daily our job is to get an accurate picture of were that prisoner came from and by deception methods find out what the enemy is planning. Our concentration probably will not be the rank and file but more on higher ranking officers from the various branches of the German Military Services?" Karl spent about another ninety minutes outlining how the training they were currently undertaking, would change from survival skills to classroom studies perfecting their languages and dialects abilities. The final part of their training would be honing their skills in these new interrogation methods. "Some of you could be asked to volunteer for field assignments outside of England another reason you are still being trained in survival technics." Concluded Major Vita.

Karl spent the next ten days working with his staff to build a plan that would become their bible for future operations. During that time, he tried to spend time with each of the teams twenty men, encouraged by their enthusiasm and knowledge to be of the highest standards. Each night he would call Claire assuring her he was in no danger, always ending by saying, "Wish you could be here to handle those special needs I have, love you darling I will be home real soon." On his final day he met with Captain Meyers to discuss the transfer of the team back to Slough. "Meyers when you arrive back it will be your assignment to settle them into the barracks that has been assigned to this team. As for me I'll be back in the camp already, so I'll coordinate with the camp Commander, Major Willian Lowes to officially welcome them and give them his direction for integration into camp life and camp operations." Instructed Karl, confident that as he left the division would excel in their duties. Walked Karl to the staff car Meyers said, "Sir I am so pleased to be reporting to you I'll take care of making sure all goes smoothly from here on see you back in Slough." Stepping back from the car he saluted his Commanding Officer, Karl reciprocating the gesture by tapping the edge of his cap as the car drove off. The last leg of the return trip would be to Duxford with any luck Ronny would still be there to give him a lift back to Hitchin and Claire. Karl was worn out sleep coming quickly he did not wake until the pilot announced. "Buckle up sir, we are making our approach into Duxford." Said the pilot of the old Avro Anson. After a bumpy landing the plane taxied up to the front of the hanger, then silence as the prop's windmilled to a stop. An RAF Private moved quickly to open the rear fuselage door folding down the ladder from inside. Karl thanked the pilots then grabbing his case stepped out into the drizzling rain. Walking quickly, he opened the hanger door hoping to catch Ronny before he left for the day. Inside the enormous hanger crews were working on battle warn Spitfire aircraft one of which was badly shot up. "Excuse me can you direct me to Lieutenant Whiting's office." Asked Karl not sure which hallway to take. "Right down the middle corridor sir his office will be on the left, did you just arrive on that Anson outside?" Asked the friendly aircraft fitter. "Yes, I did." Replied Karl walking off to find Ronny's office at the end of the corridor, knocking on the door a voice on the opposite side said. "Come." Karl opened the door to find his brother-in-Law buried under a pile of service request. "What can I help you with." Ronny said without looking up. "How about a ride to Baldock in that little Austin of yours." Said Karl happily. "Karl when did you arrive, don't tell me you were on that old string bag Anson that arrived fifteen minutes ago were you?" Ronny getting up and coming around to the front of the desk his arms out stretch so please to see Karl. "I'm having a hard time getting my head around your already a Major and I'm still a lieutenant. Let's call Claire she can come over to pick you up from the bungalow, how does that sound?" Said Ronny as he phoned Claire in Hitchin. "Claire, Ronny here, guess who I have in my office? It's a Major giving me the eye to get going, I think he's in a rush to see his fiancée?" Said Ronny handing Karl the phone. "Claire he's so right I'm in rush to sweep you off your feet, see you soon darling." Karl returning the phone to its cradle, Ronny grabbing his tunic and cap they headed to the car park. Arriving back in Baldock Ronny turned into *Brushnell Way* and there parked in front of the house was the Wolsey, no sooner had Ronny shut the engine off when the front door opened out ran Claire ahead of the others. "My Lover Boy your back come here and kiss me you good looking man." Claire happy as she could be now Karl was home. Back inside Mama made them all some strong coffee before serving a light supper and announcing her supply of paprika was almost depleted. "Karl, you have contacts in the supply service maybe you can be persuasive and try to get us some more?" Asked Claire knowing he could always find things that were impossible to obtain. Changing the subject Mama asked, "Well did everything go as planned?" knowing Karl would not elaborate too much, "Very satisfactory glad to be home though." After supper Claire could see Karl was tiring very quickly standing, she announced, "Karl has had a taxing ten days would you mind if I take him home for an early night, look at him he's exhausted, is that alright with all of you?" Mama smiled and quietly said, "Of course dear you are talking about sleeping are you not?" Mama thought the world of Karl and now that love included Claire. "Mama sometimes you really shock me with the things you say." Claire reached for Mama saying in her ear, "I love you so much Mama it's good to know I have a Mother again, now let me softly wake Karl he has a habit of reacting if shooked while he is sleeping." Claire took his hand gently squeezing it till his eyes opened, "Ready to head home Sailor I think you need a good night sleep and tomorrow morning there is no getting up to exercise or going running and that's a Claire order up you get." Mama's heart was warmed by the way Claire took care of Karl, if only they could've found each other sooner before that time when they both had their heart broken by tragic loses, it's their second chance, God don't take that away from them a second time? Thought Mama as she followed them out to the car. Driving home Claire looked over at Karl fast asleep his head resting against the door frame, she was thinking and feeling whole again knowing her life and future would be shared by this man sleeping in her car, thinking that she quietly giggled as she turned into the driveway. Walking around to the passenger side she removed his case from the back seat then ever so carefully woke Karl saying, "Let's get you to bed shall we, I'll take care of putting your things away later." Upstairs Karl went to the bathroom then stripping off and climbed into bed. By the time Claire entered the bedroom Karl was out cold so she got herself ready for bed then stealthily climbed into bed wrapping her arm around his waist.

Claire woke first, quietly she got out of bed putting her house coat and slippers on then slowly opened the door and went downstairs. After putting the coffee on she went outside to recover the morning paper. There on the front page in bold letters she read. All Norwegian civilian radios confiscated by Germans. Another story told about the escalating tension, between America and Japan, the article went on to say America and Great Britain warned if Japan attacked Thailand, there would be severe consequences. Claire still standing in the driveway reading the headlines, shook her head thinking day after day the news is always negative, this world is out of control, unfortunately most of this will sooner than later involve the BIS and that will include Karl's new division? Back inside she poured herself a mug of coffee, feeling a sensation of strong arms encircling her waist followed by a male voice with a very distinct accent announcing, "That aroma of coffee woke me up would you pour one for me as well dear." Karl turned her around and slide his hand inside her house coat. "Karl Vita behave yourself I haven't even had a sip of my coffee yet, I think I'm going to start putting you to bed early from now on, you know how I'm a morning person so remember that you animal you. Is this to be just a quicky or should I be preparing myself for a long morning?" Karl hearing her kidding around like that kissed her on the forehead responding, "My sweet Claire how much I miss our quiet times together they are the medicine I miss most now come here and kiss me properly." Karl in high spirits was over the moon with joy with this woman. Seating in the living room they sat drinking their coffee, Claire, reach over to the coffee table and picked up the morning paper saying, "Karl, look at the front page of the *Daily Mirror* it looks like the Japanese are saber rattling the Americans, do you think the Americans are preparing to enter the war or are you not in a position to comment on that yet?" Asked Claire. "Correct darling however I can tell you this the American Navy has already lost several destroyers to U-Boat torpedoes, I can't imagine President Roosevelt would allow that to continue very much longer. What is helping England, Russia and China is the *Marshal Plan* which enables these countries to purchase war material and equipment on a *deferred lend lease* basis, just in time for us, without that we would have been forced into a cease fire. As for the Japanese movements well their raw materials and oil supplies are being slowly chocked off by the America Government and President Roosevelt has instructed a freeze on all Japanese holdings in the United States, that move has effectively destroyed their currency. So, it's no surprise they are looking elsewhere for their oil and raw materials supplies, they have no qualms about using force to obtain them either. We at the BIS expect reprisals to happen within the next twelve months but more than likely much sooner. The British government is hoping these actions will force America to declare war and by doing so save England, there I said to much but there again much of this is public knowledge. As for The Axis powers, they think they are invincible well maybe they are, but right now England and the Russian are fighting them on multiple fronts. *Operation Barbarossa* back in June put Russia firmly on our side." Karl kept talking and reading the newspaper totally in a relaxed mode Claire by his side on the couch.

That evening they walked to the *Cock and Kettle* for a light supper and drinks, sitting at the bar was a place Karl always enjoyed being, less formal and having a very striking lady at his side made it that much more enjoyable. The weekend seemed to evaporate and now Karl would have to refocus on the many tasks that awaited him back in Slough. Sunday evening Karl packed his case ready to leave very early the following morning. Returning downstairs, he entered the lounge, standing momentarily to observe Claire sitting on the couch engrossed in her book, Claire looked up at Karl smiling saying, "Come sit next to me, do you want some coffee and biscuits to nibble on before we retire early to bed, we need to get up early for me to get you to the train station tomorrow morning. Karl, I noticed you did not apply your medication last night you are starting to get sloppy in your medication schedule, don't forget tonight darling." Claire would remind him of that whenever he was home, she also wondered if he kept forgetting back in the camp? Karl excused himself and went back upstairs to apply the medication, looking in the bathroom mirror he started smiling that turned into a chuckle thinking she is like a mother hen always making sure things are done correctly do I object, not at all she is the medicine I need most in my life. Back downstairs Claire had made a pot of tea carrying it on a tray with a plate of biscuits to the coffee table in front of the couch. Patting the couch Karl sat down next to her as she poured two cups of tea served in elegant bone china cups and sources with matching plates. "Claire you are truly a classy English lady nothing is ever done incorrectly, never anything out of place, except me perhaps?" Karl knew by teasing her like this she would have a comeback, she always did. "This home needs a little mess to remind me, it's a home not a museum you're my adorable mess, don't you ever change on me? Now why don't you hold me we only have tonight till you are off again." Saying that she felt those familiar strong arms encircle her waist and the sensation of Karl kissing her neck, she of course responded by kissing him back passionately her tongue finding his ready. Karl softly laid Claire down on the couch his hand under her head kissing her tenderly he could feel her becoming aroused, with his free arm he moved her legs up close to him, he could feel the soft skin of her thighs her breathing becoming shallow as he continued to stroke her. "Darling, you're driving me crazy do something before I explode." Claire was anxious to have him inside of her, those ladylike manners gone along with her inhibitions. Karl pushed her skirt up high then removed her panties followed by his trousers and underpants. Laying on top of her he continued to tease her by touching but not entering her, doing this was making Claire push to make that happened but Karl, simple maintained this contact. Claire could not contain herself any longer she was about to beg him when Karl slide all the way into her making her gasp at the sensation. He maintained a steady rhythm until arching her back she started trembling crying out, "Darling I'm going to come please let me feel you inside me, please." Karl had been holding back until she was close, he felt her pushing into him and that sensation made him thrust that one more time giving into a climatic orgasm. They laid there on the couch trembling in each other arms until Karl kiddingly said. "Guess our tea has gone cold?" They both looked at each other grinning like Cheshire cats. "Let me go make some more shall I then we can go to bed to sleep that is, you sex mad Austrian." Claire stood up straighten her skirt and buttoning her blouse doing so she started laughing saying. "Am I glad I took my nylons and suspenders off when we came home, for sure they would have runs in them by now, have you any idea how hard it is to find nylons and when you do they cost a fortune." Claire the ever, proper lady walked out into the kitchen leaving Karl lying on the couch relaxing, in the back of his mind a thought crossed his mind. Is Claire trying to get pregnant?

The following morning Claire insisted on walking him up onto the platform, holding hands he kissed her as the smoking monster chuffed into the station. "Call me tonight darling I pray this week goes by quickly." Claire reached up to kiss him then released him to climb into the compartment. From the window Karl waved, silently saying he loved her as the train pulled out of the station, like those times before she stayed till the train was out of sight, only then did she head back to the car and an empty house.

Karl entered the new quarters assigned to his division, only four clerical staff manned the main area all the other stations and offices were empty but why? Looking around he spotted his corner office with its new shingle, *Major K. Vita* prominently displayed on the door? "Where is everyone?" asked Karl to one of the clerical girls. "Oh, Major Vita sorry we have our backs to you, we did not hear you open the door, may I introduce you to, *Lora, Beth, Gloria and my name is Ruth.* We are civilian contractors employed to help your command get established. Your staff is at a group meeting in Major Lowes building, will you be joining them?" Karl spoke briefly to the clerical staff asking questions about where they all live and how long would they be working for him. "Ladies please to make your acquaintance, Ruth would you please hang up my raincoat and put this case in my office, I'm off to join the others. Walking briskly Karl entered the main meeting room, quietly finding a seat at the back of the room he listened to Major Lowes welcoming the new trainees to the camp and what he expected from each of them. Looking towards the back of the room Bill pointed his swagger stick at Karl saying. "Welcome Major Vita please join us up here on the podium, for those of you that have not met or heard of Major Vita he is one of our most valued assets in the Intelligence Service, over the next few months you will invariably be training with him in the latest interrogation methods, deception techniques and staying alive while operating in harm's way." Please welcoming Major Vita to this gathering. Everyone in the room stood up clapping as Karl made his way to the podium. "Gentleman tomorrow morning we will start in earnest to understand and learn the many facets of being a BIS agent. Major Lowes like myself has suffered under the torturous conditions of the Gestapo." Pointing to Bills leg and his eye. "That training you received in Scotland was to give you survival techniques that included hand to hand combat against the enemy. From here on we will train your brain and your language skills to second guess the Hun, see you all tomorrow."

For the next three months they trained all week and sometimes weekends, Karl's routine kept him at the camp Monday through Friday then home to Claire for the weekend. America although still a neutral country was increasingly becoming involved in convoy protection, its navy protecting Allied convoys and in many cases permission to open fire on marauding U-Boats, that command given by President Roosevelt. As for America's relationship with the Empire of Japan, it was near the boiling point negotiations were rapidly deteriorating, in the final month of 1941 Japan made its move by an undeclared attack on the America Pacific fleet in Pearl Harbor. Prime Minister Winston Churchill on the other hand was praying for a political flash point to trigger the United State to join forces with England to combat the tyranny being wagged across Europe by Germany and its Axis Powers. Daily announcements were being send back about the thousands of Jews in all occupied countries being stripped of their possessions and dignity before being thrown into concentration camps to be used as slave labor and worst.

Chapter Seventeen
A Day Which Will Live
In Infamy.
December 7th 1941

The ingenious lend lease program signed on October 30th by Franklin D. Roosevelt started paying off by providing over One Billion dollars of US aid to allied countries in desperate need of vital supplies.

Unbeknown to the American's Japan in anticipation of a complete collapse in peace negotiations, dispatched in secrecy a sizable naval force destination the American Naval base of *Oahu* in the *Hawaiian Island*. This naval force set sail from *Hitokappu Bay in Kurile Islands* the Northern Island of Japan on November 26 1941. Of the thirty-three vessels in that flotilla six were aircraft carriers. December 7th started as a normal sunny day in Pearl Harbor that would change violently at 0800 hrs when the first wave of one hundred eighty Japanese fighters, torpedo bombers and bombers attacked without a declaration of war, not given till hours later. The attack lasted over two hours when they retired the Japanese had left behind 2,403 dead American service men and women along with another 1,178 wounded. The mighty *USS Arizona* blew up taking over 1,000 sailors with her to the bottom. Six other ships were also sunk or destroyed. As for the aircraft stationed in the Hawaiian Island more than 169 US Navy and Army Air Corp were destroyed that day.

Fate intervened that day, the US aircraft carriers were out at sea. In the months ahead that blunder would prove to be a devastating blow to the Japanese Navy. This attack devised by *Admiral Isoroku Yamamota*, ironically a former student at Harvard University and a Japanese Military attaché in Washington wrote in his diary. *My fear is, that all we have done is to wake a Sleeping Giant.*
The newspapers and radio broadcast around the world painted a gruesome story of a cowardly sneak attack by the Empire of Japanese, that would forever brand them as ruthless killers. Karl along with other officer sat in disbelief at what was being relayed back to them. Bill stood up to address his staff saying, "Gentlemen we are all in shock at this senseless attack, I believe this may be the push America needed to stand by our side as we fight the Germans together, I'm sure the Prime Minister will stand by our friends the Americans by declaring war against the Japanese immediately. Our work from here on will be so much more demanding, while we wait for developments, as of this meeting I am canceling any and all leaves, that also includes weekends till we know more." Bill looking at the steel

face of Karl as he said that. "Now return to your departments to update your people." Everyone stood at parade rest till Bill had left the room. Karl walked back to this department updating everyone on what to expect in the following few weeks, returning to his office he entered closing the door behind him with a heavy heart he called Claire's office asking, "Bev is Claire in her office?" Beverly could tell this was not a day for small talk. "One moment Major, I'll get her for you." Karl sat patiently till he heard her pick up the phone saying. "Karl, oh my God, this is terrible we have just heard a radio commentary by the Prime Minister to the cowardly attack on Pearl Harbor. Are the Japanese that crazed on conquering the entire Pacific, there are no better that Hitler and his thugs?" Karl listened to her crying and trying to speak to her at the same time. "Claire this madness changes everything, the American have already declared war on the Japanese, we are confident they will declare war on the Nazi regime shortly. Now to add to that news, we have been restricted to the camp so my darling it may be quite a while till we see each other, so far there is no black out on phone use, but I fear that may be coming very soon. The BIS is the center of our efforts to manipulate the war efforts so that's why the heightened security. When all else fail's we can at least write to each other, have to go darling good night and stay positive love you." Karl returned the telephone to its cradle, that black cloud had returned but for a completely different reason.

Three weeks pasted before Karl would be able to return home to Hitchin, thanks to Bill, Karl was able to call Claire most evenings unfortunately on a monitored line. Karl spent countless hours working with members of the American Military Attaché office from London coordinating these advance directives. For the most part he enjoyed their enthusiasm and eagerness towards working together. Karl being Austrian was more receptive to this arrangement than his English counterparts that had a tendency, to be a little aloof for his liking it reminded him so much of his first meeting with officers of the BIS in Aldershot, however once he gained their confidence things change for the better this would also be the case with the Americans. By mid-December numerous branches of the British Intelligence Services were gearing up to establish training programs for the American Intelligence Service known as the *O.S.S.* Karl and numerous members of his group would be assigned to the *British Security Co-ordination Group* known as the *B.S.C.* to undertake training in *Belfast Northern Ireland* commencing in January 1942.

Prior to that mission in the three weekend Karl had been away from Claire his work kept him tied to his desk sometimes up to 16 hours a day and Christmas was almost upon them, Bill with a big grin on his face entered Karl office announcing, "I have a very special mission for you today Major, you are to proceed early this afternoon to the train station to catch the 1545 hrs train to Paddington and from there to Kings Cross to catch the connecting train to Hitchin and here is your long overdue pass, enjoy Christmas Karl you have earned it. Please give Claire, Mama, and Freida a big kiss from me. Make sure the one for Claire is a long one."
Bill watched the happy smile expanding across his friend's face. Karl had been putting in those long days with his American counterpart *Major Andy Anderson* who had already informed Bill he would be returning to the Embassy for the Christmas Holidays and in his opinion Major Vita was long overdue for a Holiday pass, God knows we have earned it. "Karl, make this holiday a good one because when you return you will be flying over to Dublin to commence the training program for the O.S.S. boys arriving from Washington, January 3rd. I have been advised that you will be there for at least a month bringing these chaps up to date on our interrogation methods. Now there is one sticky area I need to share with you. You're a professional so I'm sure you will handle it with your usual professional flair. Going over with you will be three radio instructors the head of which will be Captain Hazel Collins?" Karl looked at Bill with a stone like expression on his face, an intense moment passed before Karl responded. "Well, that's going to be sticky for both of us, but your right we are both adults and officers in his Majesty's Service, I'm sure we will find a way to make it work for the time we are there, how does Hazel feel about this?" asked Karl, Bill responding by saying. "At first she was very upset then she said, "Maybe this is a good thing for us to see each other and part as friends with no hard feelings." Karl looked at Bill his facial expression changing to one of relief. "Bill, you realize I will have to tell Claire about this don't you?" Bill sat on the corner of Karl's desk placing his hand on Karl shoulder quietly responding. "I have already done that Karl, this was a decision Clive and I had to make before we finalized the team for this operation, Hazel is the very best in that arena and Clive only wanted our best for this training." Bill waited for the response he knew would come. "So, you two took it upon yourselves to tell Claire about this operation?" asked Karl thinking here we go again with that secret stuff from the bloody BIS. "Karl, we did the right thing, I told her you did not know yet and I would tell you that before you left today." Bill waited for Karl to process which came back very quickly.

"You could of, consulted me before you made that call that would have been the right thing to do?" Responded Karl holding back a very sarcastic remark. "Karl, give Claire credit she was perfectly fine with the explanation we provided. She paid you a big complement by telling me, Karl will be the perfect diplomat when he interfaces with Hazel, I'm sure she is a very professional officer that knows how to handle herself in difficult circumstances like this. Claire closed by saying now send him home Bill, I'll work him over enough that he'll be too scared to think of anything other than his assignment." Karl felt better about the whole situation, thinking with a smirk on his face, she thinks I scare that easy?

Karl before departing took the time to wish everyone a very Merry Christmas with apologies for not sharing more time with them, finally he stopped into Bill office to wish him a wonderful Christmas and to kiss Dorothy for him. Bill hugged his friend saying don't forget to go see the Doctor so he can remove that eye patch, that's going to be the greatest Christmas present for Claire." Karl had almost forgotten about his left eye and almost forgot he had an appointment with the doctor at 1330 hrs. Karl put his officer's topcoat on then reached for his case heading for the door he placed his cap under his arm. Out in the main office he again wished everyone a safe and happy Christmas, then proceeded to the medical center. Dr Phillips dimmed the lights then removed the patch and gauze dressing, "How does that feel Major? It will take a few minutes for your eyes to normalize so don't get alarmed at seeing double it will pass quickly." Said, the doctor. "Thanks' Doc for once everything is in proper focus, great Christmas gift, thanks again and please have a Merry Christmas with your family."

With that Karl headed out through the lobby to the cold weather of December, waiting in front of the main door was Charlie standing by the Hillman staff car with the rear door open. At the station he got out wishing Charlie a Merry Christmas then went into the familiar station. Karl found a compartment with four RAF rating sitting inside, seeing a Majors uniform they immediately stood saluting the superior officer, Karl waved his arm in a downward motion saying, "Thank you boys no need to stand on ceremony we are all military in this compartment. The trip to Paddington seemed to go quickly Karl enjoying the stories being told by the young RAF chaps. Changing trains in London Karl stopped to buy a card for Claire then at a corner florist he stopped to buy some flowers asking the happy florist, "Will these flowers be alright for about an hour train ride?" He asked. "They will be fine sir, she's a lucky girl to receive these from such a handsome chap, Merry Christmas sir and a very Happy New Year." Said the older lady as she wrapped the flowers in extra paper then put a colorful green and red ribbon around the top. Karl walked along the platform and finding a half empty compartment climbed aboard for the last leg back to Hitchin. Karl waited patiently for the familiar braking from the engine as the train slowed into the station. Wishing everyone in the compartment a Merry Christmas he climbed down onto the platform, turning towards the tunnel his breath was taken away by arms around his neck and soft lips kissing his cheeks then his mouth it was Claire, her excitement obvious and everyone passing them by were laughing at the attention this striking lady was giving her man. "Darling, how I've missed you so very much, Beverly threw me out early because in her opinion I was useless thinking about you arriving back home. My God Karl you look so different without that eye patch, now you can see me with two eyes, still like the picture?" Claire was over the moon thinking, it feels so good to once again being able to meet someone special at the station, for so long that privilege was taken away from her, a shiver went through her as she suppressed a feeling it could happen again!

Walking towards the tunnel she blurted out, "Darling let's stop at the Copper Kettle for a drink and a plowman's sandwich how does that sound?" Claire just wanted to be out and about with her man. "If that's what you would like, its fine with me which car are we using?" Karl saying that knew she would not take the MG out so the Wolsey it would be. Entering the bar, they found a table by the fireplace holding hands they sat side by side, talked about the thinks that occupied their time while apart. In the back of Karl's mind, he was wondering when will my solicitor ask me about Hazel? Won't be long by the look on her face. Claire still in her business suite looked wonderful her hair tied back in a French twist always the professional conservative business lady in that dark burgundy fitted suite. Karl kept looking at her as she rattled on her nervous energy keeping her going. Karl turning in towards her finally asking, "Claire your nervous because Bill called you concerning the upcoming operation in January, he also included that Captain Collins would be in that team am I correct? Let's get it out of the way so we can enjoy our time in front of the fire with our drinks, shall we?" "Karl, you always can read me like an open book I did not want to mention it in case I hit a nerve. You've had a strenuous three weeks from what Bill told me, you and your new American friend have been working almost around the clock, but since you brought up the topic of Hazel, let me say this once and only once then it's over. Look we both know you and Hazel were close I also take responsibility for the demise of that relationship. Karl if I thought for one minute that relationship was that strong I would not of made the first move. You were lost looking for something you couldn't find, I believe you and I have found that, when the time for you to interface with Hazel, I expect you to be friendly and diplomatic as the professional officer you are. What we have is that strong I would trust you in a room full of beautiful dressed women flashing their long legs at you, so don't worry anymore about Hazel everything is alright with me, are you listening to me sailor now give me a big wet kiss you sexy man, wait till I get you home, for the record and for the thousandth time I'm madly in love with you Major Vita and you are madly in love with me correct?" Claire's nervousness was no more, her confidence was back stronger than ever, Karl sat there slowly shaking his head listening to her. "Claire what did I do to disserve a lady like you?" Asked Karl as he pulled her in towards him feeling her energy that meant only one thing. "Drink up lady you have a show to put on for this tired soldier?" Claire's response was immediate. "Thought you'd never ask?" showing her not so proper side. Back home Karl stripped off his uniform removing the various insignias ready to send it to the dry cleaners in the morning. Claire poured two glasses of port taking them upstairs Karl was seating up in bed reading an old local newspaper, "Well look at you are you waiting for something your Highness? "You could say that, but you are still dressed?" replied Karl. Claire got the message, sitting next to him at the side of the bed she toasted the bedcovers back then slowly proceeded to unbutton her blouse starting the show Karl had asked for!

The following morning, they went shopping for last minute gifts then headed to Baldock for the rest of the day. Christmas Eve they all came together in Hitchin at Claire's and Karl's home, with the fire going they all sat around the Christmas tree opening gifts and enjoying young Franchot playing with his new toys. Freida had expressly asked that no soldier or toy guns were to be given. The family departed at 9:00pm, Ronny had an early morning duty call and Karl needed to spend Christmas Day alone with Claire. They both knew when he boarded that train, he would be gone a long time so this quiet time would have to carry them through those long days of separation. Boxing day they dressed warmly and went walking through the Western Hill that overlooked Baldock and finally back to the bungalow for lunch, as the sunshine gave way to the dark skies Karl and Claire made their goodbyes to Mama and family heading home for the last evening in December of 1941.

Claire like so many times before took him to the station on December 27th, waiting on the platform for the train to arrive they both started to speak simultaneously, Claire chuckling saying, "You first darling." Karl with his arms around her waist looked into her eyes with a calming voice he spoke. "Claire, this is a difficult goodbye I'm not sure when we will see each other again? The New Year will present so many hurdles for us in the BIS, keep writing those letters and if you call me, assuming you will be able to connect, please use the secure phone just to be on the safe side alright. If your still up on New Year's Eve toast me and I will do the same to you Claire. Who would have thought last New Year's Eve I did not know you although I prayed one day I would find you, fate changed that thanks to our little MG car? The next few years will be extremely challenging for both of us we must remain strong and keep that flame brightly lit till this war comes to an end and I can come home to you never to part again." Karl was preparing her for the long months she would not see him and would rarely receive a letter or a telephone call. "Karl, I have been preparing myself for over a month that you would shortly be entering a new phase of your command. I need you to know as much as my heart will ache for you, you needn't worry I will be waiting for this smoking monster to bring you back to me one fine day, kiss me Karl I need that fresh in my mind." Claire reaching for him trying very hard to suppress the tears she was holding back. Along the platform other soldier, sailors and air force chaps were saying their goodbyes, the conductors blew his whistle yelling, "All aboard, this train departing for Kings Cross Station." Karl squeezing her tightly for one more brief minute, "Claire, I love you so much, heavens know I don't deserve you, but I can't imagine life without you." One more kiss before he broke away climbing into the compartment of the train. Claire stood by the door shedding tears her emotions flowing freely as her man was leaving returning to the dangerous carrier of an Intelligence Officer. Like those times before Claire stood watching as the train disappeared in a stream of smoke, feeling completely lost and along she walked slowly back down the tunnel and out of the station. Returned to an empty house feeling sadden by Karl's departure she picked up the phone and dialed the bungalow, Mama answering. "Mama its Claire, I'm feeling so lost, and alone would it be alright if I come over today, I really don't want to be alone feeling like this, I need to be with you all," Mama could sense Claire's sorrow and the need to be around others in a similar situation in her broken English she replied, "Claire get in your car and come over right now you need to be with your family." Claire hearing this started feeling   better grabbing her coat she locked the front door and climbed into the Wolsey and headed for Baldock. Mama standing by the front door looked at the red eyes and damp cheeks she opened her arms saying, "Come here child it saddening to see you this upset lets you and I have a cup of coffee together, shall we?" Mama with her arm around Claire could not stop thinking she must get used to this and remain strong. Karl will more than likely be spending less time here at home, his job will demand more of him now the Americans have joined us.

On the train Karl was feeling melancholy and probably about the same as Claire was feeling about now. Discipling his mind, he refocused his attention on the upcoming operation. Arriving back at the camp, he met up with his American counterpart Major Anderson, "Andy old man how was your Christmas, did you get your packages from the States alright?" Asked Karl pleased to see his new friend. "Yes, I did 'pal' and kept some food items back for you to have on the flight over tomorrow, OK." Replied Andy a big smile on his face. Walking over to the main hall they met up with other members that made up the joint task force flying to Ireland, one junior officer asked Karl, "Sir do we have a specific date to when we will be returning to England?" Karl with a stern look on his face simple replied, "No, wish I could tell you more, will get you that date as soon as I find out myself and as our American friends say, OK?" Arrangements were in high gear getting ready to leave for Dublin the following day. The sky was still dark when Karl and his team boarded the vehicles that would drive them to *RAF Northolt*. The flight over to Dublin was bumpy and noisy so Karl propped his head against the side of his canvas seat, trying to get some sleep instead he started to think about the challenges they would face in the upcoming year and beyond!

Arriving in Dublin they traveled by road to the secret camp hastily constructed by the Royal Engineers outside the rural farming town of *Shanganagh*. Settled in they gathered in the large main room to meet others that had arrived from England earlier that morning. The introductions were uplifting as they all shook hands, Karl from the corner of his eye court sight of Hazel looking at him intensely, walking over to her he politely asked, "Hazel, I am really pleased to see you, never imagined we would meet here in Ireland though. Before you give me a mouth full, may I say I have been looking forward to a time when we could meet face to face, can we talk privately. Hazel I owe you an explanation more than an apology but no excuses for how I handled myself and the shock you got when you met up with Clive. Your letter touched me deeply I pray we can work together without any additional tension between us, I understand it's up to me to make that happen?" Hazel her arms crossed, her head lowered stood silent for a few minutes then looked up eyeballing Karl, "Well Major Vita it's not like I haven't been in a similar situation before, have I? But your right we have a big job ahead of us, we are both professional enough to make this work. Karl I won't lie how I feel about you it still hurts so very much and probably will for a very long time. Now, you two timing Casanova why don't you buy me a double whiskey and tell me all about Claire?"

They both smiled at that statement, the fear they both carried at confronting each other had passed. Hazel and Karl had found a common ground they both could coexist and work in. Sitting at the makeshift bar Karl in his own special way asked Hazel a comical question? "Hazel in a couple of days it will be New Year's Eve again, it reminds me of that time up in Scotland some years back, please no repeats performances on the dance floor." They both looked at each other remembering that evening so very well, Hazel looking at him with a stern face responding by giving Karl a 'V' for victory sign with her left hand then a mischievously smile. With time and the proximity of working together, they would forge a true lasting friendship. Hazel finished her drink kissing Karl on the check then excused herself returning to her group, the sorrow in her heart remaining each time she looked Karl in the eyes. Karl found a quiet place, sitting alone sipping his whiskey he started to smile thinking again about that New Year's party in the Scottish training camp, Hazel Collins under the influence of too much whiskey tried to put the moves on him only to be politely dismissed by his fiancée Kitty Johnson, the beautiful intelligent officer that would never live to see another New Year's Eve or England again!

Karl was now thinking about the challenges that lay ahead in this senseless war that would leave so many countries in ruins its people left homeless their lives shattered and so many relationships forever lost. Millions of innocent civilians killed because of their religion or political beliefs some would face torture, others forced into slavery only to be killed when their bodies could no longer serve their Nazi masters. His final thoughts would be, we must destroy this tyrant and his senseless tyranny. With our new American allies, our chances of being victorious are getting better with each passing day. Standing up he swigged back the last of his whiskey then returned to his group.

From here on England and its new allies would take the war directly to the Germans, sealing their fate and the final victory in Europe for the Allies.

Epilogue

1942 would change everything. On January 26th thousands of American service men arrived in Belfast Ireland to commence training followed by the massive build up in England of over 1.5 million additional troops. To accommodate all of them, new camps sprung up from Scotland to Cornwell and every county in between. In February, the American 8th Airforce started ferrying over 3,650 aircraft from bases in America to existing bases and many new makeshift bases springing up throughout England. To add to this buildup, huge convoys of ships started off loading mountain of supplies, to support the American military buildup as well replenishing the English and Russians stockpiles of food, military hardware including, tanks, trucks, all types of weapons and aircraft severely depleted during the last two years of fighting.

For the most part the English people adapted quickly to the free- spirited Americans that arrived with full bellies and plenty of money in their pockets creating some animosity within the English military forces that had been fighting for over two years tolerating amongst other things, poor wages, limited food, and many other basic needs. These differences would slowly fade away as the forces started helping each other, however many a fight would start over some pretty girl that took a liking to a US soldier dangling real nylons as an enticement.

In June of 1942 Claire and Karl made their matrimonial vows, their lives from here on would forever change for the better. The service was held in the Catholic church of *St. Mary's* in Hitchin.

Karl's next assignment would be with the *British Security Co-Ordination (B.S.C.) to Canada*, accompanying him would be members of his Interrogation team to train additional members of the American, *Office of Strategic Services (O.S.S)*. Claire would not see him again till March of 1943. Hazel would also be assigned to that British Intelligence contingency, the new relationship with Karl made working together tolerable but with time the proximity of their working together became more comfortable but always at arm's length.

1943 would bring another surprise for Karl and the family when Claire announcing she was expecting a baby! At first there was shock then belated joy, holding Claire tightly he could not hold back the tears at being a new father.

1943 the allied forces were hard at work preparing for the invasion of Mainland Europe, *Operation Overlord* had a tentative scheduled for June 1944 the actual date yet to be assigned and therefore was given the code name *D-Day*. This monumental undertaking would be the biggest military undertaking in World War II. Karl and ten of his top agents would be assigned to the Americans for this operation their background and language abilities would be key in determining where German prisoners originated from, their dialect would usually give them away.

1945 the German military was almost finished but not quite yet, intelligence reports were coming in with alarming information about German development of a bomb that could annihilate cities with just only one single Atomic Bomb. The allies recognizing the extreme danger of this new bomb started planning a daring elaborate scheme to steal the ship transporting heavy equipment to the secret location in Norway after it had left the German harbor of Keil. For Karl this mission would be the most dangerous mission he had ever been involved in. Leading a team of specialized merchantmen protected by elite S.A.S commando's, they would take over the ship with the help of its Captain and members of the crew that were prepared to die to stop any further development of this new weapon.

The war in Europe would come to an end on May 7th 1945 Hitler committing suicide with new wife *Ava Braun* taking the cowards way out, what he left behind was a devasted Continent. *General Alfred Jodl* of the German High Command signed the unconditional surrender in *Reims* Northern France for all German Forces.

Japan on the other hand would face the awesome might of the Americans forces and its Allies seeking revenge for the attack on Pearl Harbor and so many other places throughout the Pacific. Defeat would be forced on them by the devastating destruction of the world's first *Uranium* Atom Bomb (*Little Boy*) dropped on *Hiroshima* on August 6th, 1945 by a single B-29 bomber Commanded by *Paul Tibbets*.

As for Hazel she would finally get her posting to America, finding a new love she eventually marries making her new home in *Rhode Island*. She would not see any of her friends in the BIS again till Clive had a reunion at the Charter Arms in Slough, July 1950.

In September of 1951 Karl, Claire, and Nicholas their son Nicholas, drove to Vienna to see Mama and the family. Before arriving there, they made a diversion stopping in the small village of *St. Sebastian in upper Bavaria* in Germany to find the grave of Kitty. Staying for two days they had a new headstone made that read.

Here lies an English Rose that left this World too early for her years. October 1938
Lieutenant Kitty Johnson
of the British Intelligence Service rest in peace

Karl and Claire would remain in Hitchin raising their son in the post war peace that would be worldwide, but for how long?

Karl could not give up his dream of returning to the sea, it had been fifteen years since he said goodbye to his ship, the Tristian in Marseille France. Claire in her infinite wisdom made Karl a deal to once again, pursue that dream with the condition it would be for only three years. The circle was almost complete?

THE END

This is the second book in this series

Made in the USA
Monee, IL
16 September 2021